THE
CHARMER

Also by Ava Rani

The Biotech Billionaires Series
The Spare
The Heir

THE CHARMER

A BIOTECH BILLIONAIRES NOVEL

AVA RANI

AVON

An Imprint of HarperCollins*Publishers*

THE CHARMER. Copyright © 2025 by Ava Rani. All rights reserved. Printed in the United States of America. No part of this book may be used or reproduced in any manner whatsoever without written permission except in the case of brief quotations embodied in critical articles and reviews. For information, address HarperCollins Publishers, 195 Broadway, New York, NY 10007.

HarperCollins books may be purchased for educational, business, or sales promotional use. For information, please email the Special Markets Department at SPsales@harpercollins.com.

Avon, Avon & logo, and Avon Books & logo are registered trademarks of HarperCollins Publishers in the United States of America and other countries.

FIRST EDITION

Interior text design by Diahann Sturge-Campbell

Poppy flower illustration © b.illustrations/Stock.Adobe.com

Library of Congress Cataloging-in-Publication Data has been applied for.

ISBN: 978-0-06-341367-2

25 26 27 28 29 LBC 5 4 3 2 1

To everyone who understands and lightens the mental load

Chapter 1

PENELOPE

Xander Sutton was a dead man.

"I can get them open," Sloan Amari insisted. A fellow partner at my law firm, she'd become a good friend over the years. Her fingers wrapped around the plastic latches—what I assumed were childproof locks—fastened along the lip of the walnut drawer on my office desk. "He did this once before on my kitchen cabinets, and I figured it out then."

I huffed, frustrated. Becoming friends with Sloan Amari meant becoming friends with her friends. And they were all lovely.

Her best and oldest friend, Xander Sutton, however, was mildly infuriating. Utterly gorgeous and impossible to not like, but mildly infuriating.

I managed to get caught in the cross fire of Sloan and Xander's epic prank war. I tried to see the humor in it, but it had been a long week and I had meetings to prepare for.

"I'm so sorry, Pen." Sloan's face contorted as she turned the lock again to no avail. "It's my fault. I stole all of his left shoes, so he was just getting me back."

I pinched the bridge of my nose. Based on the stories I'd heard, she and Xander had been playing these games for over a decade. "You two are grown adults. You do know that, right?"

On the polished wood desk, my phone began to buzz. Maddox's name lit up the screen. I scooped it up, silenced it, and put it in my pocket.

This was already the week from hell before Xander added to the pile. It started with a courier dropping off an envelope of papers that outlined the process to receive my inheritance—the one left by my grandfather after he passed a few months ago. Seemingly mundane, but I knew this wasn't just some routine paperwork drop-off. My family had been nagging me to deal with this for months and apparently felt I needed a physical reminder, so they'd gone out of their way to arrange the delivery. Gritting my teeth, I'd given in and read it all through. The ink on those pages had been hanging over me all week, tinging everything with irritation.

I regretted the pitch in my voice when I saw Sloan's shoulders fall. "I know it's silly." She sighed, standing up straight and running a hand down her skirt. Her eyes dropped, embarrassed. "It's—"

"Shit." A voice from the doorway drew our attention. Xander Sutton, the engineer behind the sudden elevation in my blood pressure this afternoon, stood in the doorway. The summer light poured through the floor-to-ceiling windows of our Manhattan office, illuminating his mossy green eyes, currently wincing with guilt. "Misfire." He raked a hand through his dirty blond hair, pushing the neat coif slightly askew. "Sorry, Penelope."

In the mood I was in, I thought I might give him a piece of my mind, but the calm sincerity in his voice made me pause. Frustrating as his antics occasionally were, even I had to admit that Xander Sutton always treated others with unreasonable levels of humility and kindness, making it near impossible to remain angry with him. It was like his superpower. Xander collected friends and simply converted enemies.

I sighed and motioned to my locked desk drawers. "Can *you* get them open?"

He nodded and came over to assess the situation.

Just then, Sloan's phone started to ring. She checked the screen and frowned. The Hightower case was going to litigation, and I knew she was supposed to be meeting with the defense team today. This would be one of the biggest cases the firm had represented in years, and Hightower—one of the firm's largest and oldest clients—would not be easy to vindicate after so much public scrutiny aimed at their practices.

"Go," I insisted, seeing the indecision warring in her expression. I appreciated her wanting to make things right, but duty called.

She nodded, then turned to her friend, pointing a stern finger at him. "Xan, be more careful," she warned darkly before leaving.

"It won't take long," Xander assured me as he shrugged off his suit jacket and laid it on one of the chairs in front of my desk. He rounded it, knelt down, and silently began to remove the locks that must have been installed while I was out.

"Good," I said, meaning to hold my annoyance, but my tone had lost all its sharpness.

"Sorry," he said softly, his attention focused on turning a lock. "Your offices changed when you two became partners at the firm. I didn't account for that."

Sloan and I became senior partners at the law firm around the same time. She and I seemed to be on similar tracks, careerwise, anyway. When it came to our personal lives . . . well, she was living out a real-life fairy tale with Xander's older brother, while I was living out something entirely different.

Xander's biceps flexed beneath the perfectly ironed button-up shirt as he turned the lock. A hard *pang* and his almost inaudible grunt followed, settling low in my stomach.

"Well, I guess it's a good thing you came here to gloat," I mused, watching as he completed one end. "I was one more failed attempt away from taking a hammer to the drawer."

"Damn." He stood and brushed past the back of my chair to the other side of the desk. From that close, an initial whiff of clean citrus from his cologne gave way to a fusion of warm amber and musk. He knelt down and flashed me a quick smile before returning his attention to his task. "Showed up too early."

I gave him a hard look.

"I came by to sign the final Dawn Capital papers, too," he explained as he pulled the fastener forward and unclicked it. The entire mechanism came loose and fell into his hand. "But I think I pissed off my lawyer."

Xander and his colleagues, Rohan, Jackson, and Tristan, all used to work at the same large investment firm. Over the past ten years, the four had been responsible for most of the company's profitability. So it only made sense for them to branch out and start their own company together.

But this was no tiny start-up. Many of their old firm's largest clients were moving with them, and new accounts were flocking their way. When the final assets and investment transfers were signed this afternoon, they'd be the second largest capital investment firm in the world.

I was their counsel and personally handling the incorporation process for Xander's firm: Dawn Capital.

"Fix this expeditiously and your lawyer will forget it ever happened."

"No threats?" He chuckled again, looking straight ahead. "I think I'm growing on you."

"Like a barnacle on a sea turtle," I answered dryly, ignoring the excited buzz that ran along my skin.

I'd occasionally felt *something* around him. A quiet chemistry that never crossed a line. But given his easy grace with strangers and the fact that Xander Sutton could have chemistry with anyone,

I was sure whatever I occasionally felt was one-sided and nothing to dwell on.

The corner of his mouth tipped up and his lips parted. My pulse skittered awaiting his retort.

It never came. Instead, his lips pressed together, he blinked, and continued working on the last lock.

"And . . . done." The final lock fell into his hand. "Like it never happened."

He stood and pulled open a drawer. His gaze landed on the documents I'd been reviewing before lunch.

My inheritance. The stipulations.

"Thank you." My hand brushed past his and closed the drawer. I opened the one below.

"Just undoing the damage. I'm sorry, Penelope."

Xander was hardly ever formal outside of professional spaces, but over the past few months he was careful with every word he chose around me. He only said half the snarky comments I knew were rolling around in his head.

I found myself wondering what prompted the change. If it had anything to do with that night—the masquerade—but asking felt impossible.

I pulled out the file for Dawn Capital's incorporation. "Have Rohan, Jackson, and Tristan sign their copies. Courier them back when you're done."

He nodded and took the folder. "Come have celebratory drinks with us tonight. We owe you one."

"I'd hold on to that generous thought; you still haven't seen the firm's bill," I quipped lightly, trying to breeze past the heaviness that lingered in my chest at the recollection of the masquerade.

"Well, if you change your mind, we'll be at the Augustus." He leaned in just a hair closer. "But no pressure. We value your time."

"Well, if you value your life . . ." I threatened, holding my capped pen like a dagger. I poked him once in his unreasonably solid chest as a warning. "Take care to exclude me from your silly games."

"No need to threaten my shirt with a good time." He put his hands up and backed away slowly to my door, grabbing his suit jacket on the way, an amused smile tugged at one side of his face. "Tom Ford is innocent in all of this."

I tamed the smile that tried to creep past my defenses.

"See you later, Penelope." He turned and his footsteps receded down the hallway.

*   *   *

HOURS AFTER XANDER left the office, I was submerged in an acquisition document when a knock at the door lifted me from my work.

"Do you have a second?" Maya Malhotra peeked her head in the half-open doorway.

"Yes, please shut the door behind you."

She was a rising star. A junior associate in litigation who could outmaneuver the devil himself. An invaluable asset to the firm and Sloan's personal recommendation to join our ranks.

"What's the latest with the Hightower Energy case?" I asked.

"Sloan says the whistleblower got some heavy-duty representation for the civil case, too." Maya took a seat, tucked her voluminous jet-black hair behind her ear, and folded her hands on the envelope she brought in. "Victor Hightower may be in some trouble."

"Oh no," I murmured with marginal sarcasm. Nobody would mourn the Hightowers. They were vile people, but we represented a lot of vile people. "Is Sloan alright?"

"She seems fine." Maya squirmed in her seat. She handed the unsealed envelope—the one holding a copy of my inheritance terms—back to me. "You wanted me to review these."

While I was in London on assignment for the firm with Sloan a year ago, my family let me know they'd finally arranged my marriage. It wasn't a surprise; it was one of the requirements for all of the grandchildren to receive their inheritances. We had to get married, and I knew my father would use that stipulation to further the company—Chen Tech—or the family name. For a long time, I'd quietly accepted my fate.

"Any clever work-arounds?" I asked.

"Well, since getting your inheritance only has two stipulations, we can't really play them against each other to find a way around it," Maya began.

For years I had ignored my father and half brother's jostling and postponed the inevitable wedding, until they became a bit more forceful. Seven months ago, at the Amari Masquerade, I was notified that my mother's shares in Astor Media—her family's company—had become tied to my fulfilling the marital clause. If my mom wanted to see a cent of what rightfully belonged to her, I would need to add a ring to my finger. And I was on a timer. I had till the end of the summer this year.

"The location stipulation is easy; buy a property in Singapore. But the marriage one . . ."

The grave tone in her voice became a pit in my stomach. Maya was a mastermind when it came to finding loopholes. Especially this close to the deadline. If *she* didn't see a way out . . .

"Yes . . ." I muttered to myself. "The marriage one . . ."

My mother, Victoria Astor, married my father, Alvan Chen, as an arrangement. The wealthy Singaporean Chen family got a coveted Western title once I was born and became more than just new money from a tech fortune. And the Astors, British nobility, whose media company was floundering before the wedding, had the capital to rebuild.

It was a joint venture sealed with a wedding. But that venture was thrown into chaos when my mother filed for divorce a few years after that. By my fourth birthday, I was splitting my time between Singapore and London and bitter parents.

"You can't change the timeline. It's ironclad," she continued. "Good news is, now that your grandfather has passed, they can't change the terms again."

"I guess that's a silver lining." My grandfather passed right after the New Year, after he changed the terms. Originally, all I would have been giving up was my inheritance if I didn't follow through with the wedding. But then, right before he passed, he tied my mother's shares in Astor Media to my own. Those shares were meant to provide for Mother for the rest of her life in the manner she was accustomed to. This was their way to force my hand. Needless to say, I didn't attend the funeral services.

I'd spent the last few months trying to find a way around the terms while avoiding all their prodding. I'd been away from home for so long, I'd alienated myself from my family—even though they hardly ever acted like one. But, you only get one family, and I'd always figured one day I'd finally get around to fitting into it. If I did this, went directly against their wishes, what if there was no road back and it severed me from them forever?

It wasn't easy to simply decide you were fine going it alone.

That fact kept my thoughts on an endless loop the last few months making me distrustful of my own intuition.

"Thank you for trying." I opened my drawer and placed the copies I'd given Maya there.

"You can still win this one. Get your inheritance and the shares that are tied up in it." Maya's voice adopted a reassuring sharpness, a steely confidence emerging. One I'd heard a hundred times when she was practicing for trial. She sat up straighter. "The old-fashioned way."

"Right."

I could marry someone—just not the person they picked—for a year, the amount of time allotted before the funds could be transferred. Someone I could trust enough to go through the motions. Then I'd have my inheritance and my mother's shares. But the daunting reality that this might be the final strike that cut me off from my own blood was unnerving.

Maya stood and began to make her way to the door. "You do know quite a few bachelors that would probably be up for the task. My annoying brother included."

A laugh bubbled up and popped out of me. Maya was Rohan Malhotra's little sister. And Rohan, along with the rest of the Dawn Capital cofounders were a part of Xander Sutton's merry band of cohorts.

She grinned as she turned to leave.

"I'll see you at Sloan's engagement party on Friday night," she said as the door closed behind her.

My phone rang again and Maddox's name lit up the screen for the second time that afternoon. A sense of dread wrapped around my chest.

I wasn't sure what I'd do next, but one thing was certain: by the end of the summer, I was going to be married.

Chapter 2

XANDER

The Augustus Club on a weeknight was tame even by high-society standards.

The massive members-only social club boasted three towers that loomed gracefully over Midtown Manhattan. They housed a social space, an athletic wing, and the arts wing. Each connected by glass breezeways, so members floated seamlessly between the different offerings.

I stepped off the elevator and turned the corner to one of the many private poker rooms, glancing down at my phone when I saw a news alert come through.

The Federally Protected Hightower Energy Whistleblower Comes Forward with an Additional Civil Suit.

I smiled, appreciating karma finally coming around to bite the Hightowers in the ass.

I passed through the grand mahogany double doors to see Tristan and Rohan seated, waiting for me.

"Madison Amherst was looking for you," Rohan grumbled. He looked at his phone screen and smiled for a millisecond, then his brows wrinkled together as he read something. I arched my neck to see what he was looking at: the East Asian markets.

"She was . . . perturbed," Rohan added.

Madison Amherst, the newspaper-turned-media-company heiress, and I had dated a few months ago. She was an avid environmentalist and we sat on the board of the Central Park Conservancy together. It was how we met.

"Great," I groaned as I sat down.

Jax joined us and the dealer began handing out the cards.

The poker lounges at the Augustus sat on the twentieth floor. The sunset streamed through floor-to-ceiling windows. The south-facing view presented Manhattan in its larger-than-life glory. The west-facing view peered into the hallways that led to the club's arts tower.

"I told you not to break her heart. Hell hath no fury like an Amherst scorned," Tristan chuckled, gathering his cards.

"I didn't break it." I tilted my cards up briefly to see my hand before laying them back on the table. Everyone assumed I did since my relationships never lasted more than six months. But that was by design. In truth, Madison broke it off with me, and it didn't really affect my life in any meaningful way.

Madison was nice. Fun. Great sex.

We got together and sort of used each other for what we needed. She was mending a broken heart, and I was doing my best to avoid one. And because I could make conversation about literally anything, we never *actually* got to know each other that well in those months.

The perfect setup.

All parties left that relationship unscathed; everyone could be friendly, and nobody was hurt. It was a benefit of not letting romantic relationships move past a certain point: you could never miss what you never had.

"Well, work it all out amicably," Rohan said roughly and finally looked up from his cards. "I want to manage the Amherst Media accounts. And have you closed the SunCorp deal yet?"

"Not yet," I answered lightly, even though it was proving to be tougher than I'd expected. Alejandro Herrera, the CEO of SunCorp, needed some hand-holding to trust Dawn Capital. The wealthy Mexican landowner whose family made their money in agave was something of a tech genius and the dime-sized extended-life battery technology he developed was a clean energy feat. Revolutionary in that the battery lifetimes were decades-long and required no additional environmental impact to make them. I figured I'd convince him in the end—people tended to like me and that made closing deals a lot easier. But Alejandro had already declined what was a generous offer. I needed to figure out what exactly I could give him that would make him *want* to sign over his stake. "I invited him to the launch party this weekend. I can do it there."

"We aren't here to talk about work," Tristan complained and we placed our starting bets. "Stop staring at the markets and see if we can stop Xander from counting cards."

"I'm not counting them," I grumbled, rolling my eyes. At least, I wasn't trying to. I had a relatively exceptional memory. Once I saw, read, heard, or understood something, it was imprinted for good. It could be useful, especially paired with my aptitude for math. "Poker is a break from all of that."

Our weekly poker game was something the four of us—Jackson, Tristan, Rohan, and I—had been doing for years. Ever since we started working together fresh out of college a decade ago.

Rohan ignored Tristan. "We should keep an eye on—"

"We *should* be celebrating," I reminded him. "Come on, Ro. The fun thing about finally being at the top is that everybody else does the work."

Two years ago, the four of us got together and realized we were responsible for most of the lucrative assets at our investment firm. With that type of track record, it didn't make sense to work for anyone else. We decided—well, Rohan decided, and we agreed—to break out on our own. We started our own company and hired a full team of analysts and managers to take care of the day-to-day. While we'd been operating for months already, our official launch celebration was this weekend in the Hamptons. It marked the beginning of what everyone on Wall Street deemed our reign.

"Ro," I repeated, leaning forward and tapping his phone. "Come on, relax."

Our jobs were to steer the ship and secure the assets we wanted, and we did. With almost every asset worth having under our umbrella, Dawn Capital was a force to reckon with.

"Rohan still hasn't learned how," Tristan cooed and mockingly pinched Rohan's cheek.

* * *

AFTER A FEW hands, I checked the time and glanced out the wall of windows.

The pottery studios in the arts wing of the Augustus closed to members at eight on weeknights. An excited tremor ran through my fingers.

I put my cards down. "I should go."

"It's early." Jackson didn't look up from the table, but it was the same time I left every week.

I settled up and left with a quick wave.

Passing through one of the side entrances of the bar, I made the turn to the elevators just as Penelope was leaving one of the studios. I was *supposed* to be ignoring the chemistry that crackled between us, but that warning in my mind always seemed to shut off when she was close.

A smiled curved over the corners of her lips. Her sleek black hair was pulled back into a ponytail. Her gray fitted T-shirt and black joggers were speckled with dried clay; it trailed along her cheek, too, and just below the thick sweep of her dark lashes.

"This is why you couldn't have drinks with us?" I asked as she stopped in front of me. Without thinking or taking a second to analyze why I felt the need to do it, I brushed away the clay that was dried on her cheek. A delightful static traveled along my thumb.

She scrunched her nose and shooed my hand away.

"I wasn't going to intrude on poker night." Her soft voice laced around that British accent like a very formal melody. One I stupidly let myself get used to. "Especially since you barred Sloan from playing. She would see that as an act of war."

"We only banned her because she kept backhand slapping everyone," I defended. Sloan was downright dangerous when she got competitive. The occasional slap to the shoulder didn't hurt until my brother put a battering ram on her finger. "She's welcome to come back if she stops hitting people."

"Well, I also needed a reprieve from earlier today or I may have seriously considered taking my frustration out on a perfectly innocent Tom Ford shirt."

I smiled, having roused that playful irritation I'd grown accustomed to over the years.

Penelope, politely reserved, always seemed like she was doing her best not to make waves. But if you could disrupt that muted tide, a brilliant storm of quick wit and sharp humor was just waiting to knock you on your ass.

"You know, if you'd just *let* me make it up to you, you'd be a little less averse to having me around," I teased.

The impulse—the one I chalked up to an attempt at helpfulness—to rub off that speck of clay stuck to the top of her cheek became impossible to ignore. I brushed my thumb over it again.

She paused for a beat before shaking her head and shooing my hand away again.

"I already tried that. I still ended up on the wrong side of a juvenile game."

"It's because you *picked* the wrong side. Team Xander wins every year."

With a roll of her eyes, her mouth opened, but another voice calling from behind me stopped her.

"Xander Sutton!"

Penelope tilted her head up and looked over my shoulder. "Seems I'm not the only one you've upset today."

I grimaced; I knew that voice.

"Madison?" I whispered to Penelope.

She nodded. "One of the many ghosts of girlfriends past. I'll see you at Sloan's engagement party," she goaded in a singsong voice. Then she patted my shoulder and walked past me.

I turned, my eyes lingering on her as she walked away, before my attention was drawn squarely to the annoyed heiress marching toward me.

"How can I help you, Madison?"

It was about the ducks. It was always about the ducks.

"The conservancy keeps getting complaints." She crossed her arms. Sloan and I had a long-standing tradition of feeding the ducks in Central Park and everyone else on the conservancy wasn't a fan. "It's unfair that you and Sloan be the only two who get to—"

"How about I donate enough to make sure anyone can feed the ducks?" I offered. My eyes were still darting toward Penelope as she walked down the hallway, wondering how quickly I could get out of this conversation and run back into her. "Make it the next Amherst initiative. I'll fund the whole thing."

Her voice dropped a few decibels. "It's more about the nutritional composition of the food. People can't feed them bread."

"Purchase whatever is in line with what a growing duck needs." I really tried not to let that sound as patronizing as it did in my head. I was trying to be nice, but I was distracted.

"Well, that seems fair." She crossed her arms.

I peered over her shoulder. The lobby door closed. Penelope was gone.

A tightness in my chest lingered.

My attention snapped back to Madison when she said, "Sounds great, actually."

"I can't have *the* Madison Amherst upset with me." I smiled, glad that I had successfully disarmed her anger.

Her shoulders fell with a sigh.

"I'll have the conservancy's donation department reach out to your assistant. You're very lucky that nobody is immune to the Xander Sutton charm."

I could think of one person who was. Hell, there were times that she seemed allergic to it.

"And that's actually not the only thing I wanted to tell you." Her voice lowered as her eyes flickered around the empty hallway. "I don't get involved in the family business, but Reina Beckett just accepted a position in the newsroom at Amherst Media."

My heart stopped for a beat at the shock of it, but the momentary pain passed as quickly as it came. For years, hearing Reina's name used to slice through me. But now, it was odd, I felt nothing. I'd held on to the idea of her for so long it felt like a reflex when my heart raced, but it didn't sting like it used to.

I met Reina, my ex, a year after my parents died over a decade ago. She felt like a way out of the storm for a time. But when her life took her all over the world with no assurance she'd ever come back to Manhattan, it ended.

"I thought you might want to know," Madison added quietly into the awkward silence.

"Thanks for telling me, Madison."

"Add it to the long list of favors you owe me." She smiled. "Like that one from after the Hightower New Year's party. Are you ever going to tell me why you needed that potting soil? Burying a body?"

I couldn't help but grin. The Hightower party was a year and a half ago, but it remained burned into my memory.

"It's not nearly as interesting as you think. Just a houseplant that was in dire straits."

"Mm-hmm." She rolled her eyes. "I'll see you around, Xander."

The night of the Hightower party, and the morning after in Penelope's kitchen, changed everything I thought I wanted. But then the Amari Masquerade had reminded me why I didn't get involved past a certain point.

Chapter 3

PENELOPE

Fridays at the law firm were quiet during the summer.

"All the annual taxes and other items have been paid," I said into my phone as I walked along the windows in my office. "So, you're set until next year. All you need to do is sign the papers I've sent, like we do every year."

The late afternoon summer sun spilled into my office, filling it with a warm golden glow. I looked out at the magnificent city below. While the Singapore skyline was a comforting sight to me, New York City was something else. Domineering. Demanding.

Wonderful.

"Little flagged markers where you need a signature, I know." My mother's bored tone came through the line clearly. "You can relax, dearest. Enjoy your summer. And congratulations on your work accomplishments."

She said that same generic sentence every time we spoke, not that we spoke all that often.

I took care of most of her financial and legal affairs, including ensuring all the taxes and bills were paid. She was more than capable of doing so, but I'd taken on that responsibly so long ago, it was muscle memory. And even though she *could* do it, I knew she was happier letting me handle it.

"Thank you, Mother." I sighed, staring down at the city. At the start of the call, she'd asked how I was, and I told her I'd wrapped up some large accounts. While I knew she didn't care for the day-to-day accomplishments of a corporate lawyer, she indulged me. "There's still plenty to do. I'll be in the Hamptons this summer, working."

After years of turning down the invitation, Sloan's aggressively inviting nature won out and I planned to spend the summer working from the Hamptons in her guesthouse.

"The Hamptons?" Her voice went up an octave. It was only when her perfectly polished English accent broke with any form of emotion that I realized how much I sounded like her. "I'm glad you're finally taking some time to enjoy yourself, dearest."

The wind rustling in the background made it hard to hear the last few words. A farm outside of Glasgow wasn't where most people expected to find my mother—the Viscountess of Hastings—but she loved the solitude. She'd lived there for years now, having moved there from London months after I finished university.

"Are you doing alright, Mother?"

I hadn't told her about the developments with my inheritance yet. She was expecting to get her shares in Astor Media back eventually, and I'd make that happen, but I tried not to overwhelm her with details. She was never good with them. It was easier for me to take care of it for her and avoid the theatrics.

I knew we didn't have a normal mother-daughter relationship. Spending the summers in Singapore and winters in London, my mother often treated me like a sister rather than a daughter. I never minded, but I was sure I was the only twelve-year-old double-checking court documents about who owned which property.

"Of course, dearest. Relax. You've taken care of everything." She laughed lightly.

My father, stepmother, and half siblings in Singapore had what felt like a real family. It was the furthest thing from what my mother wanted. She'd always been rather solitary, content to live quietly and without responsibility.

"Are you sure you—"

"Turn off that busy mind for a second." She sighed into the phone and it muffled in the line. "Take a step outside and take a deep breath. Now, it's late here. I'm off to bed."

"Good night, Mother."

I was all she had, so I *had* to take care of these things, but I didn't mind. With the money from the divorce settlement dwindling, I was already taking care of her more substantial bills. It was getting to be unsustainable given all the properties and upkeep they required.

"Hey Pen, Clef International just sched—" Sloan's voice burst through the open doorway and immediately stopped when she saw me pulling the phone away from my ear. *Sorry*, she mouthed.

I waved her in and hung up the phone. "Don't worry, it was just my mother."

"How's the viscountess?" A smile curled up the side of Sloan's mouth.

Of all the friends I'd made in Manhattan, Sloan was the closest I had. She and I also spent six months in London together for work and she had an informal introduction to my mother.

"Perfectly well." I glanced down at my watch; it was already four in the afternoon. "Shouldn't you be off getting ready for this weekend?"

Friday afternoons at the firm were usually busy the rest of the year, but in the summer, it was deserted while many worked remotely. And tonight was Sloan Amari's engagement party.

She sighed. "Clef wants to meet to discuss the merger's impact on the expansion plans."

"I'll handle the Clef account," I offered. "And I can help with the Hightower litigation if you need it."

While I spent a lot of time in my personal life careful not to disrupt the peace, that was what made my work so enticing. I didn't have to play nice; in fact, playing dirty was encouraged.

"No, Clef is more than enough. Are you sure?" She handed the files over when I gestured toward them.

"Yes." I took the files out of her hand. Taking unsavory news and presenting it in a more appetizing fashion was a skill I honed as a child since I often intercepted the mail and read it first. That way I could present legal documents to my mother in a way that wouldn't elicit a meltdown. "And is there anything else you need before the party tonight?"

"Actually, yes." She chewed on her bottom lip. "Could you swing by Harry Winston for me?"

"Okay," I agreed, though not entirely sure why since her engagement ring was sitting on her finger as we spoke. It was a lovely, albeit enormous, eleven carats. Specifically designed and crafted for Sloan.

"Lily Sutton's ring is being cleaned," she explained. "And I don't want it to sit in the Harry Winston vault all summer. Can you pick it up and bring it to the Hamptons with you?"

As if living in her own version of a fairy tale, Sloan was presented with three rings when she got engaged—two family rings, and a new one. She chose the one her fiancé had custom made for her.

"Of course," I repeated, ushering her out of the office.

She stopped halfway to the door. "I would go myself, or send Xander, but—"

"No need to explain." I put my hand up, knowing the subject of Lily and William Sutton—her soon-to-be husband's late parents— was a painful one. "I'm happy to help."

Xander and Marcus Sutton lost their parents tragically, and while both had moved on since the events of that night over a decade ago, Sloan was still protective of them both. And of the memory of the Suttons.

"I'll pick it up and guard it with my life," I added.

She smiled brightly. "And we'll pick you up on the way out of the city tomorrow."

"Now, off you go." I pointed down the hall to the elevators. "Leave Clef to me."

"Are you sure?"

I nodded. "Yes. Go."

She turned and made her way down the hall. Alone, that familiar ache started to settle in my gut again. I glanced down at my phone, considering whether to call my half sister, Arabella. But it would be the middle of the night in Singapore, and Arabella hadn't answered my calls in almost a year. Still, I couldn't help wishing I could turn to her right now for support. I was always longing for the type of family that was just out of my grasp.

It was easier to stay away, not having to be reminded of the rejection I felt from my own family. It hurt my heart a little less the years I didn't visit, and now it had been three since I went to Singapore.

I tucked my phone back in my pocket, letting the feeling pass.

Chapter 4

XANDER

As man of honor, I took my role very seriously.

While the *actual* bride, Sloan, did not.

Sloan and Marcus's engagement party was held at the Met in Manhattan. The entire museum was transformed to accommodate the event.

Crystal chandeliers, hung from the high ceilings, sparkled and filled the room with facets of light. The walls were draped in sumptuous silk fabric in shades of deep red and gold, adorned with intricate embroidery and beading. The towering columns were decorated with fragrant jasmine garlands.

I banged on the door to one of the exhibit rooms that was turned into a dressing room for Sloan. "Sloan Saanvi Amari, you open this door now."

I didn't get a response.

I left her alone for what was supposed to be a few minutes. In that time, Marcus went in and proceeded to break the only two rules given to them.

Stay put. Stay dressed. Sloan and Marcus were notorious for sneaking off somewhere during parties, hence the ground rules for *this* one.

"Guys." The tiniest bit of frustration bled into my words when there was still no answer. "This is *your* party."

I met Sloan seventeen years ago when our older brothers were assigned as roommates in college. She was fourteen, and I was sixteen, and we were both less than enthusiastic about being dragged along to move our respective brothers in.

That was the start of an epic, often messy, always reliable friendship.

A minute later, the door unlocked and opened. Marcus stood with a stupid, poorly controlled grin on his face. He adjusted his tie. "We were just talking."

I crossed my arms and noted the red shadow along his mouth. "That's a lovely shade of lipstick."

He chuckled and glanced back at Sloan, who stood a few feet behind, running her hands over the skirt of the deep red *lehenga*.

"Oops." She grinned.

I looked back at Marcus. "Where is your handler?"

Henry Amari, Marcus's best man and Sloan's older brother, should have been here to help keep the lovebirds apart.

"Henry and Selena are running a little late," Marcus said plainly.

"Seriously?" I groaned. I stepped past my brother and ushered him out of the room he wasn't supposed to be in. Henry Amari had recently fallen head over heels for his PR consultant; their relationship was all anyone could talk about for months. "If anyone was wondering, I am very uncomfortable with being the only adult in the room now that all of you are acting like teenagers."

"We're sorry, Xan. Won't happen again," Sloan assured from behind me.

"She's lying," Marcus called as I shut the door. "On both counts."

I turned to look at Sloan, who was beaming. She stood in front of a large trifold vanity and adjusted her *lehenga*.

"You're not sorry," I told her, walking over to the table beside a plush couch. I took the bottle of champagne that sat on the marble table and poured a glass for her and myself.

"Orgasms have a tendency of making me care less." She shrugged.

I grimaced as I handed her a glass.

"Did you apologize to Pene—"

"Yes, Sloan," I interrupted, hoping to abate the flood of different emotions that even hearing her name brought on.

She looked over her shoulder. "Just making sure. Pen doesn't find our games as . . . adorable as everyone else."

No one found our long-standing prank tradition adorable. The reason we kept it going for so long had shifted over the years, like most of our traditions, but I didn't question it.

Especially since I won most years. There was a peace—a stability—that came with the knowledge that I could expect that game to begin at the start of every summer.

"She's been a little more on edge lately." Sloan looked back ahead. "About the wedding, I think."

"Yeah . . ." A familiar ache settled along my ribs. About a year ago, when she and Sloan got back from an assignment in London, she told us that she was getting married. To a childhood friend slash old boyfriend. She didn't wear a ring; it was more like a betrothal of sorts. One she didn't want to discuss. "I noticed."

I asked her about it at the masquerade months ago. I was going to leave it alone, but I couldn't. I told myself it was out of concern, but it was more than that. I didn't know what I was hoping to hear but it certainly wasn't what she told me. That the marriage was her choice as much as it was anyone else's and she was happy about it.

The room became quiet, filled with the sound of Sloan's golden bangles knocking against each other as she fixed her earrings. "Are you okay?"

I stood up straighter. "Yeah, of course. Why wouldn't I be?"

She shrugged. "A lot is changing. Nobody would blame you if you felt . . . overwhelmed."

My chest tightened.

There was a pitch that Sloan's voice took whenever she was worried. It summoned memories I would give every cent I had to forget. The ones where my world changed, I fell apart, and Sloan picked up the pieces. Often giving up parts of her own happiness to ensure mine.

I huffed a breath and said casually, "You moved a few miles. Not much else has changed." She was right, a lot was changing, and she knew better than anyone to check on me. "You need to stop worrying about me."

The problem with a perfect memory wasn't that I couldn't forget. It was that my mind had a habit of pushing memories I wanted to never recall to the front of my vision at the worst times.

Like the sound of my brakes when we got to the scene of the accident. Or the myriad times Sloan or Tristan or sometimes Rohan had pulled me together when I spun out with alcohol and drugs.

"I'm not worried." She rolled her eyes, her voice dropped to a mumble. "I'm just checking in. If you're not okay, you don't have to pretend you are. That's all I'm saying. Change is hard for everyone."

The room got quiet again. I tried to smother the memories of all of those terrible times I gave her a reason to be anxious. Sometimes I would pretend I was fine, save myself reliving the shame from those instances and sort of trick myself into believing it.

Things were better now, stable. I wasn't going to let anything disrupt that stability. I wasn't going to ever let myself lose control again. Fall apart and make them pick me up.

"So," Sloan said with a deep inhale, turning back around to face the vanity. "Did you see the headline? The Hightower whistle-blower has a legitimate case against them."

"Oh no." I feigned concern. It was all a part of the plan. The Hightower family was corrupt through and through but pretty good at hiding their tracks. An anonymous whistleblower came forward alleging some pretty heinous crimes—like ignoring safety concerns and modifying regulatory documents that stated their automotive division was in breach of major safety standards. "But, from what I hear, they have some powerful counsel."

Sloan—as the Hightower Energy official counsel—told them not to worry and to settle with the whistleblower. At the same time, Sloan *may have* ensured an old law school contact took up the whistleblower's civil case pro bono.

Sloan grinned like the Grinch right before he stole Christmas. "I may actually lose this one, Xan."

That was the plan. Sloan was going to throw the hand, lose the game, and give the Hightowers what was coming to them. She'd advise, after letting the case drag on a while to damage the stock price, for them to publicly pay out hundreds of millions and step down in order for the company to continue. Wounding the company and the family, irreparably. But it needed to look like a fair fight, so one of the best prosecutors in the country took up the federal case and a top firm took up the civil one.

"You're not on the hook for any of this, right?" I asked again. Sloan was counsel for the Hightowers, so this was clearly unethical. While I liked the idea of seeing them fall apart, I didn't want it to blow back on her. In Sloan's words, ethics were in the eye of the beholder. Outside of the fact that their failed braking systems in their automotive division led to many crashes—my parents' fatal one included—they were destroying the environment without any recourse. It was a win-win.

But from the second she learned of their involvement in my parents' deaths, she lost all objectivity and insisted the ends justified the means. She should have refused to take the case; the fact that she hadn't told me she had ulterior motives. And I knew better than to try to stand in Sloan Amari's way.

"For the thousandth time no." She rolled her eyes. "It's murky ethical territory but hey, I never claimed to be a saint."

Still, I said, "You're sure?"

"Yes." Sloan took a deep breath, and her smug expression began to falter, a familiar look of concern blossomed. Right on cue, Sloan's voice switched to cheery. "How do I look?"

"Stunning." I smiled. It was her party and, after years of caring for me when I wouldn't care for myself, I refused to do anything other than make sure she had a perfect engagement party—and in a year, the perfect wedding.

"Is this the part of the movie where you tell me you've secretly been in love with me the whole time?" She looked at me through the reflection in the mirror with a patronizing smile. "Because your brother beat you to it."

I swore Sloan had a radar for when I needed to get out of my head. And every time, she'd say something wild to snap me out of it.

"Eww." I grimaced. There was never anything between us. She was my family long before my older brother ever put a ring on her finger. "No, it's the part of the movie where I make a joke about your plans to wear white at the ceremony."

They were going to have two ceremonies. One Western and one more traditionally Indian.

Sloan's grin fell. "You have your charms; I have mine."

"Try keeping those charms clothed for the rest of the night?" I chuckled, walked over to the door, and glanced at my watch. "I came in here to get you for pictures; you're late."

"I make no promises," she called as I shut the door behind me.

* * *

I PASSED UNDER the elaborately engraved marble archway and through the large atrium on my way to the sculpture hall, where the engagement party was in full swing.

My eyes found Penelope like she was a magnet. She was glancing around the party, grabbing her phone from her tiny purse, like she was getting ready to leave. I crossed the room to her.

"Leaving?" I glanced at my watch. It was still pretty early in the night.

Her soft canary yellow *lehenga* shimmered among the flickering light from the candles scattered around the room in ornate brass holders. She tucked a stray lock of hair behind her ear.

"Oh yes. I have some work . . ." She trailed off, putting the small clutch back on the table and her phone on top of it. Her eyes were frozen on her phone. She snapped out of it a second later and shook her head. "I'm a bit tired; I thought maybe I'd turn in early."

"You're that bored?"

A faint floral wisp of her perfume clouded my normally clear mind. It had a habit of stalling when she was around.

"Of course not. I was talking to Selena, but then Henry walked over and . . ." She looked over to Henry Amari dancing with his girlfriend.

"You realized you were granted the power of invisibility?" I asked.

Her tense frame finally relaxed, her shoulders dropped, and she laughed airily.

"I know the feeling," I assured her. "You get used to it."

She glanced down at her phone again.

"So . . ." I put my untouched drink on the table, the sound it made yanking her attention back to me. "Should we use our invisibility for good or evil?"

She crossed her arms. "I imagine you'll use it for some stupid game."

"You're probably right. But, before you go . . ." I took her hand and felt the dull tremor. I nodded toward the couples dancing. "Come on, live a little."

Even though I knew I should have been trying to untangle myself from her, I couldn't. I kept convincing myself that one last joke, one more smile, one more eye roll at me—and I'd finally stop seeing her the way I did. That, eventually, I could just pull her out of my head and see her the way she saw me. And then everything would be fine.

Her heels clicked along the marble floor as she let me tug her forward.

"Did Xander Sutton have trouble finding a date?" An amused smile played along the delicate curve of her lips as she rested her hand on my shoulder.

I didn't. Tonight was a family event, and it felt disingenuous to ask anyone I had no intention of getting serious with to accompany me.

"Well, there's a first time for everything," I assured her. My hand slipped around her waist and rested at the small of her back, pulling her close for the few seconds that I could. "But keeping Sloan and Marcus apart during these events is a two-man job, and ever since Henry became a lovesick teenager, I'm a man down."

"Yes . . . Sloan and Marcus are rather amorous at all hours," she replied. I glanced past her to the table. The phone she'd set back down was ringing again. "It's sweet."

I momentarily pulled her closer for a turn. "We'll see how long you think that after being in their guesthouse for the rest of the summer."

The summer was already halfway over but our group of friends was planning to spend the rest of it in the Hamptons. For work and leisure. Penelope planned to stay with Sloan and Marcus.

"We'll be working," she reminded me.

"*We'll* be working," I corrected. "I don't know what Sloan and Marcus will be doing, but a piece of advice, never trust an unlocked door."

She laughed again. "Thank you, I will keep that in mind."

"I was surprised you agreed to stay with them."

Penelope was friendly but reserved. She was the friend that always left your home at an appropriate time. She never showed up uninvited. Always a little formal. Proper. Like she didn't ever want to ask for anything.

I didn't grow up in this world; it was only when I met Sloan that

I got glimpses of it. And up until my brother's company took off, we were relatively normal. I never got the high-society coating everyone else in this world did. Penelope's was tough to crack. She seemed to open up to Sloan, though.

"Why's that?" Her voice lifted in a playful volley. I tried to ignore how it made my heart race.

I raised my arm, leading her through a turn.

She never spent the summers out there with us. The most we saw her in the summer was when she'd visit for a weekend.

"Oh, I don't know," I teased as I pulled her back to me. In the corner of my eye, I could see her phone was ringing again. "Same reason you should probably invest in noise-canceling headphones. You're going to need them if you're staying at Sloan and Marcus's."

She rolled her eyes with a reluctant smile. "You're a deeply unserious man."

The song ended, and I felt her begin to pull away.

"Song's over." Her eyes darted back to the table; she stood up a little straighter. "Have I satisfied your request?"

I nodded. "You've lived exactly a little."

Her polite smile did nothing to mask the uneasiness that swelled in her eyes. She sparkled as she walked out of the sculpture hall, the soft uplighting catching the silver details on her dress.

Pushed by an urge to stop her, I took a step forward.

And then I took a step back as her words from the masquerade rang in my head.

"It's none of your concern. I am none of your concern."

I reminded myself that there was a reason I only got involved to a certain point. That kept me focused on the people I knew I wouldn't lose; everyone else was easy to let go of. Everyone but Penelope. I was supposed to be letting her go, but I couldn't help but hold on.

Chapter 5

PENELOPE

I'd retrieved Lily Sutton's ring for Sloan and found myself admiring it more than I should have. A radiant few carats in an oval stone, set along a platinum band—it was delicate and romantic, like it promised a happily-ever-after. I tucked the ring back in its velvet box and focused my attention on the spreadsheet.

I typed in another name—Carter Billings—as I sat at my kitchen island, in front of my laptop, and the warm, golden rays of the morning sun streamed through the large windows.

For me, spreadsheets felt like therapy.

Or a weighted blanket.

They were a way to organize thoughts, anxieties, or problems into something manageable. So I'd cataloged every available bachelor I knew in Manhattan that might be amenable to an *arrangement* of sorts. I didn't have much time left to make a decision and I needed to.

I knew I needed to trust my intuition, but after a lifetime of making the wrong choices—at least in my family's eyes—it was hard to do that. If I couldn't trust my own family to care for my best interest, how could I possibly have learned to do it on my own?

A knock rattled at my door and pulled my fleeting attention. I leaned back a bit from my seat and could see the solid walnut door down the hallway. I glanced up at the clock, it was a little before noon. We were leaving for the Hamptons today, but Sloan was early.

I walked down the hall, glancing over to the stairway landing to confirm my bags were ready, and without thinking, I opened the door. The warm summer air hit me, and my stomach dropped.

Every obligation I had back home in Singapore came bursting into my life. All neatly packed in one man: Maddox Xu, the man I was supposed to marry.

He stood expectantly at my door in joggers and a plain gray shirt. His black hair was ruffled like he'd just landed from a long flight. Piercing dark eyes and a handsome smile.

"I stopped by that bakery you like earlier," he said casually as if I were expecting him, and handed me a pastry box.

Reeling from the surprise, I looked in the box to see a few croissants.

I didn't like croissants; I liked the banana muffins. But Maddox didn't.

"That's very kind of you," I finally spat out once my heart slowed to normal speed and the initial shock wore off. I took the box from him and opened the door wider, allowing him in.

He wandered into my house, his hands tucked in his pockets as he glanced around the hallway and made his way to the kitchen. "What happened to that houseplant in the corner?"

I looked to the corner of the kitchen where the sunlight streamed in over the breakfast table. Disappointment squeezed my ribs. My poppy plant was dead.

"It's gone," I answered, following a few steps behind him. I took a deep breath. "Maddox, why are you here?"

"It's time to move along with our lives, love." Nostalgia floated along his Singaporean accent. The deceptive sound lured me to the less difficult path—the arranged marriage I'd resigned myself to for so long. Everyone in my family did it and it made me mistrust my own intuition, my own wants and needs, for even questioning it. He turned to face me, taking a few steps forward he closed the space between us. "I'm here to bring you home."

"I can manage to get on a plane all by myself."

"Well, pardon me, it seems like you've had quite a bit of trouble doing just that." He chuckled lightly, but humorlessly, to himself. "Besides, I can't have you dealing with a move on your own. You don't even have a staff, Penny."

Maddox felt like my way to some idyllic Norman Rockwell painting. He and I spent our childhood summers in Singapore; the ones that felt like a dream. In a time when my half sister and I had a real relationship before it went sour. His family, the Xus, were close to mine.

I took a step back; I felt the cool countertop along my waist. "You didn't need to come all the way here."

The Xu family, pillars in Singaporean high society, saw me as a rarity. A Western title, Singaporean breeding, and money; the *perfect* addition to their otherwise *perfect* bloodline.

Eastern and Western titles wrapped in a Singaporean-appearing heiress.

For Maddox, the eventuality of our union made him the favorite amongst his brothers. So much so that he parlayed that favor to usurp his older brother as presumed heir to Xu Enterprises. For me, it meant I was spared some of the ire I would have faced as the begrudgingly accepted product of a contentious divorce.

"Of course, I did." He took a step closer to me and held my chin. He said it sweetly, but a chill ran up my spine, warning me. More than anything, Maddox liked control.

I tucked a lock of hair behind my ear. Anxiety seeped through me. I wanted to trust my instincts and just rip the Band-Aid off, strike out on my own, but it was daunting because I knew that would mean going against my family in a permanent way. When I moved here, it was always under the condition I'd move back when I got married. What if there was no return from this? Maddox was my way back and maybe my way to being loved by them and having the family I always pictured in my mind.

"Maddox, I don't think we . . ." I tried to buy some time to think.

His brow furrowed. "Penelope, you can't run away from this. Arabella took her place and it's time you do, too."

Arabella was twenty-eight, three years younger than me, and she married her version of Maddox a few years ago, keeping her place as the family's favorite. She seemed content taking on the role as socialite; she always loved that sort of thing. At least she was happy, and I tried to make myself believe that I could be, too.

"Maddox, I'm happy with my life here," I stated, the answer becoming more resolute in my mind with every passing second. The more I convinced myself I could just fall in line, the more *something* inside me screamed not to. My heart raced. "I don't think we should do this."

All Maddox wanted out of life was to be the favorite son who took over Xu Enterprises. All he needed was his parents' favor, which he got in spades since I was eventually going to marry him. Those titles really meant everything to some people. I was the perfect trophy.

"You're happy? How? You're alone. I have seen the same boxes along that wall for years." He pointed to a random array of boxes that I'd never unpacked. "Do you even have an American driver's license?"

"I'll figure it out. Lots of people don't drive in the city."

As I began to see just how much I might be missing in a preordained life, I began to gently push the boundaries—like postponing my move home—it brought out a different side of him. One that looked caring, but with Maddox, control was dressed as kindness.

"You know that's not what I meant."

"Well, you're not *listening* to what I'm telling you." My words stretched as I tried to remain diplomatic.

"I am listening," he answered sharply. "You're telling me that you're breaking off our engagement."

I never had a ring. I was supposed to go home last winter to formalize the engagement. Luckily my awful grandfather decided to drop dead and that was an excuse to push things.

"I . . ." My voice lowered.

"What has possibly changed?" He moved in closer and ran his hands along my waist.

Maddox and I had known we'd sort of end up together for years, but we were practical about it, deciding between us that nothing needed to be *real* until it had to be. "We said if it didn't feel right or if we met someo—"

"An affair, Penelope?" His eyes narrowed, grip tightened. "Mere months before we're supposed to be married?"

"Be serious," I said calmly, gently pushing him an inch back. "You can't call *this* a real relationship."

"Call it what you want. But you expect me to believe and accept you're going to defy our families for some man you're seeing." He took a few steps back. I looked up, his irritation evaporated, and a smug grin replaced it. "Come on, Penny, there's no need to lie to me."

An indignant flame sparked in my stomach.

"I told you to stop calling me that." The serene timbre in my voice spiked to something more hostile. An irate burn blistered down my body.

"You're seeing someone? Someone whom I've heard nothing of. Whom your family knows nothing about?"

I swallowed against a throat that felt like it was lined with broken glass. "Yes."

"Don't lie to me," he warned but not in a menacing way; he said it like he was trusted counsel.

My gut or intuition or something screamed what it had been desperate to put into words over the last year. That if I married Maddox, that was it. Story over. I knew it wouldn't be long before I became nothing more than Mrs. Xu. My life would be dictated by his wants, his needs.

The courage that I didn't have the last time he visited—the masquerade—finally found its way to me.

I turned away from him and took a few steps along the side of the counter. "I'm not lying."

My stomach turned. A rapid tremble overcame every muscle fiber.

"Penelope . . ." he warned slowly.

My mind filled with my options.

I could go to Singapore, like I'd always planned to eventually do. Marry Maddox. Make my family happy and get the shares for my mother. Or I could blow it all up, because I liked Manhattan, and my job, and my friends, and being my own person. But would that be enough if it meant permanently cutting myself off from my family forever?

My eyes flickered around the white countertop until it stopped on the small black velvet box that sat quietly on it. The muffled noise in my ears stopped and a clarity rang through.

Sitting atop my inheritance documents was Lily Sutton's ring box. I opened it, and my fingers grabbed the ring. I pushed it on.

"It's relatively new." I turned back around, my heart hammered against my ribs, but I held my composure. Despite the delicate ring feeling like a boulder on my finger, something about wearing it was soothing.

A reassurance that charting my own path might be worth it. My fate might have lain in an anxiety-ridden spreadsheet, but the nausea began to subside.

His eyes roved over the ring, but instead of the anger I expected, his shoulders relaxed. He took another step back and looked around.

"Where is this mystery man? Or is he also of the imaginary variety, *Penny*?"

My mouth opened to respond but nothing came out. His eyes were fixed on mine, knowing I'd crumble eventually. He knew I was lying and the humiliation threatened to demolish the short-lived confidence.

A knock at the door broke through the silence, our attention turned to the entryway.

I glanced up at the clock hanging on the wall.

"Penelope." Xander's voice called from the other side of the door. He wasn't supposed to be here, but strangely, relief washed over me.

The smugness etched across Maddox's face began to diminish.

"Coming," I answered.

In that moment, finally, I had the courage to accept that having no plan might be better than living a story I didn't write for myself.

Chapter 6

XANDER

When I walked up the stone steps to Penelope's brownstone, I realized then that I hadn't been there since *that* night. The one we spent in her kitchen over a year ago.

The door opened a few inches, and a sliver of her interior peeked through. It opened a few more inches and I could see her more clearly.

Penelope's unsure smile wavered, looking like it would be swept away on the warm breeze that brushed along her white linen dress. My eyes immediately went over her shoulder. I'd only met him once, at the masquerade seven months ago, but I didn't need more than a second to recognize Maddox Xu.

The impatient heir to Xu Enterprises—a tech company that manufactured all varieties of gaming systems—and, more importantly, the man Penelope was going to marry.

A pit formed in my stomach.

"Xander." Her eyes flickered over me, she took an uneasy breath and twined her fingers. My attention was drawn to the facets of light that reflected off the diamond on her hand, and she immediately turned the ring so I could only see the band. "I was expecting Sloan."

The dress. The ring. *Maddox.*

Waiting for this—the day she stepped into her preordained life with him—was like waiting for a storm. I wanted to draw out every second before it came and get it over with all at the same time.

I knew exactly how I was supposed to react when it finally did happen.

Congratulatory, or at least casual.

Unbothered.

Instead, a thorny grip kept me in an immobilizing helplessness. "Penelope . . ."

She rolled her shoulders back. Despite the stoic facade, her smile wobbled.

Like it had that night at the masquerade. The same visceral pain at the thought brought back a memory that tortured me the last few months.

It filled my vision.

The loud clack of Penelope's heels against the marble floors echoed as she walked a few steps behind Maddox. He was leading her quickly out of the masquerade. Her golden dress sparkled under the chandelier in the empty lobby. It was close to midnight, and everyone was inside the ballroom for the countdown.

I had never met Maddox before, but she seemed to shrink in his shadow. All evening she'd been silently standing by his side while he talked to guests. Eventually I found her lingering by the bar seeming distracted. When I asked her to dance, she'd finally smiled. Until Maddox cut in, tapping her on the shoulder and saying, "I'm leaving. Let's go."

To my surprise Penelope agreed to leave with him without question. In that moment, she wilted into something else. Someone else.

"Penelope," I called, following right behind her.

"It's fine. I'm fine." She stopped and turned, pulling the mask off her face. It only proved to me that she wasn't. Her face was flushed, her

eyes darted around the room, stopping when she saw something over my shoulder. "Xander, I . . ."

"Penny, let's go," Maddox demanded in a tone that set every last nerve on edge.

A surge of possessiveness poured into my veins.

I closed the space between Penelope and me, pulling her hand into mine. "She's not going anywhere."

Penelope laid a hand on my chest. "Truly, Xander, it's fine."

Maddox pinned me with a hard stare. "This is between me and my fiancée."

Those three syllables leveled me.

Since learning about her engagement, I did my best to avoid how fucking wrecked I felt. In that moment, the full weight of it bore down on me.

She was his fiancée.

She was getting married. She was leaving. I was going to lose her.

So, I tried desperately to hold on. "Penelope, is this what you want?" I asked.

I prayed she'd say no. That I wasn't the only one that felt whatever it was between us since that night before she left for London.

"Yes," she answered firmly, taking a step away from me. Though the way her skin paled didn't seem convincing at all.

"If you need something. If something's going on . . ." My voice lowered.

"You wouldn't . . ." She looked at the floor. "You wouldn't understand."

"Then explain it to me," I begged.

"It's none of your concern." Her eyes moved over my shoulder. I could hear a few steps getting louder in the periphery. I glanced over to see Tristan, Rohan, and Jackson nearing where we stood. "I am none of your concern."

"That's too bad, because everyone our friends date gets a proper vetting," Tristan interrupted, crossing his arms unapologetically. He and Rohan flanked either side of me. I knew someone had to have seen Maddox pull Penelope away from me at the party. "And you"— Tristan looked at Maddox—"are new."

"No." Maddox wrapped a hand around Penelope's wrist, and she went back to him without hesitation. "You are."

"Look." Rohan's raised voice drew everyone's attention. "We can keep this civil, or we can make a scene."

That statement seemed to snap something in Penelope.

"No need." She yanked her arm away from Maddox but didn't move. She looked directly at me. "I appreciate you want to look out for me, but nothing is wrong. I'm telling you to leave us alone. This is between my fiancé and me."

She turned and leaned into Maddox's shoulder, whispering something into his ear. He nodded, and they left.

I watched their backs like it was happening in slow motion.

"Should we be concerned?" Tristan said, looking at me.

"You heard her," I told him, Rohan, and Jackson as they stared blankly at me. "She doesn't want our help. She'll come to us if she needs us."

The kicker was that the next day, after the masquerade, Maddox was gone. Penelope came to brunch like she normally did and apologized for snapping at me, insisting it wasn't how she'd hoped we'd meet her future husband.

"Play along, I beg of you," Penelope whispered to me, pulling me from the memory, and turned the ring a few times on her finger.

As my eyes ran over it, all the brewing emotions were muted by curiosity.

She was wearing my mom's ring. Relief flooded me.

I raised a brow. I didn't know what game we were playing. But I looked over her shoulder again and knew I wasn't about to let Maddox win.

"Not usually what women beg me for . . ." I leaned down to say it quietly in her ear, hoping to turn her manufactured smile into a genuine one. I walked past her and awaited some type of covert explanation in the doorway. "But sure."

She took my hand, giving it a quick and urgent squeeze. I tightened my grip to keep her palm against mine. She looked at me seriously, something crackling in her eye. "Thank you," she whispered, before her voice lifted and morphed into an artificial cheery one. "Darling. What a surprise. I was expecting Sloan."

Darling? The weight in my chest lifted. I glanced up to Maddox and back to Penelope.

Oh. This was going to be fun.

I snaked my arm along Penelope's waist and pulled her in close. The faint scent of orange blossoms from her perfume floated along the air between us. Her eyes widened momentarily.

"I thought I'd surprise you," I said, leaning my face toward her. If we were acting, I was going to sell it.

A mixture of gratitude and irritation filled her eyes.

There she is.

"Maddox Xu." I slowly turned my head to him and grinned. "To what do we owe the honor of a visit?"

I didn't know him well, but ever since that night I hated him.

Not just because he seemed to ignore that Penelope existed most of the time even though he was the lucky bastard that she was supposed to marry. Or because he called her *Penny* like it meant something that he had a nickname for her. It wasn't hard to think of a nickname. And Penny was the least creative way to go.

But because of *how* he talked to her.

"I'm here seeing Penny, of course." He crossed his arms, watching us with a hard stare. "Now, if you'd remove your arm from my fia—"

"Maddox was just leaving," Penelope interrupted. She began to pull me further into the house, and I kept my tight hold around her. "We're headed to the beach for a while," Penelope told him diplomatically, her head turned toward the steps where a few pieces of luggage sat at the landing.

"I think that's my Poppy's polite way of asking you to leave," I added and felt her stiffen at the sound of the new nickname. "Twice."

"Penelope." His eyes slid from me to her as he took a step closer. "We need to speak, privately. *Now.*"

Anger flared in my gut.

That tone.

He talked to her like she wasn't a person. Certainly not an equal. Like she was a pet or an ornament. It made me want to knock his fucking teeth out.

"She's asked you to leave." I took a step in front of Penelope. "I suggest you take her hint, because mine won't be nearly as polite."

His eyes flew to Penelope. She stared at him face on, her chin tilted upward, and said nothing.

"I'll see you when you come to your senses." He gave me one last filthy glance and made his way to the door. I took a step back and looped my arm back around her.

"I was trying to get a point across," Penelope whispered to me as Maddox passed through the threshold, "not throw him into a fit."

The door slammed shut.

"Well, I didn't have a lot of time to rehearse my lines," I snapped. Irritation worked its way around my words. She wanted to protect his feelings *while* breaking up with him?

That's what was happening, right?

We stood like that until the sound of his footsteps down to the street were inaudible.

"Kindly remove your hand from my backside," Penelope demanded.

"Oh." I pulled my arm back, not realizing just how far it had wandered. After a flustered second, I remembered that she was wearing my mother's ring. "Remove your hand from my mom's ring?"

I hadn't seen that ring in years. My mom left it to the estate and Marcus handled all of that after my parents died. He took care of everything while I drowned my sadness in any illicit substance that was handy.

Penelope blinked a few times, then a deep crimson ran across her face.

"Oh my God." She looked down at it then up at me. "I'm a perfect ass."

I glanced over her shoulder and shrugged. "It's fine, I guess."

I was lying. It *was* perfect.

"Right." She began to pull the ring off, but it got stuck behind her knuckle. Her face contorted as she twisted it. "I'll just . . ."

As she struggled with it, I ran back the last few minutes in my head. Maddox had always seemed inevitable because Penelope *wanted* him to be. She'd said, herself, that it was her decision.

Maybe that wasn't the case anymore.

The insidious buzzing in my head, the one that tortured me for over a year, stopped.

"So, you're . . . not getting married?"

She sucked in a deep breath and released it slowly.

"I just need time is all," she assured me through gritted teeth as she twisted the ring again to no avail. She groaned, turned around and walked to the kitchen sink at the opposite side of the island. She ran her hand under the water. "I will get this ring off and we can pretend this little incident never happened."

"Time for what?"

"To do what I need to do." Her hand slipped from the ring with no progress. The pitch in her voice was like a kettle about to whistle. It climbed higher and the words began to run into each other. Like every thought was pushing and shoving to make its way out. "It's complicated."

I walked over to her and shut off the tap. I handed her a towel and led her to the seat in front of her laptop.

"Clawing off your own hand is just going to make it harder," I told her gently. "Let it be, we have a two-hour drive. It'll loosen when you stop messing with it."

She let out a huff; her shoulders relaxed.

"I didn't mean to do that . . ." She looked up at me before absent-mindedly running her hand along the trackpad of her laptop. "It seemed, I don't know, serendipitous that the ring was there. I'm sorry."

"Don't worry about it." I sat down next to her. "I wasn't using it."

The laptop screen illuminated a spreadsheet; I ran over it once. Then again. My heart beat a few too many times in a millisecond. Seconds later, she realized I was looking and slammed it shut with a sharp inhale.

"What was that?" I tried to keep a steady timbre in my voice even though I saw all I needed.

"Nothing."

A spreadsheet, twenty-four rows, four columns. The columns were name, age, occupation, and "ick factor." Each row had a different name. Sebastian Amherst, Preston Scott, Carter Billings, and an entire list of men I happened to know.

My name wasn't on it.

And just like that, the buzzing was back.

She sighed. "If you must know, I have a plan."

A carefully categorized one. "And that plan is . . ."

She stood and dropped the towel on the counter.

"Once I return your mother's ring to Sloan and Marcus, I'll settle the requirements for my inheritance." Penelope tucked her laptop into the side pocket of her purse and motioned toward the foyer.

"Settle the requirements?" I echoed blankly, pushing past the gnawing in my chest. "And what does every bachelor in Manhattan have to do with your inheritance?"

"One of the requirements," Penelope said, turning her face toward the opposite wall. "I need a husband. I prefer it not be Maddox, but really it's not about finding love. This will just be business."

"How romantic." I glanced at the time. My head was spinning and we needed to get going.

I brushed past her and nodded my head in the direction of the door. I picked up the bags that were neatly arranged next to the landing on my way out to the car.

I released a heavy breath as I walked down her entryway steps.

Chapter 7

PENELOPE

Xander was uncharacteristically quiet for the first thirty minutes of the drive. I'd seen the man strike up a conversation about literally anything, birding, boat racing, international trade deals, the migratory patterns of monarch butterflies. Extremely adept at small talk, yet he was silent.

With the city behind us, the Aston Martin's engine hummed smoothly along the Long Island Expressway. That and the occasional sound of the gearshift filled the intimate space inside the car.

"Why did you call me *Poppy*?" I ventured into the silence.

Why, of all the random pet names he could have chosen, did he choose that one? Why did he bring up the poppies?

His eyes scanned the road and flickered to me momentarily.

"I dunno," he answered, the shadows in the divots outlining his biceps flexed as he upshifted. The engine roared as the car picked up speed on the nearly open stretch of highway. "It's a nickname for Penelope, right?"

"Mm-hmm." I twisted the ring again. "I never liked 'Penny.'"

"Neither did I," he mumbled and glanced over to me again. His voice lifted to a less serious one. "Try not to rip off your finger."

"Oh." I looked down and hadn't realized how hard I was pulling at my hand to get the ring off; it was red and scratched along the side. I stacked my hands neatly on my lap.

It went quiet again for another few minutes before he spoke up. "What's the endgame here?"

"I just need time." I repeated the sentiment from the kitchen.

I didn't talk much to anyone about the circumstances around my inheritance because I often became overwhelmed in trying to figure out what I wanted. Mix in the ticking clock, and it was a lot to think about.

"Time for what?" His question was delivered in the tone I was accustomed to. Sweet and reassuring. The one that enchanted every woman in Manhattan.

When I got back from my London assignment with Sloan last summer, I told them, the whole group, about my arranged marriage. That it was always something I knew would come up. I also told them it wasn't really something I wanted to litigate so they respected my wishes.

Up until the night of the Amari Masquerade when Maddox showed up, unexpectedly, only hours after I was informed that my mother's financial well-being rested on my shoulders.

"I want the fairy tale," I told him. After a childhood that taught me those didn't exist, the last couple of years here provided evidence that they might. I began to reconsider my options and I convinced my family to postpone awhile. "If I have to settle on marrying a frog for a while to eventually have it, I will."

I wasn't like Xander. I didn't want to have strings of amicable affairs but keep my heart to myself.

I wanted the real thing. The real fairy tale.

I didn't recognize all the concessions I'd made until I saw the real thing unfold before me when Sloan and Marcus fell in love. Or when Henry and Selena dropped their respective emotional walls for each other.

After all that, quiet resignation to my fate felt insulting. It became harder to convince myself it would be fine. Seeing Maddox again today affirmed all of that for me.

"And that fairy tale is your inheritance?" Xander asked, not judgmentally, but curiously.

"The fairy tale is me controlling my own future, and having the means to protect the people I love." I looked out the window. "I want to find love, eventually. For now, I just need a husband to satisfy the terms of my inheritance, and then we can part our own ways when it's done."

"If Maddox isn't the fairy tale"—he shifted gears, the engine rumbling in a smooth, mechanical hum—"then, why not have him be the frog?"

I'd considered asking Maddox to entertain an arrangement to get my inheritance, but I wasn't sure he'd actually go through with the divorce when the time came. Divorce was an albatross and the Xu family—exceedingly traditional—wouldn't allow it.

"Maddox was . . . I don't know," I failed to explain. All I knew was that I wanted a chance at my own story. "I wouldn't be happy with him."

"That's not what you said at the masquerade." His even tone was soothing, calm. But I did feel like I was at the firm acting as a target for Maya as she prepared to litigate in court.

"You remember that?" I mumbled to myself, ignoring the way my stomach churned.

His head swiveled to me, giving me an unamused look before swiveling back to the road. "I was cursed with a good memory."

"A lady is allowed to change her mind." I turned the ring slowly around my finger, pulling it forward just as it loosened. It stopped abruptly at my knuckle.

"Fair enough." His brows furrowed, but he kept his eyes fixed on the road. "What happens to the Xu Enterprises/Chen Tech merger when your family finds out your husband's not Maddox?"

My eyes widened. The merger was news, but not international news.

"How did you know?" My heart danced in a probably unhealthy rhythm.

"You've met Rohan, right? Tall, serious, knows about anything and everything that might affect the markets." A smile crept past his poorly constructed seriousness. "Two competing technology companies merging would do that."

Right. My shoulders fell, arrhythmia averted.

He knew about it because of the markets, obviously.

"I don't know what happens with the merger or my family. Xu Enterprises will still get Chen Tech's market share for their eventual line of extended life handheld gaming devices." I waved my hand casually. I didn't know much outside that in terms of the actual merger. The marriage was for prestige, but the merger probably had other benefits to the Xus.

Xander's brow furrowed, mouth hung open just slightly, but he didn't say anything, so I went on. "But I think they assumed I'd eventually fall in line."

Silas, my half brother, had taken over as CEO five years ago. When my little sister, Arabella, was married, that sealed a joint venture with the Lau family. Silas was credited even though it was Arabella's wedding that made it happen. He wouldn't be happy that I was putting another victory in jeopardy for him.

"You realize Maddox thinks you're marrying me . . ."

I trusted Maddox not to make things worse. He would be motivated by self-preservation, because these weren't great optics for him. "He won't say anything before I do, at least not publicly."

He nodded and the car became quiet for an extended beat.

"So, you're going to drag the frog around while you look for Prince Charming?" he mused.

"I'm not looking for Prince Charming. Just, I don't know . . . I want something *real*." I shrugged. "For now, all I need is a marriage on paper. Outside of that, I don't care what the frog does or where he does it."

I didn't like asking for help, not because I was proud, but I hated putting myself in a position to be in need, to trust someone or, worse, open myself up to rejection. I had a lifetime of feeling rejected from my family, who could never be trusted with my best interests—only their own. Whatever this arrangement was and with whomever it was with, I wanted it to be as simple and straightforward as possible.

He nodded and became quiet again.

It was odd seeing him serious. I'd witnessed it a few times for Dawn Capital–related items but never like this.

"No snarky remark?" I teased in the silence.

"Nope." He smiled. It always seemed to lift the heaviness in a situation, if only momentarily.

Chapter 8

PENELOPE

Bathed in the sunset's golden hues, Tristan's home in the Hamptons was the venue for the Dawn Capital launch party. The outdoor terrace overlooked the beach and the ocean was a few hundred feet away. The sea doused the shore with slowly growing waves as high tide approached.

"So." Xander's eyes wandered along the party guests who were dispersed, embroiled in conversation, along the stone patio. "Who's on that psychotic spreadsheet?"

This was not a conversation I ever wanted to have with Xander. Mostly because I couldn't trust how I felt around him. Usually friendly, sometimes annoyed, and occasionally there was *something*. Regardless, it went unacknowledged and that was for the best.

I was simply drawn to him like most people were. He had a charisma about him. A way of being that made you feel important and a part of something.

He was an aberration. A heart of gold, coated in steel.

Yet, for all his wonderful qualities, he'd never settled down. It was like he was allergic to anything meaningful. I didn't know much about why, but from a few stories Sloan told me, he'd only ever been serious with one person.

Maybe it wasn't an unwillingness to share his heart, maybe it was already taken.

Either way, some things were best left alone.

"You got a look at my spreadsheet, did you?" I sighed.

He nodded.

"Well . . ." I looked around. Most of Manhattan high society was well represented at the party, so I lowered my voice. "There's Carter Billings."

I turned the ring a few times. We'd arrived at the Hamptons too late to find a jeweler, and I still couldn't get it off. Given that I was affixed to his late mother's engagement ring, I figured it would probably be best to stick close to Xander until I found a way to remove it. We went directly to Xander's beach house to get changed for the party and now I was avoiding everyone we knew—making sure the diamond was turned inward and keeping my fingers clenched in a ball.

"Sloan's ex." Xander took a tiny sip from his glass and looked ahead. "Who else?" he challenged as if he were awaiting my serve, preparing his return shot across the court.

At the other side of the terrace, next to the bar, talking to Jackson Prince was another suitable candidate. "Sebastian Amherst."

My anxiety must have been apparent because he took a drink from a circulating server as they floated by and handed it to me. It also acted as a perfect way to hide the diamond.

"Our Central Park nemesis's older brother," Xander said casually, as if the statement didn't sound ridiculous coming from a grown man.

Nemesis was quite literally the opposite of what Madison Amherst, Sebastian's sister, was to Xander. They were exes and on excellent terms. So excellent, in fact, the society section loved to speculate the relationship might begin again.

"Don't you think you're a little old to have a park-related nemesis?"

"Don't you think you're a little single to be wearing an engagement ring?"

"Trust me, I am no happier about this situation than you are." I absent-mindedly tapped the stone against the glass.

Xander and Madison had a lot in common: both loved plants and gardening. They sat on the Central Park Conservancy board. I was surprised when I heard they'd broken up.

Although, not too surprised.

Xander was decidedly single but seldom lonely; there wasn't a socialite in Manhattan who wasn't hoping she'd be the one to get Xander Sutton to finally commit.

"You're drawing more attention by messing with it." Xander's hand reached out and held mine against the glass.

I knew that, but I needed to funnel the anxious buzz into something. I released a controlled sigh and ran my hand down my silky jade dress.

"Alright." I looked ahead. The soft ocean breeze cooled the mild warmth that ran through my hand. "How about Ravi Shah?"

"Mind-numbingly boring."

"Felix Sinclair."

"Cheats at golf," Xander answered gruffly.

"Tripp Kensington."

"Cheats at everything else," he grumbled. "Why not just pick names out of a hat?"

"If you're not going to be helpful then please leave me to my list."

"I'm serious, since it means so little to . . ."

I stopped paying attention to whatever quip sat at the end of his sentence because the idea Maya gave me popped back into my mind. It seemed less awkward now that Xander had poked holes in most of the candidates I felt like I'd actually consider.

My eyes scanned the terrace and found Tristan speaking to Maya by the steps that led down to the sandy beach.

"How about Tristan?" I wondered aloud. There was no way he'd find a problem with Tristan. They were close friends.

A loud gargle burst out of him as he coughed on his drink.

"Alders?" he choked out.

"Now *you're* drawing attention." I handed him a napkin. "And yes, Tristan Alders, obviously."

Tristan, to me, felt like what Xander must have felt like to Sloan. There was an ease I felt around him that I didn't really feel around Xander. Probably because there wasn't any competing attraction to muddle the friendship. A deal with Tristan would be clean and simple. It was a lot to ask of him, but I'd probably feel the least guilty in asking him a favor.

"No." Xander coughed again, muffled this time.

"*No?*" A defiant irritation crackled against my skin. "I wasn't asking your permission."

He didn't say anything, instead he took a long sip from his glass. Tension lined his jaw.

"And why not?" I pressed. Maybe Maya had the right idea. At first, I thought it might be too large a favor, but if I was going to ask it of someone, Tristan seemed fine. "Tristan is nice and I trust him. It would be easy."

His voice lowered. "You want to marry *Tristan*?"

"In so many words, sure."

He scoffed. "What part of marrying into an American political dynasty sounds *easy*?"

"You were acting like this was a fun little game until I mentioned him," I retorted, mildly offended. "Am I not good enough for *your* friend?"

He raised a brow. "Becoming First Lady might hamper your plans to move back to Singapore."

"Don't be dramatic, we all know Tristan will never run," I

snapped as he took another sip. While his grandfather—a former president—often tried to get Tristan to join the family political dynasty, Tristan was decidedly against it. "Besides, I never said I was leaving New York."

Xander paused and lowered his glass. His eyes moved from straight ahead to me then flickered across the terrace.

"Yes, you did." His voice lowered to the seriousness I witnessed on the ride over.

"Fine, I did," I conceded. That was the plan, originally, when I moved here. But I was content and I'd strongly considered walking away from the inheritance if it weren't for my mother's shares. Still, on summer nights like these—the ones spent near the water—I couldn't deny I missed Singapore. "I'm not sure, really. I haven't figured that part out yet."

That was what my plan offered, a blank slate.

Freedom to be completely without a plan.

"You've planned out this whole marriage scheme, but not where you want to live?" Xander pinched the bridge of his nose. Something broke his easygoing nature and frustration made its way through. "Do you know what you want, Penelope?"

Before I could say anything to answer, a familiar voice called from behind Xander.

"Xander, dearest." Beatrice Amari's velvet tone smoothed over the prickly conversation as she approached. She placed her hand on Xander's shoulder, and he turned to greet her.

Beatrice Amari, Sloan and Henry's mother, was something of a mother figure to Xander after all this time. She was accompanied by an older gentleman I'd never met before. His tall, athletic frame held a quiet grace. Classically handsome, his salt-and-pepper hair was meticulously combed back.

"Mr. Herrera." Xander smiled, as though all of our sniping

didn't happen. "Thank you for coming all the way from Mexico City."

My mind clicked. Alejandro Herrera. Xander was courting him to acquire SunCorp. "The pleasure is all mine." He shook Xander's hand. "And I must thank you for the invitation to the Hamptons, but I have a feeling it's more than a social call."

"I'm sure it is, but we are being terribly rude," Beatrice interrupted and turned to me.

"My apologies." Mr. Herrera's drawl, rich and smooth, floated over to me along with his full attention. "Beatrice, you must introduce me to this divine creature."

If an eye roll was audible, Xander's was deafening.

"Or may I call you the future Mrs. Herrera?" He took my hand and politely ran his lips just a hair's distance from my knuckles. He began to release my hand and suddenly stopped. My heart dropped when his fingers slowly turned the ring to reveal the diamond. "It seems I'm too late."

Beatrice's eyes ran over the ring twice.

Then the loudest sound I'd ever heard her make escaped her mouth. The gasp quieted the entire party. Beatrice Amari took hold of my hand and stared at the ring in utter disbelief. "Lily's ring."

Mr. Herrera looked at Xander, then me, then Beatrice; his brow scrunched.

"Lily is Xander's late mother." Beatrice quietly answered the unspoken question. She looked to Xander, a not-so-quiet glee bubbling up inside her, so apparent it looked like she might burst. My panicked eyes scanned the terrace, hoping for something to steady me. I caught a glimpse of Sloan, Henry, and Marcus looking over to me, then exchanging the same look.

Mr. Herrera chuckled and looked at Xander brightly. "Congratulations. And my apologies, it looks like we've made the announcement for you."

My mouth hung open. I had no idea what to say, how to explain this without causing a scene. "I'm not . . ."

"We were keeping it quiet until all the festivities for the weekend were over," Xander answered with a calming assurance. I looked up at him and found a momentary equilibrium in his steady gaze before I realized what he was about to do.

Chapter 9

XANDER

Everyone liked to compare life to a game of chess, but in actuality, it was poker. No matter how strategically you planned, it was all up to chance. You played the hand you had—made your decisions in a state of disorder.

And Penelope Chen-Astor was chaos.

Without thinking, I ran an arm along her waist and pulled her to me. "Right?"

I didn't know what compelled me to do what I just did, because my mind was fixed on the uncomfortable knot in my stomach as I waited to gauge her response.

"Yes." She blinked and the sounds of the party began to pick back up. "We didn't want to make a fuss."

Beatrice released Penelope's hand and gently grasped her chin. "Always so considerate."

Beatrice looked at me with wide eyes. Whatever she was thinking was masked behind years of well-rehearsed tact. I was curious where that tact was when she practically screamed moments earlier.

"Now, Mr. Herrera, let's leave the two lovebirds alone." With a polite wave, Beatrice guided him away.

I looked over to Sloan, whose brows went from raised to knitted together.

Awaiting instruction.

Same look we gave each other whenever we needed the other to run defense.

"What was that?" Penelope whispered sharply under her breath. She turned to face me.

I had no fucking idea.

All I knew was that after months of wrapping my head around her marrying Maddox, I got to have the honor of hearing all the other men she was considering. It was a knee-jerk reaction because it hurt so fucking bad. I just wanted it to stop.

"Acting?" I tried not to sound nearly as shocked as I was and pulled my arm back to my side.

Each new implication dawned as the disbelief of what I'd done cleared. I lied straight to Alejandro Herrera's face, a man who was already reluctant to trust me. Trying to get him to sell his clean energy company to Dawn Capital was something we'd been unable to accomplish for months. It was too important to let myself fuck it up with a lie, especially when I could have just as easily told him he was mistaken.

But that would have pushed Penelope back to where she'd started: choosing between different rows on a spreadsheet. It was shortsighted, but fuck, I couldn't sit by and listen while she went through the damn list again.

Instead of letting go, I stupidly held on tighter.

"You went rogue," she chastised in a hushed tone. "That wasn't the plan."

"You have no plan," I whisper-shouted back. She was absolute fucking chaos. "You have a spreadsheet and my mom's engagement ring."

The only part of this ridiculous skit that didn't track with the "plan" was that I wasn't on that stupid list.

The ever-audible sound of Selena Montez's heels cut down the suspended moment.

Selena, Henry's girlfriend, happened to work at a large PR firm. And she sensed the need for damage control when there was one.

"Keep smiling. Act casual." Selena's tight command was firm through her cheery smile. "Everyone at this party clocked what just happened. Penelope Chen-Astor is wearing an engagement ring, Beatrice Amari is practically buzzing with excitement, and you"— Selena looked squarely at me—"are the presumed fiancé. Is that what's going on?"

I rubbed the back of my neck. "Well . . ."

Right now, the risk Penelope posed in turning my entire life upside down was dimmed completely by the prospect of having to see her marry someone on that list. Even if it was temporary, all of that could be a problem for another day.

Today, I wasn't ready to face those odds.

"I don't need to know the truth right now," Selena began again. She was getting eerily good at mimicking Henry's polite society smile. "All I need to know is what narrative you want."

"Can I just put a pin in this until I figure it out?" Penelope asked with an anxious pitch that hooked into my gut.

I was used to seeing Penelope pulled together, unwavering, confident. I was beginning to realize just how much power her family, or maybe Maddox, had over her. How suddenly her defenses were breached when they were involved.

Selena's features softened. "The longer we wait, the more people will talk and take what they do know to shape the story."

"Xander." Penelope looked up at me with an unsure smile. "I can't expect you to—"

"It's not a big deal," I told them with enough certainty to reassure them both. "Besides, we've had pranks more complicated than this."

"Okay." Selena nodded her head. "Act natural and I'll tell Sloan, Marcus, and Henry what's going on."

"And Jax, Ro, and Tristan," I added. "Nobody will believe they didn't know."

"Fine. Avoid the subject, but if pressed: you two are engaged, no details. The family is keeping it quiet until after the weekend. You can figure things out tomorrow. Spend the rest of the night together, keep a low profile, and leave early. Stay at Xander's beach house together for the duration of our visit to keep up appearances."

Without another word, Selena rejoined the party.

"Let's walk the beach," I suggested, noticing the eyes of almost everyone in attendance on us.

We made our way to the steps that led off the terrace to the sand.

Penelope didn't know what she wanted, but she knew what she didn't.

She *didn't* want to be with Maddox.

She *didn't* want to get married.

But if she had to, I'd be damned if it was to anyone else.

Chapter 10

PENELOPE

The early morning sun warmed my back as I knelt on the beach in front of an almost complete sandcastle. The sound of the waves crashing mingled with the graveled crunch of sand as I scooped it up.

When a pottery wheel wasn't available, a sandy beach was an excellent alternative to channel busy hands and ease a busy mind.

Last night, after leaving the party, Xander and I walked the beach wordlessly for a while. An uncomfortable silence followed us back to his beach house and I immediate excused myself to a guest room.

I hadn't seen him this morning, but when I got downstairs there was coffee and banana muffins waiting on the counter. I wouldn't blame him for rethinking what he agreed to in the spur of the moment.

"Is that Château de Chenonceau?" His voice came from behind me, warm and inviting.

A shadow fell along the western face of the sandcastle. I held a hand above my eyes and squinted, looking up to see Xander. His athletic body blocked the sunlight. He was holding two mugs.

He offered one to me. The sand beneath my knees shifted as I wiped my hands against my shorts and reached up for it.

"Thank you. And yes," I said, pride filling my chest. What started as five large shapeless mounds became the sweeping curves of turrets, the delicate contours of the windows, and the angular heights of the roof.

He took a seat next to me and examined the castle more closely. Then he rested his elbows on his knees and looked ahead at the horizon. "All that work for high tide to wash it away in a few hours?"

I cradled the mug in my hands, the warmth seeped into my cold fingers. "Permanence is time's prison."

The moments we'd had alone together since we'd met were usually on drives and the brief spaces between parties or other gatherings. In those instances, there was a seriousness about him. Not a menacing or off-putting one. But he was different when he wasn't masked behind an array of snarky remarks or witty comebacks.

Real.

I often found myself looking forward to that time.

"Poetic," he noted.

"I've had some time to think on it."

"Permanence can be nice," he offered so quietly it was nearly muted below the sound of the crashing waves.

He looked over to me and his eyes lingered on the ring.

Guilt snaked through me. "I'm sorry. I'll go into the city tomorrow and—"

"It's fine. My mom had an interesting sense of humor." He chuckled and looked up, glancing around the morning sky. "Maybe this is her return fire for you putting on her ring without permission."

I smiled so wide I could feel my cheeks tightly against the bottoms of my eyes. I couldn't quite put my finger on it, but the joy in his voice was contagious.

"Is that where you get it from?" I asked.

"Probably. She was the one who started the prank war tradition between me and Sloan."

I could feel that recognizable pull. The one I imagined everyone felt when they were around him. The urge to know more. To hear more outlandish stories. To be a part of his world.

"Speaking of Sloan." I cleared my throat, remembering the conversation I had this morning. "She called me." It was a short call. Sloan being her typical, well-meaning, busybody self. She wanted to help get everything sorted, fix it. It was endearing and very much in character for Sloan. Maya called minutes after we hung up; she'd been summoned by her mentor to act as my counsel. She'd be working in the Hamptons all summer as well, and now she was assigned to *my* case. "We've been summoned to Amari Manor."

Amari Manor, Henry Amari's home in the Hamptons, also happened to be next door to Sloan and Marcus's beach house.

"Yeah. She called me, too."

A couple of waves crashed closer to the shoreline, sending a salty mist against my skin. He turned his mug in his hand and shifted a bit. The sun bathed him in warmth.

It was reminiscent of that morning. The one a year and a half ago before I left for London for work, before everything changed. It was the first time I believed the attraction, the playful banter, all the things I quietly ignored might be more and maybe not one-sided.

The deep, luxurious scent of coffee woke me. Sitting up on my plush couch, still in my evening gown, my eyes adjusted to the early morning light.

I looked around my living room then to the clock. Nine A.M. New Year's Day.

It was quiet. I blinked away the sleepiness and I looked ahead at the coffee table. A to-go container of coffee sat next to a banana muffin.

Last night had been the Hightower New Year's Eve party. Before I got to the ballroom, I made the mistake of picking up a phone call from Maddox. He was going to be in London for some time while I was there with Sloan on assignment for the firm.

The rest of the night felt like vertigo, and I decided to leave the party early.

As I did, I ran into Xander. He looked dazed, almost haunted. Neither of us were in the mood for a party, but were in need of a stiff drink, so we ended up at my house.

I stood and wandered to the counter, taking my muffin and coffee with me. My evening gown trailed along the floor.

Xander and I talked for most of the night, and I guess I fell asleep on the couch. I enjoyed those hours in my kitchen more than any party I'd attended in years.

I took a bite of the muffin, then placed it on the counter as I walked down the hall toward the sound coming from the entryway.

Xander sat on the floor in front of my potted poppies. The morning light poured over him. He was in his tux from last night, minus the tie and jacket. Next to him was a to-go coffee and a bucket of soil. He gently tilled it over and around the stems.

"What are you doing to my poppies?"

He paused for a moment, then looked over at me, an entertained smile playing along his lips. "They're almost dead. When is the last time you watered them?"

I couldn't remember. That was probably a bad sign.

"Where did you get soil?" I wondered, taking a sip of the coffee he'd clearly run out for. It was from a bakery near my house.

My fingers tapped along the paper cup.

"They need water." Xander ignored my question and clapped his hands against each other, brushing off the potting soil, then picked up the entire planter. "And sunlight."

I followed a few steps behind him as he placed it in the corner of the nook where my breakfast table sat. He turned it so the flowers were in the sunlight.

"And make sure someone takes care of them when you're in London," he instructed warmly.

"Water. Sunlight. Caretaker," I counted off as the butterflies in my stomach kicked up a whirlwind. *"Understood."*

A few days after that morning, Sloan and I were off to London for six months for work.

By the time I came back, everything had changed. My family told me about the plans for me to marry Maddox and for a while, I was resigned to it.

And Xander, well, he'd gone about his life like that morning never happened. Weeks after returning and sharing the news, the society section was littered with pictures of Madison and Xander; he was very much still in his pattern of short-lived relationships.

I thought I felt *something*, but it was probably nothing. My intuition was spotty at best.

"Penelope." The serious timbre in his voice roused me from the memory. "What exactly did I sign up for?"

"Nothing," I blurted before thinking. Maybe I messed up. Maybe all this was too much, a step too far. A tremor ran through my hand as I backpedaled what I'd decided the day before. "I . . . I'll talk to Selena. We can stop all this now."

"Hey." Xander's gentle voice steadied my nerves. The reassuring look in his eye felt like a guiding light, promising me I wasn't lost. "If you want your inheritance this way, we'll do it. I just need the details. I'm part of this, too, now."

"Right." I looked at my feet as my heels dug into the sand a little deeper. I also remembered that all of what happened last night happened in front of half of high-society Manhattan. And important members of Dawn Capital's portfolio. It sort of sealed things unless he planned to have awkward conversations with everyone in attendance. "I'm sorry. I know commitments aren't really your thing."

"It's not a *real* commitment." He gave me a tilted smile, though it seemed to waver at the corners. "Really, Penelope, it's not a big deal. I want to help. Just tell me what we need to do."

I envied him for that, the ability to make a decision in a moment and feel assured in it. A lifetime of being told I was wrong in wanting things that felt natural robbed me of that confidence and riddled me with self-doubt when it came to making personal choices. Like now, when I waffled over if I'd done the right thing.

"You signed up for a year," I explained, giving him the details he asked for. "I'll get my inheritance a year from the date of my marriage. The only stipulations are: I need the marriage to happen by the end of this summer and I need to purchase a home in Singapore."

"Buy a property, get married," he counted off on his hand. "Simple."

I nodded.

We could do this. It would ensure my mother would be cared for in perpetuity. The taxes on that country estate she lived on alone were higher than my annual bonus. The shares in Astor Media were not only rightfully hers, but the dividends would provide my mother financial security for the rest of her life. And maybe loosen the pressure that caring for her always bore down on me.

Xander was silent and looked back at the water. The waves lapped gently at the shoreline, inching closer to my castle; the sound filled the quiet between us.

"I would have walked away from it, the inheritance," I told him, hoping to abate the shame I felt for dragging him into this. "I planned to. But that night, during the masquerade, Maddox told me about my family's plans to tie my mother's shares in Astor Media into that inheritance as well. And add a timeline for this summer."

Something flared in his emerald eyes. "That's why you left with him?"

I nodded and regretted the way I snapped at Xander that night for being a good friend.

"I needed to figure out what I was going to do. I hadn't really decided until right before we left for the Hamptons and"—I looked at the ring—"this."

"Why does your dad's family have control of your mom's shares in *her family's* company?"

"On paper, my father said he was concerned that my mother would misuse them. Truthfully, she isn't the best with responsibility," I explained. Even now, my mother relied on me to take care of everything. "He promised them back to her through me and in turn, he let my mother have the custody arrangement she wanted."

My mother only agreed to that because she was twenty-five and terrified that he'd take away her only child. She assumed she could live on her settlement, something she'd nearly run through by now. She had no idea the shares would one day be used as a means to control me.

"That way they keep you in line and honor a marriage to Maddox," Xander surmised quietly. "What do the Xus get out of it?"

"My mother doesn't have siblings," I explained, "so her title passes to me. I'm the last Astor."

To the Xus, I was something of a rarity. Born with a Western title, but raised in Singapore, I was a bargaining chip into every high-society family.

"Tying you to Maddox, using your mom as emotional blackmail, and no one seems to care how you feel about it." He ran his hand along his jaw, frustrated. Then he looked back to me and smiled. One of those smiles that always seemed to make my stomach flip. "Maybe we *should* use our invisibility for evil."

My heart felt lighter.

He had a knack for doing that, chasing away the heaviness with humor.

"This may not be a simple favor, Xander. My half brother, Silas, may want to fight me on my choice, or be treacherous," I warned.

He stood and dusted the sand off his legs.

"I wouldn't worry about it," he assured me with an impossible confidence. "Xander Sutton doesn't lose."

Chapter 11

XANDER

When we arrived at Amari Manor, we found Maya on the stone terrace overlooking the south lawn with a stack of papers, waiting for Penelope, alone. Penelope went to Maya immediately and they began discussing what I assumed were the terms Sloan probably drew up already.

I looked out across the rolling green lawn and spotted Henry and Sloan participating in an Amari family tradition while Selena and Marcus watched fifty feet away.

I raised my hands over my brow and squinted against the sun.

"I'll get them," I called to Maya and Penelope as I crossed the lawn, away from Amari Manor and the elaborate breakfast set up on the stone terrace.

"Pull!" Sloan's shout pierced through the silence; a metallic clacking followed as a clay disk was ejected, full speed, into the air.

Sloan and Henry were lined up next to each other. The barrel of Sloan's shotgun followed the clay disk's trajectory; she aimed and shot it dead-on. A few seconds after her bull's-eye, Henry yelled the same thing, and the same sequence of events repeated for a few more rounds. Each of them hitting their target as they switched off.

"I thought we went over firearms around Sloan," I told Marcus plainly as I walked up beside him and Selena. They stood next to each other, watching with controlled trepidation from afar as the Amari siblings competed.

"Sloan can be . . ." Marcus's eyes followed Sloan as she geared up to take out another clay disk ". . . persuasive."

"Who's winning?" I asked, skating by the disgusting implication.

"It's a very tense tie." Selena took a sip of her mimosa.

"So." Marcus crossed his arms. Knowing Sloan, he probably had to listen to her go through all the possible iterations of how all of this could turn out. She was worried, which meant Henry and Marcus were, too. "You're getting married."

"If this is when you give me the sex talk, you're *very* late. Besides, I'm pretty sure I'm the one who gave it to your fiancée."

If looks could kill, the one Marcus gave me would do it.

"I'm serious," I goaded, too tempted to see how far I could push his legendary patience. "All Beatrice told Sloan was that unplanned pregnancy was unbecoming."

"Xander," Marcus warned again, this time it sounded exasperated. "You don't need to pretend every difficult conversation isn't difficult by making it a joke."

But it made dealing with them easier.

"I'm fine," I assured him firmly. I looked over to see Henry firing the final shot. "Seriously. It's not a big deal."

If I said it enough, I was sure to believe it eventually.

Marcus looked over to Sloan then back to me, thinking. Henry joined us and right as he opened his mouth, Selena interrupted.

"Why don't we head to the terrace," she said quickly, looking up at Henry with an expectant smile when he walked over and threw an arm over her shoulders. Henry and Marcus exchanged a look and agreed. "Penelope and Maya are probably waiting."

The three made their way up the lawn toward Amari Manor. I

waited for Sloan since, clearly, everyone thought I needed to talk to someone.

Sloan finished handing her materials back to the groundskeeper and joined me.

"So." Sloan clapped her hands together, brows raised.

"Penelope needed help. I helped. That's what we do," I said quickly before she launched into whatever line of questioning she had planned. Penelope often kept us at arm's length, but she was still one of our own and if she needed something, we were going to get it for her.

Sloan nodded, didn't say anything, and strolled toward the house. I followed next to her.

"I'm just surprised." She slowed down to a stop. "Going from the guy who starts every relationship with the 'don't fall for me' talk to getting married."

"It's not a relationship, it's an arrangement," I corrected her.

"Right . . ." she wondered aloud. "It's just . . ."

She turned to me. Her eyes spanned the lawn a few times, undecided. Sloan's default setting was to push, but when it came to me, she often held back for fear she'd push too far.

"After Reina, it seemed like you'd never go through with an actual commitment again," she continued but winced when she realized she'd just said Reina's name out loud. "I know you said you'd moved past it, and I'm happy you did. I guess a part of me always wondered if you were still waiting for her."

Reina, for so long, felt like the one that should have been.

For a fleeting second, I was tempted to tell Sloan that Reina was back in Manhattan after spending years abroad. The one thing, the only thing, I'd wanted for so long. Reina chased a dream to be a traveling journalist, leaving me with the choice to follow her or stay home. I chose home. Surprisingly, after years of regret, I couldn't make myself care that she'd returned.

"I'm not waiting for her."

Not anymore. Not for a long time. Not since that night and the following morning with Penelope—and the poppies—before she left for London.

"I'm glad." She squeezed my shoulder.

A silent beat passed between us, filled with the rustling sound of the wind moving through the trees at the ends of the property.

"Look . . ." I let out a heavy breath and tried to think of how I was going to ask this without raising a thousand alarms in Sloan's head. My weight shuffled between my feet. "I need a favor."

Sloan not acting in the best interest of the Hightowers was nice in that it was satisfying to see them get what was coming to them, but that thrill was short-lived. It had been so long since my parents died, the fury of it faded for me even though the desire for retribution burned bright for Sloan.

"Okay . . ." Sloan looked at the terrace to see everyone there along the table, very far out of earshot. Like she knew something was coming. "What do you need?"

It all came together in my mind in pieces.

The drive to the Hamptons. The terrace. The beach this morning.

I'd looked into Maddox when I'd first met him, but I didn't do anything with that information because Penelope had told me to stay out of it. But that was how I knew a merger was brewing. Every tech company would want a piece of SunCorp once Herrera's novel extended-battery tech was made public. Especially someone who planned to make extended-life portable gaming systems—that little piece of information Penelope mentioned in the car. All this time Maddox had power over Penelope, but now, I had a chance to have some over him.

"Speed up the Hightower case. You probably have the proof that the whistleblower needs to support their claims, right?"

She had to. It was how she knew the Hightowers were guilty. But her job was to protect them.

"Yes," Sloan answered speculatively.

I had a feeling if I could promise Herrera the seat at the head of the world's largest energy company and the capital to get his technology up and running sooner than anyone planned, he'd agree to Dawn Capital acquiring his company.

And that happened to put me directly in the same market that Maddox would need. It gave me a seat at the table and an impossibly good hand.

All I needed was Sloan to agree to stack the deck.

"And you know how we call in favors with each other—no questions asked?" I reminded her. "I'm calling one in."

Her lips straightened. Breath stilled. Shoulders lined up. She knew it was serious and now she knew she couldn't ask me about it.

Over the years, through endless shenanigans, Sloan and I accrued favors for each other by getting the other out of an unsavory situation. The game of I-owe-yous was originally lighthearted. But occasionally, when things got heavy and we weren't able to talk about them, one of us would call in a favor—named after the location that favor was earned—and the other would grant it without question.

That's how she knew it was serious and I wasn't ready to talk about it. For so many reasons. It was far riskier now—unethical and probably *a little* illegal—so I'd understand if she wanted to know more for putting her in a precarious position. But Sloan also knew I wouldn't ask if it weren't important.

"I'm going to put Herrera on that open throne," I told her, resolutely.

Hightower Energy needed to collapse. Originally, that's where the plan ended. But now, I'd buy it out and use the open CEO seat as bait for Herrera to finally sell SunCorp's assets to Dawn Capital.

Assuming it went according to plan, the world's largest carbon emitter would become the leader in clean energy. The world would benefit. And, as an added bonus, Dawn Capital would be well set up to profit from it all. Having the patent on extended-life battery technology decades ahead of any viable competition would give us power over anyone who wanted to buy it.

The Chens. The Xus. Anyone that might try to pull the strings in Penelope's life again.

Sloan's lips twisted to the side in thought. Her brow crinkled with a thousand withheld questions.

"Since this is headed to the Justice Department, I can have Senator Fitzgerald Alders *happen upon* the documents that would be the smoking gun to the whistleblower's accusations." Fitzgerald Alders, Tristan's cousin, was a friend with his eyes on the White House. Being the public face of taking down the Hightowers would make him look like a hero. "A full-blown Senate inquiry would give me enough plausible cover to advise Hightower Energy's board to vote him down. Once they do, you need to be ready to buy them out." She went on, looking at me with concern etched all over her face, "Does that work?"

"Yes," I answered, and we began making our way back to the rest of the group. "Thank you."

She nodded and went on in a firm, unemotional cadence. "And you'll need new representation—I'll get you a good name. The same firm that represents Hightower cannot help you buy them out."

"Okay."

"And you'll tell me the real reason eventually. Whenever you're ready," she added sternly, looking at everyone on the terrace, then back at me, "because I know this isn't only to close a deal."

If Sloan knew how tangled up I was in Penelope, it would mean spending the next year watching her and everyone that cared about me treat me like I was made of glass. Terrified that the end would break me.

"I will," I promised.

Once I was past all of this, I'd tell her with the same ease I told her I was over Reina. I just needed some time.

"And be careful, okay? With Pen, I mean. Her family in Singapore is tough. Then there's her mom, who isn't the best when it comes to support."

"Yeah . . ." I didn't know much about Penelope's family other than she had half siblings. All I knew about them was that they existed.

"Her half sister, Arabella, doesn't really talk to her." Sloan's shoulders slouched. "I met Silas while Pen and I were in London and he's a trip."

I tried not to linger on how broken I felt when she came back from London and told us about her engagement, so I started seeing Madison. I knew what I needed: short, amicable relationships with an expiration date. Nothing that would be painful to lose.

I could do with Penelope what I did with every other relationship. *Right?* Use this time to move past her, try not to get pulled any deeper than I already was. All without having to see her married to someone else. Win-win.

"I don't want her to get hurt and keep her distance," Sloan warned me. "I don't want to lose her."

Neither did I.

In fact, I was constantly surprising myself with the lengths I'd go to just to hold on to even a piece of Penelope.

* * *

WE WALKED BACK up to the terrace to join everyone already seated around the large circular outdoor dining table.

I took the empty seat next to Penelope and looked over her shoulder to see what she was reading.

Sorry, Ladies, He's Taken!
Billionaire Cofounder of Dawn Capital,
Alexander Sutton, Engaged to Manhattan-
based Attorney Penelope Chen-Astor.

Penelope tilted her phone screen in my direction, the warm breeze rustling through her silky hair and into my face as I leaned in to read the headline on her phone.

"Good news is this article is highly complimentary," Selena began cheerily from next to Henry. "Bad news, now there's press interest in you two."

"And as long as there's interest, someone will try to find a story." Henry ran a hand through his hair. "Trust me."

"At least they called you an attorney." Sloan looked at the headline above the picture of the two of us. It must have been taken moments after the gasp that launched a thousand rumors. "They always call me *an heiress*."

"Well . . ." Penelope's eyes kept running over the headshots of us, side by side. Her shoulders slumped down. Her voice lowered to a decibel I could hardly hear. "I guess there's no turning back now. It has to be you."

I sat down beside her and glanced at the stack of papers in front of me. Sloan already had the contracts written. And she'd thought of everything.

An agreement, terms, and a divorce date.

Everything.

Not that I needed the reminder that this was strictly an arrangement, but if I did, Penelope's tone—the one bordering on resigned disappointment—did a good job.

Henry chuckled and laid a supportive hand on her shoulder. "Don't worry, it's just a year. We've had him for eighteen and we're mostly fine."

"Henry," Marcus, who'd sat silently next to Sloan, warned.

"What? He's been a smart-ass since the day I met him. I'm not pulling any punches."

I leaned toward Penelope. "Consider yourself lucky. You get to leave me when this is done." I pointed around the table. "These suckers can't."

"That's not what I meant," she snapped, sitting up straighter. "And you know it."

I always found that pissing her off was the fastest way to eventually get a smile out of her. And those smiles were like a drug.

Focus.

I sat up straighter and reminded myself not to fall in any deeper than I already had. That every protection I'd built for myself seemed to crumble when she was around. I needed those.

"We can use the press interest to our advantage." Selena drew our attention back to her. "We play into the whole whirlwind-romance thing. You fell in love, just had to get married. Then in a year or so, you have an amicable split."

"Which is an easy sell with Xander," Sloan pointed out.

"Thanks?" I crossed my arms, unsure if I should be offended.

"It's simplicity itself," Selena insisted.

"Sounds perfect, honey." Henry grinned up at Selena from his seat. Selena could have just as easily regurgitated incoherent nonsense and I was sure he'd look at her the same way. Pure love and unwavering devotion.

It was sweet. The kind of sweet that decayed your teeth, but sweet, nonetheless.

"You're married for a year. Once Penelope's inheritance is transferred to her, the clause in the divorce agreement goes into effect," Sloan explained, handing me a small stack of documents. The signature lines all flagged. "Then you're divorced with all the assets you came into this with."

I swiped my pen along the signature lines, signing both my marriage contract and the divorce papers.

"One last thing," Maya added. She hesitated for a second. "There is no fidelity agreement written into the contracts. They're sealed and the only thing that's publicly available is the marriage license."

The table became quiet.

"But . . ." Selena picked up for her. "It would be a mess if either of you are caught with your pants down . . . so to speak."

"Understood," I said as I looked up and the sudden realization that I just signed up to be fucking celibate for a year hit me. But if it meant not having to sit by and watch as she married someone else, I'd take that bet.

"Great. The wedding is in two weeks." Selena didn't wait for either of us to ask a question. "The whirlwind romance with a whirlwind beach wedding is perfect. Nobody is going to go looking for plot holes in such an adorable story."

"A wedding?" Penelope turned the ring around on her finger. "Is all that necessary? Why not sign these, call a judge, and get it all over with?"

Henry chuckled again but didn't say anything.

"I just mean . . ." Penelope moved her hands to her lap and shifted in her seat. "I don't want to make a fuss."

"The more real it looks, the fewer questions, the less interest from the press." Selena walked back to the empty seat next to Henry. "Everyone at this table, plus CeCe and the Dawn Capital cofounders, know the truth. Everyone else doesn't."

After we finished talking about the terms, Selena went to meet CeCe—a friend of ours who practically ran every high-society party in Manhattan. The two had taken it upon themselves to plan everything. By the time we got back to my beach house late that afternoon, the date, venue, and most of the other big details were being settled.

In two weeks, I'd be a married man. Fake-married man.

"Look." Penelope turned to me in the foyer. She was silent for almost the entire afternoon. "I know this isn't fair to you."

"Seriously." I put a hand on her shoulder and leaned down. "It's not a big deal, this kind of thing happens more than you'd think. Besides, now you owe me a favor."

She smiled but it faded almost as quickly as it came.

"Yes, but." She looked down at her fingers twined between each other. "If you find yourself *with* someone."

"With someone?"

"I just mean, it's fine. Fair. I wouldn't expect you to . . ."

A thorny grip constricted around my lungs as I processed that her words went both ways. "You *want* to have affairs?"

Of course she did. I was the frog. Not the prince.

"I just mean," she clarified with a sharp undercurrent, "this isn't real, so I don't expect fidelity or anything silly like that."

"What do you expect?"

"Nothing," she said firmly but her eyes refused to look at mine. "That's my point. Outside of what's on paper, I expect nothing from you."

My jaw sat on edge, trying not to react. I couldn't figure out how she managed to get under my skin so fast. Nobody else could. But fuck, Penelope made me feel anger, jealousy, *real* desire, everything I tried to avoid.

"Once is more than enough to be a headline." I lifted her chin to force her to look at me, trying to get across what I couldn't put into words—that I wasn't about to sit here and have a front row seat to her doing exactly what she so kindly offered to me. Irritation pricked against my skin. "I know this isn't real, but there's risk for me, too. I am not signing on to this, lying to everyone I know, all for you to blow it because you can't keep—"

"I have no plans to blow it." Indignation sparked in her eyes. She pushed my hand away and took a step back. "God you're infuriating. I'm trying to make this entire mess less of a burden on *you*."

It was so clear that Penelope accepting help made her viscerally uncomfortable. I wasn't sure why; it didn't seem like pride. But I never wanted her to feel that way around me. And I didn't want to *ever* have this conversation again.

I tried to rein in all of it. Go back to the setting that felt safe, one I could rely on—carefree, unbothered. Diffuse this entire conversation, the one that was getting *way* too close to somewhere that I knew would hurt.

So, skirting around it with a joke seemed like the perfect fix.

"How about this. If you want something"—I leaned in and playfully threw my arm around her shoulders, dissolving all the anguish that the reality of the situation brought up—"all you have to do is ask."

The teasing suggestion got exactly the response I was expecting.

With a sigh that couldn't hide the smile or conceal the laugh, Penelope gave me a gentle shove. "Are you ever serious?"

"What makes you think I'm not serious?" I grinned down at her as she stepped out from under my arm.

She rolled her eyes and waved as she walked down the hall, her lithe frame cutting though the evening light as she walked to her bedroom.

I watched, realizing just how difficult this year was going to be.

Chapter 12

PENELOPE

The best part of working from the Hamptons for the summer was that everyone made themselves available for the social events during the season. Today, that was the Annual Augustus Charity Regatta at the society club's outpost in the Hamptons.

My wide-brimmed sun hat gave me some shade as I walked out of the clubhouse toward the docks where everyone had congregated for today's races. All for charity, the different age groups of rowers competed in the regatta for the afternoon and then there was a reception that would be sprawled across the club's green and indoor spaces.

"Why aren't you three competing today?" I asked when I joined Henry, Sloan, Marcus, and Selena, all standing along the wooden walkway that extended over the water's edge.

I looked out onto the water. It glimmered in the afternoon sun as the faint salty spray from the waves lapping against the rocks and the patio misted around my feet.

Lined up a hundred feet away, bobbing along the tranquil water, were the sculls—the boats—for today's races.

"See that marker?" Sloan asked, nodding her head in the direction of the water. Marcus pointed to the red one a few hundred feet behind.

"Yes."

"I took an oar to the back of the head from the shell during a race right there," Henry explained. "From Sloan."

"*During* a race?" I clarified. The Amaris always surprised me. From the outside they were a powerful, seemingly perfect family. From the inside they were surprisingly comfortable with their dysfunction.

It was refreshing.

"Needless to say, they lost," Marcus added. "And have been banned from competing."

"In my defense it was a few months after the formal succession plans were announced and I wasn't taking it well," Sloan added.

I smiled and leaned against the dock; the warm summer breeze sent ripples across the water as the boats took their places at the starting line.

"I didn't know Xander rowed crew," I said aloud, seeing the four rows to the starting line. He, Tristan, Rohan, and Jackson were all on a team competing today.

This past week was interesting. I was learning a lot of little things about Xander.

There was an alluring duality about him. An extrovert by nature, yet he spent his free time alone in quiet solitude. A charismatic jokester when in public, but surprisingly serious when in a more intimate setting.

"He didn't for a long time," Sloan explained, watching the water as the starting gun blared through the tranquil air and they were off. "But when he moved to Manhattan after college he met Ro and Tristan. It was something they started doing together to help—"

She stopped. I looked over to her and saw her glancing at Henry and Marcus.

"It got his mind off things," Marcus finished for her.

Neither of the three said anything else and I could see Selena fidget uncomfortably before turning her attention back to the water. The time directly after he graduated college was when his parents passed tragically in a car accident. The details of that period weren't often discussed.

The silence was interrupted by a loud cheer. Tristan's team crossed the finish line to win the race, earning them advancement to the next round.

"I'm going to head in." Marcus pressed a kiss against Sloan's head and nodded to Henry to follow. "They may actually win this thing."

"Oh good." Henry finished his drink and followed Marcus as they made their way into the clubhouse. "Their egos weren't nearly inflated enough as it is."

"Huh." I looked over to Xander, the water that had sprayed on him during the race made his shirt cling to the defined muscles below. My eyes *lingered*. "I never really enjoyed watching rowing . . ."

"I didn't understand the whole polo thing . . ." Selena took a sip of her champagne and leaned against the railing of the dock, nudging my shoulder. "Then I saw Henry in the uniform."

* * *

"Aren't you going to congratulate me?" Xander threw his arm around my shoulders. The weight sent a delightful wave through my body.

A few hours after the last race, all the participants changed and joined the festivities.

"I'm fresh out of gold stars, I'm afraid." I turned the drink in my hand as we walked outside, the extensive lawn was punctuated with tents and lanterns.

"You know, this is our first public outing since the engagement," he teased with a coltish grin. "Instead of Proper Penelope, why don't you try 'doting fiancée'?"

Either he was exceptionally talented at compartmentalizing or everything about the marriage didn't faze him at all.

He was still so carefree, like it was all a game.

"Fine." I turned to face him and patronizingly patted his shoulder; I could play along. Maybe even win a round. I glanced through the partygoers socializing around us then looked right back at him. "Usually, men don't like to be known for how quickly they finish, but good for you. Congratulations."

He chuckled; a boyish excitement passed through his eyes. "Try again."

That was the thing about Xander, despite how you'd fight his magnetism, it was quicksand. The more you rebelled, the tighter its hold.

"*Darling*," I drawled. We took a few steps closer to the patio railing overlooking the water. "You did such a good job paddling your little boat faster than all the other little boats."

A smile curved along his lips; his eyes stayed fixed on mine. "Almost."

"And in a straight line, no less," I added sarcastically. His arm moved from my shoulders, his hand slowly glided down, resting at the small of my back. My breath hitched. "I . . . I imagine it was rather difficult."

"Come on. You can do better than that."

"Well, I don't see you tryin—"

He took a quick look around us before taking a gentle hold of my chin with his thumb and index finger. He leaned in. "You look intoxicating."

A flutter I refused to acknowledge lapped *low* in my belly. I'd never been on the receiving side of his flirting, but I could see why every woman fell for him so quickly.

"I . . ."

"Directionality is a lot harder when you're standing there, in view . . ." His eyes flickered down my dress. His jaw flexed for a moment. ". . . looking the way you do. So, thank you, Poppy, it *was* difficult."

He released my chin and looked straight ahead, acknowledging someone behind me. I turned to see it was Alejandro Herrera walking in our direction.

Of course, he was performing for an observer, and I stupidly almost believed it. Then I reminded myself that Xander could probably have chemistry with an inanimate object.

"If we're going to sell this thing," he whispered as Herrera approached us both, "you're going to have to try a little harder."

His flirtatious playfulness was swept away. The warm buzz dissipated.

I shook my head. All of this was in service to my inheritance. The least I could do was play along as well as he did.

"You're right. I'm sorry," I stammered after an extended, awkward silence.

His gaze softened and his shoulders relaxed. He opened his mouth as if to say something when another voice filled the air between us.

"If it isn't the couple everyone is talking about." Alejandro Herrera let out a deep bellow of a laugh. "You'll have to excuse my forward introduction to your fiancée."

Xander's hand gently slid along my hip to my back again, finding its original place. "Who could blame you? My Poppy is . . ."

"Intoxicating?" I smiled politely, taking his lead, and playing along.

His brows lifted momentarily; a smile arched up his cheek. It was different this time, it looked genuine, unacted, but it wasn't as though I was any good at deciphering what was real and what wasn't.

"Exactly," Xander added.

"That's very kind, darling." I gently patted his chest and leaned into him.

Alejandro began to talk about something related to a deal Xander was trying to convince him to complete, but I had trouble hearing it. Xander's fingers gently moving up and down an inch or two along my back became thunderous.

"Where did you two meet?" Alejandro looked at me warmly, the question snapping me back to the conversation. Then he looked back squarely at Xander. "The mark of a man in love is how he tells this story."

Xander's arm moved up my back to rest along my shoulders again. His fingers passed the dangling gem on my earring between them. A gentle shiver rolled down my back.

"It was the summer, years ago, when she started at the firm. I was visiting a friend who works there, and Poppy was wearing this pastel yellow dress with adorable short, ruffled sleeves. She kept running her hand over it, like she was nervous." He spoke with a wistfulness that was so convincing that I had to remind myself not to believe him. "Her desk looked like a windstorm passed over it. She was reading the files she had in one hand with more tucked under her other arm. Distracted . . ."

He turned his attention to me. The emerald in his eyes shimmered in the setting sunlight.

I smiled and tried to think of anything to say but couldn't. He wasn't fabricating some adorable anecdote. I remembered that day. The yellow dress. It had been my favorite dress for years.

I wore it on my first day at the firm. I spilled red wine on it during the new associate mixer after work that night and the cleaners couldn't get the stain out.

I never wore that dress again.

But that wasn't the day I met Xander.

We met at a bar near the firm a few weeks after my first day.

He'd come to meet Sloan when all the associates went out for drinks. Had he actually seen me before then?

Xander looked back to Alejandro and exchanged a few more pleasantries, but it all felt muffled under the realization that began to dawn.

My heart skipped a beat.

It wasn't until Alejandro began to walk back toward the patio that I blinked away the haze.

"Poppy?" The slow, teasing drawl pulled me from the memory completely.

"You remember the yellow dress?" I murmured.

"I wouldn't read into it," he advised me, his arm around my shoulders led us as we began to walk toward the rest of the party. "I have a good memory."

I stopped and turned to face him directly. His arm fell to his side. "I won't because you're wrong."

"No, I'm not." Xander looked down at me with a competitive smile. "You were in a yellow dress at the firm, arms full of papers and folders. You were talking to . . ."

His eyes flickered to the floor and his throat shifted with a noticeably hard swallow.

He had come to the same realization I had.

Xander couldn't have been recalling the first time we met; he must have been remembering the first time he saw me.

Xander looked at me, deep in thought, like he was debating saying something. Then, after a beat, the seriousness faded from his eyes, and the tension that lined his body relaxed. It was like he flipped a switch. And we were playing a game.

"Point, Poppy," he answered.

Chapter 13

PENELOPE

Custom Chanel. Lotus silk. Handcrafted stitch by stitch.

My wedding dress required three dressmakers working around the clock in order to have it ready in time for this weekend. Between CeCe and Selena, this wedding was certainly going to *look* like a real one.

"We'll put a couple of satin buttons along the back of this collar to fasten it," the seamstress from Chanel, Griselda, said through closed teeth that held a few silk pins.

I'd been standing on a pedestal in front of the mirror in the primary bedroom—Xander's bedroom—of the beach house for almost an hour as Griselda made some of her final adjustments. It was the only room with a full-length mirror.

"Alright." I nodded; I'd spent most of my time in this dress nodding obediently to the elderly seamstress.

Of the five designs the artists at Chanel created, CeCe fell in love with this one and insisted that even if I didn't choose for it to be my wedding dress design, I have it made in another color.

The sleek high halter neck left my shoulders and back completely bare.

It was a departure from my demure taste in its provocative backless dip that ended just above the curve of my backside; it seemed perfect for a fake wedding because I'd never choose something like this for my *actual* wedding.

I looked at myself, running my hands down the luxurious silk.

It had to be a fortune. Xander simply gave his black card to CeCe, so I had no idea what it cost, but I owned enough custom Chanel to know it was at least a couple hundred thousand dollars.

"Wow." Sloan stopped in the doorway, holding a yellow envelope in her hands. "Va-va-voom, Pen."

Every drop of blood found its way to my face. I'd never really seen myself as sexy before. Pretty, of course. But sexy? My eyes wandered along my reflection again and I couldn't help but feel that way.

"What are you doing here?" I asked.

"I came to drop off a few things for work and ask you something." Sloan handed me a yellow envelope. I opened it slowly, tried to remain completely still as my eyes ran over it. The last time I moved to take a bite of my banana muffin Griselda pricked me and I was sure it was on purpose. "And that yellow envelope was being delivered when I was walking in."

I looked up at Sloan, pausing my assessment of the document. "What did you need to ask?"

"Your mom." She looked down at the floor then around the room. Sloan met my mother, so she had firsthand experience to understand why I hadn't even thought to include her in this. "I know this is sort of a surprise for the Chen side, but as for Victoria . . . Do you want to invite her to the wedding?"

"No," I said reflexively. My mother would come but only because she knew she should. I loved her, dearly, but my mother wasn't the doting kind. "I'll tell her about it after it's done."

"Are you sure? Are you worried about . . ." Sloan looked at Griselda, who was busy around the short train of the dress. Sloan mouthed: *Lying?*

I couldn't help but laugh a bit, then immediately stopped when a cool metal pin scraped along my skin. I wouldn't have to lie that much to my mother; she wasn't the type to ask questions. As long as I took care of logistics like I had since I was a child, she was happy.

I nodded as I carefully opened the envelope.

"Good news! Tristan's grandfather would love to officiate," she added cheerfully.

While mundane for Sloan, the former president of the United States officiating my wedding made my pulse race with worry. This lie was going all the way to the top of the federal government.

I scanned the document Sloan brought in with her. An anxious skitter prickled along my skin.

"They're taking control of their Manhattan property," I explained after a quick review. "The Chen family lawyer states I need to be out by the end of the month."

It wasn't as much of a shock as it should've been. I'd always known that home didn't belong to me. That's why I'd never fully unpacked.

"They're trying to force me back home," I said, handing Sloan the file.

"Is that the best they have?" Sloan's lips pursed for a moment as she looked down at the paper. "All we have to do is move your things into Xander's place. Either here or his place in the city. We were going to do that anyway, right?"

Yes, it was an easy fix, and my family must have known that. This wasn't meant to stop me. It was meant to make me nervous. And it did.

It also meant that Maddox had told someone what happened, and I suspected it was Silas since this development reeked of him. My half brother, the engineer behind the nickname I reviled, was an expert in torturing me. He knew nothing worked more efficiently at bringing me down than my own head.

"It's a warning shot," I explained.

Ever since Silas took over Chen Tech as CEO, he'd been out to prove himself. And since he had little talent, he needed to rely on other methods to close deals, like the Xu family's obsession with ornamental titles.

"A pretty bad one." Sloan shrugged, a soft smile curving her lips. She took the envelope and dropped it on the dresser next to the door.

"Alright." Griselda snapped our attention to her. "Turn now."

I slowly turned, my back to Sloan and the doorway, being careful not to move any of the precariously placed pins.

The sound of the front door opening and closing echoed through the open foyer and up to us.

"You can't come up here," Sloan shouted into the hallway.

The sound of keys dropping against the marble entryway table and a scoff could be heard from downstairs.

"It's my house," Xander answered.

"Penelope is in her wedding dress." Sloan stood in the doorway, her attention to the staircase that overlooked the foyer. "It's bad luck."

His chuckle bounced through the hallway, getting incrementally louder. My back was turned but I could hear him nearing the bedroom. "I think the divorce papers might be—"

The blunt end to the sentence made me look over my shoulder at him.

Electricity sparked in emerald, illuminating every corner. His playful gaze concentrated into something entirely different.

A warmth spread like wildfire, consuming every last bit of oxygen between us.

The air in my lungs became stagnant.

"I . . ." I faltered, stammering over my words. "We . . . needed your room for the mirror. For the dress."

The room felt stifling and freezing at the same time. My pulse ticked away, up and up, out of control.

"It's . . ." He gripped the back of his neck, the column of his throat shifted with a hard swallow. "White."

"You need to remove these buttons one at a time." Griselda's irritated command was a cold deluge that washed away the tension. I quickly stood up straighter and was rewarded with a needle digging into my side.

She looked at Xander from above the glasses that slid down her nose.

"One at a time." Griselda began removing the pins one by one and I held the fabric against my chest. "No matter how important whatever else you'd like to do feels."

Sloan stifled a laugh as she handed me my robe.

"Got it." Xander cleared his throat and looked down at the floor.

"One button at a time," Sloan teased. Her grin stretched from ear to ear. "No cheating."

"Shut up, Sloan," Xander grumbled and made his way to his bathroom, keeping his eyes on the floor the whole time. "And get out."

* * *

AN HOUR LATER, Sloan and Griselda were gone. The dress was on its way for its final alterations and I went to the kitchen and tried to tidy up the mess I'd made in unpacking one of my suitcases. Since I was planning to stay in Sloan and Marcus's guesthouse, I packed enough clothing and other odds and ends I'd need for summer.

My things littered the kitchen, and even bled into the open-concept living room. The general disorder I seemed to unleash was a stark contrast to Xander's neat and tidy house, but he didn't seem to mind.

He was almost a different person on his own.

When he was around other people, his light was so bright it was nearly blinding. Alone, he was quiet and kept to himself, like he was recharging.

"I see why you keep so much in boxes," Xander said as he joined me at the large kitchen island, his hair still damp from the shower. He looked at the living room from our spot in the kitchen; it was filled with my things. "All of these are for the summer?"

Journals were spread across the kitchen island, my work laptop and a few notebooks with some other items were everywhere.

"Sorry." I walked around to the counter to begin gathering them.

"Most of these are empty," he noted, giving me a quizzical look as he picked one up and flipped through it.

"Well, you know that thing. Where you can't remember something and then you do. But you don't have a piece of paper, and you don't know where your phone went, so you get a notebook. But then you decide that notebook should be specifically for that specific category of thoughts, so you get a new notebook and then . . ."

His gaze lifted slowly from perusing the notebook to me, brows arched up. He remained silent.

"I'm guessing that's never happened to you?" I surmised.

"No, but the spreadsheet makes a lot more sense now." He took a step closer and leaned into me, gently tapping at my forehead teasingly. My skin prickled at his proximity. "It's busy in there, huh?"

I scrunched my nose and shooed his hand. "Like Grand Central Station if none of the trains ran on time. Except on certain days when they ran like clockwork."

With a gentle laugh he began to neatly stack the at least thirty journals that were strewn all over the countertop. I tried to do the same. "And all the other days?"

"They tend to crash into each other."

"What is . . ." His voice dropped, becoming graveled. "*This?*"

"Hmm?"

I looked up to see what he was holding. A note card must have fallen out of one of the journals. He read the front, then his mouth hung open as he read the back.

My heart fell into my stomach. I was mortified. It was my . . .

Well, it was a list of things I wanted to do.

- Live on the edge
- Learn to surf
- See a shooting star
- Norman Rockwell Museum
- See the aurora borealis

But he was looking at the *back side*. On the back were more things, but mostly things I wanted done *to me*.

- Have an orgasm without a vibrator
- Get tied up
- Get blindfolded
- Have sex in a public place

"Is this a . . ." His voice lowered and became hoarse. I crossed the counter as he read it. "Fuck-it list?"

I pulled it from his hand. Bumping into his chest with my own, briefly.

Something came alive in his eyes. Like a debate was happening in his mind. This close, his breath caressed my neck, igniting tiny sparks along my skin.

"I wouldn't call it that," I answered quickly, even though that was a fair assessment. One side was most certainly how I'd like to be . . . *fucked*.

My heart beat frantically. The fact that he'd read it and had a near perfect memory meant he knew *exactly* what it was.

"Oh." He took a couple steps back, shaking his head like he'd been knocked out. "Sorry. I didn't realize . . . I was reading—" He stammered to a stop.

I'd never seen him so thrown. Mind adrift and practically stumbling over his words.

Viscerally uncomfortable like he was desperately trying to forget everything he'd just read.

His reluctant eyes met mine for a moment and immediately softened at the corners when they registered the outright mortification that probably painted my face.

He rubbed the back of his neck. "It's nothing to be embarrassed abo—"

"Hardly matters." The words popped out of my mouth, trying to avoid the humiliation of both him finding my list of *proclivities* and his generally horrified reaction. I tried not to take that too personally. Or the fact that he was trying to make me feel better about it *after* his generally horrified reaction. "I'll clean all this up."

He blinked a few times. "Yeah . . ."

"Sorry for the mess." I patted him politely on the shoulder, the other arm filled with journals.

Chapter 14

XANDER

I never imagined a wedding day for myself.

But if I had, former President Alders marrying me to my friend in order to buy her some time so she could do all of this again someday with someone she actually wanted to marry was not how I thought it would go.

Two weeks after our arrival in the Hamptons, on the beach at sunset with waves crashing a hundred feet away, Penelope and I got married. A scheme that the entire front row, all the people who happened to know the truth, watched with mild apprehension.

After the fuck-it list incident, Penelope avoided me for a couple days until I teased her about how a woman who had a spreadsheet for everything was a little disorganized everywhere else. That led to a slightly irritated snap back at me and after a few rounds of light banter things settled out into what they always were: Penelope marginally irritated, but at ease. Or as close to ease as Penelope got.

And I tried—and failed—to forget about *that list*.

"You may kiss the bride," former President Alders announced cheerfully in front us, beneath the altar decorated with an array of tropical flowers.

I wrapped my arm around her waist and pulled her close.

Her silk white dress was conservative in the front, a high neckline and sleeveless. But the back, *fuck*, it was backless. I didn't know why prim-and-proper Penelope chose it but a part of me was sure it had to be payback for something. I hadn't stopped thinking about that dress since I saw her in it in my bedroom.

My hand splayed along her lower back, and I pulled her in for the kiss. I could feel her hesitate briefly as I pressed my lips against hers, but a moment later she relaxed.

Her supple lips loosened, and her hands closed along my lapel. Like molten caramel, her lips were warm and sweet. Chills rolled down my body, wanting nothing more than to deepen it. When I began to pull away, she held me there. Kept me close.

So, I kept going. She tipped her head back and her lips parted—baiting me to push a little further. And I did.

She'd made her intentions incredibly clear about what she wanted and what she didn't. Who she didn't. But, as long as we were acting . . .

I ran my hand along her waist, she moaned softly against my mouth. My blood heated at the sound; electricity sparked through every muscle in my body.

Our tongues swept along each other's, tentative and unsure, but as the rest of the world melted away around us—they found a more confident rhythm.

A groan ran up my throat and I kissed her deeper.

The memory of that list she had ran through my mind, teasing me with mental images of how I could help her with it if she'd let me. Tied up. Blindfolded. In public. Her orgasms on my mouth, my hand, my cock.

Fuck, I imagined all of it.

Her nails scraped against my scalp as we fell hopelessly into the kiss. My fingers pressed desperately against her skin, never wanting this to end.

Fuck. She tasted so good.

The sound of the former president clearing his throat loudly finally lifted the spell. But I didn't pull away until I felt an insistent tapping on my shoulder.

"Guys," Sloan whispered. "We get it."

I silently cursed not making Marcus my best person; he'd have probably let that go on a little longer.

Penelope's eyes opened and stared into mine. Hazy and dilated. She blinked a few times.

"Not the plan," she whispered against my lips as she pulled away, her face flushed.

"You don't have a plan," I mumbled under my breath.

Her grip loosened and she smoothed a hand over my tux jacket, with a delicate shift along the column of her throat, the fog lifted. Sitting just below the blush that ran across her cheeks, she put on a smile that looked real. So fucking real my heart skipped and I couldn't look away.

We turned to face the photographer standing in the aisle. We smiled at the camera as we walked down it.

* * *

"Are we going to talk about that kiss?" Sloan asked as she walked over to me with a teasing grin.

The reception was on a platform constructed along the beach behind Amari Manor for the event. Lanterns and the moon lit up the night. Tables were scattered across the sand.

I couldn't think of a good excuse for kissing her like *that* in front of everyone we knew. I couldn't think of anything other than how good it felt. In fact, my mind replayed it every couple of seconds. "I was instructed to sell it."

"Well, mission accomplished." She clapped tauntingly.

"It was for the crowd."

"You're telling me there's nothing there? Because that kiss was . . ." She fanned herself.

"Selena was clear: sell it," I repeated.

"That's it, then?" she asked disbelievingly.

"Yeah. That's it."

Penelope needed to figure out her future and I needed to untangle myself from her—which became infinitely more difficult now that I knew how good it felt to kiss her.

"If you say so," Sloan huffed quietly. She glanced around the party and smiled as Marcus walked over to us, handing Sloan a drink.

"I think it may be time to take the bride home," Marcus said as he ran an arm around Sloan's waist. He nodded his head in the direction he'd just walked over from.

I looked over to Penelope, who'd spent the entire reception politely mingling with every guest in attendance that wasn't me. The champagne seemed to take the edge off her nerves.

Talking to CeCe, Henry, and Selena, she took the full glass of champagne and emptied it in seconds. She wobbled just a bit between CeCe and Henry.

Sloan looked back at me; her mouth hung open. "I don't think I've ever seen her drunk."

"CeCe kept her occupied, so nobody knows," Marcus attested. "At least she's having fun?"

"Yeah," I grumbled and began walking over to her. Sloan and Marcus followed a few steps behind, exchanging a few whispers between them.

When I was next to Penelope, I realized she was swaying her weight between her feet.

The only other night I saw Penelope even close to drunk was that night when it was just us in her kitchen after the Hightower party, before she left for London.

"They believe it." Penelope scrunched her hand around my lapels again when I was in arm's reach. Her voice lowered and she got on her toes to whisper the rest in my ear. "We lied to a former president."

Her warm breath, mingled with the scent of champagne, lingered along my neck.

"This fascination with the Alders family dynasty is a little weird."

And mildly maddening.

She giggled and hiccupped at the same time, lowering herself and releasing her grip. "I've never lied like this before; it's rather exciting."

Being close friends with Sloan and CeCe over the years got me and the guys adept at caring for drunk women. It was simple: have food, have water, and never underestimate how fast a woman will run for pizza even in four-inch heels.

"I'm glad your first scheme is going well, Penelope."

When CeCe was drunk, she got a little dark. When Sloan was drunk, she got a little violent. Neither really bothered me; both were relatively easy to steer to safety.

But Penelope?

When champagne lifted the polite veil, she was fucking adorable.

A smile spread across her face; her spilled-ink eyes stared up at me. "I prefer Poppy."

My heart jumped. "Oh yeah?"

"Who knew you were so creative?" She laid a hand on my chest to steady herself. She giggled loud enough to draw attention from the mayor and the former president a few feet away.

"Maybe it's time we say good night to the Suttons." Henry politely offered to take Penelope's empty champagne flute.

"Car's ready for you," Selena said from beneath Henry's arm. "Leaving early plays into whirlwind narrative anyway."

"Great." I forced a smile.

I wrapped an arm around her waist as she took a few unsteady steps. She was like Bambi on ice.

She leaned in, the scent of orange blossoms bounced around her hair. "You are shaping up to be an excellent first husband."

I flinched; she didn't notice.

"And you're starting to look like a lot of first wives in the Hamptons." I carried more of her weight and helped her to the car waiting for us. She looked up at me, her brows scrunched. "Visibly intoxicated."

She grinned widely and I felt a little lighter.

For the next year, all that was promised to me—and all I was prepared to want—was that I could make her smile.

Chapter 15

PENELOPE

The next morning, I woke up with a splitting headache.

That kiss knocked me off my axis and champagne was the only thing that quieted all the discordant confusion in my mind. Because that spark I often felt around him—the one that didn't even seem to register to Xander—had always felt like it was one-sided.

But the kiss made me question everything. Was it all for show? Did he feel like electricity passed through him like I did? Or was it the humiliating reality that my intuition was wrong and I was the only one worked up about it?

From my seat on the couch, I heard the double doors that led out to the terrace open.

I vaguely remembered trying to get out of my dress and failing. So I gave up, fell asleep, and woke up in it. After thirty minutes trying to get out of it again this morning, I gave up and settled on the couch with a coffee and banana muffin, in a wrinkled silk Chanel dress.

"Soaking up the champagne from last night?" Xander's voice asked from behind me.

"Yes and I never realized you liked banana muffins, too," I stated quietly, mildly amused, trying not to replay the sound of his groan when it rumbled up his chest. Or the way his fingers pressed into my skin.

I turned and bent an arm over the back of the couch, determined to act casual. If he could do it, so could I.

And then, I lost my train of thought.

Xander walked, shirtless, from the terrace doors to the kitchen island. The morning light poured over him, leaving devious shadows in the divots between his muscles along his arms and sculpted chest.

"You . . . you were at the beach?" I stammered when every thought in my mind turned to what lay below the swim trunks.

"Decided to swim some laps in the pool. Had my coffee out there after," he explained and cocked his head in the direction of the French doors that led out to the pool overlooking the ocean. He walked over to the kitchen counter and threw on a shirt. "Still in the dress, huh?"

"Yes. I had some trouble with it this morning." I felt my cheeks heat as he walked down the hallway to the laundry room, his thumbs slipped under the sides of his trunks on the way. Moments later he came back with a pair of gray joggers on.

If the swim trunks were distracting, those were—I swallowed hard—something else.

"I did try to help last night, but you said, and I quote"—he playfully threw an arm around my shoulders as he collapsed onto the couch next to me—"'Only an imbecile cannot remove an item of clothing, Xander.'"

His impression of me was terrible. "Your British accent needs work."

I tried to distract myself from the fact that his muscular chest was right up against my side. His teasing chuckle temporarily halted the banging in my head.

"I don't think I've ever seen you drink that much."

"Yes . . ." I turned to him. Emerald eyes sparkled in the morning light. They followed me when I tried to look away. "Well, we were . . ."

His voice lowered. "Celebrating?"

"Well, the world . . ." My mind became transfixed with the feel of his thumb slowly moving up and down my shoulder. Each stroke sent a warm buzz down my arms. "Thinks . . ."

"Thinks?" he repeated in a whisper.

That we were married. Because we were.

Suddenly everything felt topsy-turvy again. And despite itself, my mind filled with the memory of *that* kiss.

I gave him an opening and he took it. He made it more intense and I spent hours wondering if it was just for show because it felt like *something* else. One kiss had my entire body on pins and needles, which was dizzying since my mind was like that at baseline.

"I should probably make a list of all the things I need to get from the boxes in my house." I blinked away the daze, and with a deep inhale I pushed myself back from him. "If they're being moved, I may need something."

His gaze dropped; the muscles along his jaw flexed. "The boxes you haven't opened in years?"

"Well, I might need something," I reasoned and stood up from the couch. "And I should probably work on getting a property in Singapore." I began to pace, the length of the dress occasionally getting caught between my legs. A familiar feeling, a quaking restlessness, began to overcome my muscles with a slight tremor.

"Come on." Xander stood from the couch and took my hand.

"What?"

"Come on," he repeated, leading me away from the living area toward the hallway that led to the foyer.

"Selena told us to either go on a trip to look like a honeymoon or keep a low profile," I reminded him even though I followed him without much resistance.

"Come on," he repeated more softly this time, turning to me.

The look in his eyes felt heavy. Smothering everything else around me until it was just him.

His fingers laced into mine.

"I can't." I snapped my hand back and tried to think of a reason not to go when my entire body wanted to follow him. My brain wouldn't let me. "The dress."

"Oh." His eyes wandered up the dress. "Right."

Before I could say anything, he closed the space between us, put his hands on my waist, and turned me around. The sudden, commanding shift made my stomach dip.

His fingers ran across the back of my neck to the tiny buttons that fastened the collar. "These buttons are the only things keeping this dress on?"

The warm caress of his breath floated along the crook of my neck, leaving chills in its wake.

"Yes," I whispered, unable to find my voice.

His fingers traced along the lining all the way down my back to where it ended just below my hips.

"How attached are you to it?" He leaned in closer, a hand spreading across the base of my throat.

My breath caught.

"Not very, but it's custom Chanel." My nipples hardened against the silky fabric.

I found a spot on the wall and tried to focus on something, anything other than the fact that I reveled in the feel of his hands touching me. His fingers ran along the delicate fabric and gripped the collar on each side.

"It's worth—"

A low grunt was immediately followed by the sound of fabric tearing. A frisson of excitement shot down my body and settled deep in my naval.

I gasped. The fabric cascaded down my neck; my arms immediately held it up against my chest.

With one touch, one quick motion, he managed to awaken a heat inside me that I couldn't achieve with lovers, vibrators, or any combination of the two.

I turned around, eyes wide. My jaw hung open.

"You said you weren't attached to it." He put his hands in the air.

"I'm not, but CeCe may murder you," I snapped, a little frustrated. Not so much at the dress—although it was the perfect excuse. It was at him for being so casual when I felt like I'd pass out at any moment—none of *this* even fazed him. I turned and examined the back of the dress. From the looks of it, the only damage was to the collar. "It's a crime against fashion."

"Oops," he mumbled. I looked back over to him as his gaze lingered on the back of my dress. "Come on, get changed. Let's go."

I held the silk more deliberately against my chest, recognizing the only thing under this dress was the lace thong I wore because it didn't leave panty lines. "What?"

"Get changed. We're going out."

"We're supposed to keep a low—"

The door to his bedroom closed behind him.

* * *

AFTER A QUIET twenty-minute ride up the coast, one where Xander refused to tell me where we were going, we arrived at a trail that led up to a lighthouse that stood proudly on a cliff a few hundred feet away.

"Pink noise," he explained, opening his car door as I reached for mine.

"Is that supposed to mean something to me?"

He smiled. "Come on."

He was being frustratingly mysterious. I hated how it sent an electric wisp along every neuron.

"Is this one of your games?" I was a few steps behind him and he walked the path as if he'd memorized it.

"No." He turned around and walked backward a short distance, a teasing smile playing along his mouth. "I already know that I'm not allowed to play with you. But your aversion to fun is noted."

I heaved a breath at the idea of him *playing* with me. "Your games are not fun."

They were. I hated to admit it, but what I initially thought was juvenile when I first met him years ago was actually a way to keep strong relationships thriving. And Xander, when he chose to be close to someone, he didn't lose them. Those bonds were seemingly unbreakable.

"And what's your idea of fun?" he asked. Taking my hand, he began to lead me up the stony walk toward the lighthouse. "Don't say making a spreadsheet."

"Spreadsheets *are* fun."

They were orderly, calming. Life was the opposite.

He walked up to the door, stopped a moment to think, then walked a few feet to a window that opened with little effort.

"Your idea of fun is breaking into private property?" I mused.

"It's not breaking in." He gripped the stony ledge above the window, his biceps flexed against his short sleeves as he pulled himself up. "I have a key."

"Of course, you do." I tried to sound disinterested even though I found myself fixated on watching him. He pulled himself up and through the window with ease. "Most people who have permission to enter a building prefer shimmying through a window."

"I forgot it," he called; the echo of his voice rang through the tower.

Moments later, the door opened.

"I thought Xander Sutton didn't forget anything." I pressed a finger into his shoulder a couple of times and swept past him to the base of the stairwell.

"I got a little distracted." He rubbed the back of his neck. "Surprise wedding and all."

I knew I should probably ask a few follow-up questions. But, staring up at the spiral stairs that lined the gray stone walls, I didn't want to talk myself out of doing whatever he had planned.

It was an adventure, and my life was so hermetically sealed for so long, that I never had those.

"Ten stories," he told me, pointing to the steps, motioning for me to go first. "I'll walk behind you."

I raised a brow. "Very gentlemanly of you."

He grinned. "Something like that."

The warm salty air passed through the large open archways at the top of the structure, whistling down the tower. We began walking up the steps, stopping every story or two to look out a window.

"Why are we here?" I asked, glancing over my shoulder for a moment.

"This lighthouse is the furthest point in the Hamptons. No land directly ahead until the Azores," he explained. "So technically, for now, you're living on the edge."

I stopped.

My heart skipped too many beats to be safe. Maybe from the mortification that he remembered the fuck-it list—as he called it—and was bringing it up. Or that he was trying to help me with it, the less salacious side anyway.

"And." His hand gently pushed against the small of my back, encouraging me to keep going. We were only a few more stories to the top. "I thought you might like this."

"You did?"

He didn't say anything else as we ascended the last few spirals. Once we reached the top, I understood.

The wide, arched windows, the ocean spread out before me like a canvas painted with ever-changing shades of blue. To the east, the morning sun cast a golden sheen on the water's surface. To the west, the coastline stretched out, disappearing into the horizon, dotted with picturesque seaside cottages and sandy beaches.

"Pink noise." He leaned against the stone frame of the window opposite me. "Sounds of nature, thunderstorms, waves, rainfall, tend to help people relax."

I took a deep inhale of the salty air. He was right.

This far up you couldn't feel the mist from the waves, but the crashing was so present, it felt like you were next to them. The vast expanse of the ocean ahead. My problems seemed rather small.

"This does put things into perspective, doesn't it?"

He nodded.

"It's even nicer at night," he stated, watching the tide push and pull below. "I used to come up here in the summer when things got to be a lot."

"Coping mechanisms," I noted, wanting to know more. "It reeks of a beautiful childhood."

I said it as though mine was terrible when it only sort of was. Growing up, my half sister and I were close. But as we got older, my half brother often drove a wedge between us. Silas would give her one expectation that she'd feel forced to follow and when I balked at it, I was punished or ridiculed. Eventually, I fell in line to keep the peace, to maybe be accepted—loved. It never helped.

"Guilty." He chuckled. "But I went through a lot of shitty coping mechanisms before I found this one."

I smiled and leaned against the window's stone frame, looking out at the horizon. He did the same, the sounds of the ocean filling the space between us. I wondered when he'd come here in the past. I never really heard Sloan mention it and they'd been coming to the Hamptons together since she was sixteen.

"Did you come here alone?" I asked.

He said he came here at night, it was probably very romantic.

This little trip, the attempt to lighten my mental load, fulfilling an innocent item on the list. All reminded me that at his core, he was a good and loyal friend—up until yesterday, that felt like an indisputable fact in my mind.

But now everything felt scrambled.

Because of *that* kiss. How he kissed, how he deepened it, and how I let him.

I thought knowing, empirically, that his heart was unavailable or simply taken might help my head reel in my body because— after that kiss—it wanted more.

He raised a brow, but the stillness along his features gave me no indication of what he was thinking.

I could feel the self-imposed pressure to somehow explain my way out of prying. "I only ask because it's nice. Romantic."

I took a few steps forward, glancing around the domed ceiling. When he didn't say anything, I felt the persistent need to bolster an argument I wasn't even sure I was making. "I'm sure a date would like it."

The thunderous silence continued. I looked over to him; he blinked a couple of times. Confusion ran lines across his forehead.

"Not *me*. Someone else," I asserted, feeling the embarrassment warm my face. The overwhelming fear that he'd somehow know I was having conflicting feelings began to spin up a tornado in my head. It forced some reasonable explanation to why I was prying. "Like Madison."

Oh my God, stop talking.

"Madison?" He pushed himself off the wall, the calm timbre was giving way to something thornier.

"You two seemed happy, is all." I took a deep, steadying breath and shook off the nerves. I tried to imagine I was at work; I was a different Penelope there. Strong, confident, self-assured. I took a few steps toward the spiral staircase. Without any real indication of how long he planned to stay here, I began walking down. "Happy and in love."

"Falling in love is overrated." He followed behind me.

The sentiment from him wasn't surprising given all of his relationships ended as if on a timer. Except for the one with a woman I dubbed She-Who-Cannot-Be-Named in my head because the one time I heard her name—Reina—the entire room went silent. It was at brunch and CeCe let it slip; everyone looked at each other, then at Xander, and then picked up like it never happened. I knew better than to ask about it.

"A man who thinks love is overrated," I drawled lightly, mimicking casual as closely as I could. "How original."

I sometimes wondered if Madison was why he never brought up *that* night and the next morning before I left for London, with the poppies. If her light dimmed that memory for him. Or maybe, it was really just me who felt it and it was simply a regular day for Xander.

Do something nice. Be charming. Rinse. Repeat.

He laughed quietly and I took a few more steps down.

We reached the landing and he walked past a few steps to open the large wooden door.

The poppies I'd given to Maya to care for while I was in London stayed with her. I never asked for them back. I didn't need the reminder.

I tried to trust myself and enter into this arrangement because my autonomy was worth it. But now, this choice was becoming similar to my decision to stay in Manhattan instead of going home. Riddled with complications, making me second-guess a path when I was already so far down it.

The arrangement was supposed to be simple, but this was quickly becoming the opposite.

Chapter 16

XANDER

**Is the Honeymoon Over?
The Newest Mrs. Sutton Seen Leaving
the Home of American Royalty.**

I arrived at the newly purchased Dawn Capital building in lower Manhattan.

The elevator doors opened, and I folded the paper in half in my hands.

It was a stupid headline above pictures of Penelope leaving Tristan's Hamptons house early in the morning a few days ago. It was for work; she needed Tristan to sign some disclosures to finish off her tenure with Dawn Capital since she couldn't continue being our counsel, given the wedding and Sloan's warning. Sloan recommended counsel at a separate firm and that was taken care of quickly, under the guise of a conflict of interest.

And Maya stayed with Tristan most summers; it was some bizarre tradition they had. So Penelope and Maya worked there a lot.

It made sense, even though it felt like Penelope was avoiding me.

None of that perfectly reasonable information abated the unfamiliar urge to strangle one of my closest friends.

"Don't read that trash," CeCe insisted from behind the reception desk on the top floor.

"What are you doing here?" I asked. When I got close enough to her, she reached over the desk, grabbed the paper, and threw it out.

"It's a long story, but I work here now."

CeCe was often unsure of where to go but she was never lost. She and I had developed a kinship over the years, one rooted in the fact that we were the ones everyone worried about for a period of time.

"Got it." I took the hint to not ask why she was there and if it had anything to do with her abrupt departure from *Vogue* last summer. I looked into my office and saw Rohan and Tristan seated, waiting.

"Jackson is still in Dubai, so it's just you three," CeCe explained as she sat back down and pointed to my door. "They're waiting for you."

The morning light streamed through the floor-to-ceiling windows of my sparsely decorated office, offering a view of Lower Manhattan.

"Any reason we don't manage majority stake in SunCorp yet?" Rohan inquired from his seat in front of my desk. He was the obvious choice for CEO of Dawn Capital since none of the other cofounders—myself included—wanted anything to do with that job. Tristan and I oversaw operations, and Jackson ran the financials.

"I can handle it if you've got too much going on," Tristan offered as I walked into my office, rounded the side of my desk, and took a seat.

"No, I'll take care of it," I told him with a new urgency to get the SunCorp deal locked up.

My phone buzzed on my desk, I glanced to see the same headline pop up there, too. I swiped it off my screen.

"I mean it, I don't mind." Tristan glanced up from the papers he was reviewing, the corners of his mouth tipped up. "Maybe plan a few date nights."

"That's not funny," I retorted quietly. "You wouldn't make that joke if it were Sloan or CeCe."

It had to be some sort of sick karma that his joke was the exact one I would have made if it were anyone else in my situation.

"You wouldn't be so flustered if it were Sloan or CeCe. You wouldn't have kissed either of them like you did at the wedding if it were Sloan or CeCe." He put the papers down and leaned back into his seat. I glanced over to Rohan, who was still reading, ignoring us. An uncomfortable shiver ran up my spine at the idea of having to kiss either Sloan or CeCe. "Or flirt with them like you do with *Poppy*."

I looked up at him and tried not to react, even though my mind replayed that kiss every chance it got—torturing me with the memory of what she tasted like. I knew he was joking, and using the nickname to prove a point, but an uncomfortable tightness moved through my muscles. Only *I* called her Poppy.

"I didn't think so," Tristan said, seeing my expression. He pushed himself forward and neatly placed the stack of papers on my desk. "If you were wondering when we called your bluff, it was the masquerade. The way you stormed after her and got in Xu's face."

"I was vetting him," I barked, looking down at my phone.

That part was true. I was. Penelope hadn't looked like herself; she'd looked a little scared. I couldn't just let that go. It didn't sit right. My gut told me to do *something*.

"No, *we* were trying to vet him," Rohan, for the first time in weeks, answered with a lightness that had long since left him. Dawn Capital's success meant a lot to all of us for different reasons. Rohan's drove him to a relentless pursuit of perfection. "*You were trying—*"

"Drop it," I snapped.

I knew now that Penelope found out about her mother's shares being tied up in her inheritance that night. But at the time, watching her walk away, despite me trying to hold on, felt like . . .

Like more than I ever wanted to feel again.

"Fine," Rohan agreed and looked at Tristan sternly.

They both stood and made their way to the door, and an awkward silence filled the room. Rohan walked in the direction of his office, but Tristan lingered in the doorway.

"I mean it." I stared at my phone screen. "Drop it."

"Hey." Tristan waited until I finally gave in and looked at him. "After everything we've been through, the last thing you need is—"

"To be reminded of every time I fucked up?" I snapped again; guilt curdled in my stomach.

"To pretend nothing bothers you," Tristan answered back calmly.

I did that a lot. Pretend.

Pretend that my mind didn't replay all the worst memories I had like some sick highlight reel. That—for a long time—I wasn't being crushed under the weight of my own sadness. That I was okay when I wasn't.

It happened for years and always had a way of coming to the surface at the worst times.

Tristan let out a frustrated sigh when I didn't say anything. He continued. "You looked lost and wrecked that night."

I loved them for caring, but I hated myself for being such a fucking mess for so long that their initial reaction to a change in my life was outright panic.

"Well, I'm fine now." I gave him a tight smile.

What was I going to say? That I still had no fucking idea how

I felt? Because I didn't. Every day I was finding new ways that this feeling I had for her ran deeper than I ever thought it did. And every day, I was reminded that she'd never see me the way I saw her—the lighthouse was the perfect example. I took her there thinking she'd like the peace. Then, as we left, it felt like she was trying to convince me to get back together with Madison.

The arrangement didn't just buy her time, but it gave me some, too. Time to untangle whatever it was I felt for her and move past it. Past her.

He turned on his heels, shaking his head, and walked out of the office. My phone chimed and a couple messages lit up the screen.

Selena: Did you see the headline?

Selena: This is supposed to be my summer off.

Xander: Sorry, I'll fix it.

Selena: If you and Penelope can't sell it here, go on a "honeymoon."

Chapter 17

PENELOPE

While walking through Xander's beach house, I was distracted and carrying too much.

Distracted from the call I just ended with my mother. My hands full with a banana muffin and an iced coffee in one hand, my laptop in the other hand with my water bottle dangling precariously from my pinkie.

I called my mother to tell her the news and was met with very little in the way of conversation. She congratulated me, told me marriage was silly, and that was about it. She didn't question any of it, she never did, and it was a relief.

As I crossed that item off the mental checklist, the sound of my refillable water swinging off my pinkie and crashing down on a large ceramic globe that sat in the living area yanked me right out of my head.

"Oh God." I placed all my things on the table behind the couch and assessed the damage. The pieces were large, maybe I could fix it. Although mending ceramic usually left noticeable seams—not something you'd really like on a globe.

The sunlight streaking through the windows highlighted every jagged edge.

"Are you—" Xander came rushing down the hall and stopped

abruptly when he saw me knelt over, looking nervously at the mess. His eyes drifted down to the large broken pieces, his shoulders relaxed. "Oh."

"I'm so sorry." My heart raced with anxiety.

My head began to run through all the ways I ruined something in his home. Was it important? Did it mean something? I prayed it was some throwaway piece that a designer stuck in the corner.

He ran a hand through his hair, the bottom of his crew neck T-shirt lifted a few inches from the waistband of the gray joggers. The quick flash of his abs distracted my busy mind for a delightful second.

But only for that one second.

He shrugged and walked over to me. "Things break."

"Was it important?"

"Not really." Xander knelt down beside me and began helping me pick up the large pieces carefully. "It was actually stolen. I'm no lawyer, but I think that makes you an accessory to destroying evidence."

I paused and stared at him for a moment. He was joking to make me feel better. He had to be.

"You're not serious."

"I am. The original owner was a French photographer. He broke CeCe's heart, so Sloan stole this from his studio," Xander told me as he stacked the three largest shards together. "Then Rohan broke his nose."

"And now it's here?"

"It used to be in Manhattan, but it must have been moved here with some of my things when I bought the place." He smiled as he ran a thumb over the smooth glazed piece he picked up. It was the shattered remains of Brazil. "Occasionally, the group of us used it to decide where we wanted to go next. Spin the globe, pick a spot, get on the plane."

I envied him. Xander, in his thirty-four years of life, was never bored. Always a new adventure whether here or abroad. He was a man with a story for everything. It was like when one adventure ended a new one began. No respite.

"What if you land in an ocean?" I wondered.

"Spin again."

"What if it's a place you can't travel to?" I took the smaller pieces and left the tiny ones to sweep up.

"Spin again."

"What if—"

"It's a pretty simple game." He stood with the broken pieces neatly stacked in one hand. "Just spin again."

Even when I didn't want to be happy, like when I wanted to stew in shame, he had a way to pull a smile out of me.

I carefully held the pieces and got up, looking around the floor for anything else I might have missed. "Traveling around the world, stealing with your merry band of cohorts. You've lived quite the life, Xander Sutton."

Caught in the magnetic pull, I felt myself draw closer.

His eyes locked on mine.

He smiled, took a step toward me until something passed over him and he pulled away.

Looking down at the floor as he cleared his throat.

The static dissolved into the air and I felt silly for acknowledging— to myself—that the static was there in the first place.

"I'll throw these out," he said as he turned and walked to the kitchen in the direction of the trash can.

"No!" I ignored the rapid thumping in my chest and followed him. I took the pieces and laid the broken ceramic on the cool marble countertop. The words began to feel jumbled in my mind and the seductive ease I felt a few seconds ago was replaced with a thorny apprehension. "I can find someone who might be able to put it back together. If not that, then—"

"Hey. It's okay." He put a steady hand on my shoulder. "Things break."

That was something I'd come to expect with him. No matter the circumstances, he always reset to where he was before as if nothing happened. Like at the masquerade. I couldn't tell if he was pretending or if it was real, but it was like a switch.

"Okay." I turned the ring around on my finger. "Are you sure you're not upset?"

I tried to move about the world quietly, without incident, but I was always breaking things. Or blamed for breaking them. My stepmother, Eleanor, complained that my social graces were wobbly—it made me the target of her ire.

Overthinking every step—because my life felt like a field of land mines—made me clumsy.

"Who needs a globe, anyway? The Internet exists." His contagious good humor made it difficult to be hard on myself.

I smiled. "How are you like this?"

"Like what?"

There wasn't much that disrupted his calm tide. Even when something managed to make a ripple in the still waters, it didn't last long. Was it an act? Or was he this pathologically easygoing?

"Why doesn't anything bother you?"

"Things bother me," he countered softly.

"Like what?"

He paused, opened his mouth, then closed it. Something warred in his eyes. I could tell he wanted to say something, but he didn't.

"Maddox bothers me," he answered quietly. His brows lifted, like he was surprised he said it.

"Maddox?" Butterflies in my stomach spun up a whirlwind.

"I didn't like how he talked to you," he noted casually, leaning against the countertop.

"Me neither," I murmured. "And I know he can seem difficult, but he's been a friend to me."

I knew I'd rationalized a lot of Maddox's behaviors to myself, but he wasn't a bad person. He'd been honest with me about what he wanted out of marriage, and what our future would look like together. His primary draw had been that I could have it all. My family would be happy, and I would finally be accepted rather than rejected. It was never love, but I told myself it could be enough.

Xander's eyes moved around the kitchen as he turned his wedding band a few times.

"You're sure that's all?" he asked quietly.

For a man who never forgot anything, he had a habit of asking that question in one way or another. He didn't move, but there was a subtle change in his demeanor.

Trusting others felt impossible when I hadn't even perfected trusting myself, but Maddox was the only person I had growing up—aside from my sister and cousin, Olivia—that seemed to care, at least a little, about my quality of life.

"Yes," I repeated. "I want my chance to find happiness."

"Something you haven't found yet?" His voice lowered; it sounded like he was talking to himself. He took a step away from the countertop.

The air shifted. "Yes, I guess."

He nodded again, taking another step back.

"Then, why wait so long to walk away?" Seriousness hardened his tone to something that sounded stern. "Why put m—" He faltered. "Why put yourself through all of this?"

The tempting warmth that the encounter originally started with evaporated.

"You have a supportive family," I reminded him with the same irritation I had at the masquerade. He and the rest of them came out to tell me what I could and couldn't do out of some well-meaning protectiveness. But they didn't understand what I was up against. They'd never felt completely rejected by the people who were *supposed* to care for them. "You wouldn't understand."

I felt the brunt of the blame for everything no matter what I did. I moved to New York to pursue my own goals and I was selfish. But when I was in Singapore, in my father and stepmother's home, I was treated like a burden. Yet, I was expected to be grateful because I was still raised in the upper echelons of society thanks to the Chen fortune.

"What does that mean?" His brows scrunched together.

"It's not easy to decide you want to go it alone," I snapped. An angry flame burst alive in my stomach. He had no idea what it was like to tiptoe through life. He could live as raucously as he liked without fear of recourse. "You don't know how paralyzing it can be."

A familiar feeling began to swell. It always started the same way. A quiet whisper in my mind. A subtle shiver deep in my bones before it would blossom into an all-consuming whirlwind. Weeks of repressed anxiety began to claw its way out.

"Every decision. All the time. Worrying who you might affect. Who you might hurt. Who you have already hurt," I rattled off, feeling my chest tighten. "Questioning *everything*, constantly."

What was to come now that I'd ruined my family's plans? Would I ever find a place there with them?

A maelstrom of implications whirled like leaves in a storm, a mess of fears and doubts that I could neither fully understand nor silence. Each concern speeding past my vision, too quick to grasp, blurring it entirely.

"All while hoping whatever you're blamed for isn't irreparable.

Knowing some of it probably is." I drew in a deep uneasy breath trying to prevent the inevitable. "You've never had to weigh a life you wanted against losing your family."

My vison distorted into a hazy abyss behind tears I tried not to shed, while the air thickened, choking my lungs.

"Penelope . . ."

I could vaguely hear him, but everything blended together like waves in the ocean.

Tears pricked along the side of my cheek.

And then, everything began to settle. I hadn't realized he'd moved until his arms were wrapped around me, my head buried in his chest, his fingers gently stroking my head.

I didn't say anything. I listened to his heartbeat and found some balance in its metronome.

The time passed and I ran my final words through my head again as the fog lifted.

"You've never had to weigh a life you wanted against losing your family."

He didn't have to make that choice, but he'd already lost enough of the loved ones in his life and in my own frenzy I didn't see how this conversation might hurt him.

"I didn't mean it like . . . I'm sorry," I murmured into his chest.

"Don't be."

He continued to gently run a few fingers through my hair, and I let him. After weeks of trying to have everything together, I was no closer to actually having a plan for my future. But I felt better. Calm.

"Just so you know," he whispered softly, his fingers continuing their gentle caress. Once again, his warmth took over despite how I may have rattled it. "You have a family here, and it's not going anywhere."

The truth of it resonated through my chest. He was right.

They were always there, and I kept them at a distance. It felt safer. When the people in my life who were supposed to care about my happiness—my family—didn't see me as anything more than a pawn, it was survival to keep others at a distance. Fearing their judgment or maybe rejection if you happened to show any part of yourself that they didn't agree with.

But as each day passed with Xander, I was reminded of how safe I was.

That I could simply be myself without recourse.

It was freeing and somehow even more terrifying.

Chapter 18

XANDER

A few days after the globe incident, Penelope and I boarded the jet to Singapore. Under the guise of a honeymoon, we'd secure the property piece of the inheritance stipulation.

We packed the bags we had at my beach house and had them sent back to my Manhattan penthouse. Her things were all over the house. Like the second she let herself unpack, she sprawled out.

I normally enjoyed my time alone; it was nice to turn off for a little while. I always thought I'd have trouble having someone else around during those moments of solitude, but I didn't. These past few weeks living together, I was seeing a side of her that I never got to see. Penelope, while pulled together and organized in front of others, was kind of a mess when she was alone. The brave face she put on disappeared when she was in the comfort of her own home.

Literally and figuratively.

"Anything I should know before we get there?" I eventually asked, even though I wasn't all that worried. People tended to like me.

Despite being confined to a jet for the last fifteen hours, she didn't say more than a few words to me. When she wasn't sleeping, she was either working with her headphones or pacing. I didn't mind, I liked the quiet, but it seemed like she might need someone to talk to.

"Actually, yes. That's what I was working on." With a deep breath she looked back down at her laptop. "You were right."

"Right about what?"

"We need to be convincing. To some degree. Even the tabloids seem disbelieving. So I'm making a spreadsheet of our interests and preferences. We haven't needed it much since we've been spending time around people who know the truth, but still." Her fingers moved along the trackpad. "I should learn the pieces of information a wife would know."

Penelope had been in my life for five years now, but I wasn't as close to her as I was everyone else, because she kept a distance from all of us. Even so, she knew where I grew up, the broad strokes of what happened to my parents, my general interests. I knew about her mom, and that she had two half siblings who never visited. Silas made sense because it seemed like he was an antagonist to her. But she had a half sister.

"You have siblings," I stated, wondering if she'd tell me more, knowing that I was supposed to stop myself from doing that. I wasn't supposed to be getting in deeper, I was supposed to be *trying* to move past her. But dammit, I couldn't help it.

And after what happened with the globe, I wanted her to know that she didn't need to worry about being perfect or anything other than what she was, not with me. She had a safe place if she needed it. One she could trust to see and accept her for exactly who she was.

"Silas is a terror," she noted quickly. "And Arabella."

She sighed.

"Arabella?"

"Arabella is utterly perfect." She smiled, almost proud but a sadness rang through. She looked up from her screen. "Beautiful, graceful, and happy to marry the man chosen for her."

"Do you miss her?"

She shrugged. "We grew apart after I went to uni."

"Why?" I pressed quietly.

She shuffled in her seat again, struggling to answer. "She wore her marriage like a medal when I saw her last, at her wedding. And I . . . obviously, I took a different approach. We became different people."

"Were you close before?"

"As girls, yes." A melancholic smile drifted along her cheeks. "I did her homework because she always struggled in school and she'd sneak me treats and gifts whenever she was showered with them. We were thick as thieves. After university, I was supposed to move back to Singapore, but I didn't . . ."

"Why not?"

"It's hard to go back, but at the same time it's the place that feels . . ." A distant look passed over her. She looked out the window for an extended beat. Then, she took a deep breath, rolled her shoulders back, and shuffled in her seat. "We should also know more basic things."

I wanted to know more, but I took the hint. I quietly reveled in the fact that after years of knowing her and stringing together the parts I got piecemeal, I got to know all of that at once.

She was uncomfortable, so I switched to what was easy and safe and my default setting. A playful banter. "Like . . ."

"Like where we met," she answered.

I leaned forward, resting my elbows on my knees, and waited until she looked at me. "You remember when we met."

She remembered that the yellow dress was her first day at the firm, so she had to remember when we met at the bar. I took that moment to remind myself that there were a lot of nights that meant something to me that seemed to fade in her memory.

She sat up straighter in her chair and looked down. "I'm only trying to make sure we're on the same page."

"We got together a few months ago; fell madly in love. This summer we decided why wait?" I rattled off a perfectly reasonable love story.

Her eye twitched just slightly at the ambiguity of that short answer.

She let out a quiet huff and typed a few things into her laptop then looked back at me. "What is your favorite color?"

"Who is going to call our marriage into question if you don't know my favorite color?"

"What is the harm in just picking one?" Her tone tightened.

"Fine, green."

"Green?" She raised an unamused brow. "Like *your* eyes? Isn't that a bit on the nose?"

I had to stop instigating, but with her, it was so damn hard. "Spend a lot of time thinking about my eyes, Poppy?"

My attempt to make her smile failed. "Pick any other color," she demanded.

"Fine, yellow."

"Yellow?" She looked up, her fingers tapped along the side of the table. "Why yellow?"

"You told me to pick one." I tilted my head back against the leather seat with a groan.

"Fine." She looked down at her screen. "Your favorite color is yellow. How did we get engaged?"

"That one's easy," I answered and snapped my fingers. "You blindsided me in your foyer."

She closed her laptop. "This isn't a game."

"Then why am I having so much fun?" I laughed.

Just as I was about to apologize, noticing her patience waning, I caught it.

The tiny reward I got when I managed to successfully disarm her. The smile that played tug-of-war against the side of her cheek.

"Send me your psychotic spreadsheet. I won't mess this up for you," I leaned forward and whispered.

Her eyes met mine and my entire chest warmed when her grin broke loose. Whenever I did that—made her smile, really smile—time stilled. And my mind would go completely blank; a blissful state of amnesia for the fleeting second she granted it to me.

It was always gone too soon.

Her eyes left mine and she straightened in her seat.

"Fine." She tucked her laptop into the side pocket of her purse and glanced out the window. She twisted the handle between her fingers.

The plane began to make a few gradual dips and we got the alert we'd be landing soon.

I ignored the dull ache that always followed after those moments. "Don't worry, Poppy. Families love me."

Chapter 19

PENELOPE

I wasn't nearly as nervous as I thought I'd be landing in Singapore. In fact, seeing it again—feeling the warm breeze, smelling the occasional floral fragrance that wafted through the air, watching the broad palm leaves sway—felt like coming home. Right after landing, our things were taken to the Four Seasons suite we were staying in and Xander and I went right to Marina Bay.

Despite the humidity that hung on the air, the metropolitan hub of the city pulsed with activity: honking cars; the chatter of locals and tourists alike; and the rhythmic clinking of utensils at bustling food stalls that wafted the tantalizing scents of Hainanese chicken, chili crab, and all manner of stir-fried favorites.

It was a perfect place to purchase a property. Since real estate moved fast in Singapore, I planned to make a purchase that afternoon.

"That was easy," Xander said, sounding carefree as he threw an arm around my shoulders, and we walked out of the lobby of a new luxury condo tower. I held a stack of papers in my hand.

While touring the properties that both fit my budget and were still available, I was beginning to feel a little overwhelmed. I didn't know if he could tell or not, but he left to make a call and five minutes later I was the owner of the entire building.

Worth a little over five hundred million US dollars, it was mine now.

"Thank you, Xander, but I didn't need the entire tower to meet the terms." I rolled my eyes.

"Okay. Take your time to pick the one you want," Xander suggested. "You can sign the rest over to me when you're done. This way you can choose with the pressure off."

I looked up at him, suddenly overwhelmed with feeling. He did it to give me time, knowing I was probably a bit overcome. While I didn't need things to be taken care of for me, it was nice for my worries to be handled with care. For someone to look out for *my* well-being.

The humid air hit me the second we walked out of the lobby. I let it fill my lungs and smiled. My shoulders relaxed. The cacophony of thoughts muted, the mental burden of it all suddenly off my mind.

Then, I saw a familiar face waiting for us outside.

My cousin Olivia.

Before I could say anything, Olivia was running toward us, linking my arm in hers, all while Xander's remained along my shoulders.

"I'm so glad you called me." Olivia beamed, her short hair brushing along her chin. "It's so good to see you!"

Olivia Chen was a couple of years older than me, but she and I had a kinship in that we were both black sheep of sorts. Olivia, who had come out years ago, was given what my family believed to be a generous offer.

As long as she never married or made her truth public, she was still a part of the family. A begrudgingly accepted one, but still a part. Her decision often influenced my reluctance to fully pull away from the family. Even someone as independent as Olivia knew that you only got one.

"I couldn't visit without seeing you," I told her, holding her arm a bit tighter, reveling in this feeling. One that felt like finding something I'd lost. Despite having avoided home for years, being around Olivia felt like I'd never left.

We spent the rest of the day having a decadent three-course lunch, then stopping at places along the waterfront that she and I used to sneak off to when we were younger. Xander mostly followed along and took pictures obediently at Olivia's instruction.

"See that building?" she said, pointing at a skyscraper at least fifty-stories high. "One of mine."

While our family business was in the technology sphere, Olivia branched out into real estate. She went from boutique developer to buying out one of the larger development firms in Singapore.

"That's amazing," I said. "I've missed so much of your life these past few years."

"Same here. I wish I'd known about the wedding early enough to sneak off and attend." She gave me a scolding look as we walked along the path overlooking the bay.

The warm ocean air whipped along my face. "I should have told you sooner."

"It's my fault." Xander leaned forward to give her an enchanting smile. The muggy breeze swept along his shirt and rustled through his tawny blond hair. He'd been relatively quiet all day, allowing for Olivia and me to fill the air with everything we'd missed in each other's lives. "I couldn't wait anymore."

"This man," Olivia cooed, smacking an exaggerated hand over her chest. "Now that you've purchased a building, do you plan on moving back?"

I spent so long feeling rejected by this place that I forgot how good it felt, too. In protecting myself from the pain, I missed out on the joy that was here.

I looked to Xander for help, but he looked just as interested in my answer as Liv. "I'm not entirely sure."

"Oh." Olivia's shoulders fell. "Well, tell me you're going to at least come to the Chen Charity Gala this weekend."

"It's an annual event at the family's house," I explained to Xander, seeing his quizzical look. "I wasn't invited." I also didn't have anything to wear and there was the glaring issue of being persona non grata now that I'd jilted Maddox.

"You're a Chen, so you're always invited." She stopped and looked me squarely in the eye. "I don't know if Silas will attend, but he's usually a no-show anyway. Your father and stepmother are hardly in Singapore anymore. They're mostly in Hong Kong now."

"And Bella?"

Olivia's face brightened. "She's never really out at social events these days, but I believe she's coming. It is at the old Chen house after all."

Arabella and I didn't really have a relationship now, but that didn't mean I didn't want one. And in the last day, being here and seeing Singapore with fresh eyes, I wanted to try.

Hope fluttered in my chest.

"It might be fun." Xander's arm moved from my shoulders to slowly run up and down my back reassuringly. Then he glanced over to Liv. "But she's not just a Chen. She's also a Sutton now."

"Ooh, I like him." Olivia smirked.

"He's a bit of a charmer." I rolled my eyes.

Xander's chuckle settled in my chest like an anchor; it kept me steady.

Chapter 20

XANDER

The Hightower Energy board meets in a month." Sloan's voice came through over the sound of a dinner party in the background that got progressively quieter. "The Senate is conducting hearings next week."

The humid air of a Singaporean summer practically adhered to my skin. I was hoping the unrelenting heat would wake me up. The jet lag and the fact that we were staying in the honeymoon suite, so I was sleeping on the couch, meant my sleep schedule was fucked.

"Really?" I said through a deep yawn. It was already well into the afternoon by the time I woke up. "That was fast."

I took a few steps to the edge of the terrace and looked at the city on one end and the bay on the other. Our suite at the Four Seasons came with a pool on a large terrace, outfitted with tables and lounge chairs and enough space to throw a party.

"Mm-hmm," Sloan affirmed. The sound of a door closing behind her could be heard on my end. "Victor Hightower will be voted down. I'll advise the family to take a step back in order to meet the restitution mandated by the Feds, which I'm sure will be hefty."

"Victor is out." I glanced over my shoulder, through the glass doors that led into the hotel suite. I could see Penelope walking around inside.

In a bikini.

Fuck.

Sunlight drenched her warm sandy skin, light streams from the blinds cutting shadows along her gentle curves as she walked around. The modest bikini bottom and top did nothing to stop the heat that ran through my veins at the sight of her.

But Sloan's voice did. It was a fucking ice bucket when she cheerily replied, "A new direction for Hightower Energy is in."

I smiled. One step closer.

Once I took control of Hightower Energy, their global reach combined with Herrera's revolutionary battery technology would make the newly merged company a leader in clean energy. It would be the only leader in an open field for decades, until others could catch up. All tucked neatly under Dawn Capital's umbrella.

"Next step will be the acquisition," Sloan told me, as if I needed a reminder. Take out Victor. Take over. Sit whomever I chose on the open throne. It was child's play. "It's going to be a bloodbath once those shares hit the market. You'll need to act fast to take Hightower."

My eyes flicked to the side when I heard the sound of a smooth swipe from the glass door. Penelope stepped outside with her laptop tucked under her arm.

"I know." My voice lowered to a whisper now that Penelope was in earshot. What Sloan was doing for me wasn't exactly ethical.

After a long pause, Sloan must have known I got distracted.

"I'm gonna go, but enjoy your honeymoon." She hung up before I could correct her.

All the things normal couples did on a honeymoon were just out of my reach. Yet, it was the only thing I could think about when a sultry breeze danced along her sheer cover-up.

Flimsy, it opened completely, giving me a better look at her curves.

I walked over to her once she sat down. I dropped my phone on the teak table beside her.

"Save whatever you're doing," I told her, gently tapping the top of her screen.

"I beg your pardon?"

"Show me around Singapore."

We were out yesterday, but most of the day was spent with Olivia leading the way. Penelope didn't really say much in the direction of things.

"If you'd like a tour guide, Xander, I am sure the concierge can help you."

"I'm calling in that favor. You know, the little one where we save your inheritance," I teased.

We were in her home city, and she didn't want to leave the hotel? We weren't doing anything interesting in here. She deserved to have some fun.

And, fuck, I missed her smile.

"I know what you're doing, being all meddlesome, and I'd just like to point out"—she leaned in closer and shut the laptop—"you are exactly like your best friend when you do that."

"Should I be offended?" I kind of was.

She stood up and walked back inside. "Entirely up to you. Be ready in ten minutes."

Chapter 21

XANDER

A lush green canopy overhead provided shade from the late afternoon sun as Penelope and I entered the garden. The spindling vines climbed up and along the broad palm leaves creating a giant interconnected umbrella.

"Why the Singapore Botanic Garden?" I walked a few steps behind Penelope, who traversed the path like she'd memorized it: her head was on a swivel.

Penelope shrugged. "I wasn't allowed to go to many places as a child. But I was allowed to come here.

"Everyone likes to go to the Gardens at the Bay," Penelope explained as she walked ahead, reading the signs next to the flowers carefully. "And it's lovely." She kept walking, scanning the landscapes along the path for something. "But this one is . . ."

She stopped in front of a patch of flowers that didn't look like they had much adornment around them. A little bit away from the orchid gardens, the landscape was mostly filler flowers and foliage as a bland contrast to the opulent orchids that awaited us up the path.

The flowers in question were red with black centers.

My heart dipped.

She stopped in front of poppies.

I always wanted to know why, of all the things she could have grown and killed in her house, she chose poppies.

"Poppies?" I caught up to her and looked at the patch of unassuming flowers.

"They grow everywhere. Here, London, Scotland. In the snow. In the sun."

She took a deep, shuddered breath and knelt down. It made a little more sense now. Shuttled between homes on different continents. Poppies were there regardless. Something *she* could expect in a life where so much was expected of her.

"Everywhere except your house," I teased.

She looked up, passing her fingers over the velvet petals. Her eyes widened and something about that made that statement twinkle for a fleeting second; her mouth opened and immediately closed before she blinked it away.

"Yes, well." She stood up and ran a hand down her dandelion-colored dress a few times. "Not everyone has a green thumb."

"You don't really need a green thumb to take care of them," I quipped, throwing an arm over her shoulders, unable to resist touching her in any way I was allowed to. "It's hard to destroy poppies, they're tenacious."

Mine certainly was.

"I'm an overachiever." She didn't do anything to move my arm, so I left it there.

"Well, I like your choice of venue." I breathed in the citrus scent as we passed the fragrant lemon trees a few feet from the orchid gardens.

"I thought you might like it here; the conservancy and all."

Originally, working with the Central Park Conservancy was Beatrice Amari's way of trying to help me deal with my parents' death. My mom loved to garden. The house I grew up in was always surrounded by flowers and my mom had a pretty extensive garden in the backyard.

"I do," I admitted. "My mom liked to garden. She'd have loved this. We had peonies and roses all along our house growing up."

"Yeah?" Her eyes flickered around the high canopy, brows lifted and her chest filled with a deep contented breath.

"She and Marcus enjoyed reading. And she and I would garden," I explained. Growing up, I was in all the gifted programs and while it was a blessing in the opportunities I was given, a mind that never stopped could be overwhelming. My mom was good at finding ways to help slow it down when it moved too fast. "When things got to be too much, it was calming."

"That sounds . . . she sounds . . ." She trailed off. "Wonderful."

"She was."

I paused when I realized that I talked to Penelope more about my parents than anyone that wasn't my family—Sloan, Marcus, Henry. I couldn't help it. With anyone else, my mind never even considered getting that close, that personal. I was the king of small talk. I never needed to get that deep. But with Penelope . . . I found myself wanting to tell her everything, in the hopes she'd do the same.

"Did your mom ever come back here with you over the summers?" I asked, since I knew almost nothing about Victoria Astor. Penelope went to school in London, so I assumed she spent time with her mom then. And she was in Singapore for the summers.

"No, she was happy where she was. So she didn't come to Singapore at all after the divorce."

"Really?"

I wasn't in any place to judge, as Penelope rightly pointed out when we were in the lighthouse, I had a great childhood. I had amazing parents who sat through every one of my games regardless of the weather. They were at every school activity, no matter how boring.

"Mm-hmm," Penelope affirmed with casualness, like I'd asked her a mundane question. "She's always been happier on her own. After I went to university, she left London. She lives on a small farm outside of Glasgow now. We used to go there when I was younger for the winter holidays."

"Did that ever bother you? Seeing her so little?" I prodded carefully, like walking a tightrope, she was finally letting me see pieces of her and I didn't want it to stop.

"It's fine." She shrugged, not answering the question. "I was with her in the winter months and as long as I kept everything organized, she was easy to please."

"What do you mean?"

"She was never good with details." Penelope looked up at me. "So, I took care of things."

She gauged my reaction, one that was honestly a little confused with how indifferently she felt about a mom who, from what I could surmise, treated her like a sibling. Or an assistant.

"My mother is a little different, I guess," she defended. "But it's fine. She never really wanted the whole family-life thing. So she goes about it a little differently."

I nodded.

"And it was easy," she insisted. "Taking care of her meant no melodramatic breakdowns. Win-win."

"And who takes care of Penelope?" I murmured.

She straightened and looked ahead. A bob in her throat was the only indication that I'd probably pried too deep. "I don't need to be taken care of."

I moved my hand down her back. "Why don't we do something *you* want to do."

She took a deep breath and looked around. Her head tilted

slightly, like the idea had never crossed her mind. "What do you mean?"

Always accommodating and never an imposition on anyone; it had to get exhausting. After a lifetime of walking on eggshells, she should be allowed to break a few.

"What do you want to do?" I repeated.

The question seemed to do more harm than good. I could practically see all the ideas running through her head.

"Well," she said, deep in thought. She took a few steps ahead of me, then paced back. "We could go to the bay if you like—"

"Poppy." I held her shoulders and leaned down to meet and hold her attention. "*Your* preference."

"The night markets." The answer shot out of her mouth so fast that I was sure it was loaded for years, waiting for the day when someone actually gave her the chance to decide.

* * *

"Slow down," I said over the hiss of hot oil in the woks at the stand next to us. Prawns and marinated chicken skewers sizzled and popped on open flames. The scent of garlic and charred chilis wafted around us.

"God, I missed this food." She tore a few prawns off their skewer with a ravenous speed. Peanut sauce from the satay she'd finished in what had to be record time was smeared across her mouth.

"People are going to think I don't feed you." I handed her a few more skewers and a napkin.

We were only at the Newton Centre night markets for an hour and she'd already downed a bowl of stir-fry, a few desserts, and now she'd moved on to some items off the grill. High-society Penelope was nowhere to be found as she polished off another satay.

"I never got to come here," she confessed, then took a long sip from another Penicillin Cocktail. It was a type of scotch mixed with honey and ginger. "I always wanted to go. My nannies would have some food picked up for me."

I'd been to Singapore twice before, both for work. I'd never been able to actually enjoy the city like this. And Penelope seemed completely at ease. Seeing her relaxed made my chest tighten with the recognition that she was probably walking through life pretending. I knew exactly how hard that was.

"Why not?" I asked.

"It was considered unseemly. My father and stepmother wanted to keep the illusion of nobility up as long as they could."

She handed me the empty cup and took the full one in my hand.

"And princesses don't eat street food?" I teased.

She shook her head, taking another sip. "Technically, I'll eventually be a viscountess. But, yes."

"Not even when it's Michelin-star street food?"

She grinned and shook her head again. She looked up at the sky, something she did a lot.

"I'm having fun," she piped out with a contented sigh.

"Well, it's no spreadsheet." I threw out the trash we'd collected over the last hour and put an arm over her shoulder. "But me, too."

"You tease me about my spreadsheets, but for those of us not gifted with a perfect memory," she said, yanking on my shirt and looking up at me impishly, "it's helpful to organize your thoughts. Peaceful even."

"Just because I remember it all doesn't mean it makes any sort of sense."

"Hmm. Cryptic." She didn't look away but brought the straw to her mouth and took a large, loud sip, pulling up every drop from the bottom. "What does that mean?"

We began walking down the narrow street, through the kaleidoscope of colorful food stalls. I looked down at her. "Sometimes it's useful."

"And other times?" she asked.

"It's chaos."

"Sounds like *you* need a spreadsheet." She poked her index finger into my chest. Her voice dropped to a whisper. "And you know, an organized list can be fun."

Despite the cacophony of languages, food, colors, lights, everything muted, and I could hear her with perfect clarity.

"Oh?" I stopped walking but my heart raced, wondering if we were thinking about the same list. She hadn't brought up the fuck-it list—or whatever she'd like to call it—since that night. Not even when I took her to the lighthouse to cross off an item. "What kind of list?"

She looked up at me from beneath my arm and rolled her bottom lip under her teeth. "Well, maybe one with . . . *activities*."

"Activities?" My voice lowered.

A part of my brain switched off. The reasonable part. All that was left was everything I wanted to say, do, feel.

"The kind you might need a partner for?" I ventured when she didn't answer, feeling dizzy even though I hadn't had a single drink.

A hard swallow shifted down her throat. She leaned back on her heels, precariously. "You remember it?"

Blood rushed in my ears, a spark ran down my spine.

"Every last letter," I whispered, leaning in closer until my lips just barely grazed her earring. She swayed ever so slightly on her heels. My hand moved down to the small of her back to keep her close. Then, I listed off the few deeds that had my brain completely foggy for days after reading them. "Tied up. In public. Blindfolded."

Her breath gently hitched along my neck.

Fuck.

"Oh." Her lips parted just slightly as I pulled back to look at her; her irises were spilled ink that glittered in the moonlight.

The air thinned, making me lightheaded in the most exhilarating way.

I pulled her closer, my lips a hair's distance from hers.

She sighed softly. "Do you w—"

A quick hiccup and a slip shattered the tension as she stumbled back—losing balance on her high heels.

My hand pressed against her back to catch her while her hands closed to fists around my shirt. I pulled her forward and the scent of scotch and honey brushed against my cheek, reminding me that I wasn't intoxicated but she probably was.

A blush ran across her cheeks.

"Sorry." She looked up at me with wide eyes that fell slightly at the corners. Her mouth did the same, like she was disappointed with how the moment ended. She took an extra few seconds, frozen, before her fists loosened against the fabric of my shirt. "I'm a bit unsteady."

The tension from that moment floated away on the night's warm breeze.

"Don't be sorry." I pulled back enough to try to clear my head. But I kept my arm wrapped around her waist to give her some balance. "Gives me an excuse to steady you."

A smile curved up her still crimson cheeks, but she didn't say anything. We wandered through the crowded market for a few more minutes before I figured it was probably time to head back.

Twenty minutes later, she leaned on me as we walked into our suite. Her heels clacked in a wobbly cadence against the floor.

Penelope swayed as she took a few steps into the bedroom.

"Should I be offended that the only time you feel the need to drink is around me?" I followed close behind her.

"You should be honored." She shook her head. "I haven't had that much fun in a long time. I forgot how much I enjoy the occasional cocktail."

I smiled. Penelope was letting loose, and she didn't do that very often.

Looking at the bed, I ran a hand against my neck, fighting every urge I had to go to sleep next to her. She walked into the bathroom, and I went to grab a few things from my bag and sleep on the couch in the living room outside.

"Where are you going?" She rocked a bit as she crossed the room and took off her earrings in front of the antique floor-length mirror beside the nightstand. Her eyes caught mine in the reflection.

"I'll be on the couch if you need anything."

"Xander," she called quietly, turned, and slid a hand across my chest as I passed behind her. "Stay."

"Penelope . . ."

She took a step closer. "You can help me out of this dress."

"I don't have a great track record with your dresses," I reminded her.

Her hands slowly closed to a relaxed fist around my shirt. "You can rip this one."

My heart roared in my chest.

"Poppy . . ." I let out a deep, slow groan. My forehead leaned against hers, our eyes caught in an unbroken stare.

"Thank you for tonight," she whispered.

"I should be thanking you for showing me around." My hands sat firmly on her waist, knowing better than to move anywhere else.

"You're really not that clever. I know it was for me."

She pulled me and I followed without hesitation. Step for step until she'd backed herself against the side of the bed.

She leaned forward, her chin tilting up toward my face. I couldn't bring myself to back away. Her lips brushed against mine. Her breath sent heat down my spine. I held very still, afraid that if I moved I might not be able to stop myself. "I think you should stay," she whispered.

"I can't," I stammered, trying to get control of my heart rate. I couldn't for so many reasons, the primary one being that she was drunk. Sober Penelope wanted very different things than Drunk Penelope. The chemistry was undeniable, but past that I wasn't sure what Penelope wanted.

"Why?" Her hips rolled against mine.

Fuck. My cock strained against my pants. I wanted her. I wanted to hear what she sounded like when I crossed off every item on that list.

I took a shuddering breath.

"You have plans that . . ." I began, telling myself more than I was telling her.

She had plans that didn't involve me. I didn't know how many times I needed to be told the same thing before it stopped feeling as sharp as it did. She was looking for something she hadn't found yet and I'd been in her field of vision for years. She didn't *want* to be with me and as good as it felt to feel her in ways I'd only dreamt about, it wasn't real.

"I don't have plans," she murmured. Her eyes closed slowly. "Just a spreadsheet and your mother's engagement ring."

She gave me a teasing smile, repeating the words I said to her on the terrace, engaging in a little game between the two of us. My heart dipped.

I tried to figure out which would be worse: giving in to the chemistry and accepting the free fall that would follow, or taking solace in knowing I couldn't possibly miss what I never had.

"You're drunk, Poppy," I reminded her.

Her hand slid down my chest, to my groin. She stroked my erection through my pants. "You're hard, darling."

My breath faltered. Everything felt cloudy. The only clarity I had was that whatever *this* was . . . it wasn't happening tonight.

"So, what if I'm drunk?" She smiled, running her hands up my neck and raking her fingers through my hair. Electricity shot down my back. "I still want you to stay with me."

I wasn't going anywhere.

I'd known that since that night in her kitchen.

I was going to be stuck here, in this purgatory. Caught between what I wanted, what I needed, and what I could never have.

I was here. She had me and that wouldn't change.

"Let's go to bed, Poppy." I slowly maneuvered her to the mattress, knowing she was exhausted, and she'd probably fall asleep quickly. She gave me a slow grin and hummed quietly. "For *sleep*."

I pressed a gentle kiss against her lips, using all the effort in the world to keep it at that. She sighed again and complied without another word. I lay next to her.

"What a gentleman," she said through a soft yawn.

I pushed a few hairs out of her face, my thumb grazed slowly against her cheek. I didn't say anything, only smiled and watched as she drifted to sleep.

Chapter 22

PENELOPE

My heels clicked along the hardwood floors. Xander stood by the entryway, reading something on his phone when I walked out to the living area from the bedroom.

"Sorry, I was having trouble with my dress," I lied.

I was pacing in there for an hour.

The truth was that I woke up this morning, in my dress from last night, wrapped in Xander's arms. My memory got a bit foggy after getting in the car to return to the hotel, but the flashes I remember were of me coming on to him. Based on how I woke up this morning, he must have declined. Obviously, it was the right thing to do given my state, but God, was it humiliating.

So I left early in the morning, before he woke, to find a dress. Avoiding the ache to feel his touch. Grappling with the realization that maybe we could *explore* our chemistry while we were married. After groping him last night, at least I knew with absolute certainty that the chemistry wasn't one-sided.

"Don't worry about it," Xander said casually, looking at me from over his phone. "I was just returning a few—"

His eyes wandered down the dress then back up to me. His languid gaze weighed heavy on every inch of skin. In three seconds, every single emotion I'd tried to bury since waking up in his arms this morning flooded back to me.

"All set now," I added easily as I adjusted the bracelet on my wrist and closed the space between us, trying and failing to not gawk at how *good* he looked.

I'd seen him in all manner of attire. Suits mostly, given the nature of his work. Casual in a T-shirt and joggers, distracting in swim trunks, and then dapper and refined in formal wear.

I didn't know which version drew me to him the most, but this tux was something new. His hair was neatly arranged to the side. His sharp, chiseled cheekbones contradicted his sweet, affable nature.

He stood up and closed the distance between us, looking me over appreciatively. He blinked a few times, leaned in closer, and his voice lowered. "Do you know how to get out of this one?"

At the baritone in his voice, an excited chill ran across my skin.

There was no playfulness in those words. He was being . . . forward. And it sent an electric spark through my entire body.

"I'd better, it's vintage Valentino." My legs began to wilt under his unwavering attention. He ran an open hand along the small of my back and let it rest there. "And if you rip another piece of couture, CeCe will murder you."

I glanced at my reflection in the window.

Tonight's gown was similar to the one I'd chosen for the wedding. Silk and nearly backless with two tiny straps along my shoulders. A deep hunter green, a little more revealing than I was used to, with a slit that ran all the way up my thigh. I thought it would make me self-conscious. In reality, I felt the opposite.

Like finally, I wasn't hiding.

"I can think of worse reasons," he whispered. His fingers tapped along my bare spine, sending down delightful sparks with each gentle thud. It felt like he was testing the waters, and I wanted him to.

His eyes moved across my shoulder, then his fingers followed. Gently stroking an old scar just along my collarbone. It was faint and usually covered but my newfound preference for shoulder-baring dresses made it more visible.

"It was a wine bottle," I told him, trying to regain some composure. His eyes snapped back up to meet mine. "When I was younger, Arabella and I would play hide-and-seek and I'd always hide in the wine cellar."

"I didn't notice it last night." His gentle reminder brushed against my skin, like he wanted to talk about it but wasn't sure how. I wasn't either.

"Arabella would always find me since I hid in the same place. But once she snuck up behind me, gave me a fright, and I jumped. The entire shelf of bottles came crashing down and one shattered along my shoulder."

His fingers ran along the scar again.

"Ouch." He winced. "Were you okay?"

"No, unfortunately I passed away," I answered dryly, realizing it was fun to instigate even if that was a little dark. I liked playing along, being a part of our little game.

His brows rose. His cheek twitched.

"A few stitches, and we weren't allowed to play hide-and-seek again," I added, answering the actual question.

"Did it ever occur to you to find a different hiding spot?" he teased.

It wasn't about winning the game, not for me. "I liked knowing she'd find me."

That I wouldn't be alone, waiting for someone who wasn't coming.

*　*　*

I WALKED UP the stone entrance to my childhood home and felt a foreboding prickle through my chest. Suddenly, I wanted to go back and change.

"It'll be fun," Xander encouraged. He squeezed my hand, holding it tight as we made our way up the steps. The attendants stationed at either side of the grand mahogany doors opened them as we reached the final step. "And if it's not, we'll leave."

I nodded. His light demeanor almost lifted the oppressive anxiety as the doors swung open, but just as they did, my eyes met Olivia's, and Xander's sentiment felt like it might be true.

This might be fun.

"You look captivating!" Olivia gushed. Before I knew it, I was wrapped in a hug. Olivia had to have been watching the door, she got to me so quickly.

"Olivia, you've outdone yourself," I told her as I glanced around the room. The grand staircase welcomed guests as they filed around either side of it to the courtyard.

Everyone in attendance dressed in white-tie formal attire. The men in dashing tuxedos and the women in gowns one might see along the French Riviera at the ornate celebrations after the Grand Prix.

"Thank you." She beamed then looked over to Xander then me. "Mrs. Sutton."

The two had only known each other for hours and were already thick as thieves. The Xander Sutton magnetism never missed.

"Olivia, you look lovely." Xander greeted her with a warm hug. "If I wasn't already married," he jested and stood back at my side. His hand spread across my bare back.

"He is too delightful for his own good, Penny." Olivia grinned as she looked at me, then froze. "Penelope," she immediately corrected; her face fell. "Sorry."

Xander looked at me, but I breezed past it.

"It's quite alright." I hooked my arm in hers and she guided us through the rooms that were transformed for the party. "Where are we going?"

Inside, the rooms directly adjacent to the courtyard hosted neatly arranged table games. Poker, baccarat, blackjack, seemingly any high-stakes game was available for play. Fresco-style paintings adorned the walls, crystal chandeliers were hung along the center of the high vaulted ceiling, sending soft uplighting along the walls and floors.

"The courtyard, so I can get you both a drink." She pulled me past the guests, who quickly recognized me. I could hear an up-swell in whispers as I passed.

Xander followed a few steps behind.

Olivia led us to the courtyard where guests enjoyed drinks and some quiet conversation. Each corner featured a bar and the center of the courtyard held an elegant fountain.

"Xander." She handed us both a drink. "All of the boys are play-ing poker, if you'd like to join them."

"Is that your way of dismissing me?" He took the drink but didn't take a sip.

"I haven't seen this woman in over a year. And she comes here married to what I can only describe as a *GQ* model." She motioned for him to go. "You've had more than enough time with her. She and I need to gossip, so off you go."

"I knew I liked you," he chuckled, then leaned in to whisper in my ear. "Are you going to be alright?"

I nodded and he glanced back at Olivia, gave her a wink, and walked to the poker tables.

"Please tell me he's terrible in bed, otherwise that's just not fair," Olivia demanded when he was out of earshot. God, I hoped he was out of earshot.

"Liv!" I looked around to see if anyone else had heard her. "That's not appropriate party conversation."

"The sex is great, isn't it?" She grinned wildly. "Well, of course it is, look at that dress you're wearing."

"Liv!"

"He looks like the tie-you-up, tie-you-down type," she mused.

"Liv!" My face heated.

"I'm right, aren't I?" She giggled into her glass as she took a healthy sip of champagne.

"Oh my God." I shuffled my feet a few inches back and forth.

"Come on now, tell me what happened. Last we saw each other, the Xu family ring was being resized for you," Olivia recalled. She came to visit me while I was in London while Maddox was there. "That gorgeous man fucked all the sense right out of you, didn't he?"

"It's quite simple really. We fell in love, and I couldn't be with anyone else."

It felt like it could be true and that, maybe, the inescapable draw was worth exploring.

She put her empty glass on a high top next to us and took my hands in hers. "I'm glad, Penelope. You seem happy."

"I am." I took a gulp of my champagne.

It was the truth.

"Xander is wonderful," I added.

When I wasn't worrying about my family or how all of this would play out, I was having a nice time. Those moments in between plot twists were fun; I was enjoying pretending with him.

"Penelope." My heart stopped at the sound of a soft voice.

Then it restarted at twice the speed. I looked over my shoulder to see Arabella taking a few steps toward us.

Her pin-straight black hair was neatly tucked behind a bejeweled headband, not a strand out of place. She folded her hands in front of her, along the simple blue gown.

"Bella." I unfroze. I didn't know if I should be excited or not.

Olivia wasn't sure if she'd come. The two hardly spoke, and I hadn't figured out how I'd even begin to talk to my little sister. We hadn't spoken in years, but the silent anger that bounced off of her was palpable.

"What are you doing here?" she demanded quietly. Her frame was tense and her eyes narrowed on me.

"I wanted to . . ." My eyes fell to the floor. "I was hoping to see you."

That was true, even though I knew Arabella was asking why I was back in Singapore after years away.

"Were you?" Her features sharpened after a moment of softness, like she felt the same longing to be close that I did. But only for a flash.

"Of course," I added sincerely. I took a step forward and put my glass aside to take her hands but she pulled them back quickly.

"I'm guessing the visit has something to do with your inheritance." She rolled her eyes and waved her hand at me once, dismissively. My stomach hollowed because she was right. "A home in Singapore, right?"

"Yes, but—"

"Why else come back here?" she said plainly, an innocent undertone. She was punishing me for being away. "Unless it's something for yourself."

I tried not to flinch.

I was selfish for choosing something different than her? Phone calls worked both ways, she could have called. At the very least she could have understood that while she wanted this life maybe I wanted to try something different. She knew that I was so often scorned it was hard to fit in here. That toggling between wanting to stay away to spare myself the pain and wanting desperately to be accepted by my family hurt.

I swallowed the anger. I was the older sister, I should've been the one to be the bigger person. "Can we talk?"

"Now that it's convenient for you, you'd like to talk?" she answered quietly.

"Bella . . ." I began, almost pleading.

"Sorry, I forgot the rules." She put her hands up, a purposeful scowl on her face. "Whatever you want, you get."

A ringing struck through my ears. Indignation lit a controlled burn in my stomach. I had to endure growing up the begrudgingly accepted half sister to Arabella and Silas. The ire I faced from my father and stepmother eventually bled into those relationships. I was still a Chen, so I was family, but nobody ever tried to conceal the fact that my father's kindness—if it could be called that—was because of my Astor title.

That simple fact drove me away and kept me away, despite feeling like a part of myself was missing. The part that remembered all the wonderful childhood memories with Liv and Bella. The part that wished there was a way back to that.

"I get what I want?" I repeated. "Coming from you, that's rich."

Arabella always got what she wanted because what she wanted was here and readily available. I wasn't the same.

"Alright, you two," Olivia whispered between us. I took a second to look around, but nobody seemed to notice us bickering quietly, like proper ladies. "That's enough."

Arabella ignored Olivia, not bothering to acknowledge she was there. "I had to stay. I had to marry the man chosen for me. *I* didn't get to run off to the States without a second thought to my family or how my choices would affect them."

Suddenly, the buried resentment I had for all my attempts to reach her going unanswered bubbled up.

"Get to? Don't be angry with me because you weren't clever enough to do it yourself." The words settled all along her face and I immediately regretted them. Arabella, while so perfect, might not have been the best in school. It never mattered; she was always so happy to take on this life. "I'm sorry, Bella. I shouldn't have said that."

"No, you're right. You were the clever one." Her voice cracked. "Count yourself fortunate."

She took a deep breath, looked down for a moment, and fluttered her lashes to brush the glassiness from her eyes.

The words settled in my chest, making it ache. "Bella . . ."

She shooed my hands away, taking a step back. "Go home, Penelope."

Olivia said something to me, but I couldn't hear anything; I blinked a few times, registering her walking into the house after Arabella.

Chapter 23

PENELOPE

My entire body shook as I took a glass of water from a circulating waiter. The anxiety from the encounter with Arabella set every nerve into panic. I moved through a blur of faces as they passed my field of vision until I'd walked all the way through the courtyard and was at the terrace at the western face of the house.

In the distance I could distinctly hear the sound of occasional cheers from a table game.

The serenity enveloped me as I leaned on the marble railing that overlooked the lawn and the gardens. I wasn't sure how long I was there, lost in thought, but a familiar voice pulled me from it all.

"Are you alright?" A shiver rolled up my spine in warning from simply hearing his voice. Comforting in its familiarity but devastating in the consequences. "I saw what happened in the courtyard. You and Bella were always very good at the covert argument."

"Maddox." I didn't need to turn to know it was him. I set my now empty coupe glass to the side.

Maddox Xu. His jet-black hair slicked back neatly; dark brown eyes affixed on me.

"Yes. It's expected," I noted calmly, turning to face him. I hated that I got so worked up and snapped at her, but at least we spoke. That was more than we'd done in a while.

"Remember all those summers we'd spend out on that lawn?" he asked with a wistfulness I hadn't heard in years. "We used to plan all the places we'd go after university."

I was always told that I was allowed to see the world once I was married. So I would often tell Maddox of all the things I wanted to do and the places I wanted to see.

Eventually it became a list I kept to myself. Then, much later, other things were added to that list, too . . .

"That was a long time ago," I told him blankly. "No point in reminiscing about the past."

He let out an exasperated sigh and took a step closer.

"Do you think I like this? Having to come home and explain to my family that I couldn't even control my own—" He stopped himself. "That you've gone mad and married some American. All the while, you're traipsing around looking like . . ."

His eyes wandered down my dress.

This side of him, the one that became controlling, was usually concealed. It hid behind well-meaning advisement, but I could see it clearly in these moments.

As a teenager and young adult, I didn't think much of it because he'd always been a good friend, but seeing it now, there was clarity. It made me more confident in my decision to pursue my inheritance through other measures.

"Plans change," I told him calmly. I had a hard time believing he was at home pining for a life that could have been. He saw me as a means to an end; it was never clearer than right now. "You never wanted me either, Maddox."

"That's not the point." He took a step closer, his voice lowered. "Sometimes it's what's good for everyone. And you can't tell me you don't miss it here."

He was right in that I did miss Singapore.

What kept me from returning wasn't the place. The rejection I felt here was a product of the circumstances. Now that those had changed, I could see a life here. It was riddled with all the questions of what happened next. But I could see it.

"You'll still lead Xu Enterprises," I consoled softly. That was always what he wanted. To be the one his family chose as the leader, the favorite amongst his own brothers. He didn't need me to secure his future the way I had.

"Will I? With a family full of brothers just waiting for the moment to knock me down, it won't make convincing my family I should lead any easier, will it?" He laughed humorlessly. "The optics of my fiancée running off are humiliating, but at least we've been able to keep that news contained." He seethed to himself, under his breath, before looking up at me. His features softened. "What have I ever done to deserve all of this?"

My heart squeezed for a moment. I took a step forward, recognizing my childhood friend, the one that helped me feel less rejected. "I'm sorry it all unraveled like it did."

"I know you want to come home." Maddox put his hands on my waist and stepped closer. "Penny, it's not too late to salvage things, end all of this nonsense."

The nickname—the one I asked him a million times not to call me—cut against my skin.

"This nonsense?" I spat. "I'm married, Maddox. It's done. *We're done.*"

The heaviness in my chest lifted. Choosing myself felt freeing no matter how many times I did it.

"Poppy." Xander's voice was finely sharpened steel as it cut through the conversation.

My heart fell into my stomach. I looked past Maddox to see Xander crossing the threshold. I immediately walked to his side.

He threw an unsure look to Maddox but once his eyes met mine, they didn't let them go.

"Are you okay?" His tone lost all its edge when he addressed only me. A look I'd never seen passed over his features, disappearing as quickly as it came.

"We were just talking," I whispered. I knew, from his vantage point, it must have looked like something else.

"Are you okay?" he repeated, grasping my chin gently.

"Yes. Of course."

"Good." His arm circled my lower back and pulled me close. The tone in his voice became alluringly smug when his eyes lifted to Maddox. "Didn't see you come in. We should put a bell on you."

"Hardly seems necessary," Maddox shot back. "I'm not the one who keeps showing up where he doesn't belong."

"Why don't we fix that?" Xander answered politely, a tactful venom in his words. He looked down at me. "Let's go inside."

I could feel the tense muscles beneath the buttery fabric of his tux. I nodded and we made our way back inside.

Chapter 24

XANDER

I didn't hate many people, but I *hated* Maddox.

I hated that he got to have a piece of Penelope's life.

I hated how viciously jealous it made me.

I hated being reminded that they had a history I couldn't compete with. Especially after waking up alone this morning. The faint candied citrus scent on the pillow was the only thing she'd left behind when she scurried out of bed.

"Nothing happened," Penelope said offhandedly as we walked back inside.

Not that it stopped my mind from going wild thinking of all the things that could have happened.

We stopped at the bar. I didn't care where we went, I just needed to get her away from Maddox so that my mind would stop creating mental images of them to torture me.

"I didn't ask," I answered curtly, ordering a drink even though I didn't want one. All I wanted was to keep my mind busy. She took a step back and turned to look at me squarely.

"Well, I thought you should know." Penelope took a sip of water and glanced around the room, calmly.

She'd said so many times it was nothing, but he loomed like a shadow. That thought, coupled with the subversive allure of the deep green dress, made me fucking crazy.

That dress. Practically seamless, the silk draped over her shoulders in thin straps, bared her back all the way down to where it came together right above where I would have expected her panties to begin.

"Well, thank you for telling me, Poppy." I tried to rein it all in. Tried to put up a happy face and keep moving. There was no point in being annoyed or upset over information that was hardly news.

If I could act unbothered, maybe I'd believe I was, and it would hurt less.

I glanced around the room and remembered what we were *supposed* to look like.

"As a reminder. We're on our honeymoon," I murmured. I ran my hand down her waist and kept her close. "We should look like it."

Her eyes widened. She shuffled a bit more.

It was petty and juvenile, but the possessiveness seeped into my bloodstream with every passing second. Spurred on by the fact that she felt so good next to me, the memory of last night flashed in my mind.

"Come on," she said with a frustrated sigh.

Her warm breath lingered along my neck.

She put her drink down, took my hand and led me away from the bar.

* * *

PENELOPE

"Come on," I said and placed my drink along the bar.

He was annoyed but masked it in cordiality. It would be easier to talk freely where nobody was around, and I didn't want this unnecessary tension all night.

I led Xander down the hallway at the side of the staircase, knowing the den was probably empty. We passed the clean lines of the moldings along the wall. Each framed a different patriarch of the Chen family.

I opened the door and he followed, shutting it behind us.

The large, empty room was a den that Olivia used as a staging area. A few card tables, props, and decorations that weren't used for the party were strewn about. I didn't know where to find a light switch, but the moonlight streamed in over the large windows that looked out onto the gardens, filling the room with light.

"You're angry," I noted.

"Why would I be angry?" he asked so plainly, I was almost convinced he wasn't.

"Because clearly you're not a fan of my relationship with Maddox."

That lit a spark in his eyes. His jaw flexed at the mention of Maddox's name.

"And what relationship is that?" He took a couple steps forward; I matched them with a few steps back.

"My *previous* relationship with him," I corrected.

Xander's lips thinned. He passed a quick glance around the room, then took a slow prowl toward me to close the space between us.

His voice became stiff as he drew closer. "Why do all of this if Maddox was still—"

"He's not." I backed up instinctively until I felt a table behind me. I understood how it looked out there and, given my long history with Maddox, it wasn't entirely far-fetched. "There is nothing between us."

My hands braced back against the soft felt surface.

"Then why are you so close to a man you practically ran away from?" he demanded, his tone was low and heavy, settling deep in my stomach. I wobbled when his arms stretched to either side of me and he leaned in with a look I'd never seen from him before.

He wasn't hiding behind charm or pleasantness or humor.

He was upset. Hurt.

Avoiding his question, I scoffed. "That's interesting, coming from *you*."

He didn't have a single ex with a critical thing to say about him. Hell, I wouldn't be surprised if he were to be invited to their future weddings, the great indisputably likable Xander Sutton.

His brows lifted. His shoulders relaxed.

He didn't move even a centimeter away. "Jealous, Poppy?"

I scoffed again, except this time it got lost in a faltering breath.

He was the one who was jealous.

I didn't know if it was purely physical or something more, but Maddox and his closeness to me roused *something*.

His eyes stayed fixed on mine as he tucked a strand of hair behind my ear, his fingers brushing against my earlobe. My heart roared in my ears.

"I'm pointing out the hypocrisy." My voice tried to remain steady despite the quiver that ran through every muscle fiber. Sparks ran along my neck where his fingers had just brushed against it.

"It's different," he whispered.

Every nerve ending in my body became aware of just how good his proximity felt. From the hair he gently pushed over my shoulder, to my legs that began to feel like they were made of jelly.

"How?"

"It's easy to be civil when the feelings were hollow," Xander pointed out. It was something I'd known to some degree. Somehow, hearing it now in that graveled voice made my stomach flip. "I never planned to marry any of them."

"I'm only saying . . ." I stammered, trying and failing to remember what we were talking about. "You don't have a reason to be wary of him. It's unnecessary."

He passed my dangling earring between his fingers and drew closer. My breath shallowed against his skin.

"Is it?" he whispered. His lips moved to my ear and his fingers released my earring and curled around the back of my neck instead. "He wants one thing; you want the other. I'm on your team, so I'm going to do what it takes to win."

His demeanor was serious, but the volley in his tone made me feel like I was part of a game, one he was playing with a smug assurance of victory. Reducing it to that made me think the jealousy was more physical than something deeper, but either way, it felt *good*.

"Not everything is a game, there's nothing to win here." My body trembled lightly beneath his touch. "That little competition with Maddox is some juvenile reaction to him wanting to play with *your* toy."

"That's where you're wrong." His hand traveled down my side and slipped through the slit in my dress at my thigh. I flinched despite the growing ache between my legs.

My breath hitched.

"You can't be *jealous* because . . ." I tried to reason, mostly with myself. I tried to make sense of the feelings that bloomed inside me, the ones that had been more vocal the last few days; I wasn't sure what I wanted. The chemistry or more—but in that moment, all I wanted was him. I swallowed hard as his hand skimmed up my thigh. "You don't really want me. It's not real."

"This doesn't feel real to you?" His fingers dragged across the lacy panties that lay along the curve of my hip. "If it doesn't, say the word. Tell me to stop."

A slow shudder worked its way down my body.

My hips bucked. God, I wanted to give in. To shut my busy mind off for a moment and drown in how good it all felt. To release some of this pressure.

"I . . ." The dark room began to blur; the only part of my vision that was clear was him.

His body pressed against mine; an arm wrapped around my waist, keeping me close. His hand moved closer to where I ached for it as his thumb just barely grazed my clit over the lacy material of my panties a few more times, slowly.

I jerked forward.

He continued with the slow presses against my clit. Each one sending a small shock wave through my muscles, making me arch my back, but he held me tightly against him.

I closed my eyes. His strokes became more intentional. A slickness began to gather between my thighs.

"Poppy." His mouth hovered a hair's breadth from my shoulder, up the curve of my neck. "Tell. Me. To. Stop."

My hips rolled into him again. "Xander . . ."

He pushed my panties aside and sank a finger into me slowly, holding me so close I could feel his thick arousal pressed against my thigh.

"And as far as this *game* goes," he groaned roughly in my ear.

My head tipped back, the shudders became more pronounced, and I reached a hand to his shoulder to steady myself.

"You're not a toy." He pressed another finger into me.

The roar of the party down the hall was completely muffled by the downright filthy chorus of my breathy moans intermingled with the slick sounds of his fingers stroking and curling until he found *that* spot.

I gasped. My leg swung around his waist. Shamelessly grinding against him for more.

My fingernails dug into his shoulders, a static began to move through my legs, concentrating at my core.

"You're *my wife*," he told me through gritted teeth. "Only I get to play with you."

My eyes opened momentarily to catch the way he studied me.

He moved faster and deeper, my hips rolled in rhythm with his hand.

"Xander." I cried out for the release his fingers promised.

He increased his pace to a maddening speed, curling and twisting, all while his thumb stroked my clit firmly. The tightness along my core finally released. The pleasure burst indiscriminately along my navel, moving through my legs and torso.

With a quiet sob, my body rocked against him. Holding me flush against him, he continued his strokes until every ripple from my climax subsided.

"This might be a game, but for the next year, we're a team," he reminded me, softly. Gently.

His chest rose and fell with swallow breaths.

I nodded slowly; the haze began to lift from his eyes. My hands slid from his shoulders, hanging weakly onto his lapels.

His lips dropped to press a tender kiss along mine.

"And don't worry, Poppy. Xander Sutton does not lose."

Chapter 25

PENELOPE

Before Xander could pull me into another tryst on a poker table with a party going on just fifty feet away, I excused myself and tried to regain some composure in the bathroom.

After fifteen minutes of staring in the mirror and running through every possible repercussion in my head, I was no closer to figuring out what exactly I was feeling. It was a mix of a thousand emotions ranging from concerned to downright giddy.

The sconces' dim light cast shadows along the corners of the hallway as I walked down it slowly, twisting my fingers with excitement and nerves, knowing I was going to stand beside Xander and act as though all of that didn't just happen.

"You disappeared, are you alright?" Olivia's voice pierced through the constant replays of his touch and heavy breaths baiting me to an unbelievable orgasm.

"What?" I shook away the mental image. My entire body was still buzzing from what happened.

"Well, I just ran into your husband, who, by the way, is making polite conversation with Aunt Agnes." Her brows rose with a humor-filled look. "So give that man a medal."

I let out a short breath. Xander was making friends, the least shocking thing to happen all night.

"I told him you and Bella had a tiff and I couldn't find you. He said you'd gone to freshen up." She put her hands on mine. "Are you alright?"

The last couple of hours settled in my mind, after Xander wiped it clear. Despite how it went, at least Bella and I spoke. It would take time to mend things, but I was hopeful maybe we could. She could have walked away and ignored me, but she didn't.

I wanted to clear things up with my sister, but the tension was something I probably shouldn't inflame tonight, and I was sure she'd left.

"Oh." I blinked a few times. "Everything's fine. Xander and I played a hand of poker."

"Played a hand of poker?" Olivia's eyes narrowed. "Is that code for something?"

More than anything, I wanted to finish what Xander started. If there was one thing arguing with Arabella had taught me, it was to not wait to do something you should have done long ago.

I spent my entire life sacrificing adventures in the name of stability. Trading in spontaneity for sensibility. I deserved a chance to be a little reckless, too. And with Xander I didn't fear rejection in asking for what I wanted. My desires felt safe with him.

I felt safe with him.

"Well . . ." I turned my ring and in the periphery over Olivia's shoulder, I saw Xander. His eyes met mine.

His brows raised with delight, like he'd been searching for me. Stuck in polite conversation with my eccentric aunt Agnes, his jaw shifted slightly as his heavy stare bore down on me.

A controlled burn moved along my skin until my entire body warmed under the heat of his gaze. I was mildly overwhelmed with everything I was feeling and ached to feel one thing.

Him.

The images my mind created of him doing all of that again settled like metal at the bottom of my stomach.

Olivia turned when the staring became unreasonably noticeable.

Xander blinked away the look, his mouth raised at the corners, and he looked back to Aunt Agnes, still very much in the middle of what was surely a long-winded story.

"Oh." Olivia barely kept the laugh in as she turned back to me with a knowing smirk. "Well, I hope you won that hand of *poker*."

I most certainty did.

"I . . ." I stammered.

"Well, I can't blame you." Olivia linked her arm in mine. "Come on, let's save him before Aunt Agnes bores him to death."

* * *

XANDER

DURING A SHORT, bizarre conversation with Agnes Chen about beekeeping, Penelope found a lull in the discussion to politely pull me away.

She took my hand and led me to the same terrace I'd found her on earlier. "Poppy?"

My heart rate ticked up as I involuntarily thought about the last time she'd pulled me into a secluded area.

She turned to me, leaning against the stone balustrade. Her lips pressed together, keeping tight hold of a smile. "I wanted some air."

Her fingers laced in mine.

"Are you okay?" I pulled her a little closer. Looking up at me, her onyx irises glinted in the moonlight. Her hair picked up and gently swayed along the warm breeze. "Olivia told me you argued with your sister."

"Oh." Her shoulders fell slightly. "Nothing unexpected, I'm afraid. But I'm fine."

Everything felt up in the air. I wondered if she was okay after what Olivia told me about her argument with her half sister. Maybe she had been feeling vulnerable and I'd crossed a line. But the look in her eye, her ease around me, made me think the opposite.

"I'm sorry," I began. "I shouldn't have . . ."

Let jealousy get me so worked up that I finger-fucked her on a poker table.

"Gotten insanely jealous?" she finished for me, crimson ran across her cheeks and she pulled me a little closer.

"Poppy . . ." I leaned my head against hers, my hands ran along her hips. I had to remind myself that we were steps away from lots of people she happened to know since childhood.

"I'm not sorry," she said. A brief, wavering look passed over her before a more assured one came through. "About *that*."

The electricity in the air spread until I could feel flickers through every muscle. "No?"

She shook her head; her unbroken stare was a siren song drawing me closer. I leaned in, feeling her warm breath glide against my skin.

A tiny moan escaped her parted lips.

Fuck.

Just as I thought of all the ways I planned to elicit that sound over and over again tonight, a reminder passed through my mind. "I should call the concierge. For a few things."

The only protection I'd packed was sunscreen. I should have taken care of all of that while she was out today, but I was too busy trying to figure out what the hell was going on between us.

She shook her head and yanked me closer.

"There's no need." She ran her teeth over her full lower lip. "I'm on the pill and I haven't been with anyone in some time."

I pressed my lips against hers for a second, not wanting to know any more than that. Electricity shot down my spine.

I knew I should have been a little more restrained because her delicate hands were dangerous. And there was safety in never knowing what she felt like, what she tasted like, fuck, what she sounded like. You couldn't miss what you never had and up until tonight, in any sense, I'd never *had* Penelope. Now that I'd let it get that far, I couldn't stop. However she wanted this to go, it would go—I could deal with the aftermath later.

"You know I would never put you in any sort of risk, right?" I whispered on her lips. My fingers ran along her bare back.

"I know." She let out a short, shuddering breath. I could feel the goose bumps prickle along her skin. "But we should stay a little while longer."

I nodded. "It would be rude to leave early."

I tried to pull away from her, but fuck, I couldn't. She kept her hands, pulled into fists, around my shirt. An hour or five minutes could have passed. I had no idea. All I knew was that I didn't want to be even an inch further from her than I was now.

"My God, don't make me get the hose." Olivia's voice interrupted, clearing the fog. "The party is in here."

I cleared my throat and lifted my head to acknowledge Olivia. She gave us an expectant look and walked back inside.

"Come on, now." Penelope laid a hand on my chest but did nothing to push me away. "I'm sure Aunt Agnes misses your company."

Chapter 26

PENELOPE

The rest of the night was laced with anticipation. Every moment of small talk felt like a blur of heated stares and sultry whispers. We kept ourselves relatively composed, not so much as kissing before we entered our suite.

My heels snapped against the floor, echoing in an unsteady cadence with my heart as Xander opened the door to let me in. The heavy thud of the door closing, and the roar of my excitement hushed every other sound.

"Poppy."

But those two syllables were steel through silk.

"Yes?"

The air between us flickered with impatience, yet while my entire body felt like it would give way at any moment, I turned to see Xander standing there patiently. Watching.

"Where are we going?" His tone remained flat but stern.

A finger sank beneath his tie. He loosened it slowly as he took the few steps toward me. The lighthearted man was replaced with one whose gaze refused to move from mine.

His duality was a rip current. Deceptively calm with a furious tide that raged just below the surface.

He dropped his mouth to my ear when I didn't answer. "Kitchen, bed, pool, up against the wall, bent over the couch . . . where are we starting?"

The whisper settled between my thighs.

"I . . ."

"I need you to make a decision." He leaned his forehead against mine, electricity crackled between his words. "Because after that, I get to decide *how* you come."

His hands moved just above the curve of my ass, where the hem along my back began. "*When* you come.

"And how many times you come." He stepped forward, backing me against the wall with an unbroken stare. "So, where are we going, Poppy?"

My thighs clenched at the mental images of the veritable ways Xander could keep his word.

"Bed," I said through a shuddered whisper.

A grin pulled at the side of his cheek. His hands became fists around the lining of my dress, which was snug around my hips. "You won't need this."

With one hard rip the bottom came loose. Moisture slickened between my legs.

His finger ran slowly to my collar and pushed the thin straps off my shoulders. The fabric pooled at my feet, leaving behind a lacy thong and the diamonds I wore for the occasion.

Xander's eyes roved down my body slowly. A subtle shift in his muscles confessed his arousal.

"Poppy." His lips brushed against mine; his thumb passed tentatively over my clit. "If it's too much, tell me, okay?"

I nodded. His fingers lightly stroked the dampness along my panties.

"Are you being a gentleman, darling?" My teeth dragged over my lip fighting back a moan.

Heat flashed though his eyes. His fingers looped around my

panties and with a quick yank, they joined the tattered pieces of my dress on the floor.

"Gentle ended on the poker table." His hands ran up my side then along my collarbone, and he pulled me into a heated kiss.

The world around me melted away. I got lost in a heady mix of passion and pleasure as it spindled around every nerve ending. His hands roamed along each dip and curve of my body.

His mouth, his teeth, his tongue devoured every soft moan and whimper.

His fingers laced through my hair before gripping the base of my neck roughly. Raw and untethered, his kiss sought to claim *everything*.

He groaned as he pulled away, looped both hands under my thighs, and lifted me.

"Already so wet for me." His fingers followed the curve of my spine and teased my entrance from behind. My naked body ground against him. "You're going to ruin this tux."

"You ruined my dress." I rolled my hips.

His nostrils flared. "It won't be the last."

He pulled me back into a kiss and carried me to the bedroom. He laid me on the bed and I watched as he undressed. Beneath the perfectly crafted fabric was a man built like an athlete. Broad muscular shoulders, a sculptured torso that led down to . . .

I swallowed hard as he removed his boxers. His massive cock, long and thick, jutted out, making my stomach flip. The idea of *that* inside me felt daunting and alluring at the same time.

The mattress dipped as he hovered over me. His thumb found my aching clit again and ran progressively firmer strokes around it, being careful not to actually press it how he knew I wanted him to.

"Xander . . ." I panted.

A slow ember began to burn away along my spine, spreading in all directions. I ran a hand up his chest into his hair.

He pushed a finger into me. My head tipped back, and a short whimper rolled up my throat.

"*Fuck*," he groaned as he sank another finger into me. The slick sounds began to hasten, the static moved along my limbs.

My hips ground against his hand again, feeling the shaky precipice approaching.

"Look at me." His gravelly command nearly pushed me over the edge. But he stopped his slow circles and pulled his fingers out of me. He licked one before looking down at me like captured prey. "Open your mouth for me, Poppy."

A molten heat settled at the bottom of my stomach.

My past lovers were proper. The sex was . . . *appropriate*. And, mostly, disappointing.

This was sinful.

It ignited a desire that threatened to consume every fiber of propriety in its blaze.

I parted my lips. He slowly pushed his fingers, covered in my arousal, along my tongue.

"Suck them clean," he instructed. Leaning back a bit, he ran his other hand down my thigh. He brought my leg over his shoulder.

His jaw flexed as I felt his tip slowly stroking my entrance.

I sucked harder against his fingers, my hips jerked impatiently.

"That's my girl." He leaned in, pulled his fingers from my mouth and lifted my other leg to his shoulder. "So eager to cross everything off that list."

He entered me slowly at first, inch by inch. "One by one."

Then he pushed in all at once, knocking all the air from my lungs as I struggled to adjust to him.

The pain from his sheer size was quickly washed away by the pleasure that began to mount. Every muscle stretched to accommodate him, and I'd never felt so completely and utterly *taken*.

"Fuck . . ." He groaned deeply. His thumb ran along my clit, not pressing too firmly, teasing it over and over. "You're tight."

My slow pants began to give way to deeper, more languid breaths as I adjusted. And just as quickly as I felt completely overwhelmed by him, I *needed* more.

A whimper, overflowing with desire, escaped my parted lips.

"That's it, Poppy." He pulled himself completely out of me only to push back in—inch by inch—seconds later. "You can take it."

Each slow and brutal plunge, deep and intense, lapped over me. Wave after wave, slowly drowning me only to bring me back up for air between each stroke. He was teasing me.

"Xander, *please*."

His torturously slow rhythm felt like being so close to paradise only to have it ripped away at the last second.

"Please, what?" He pushed a little harder and deeper. The slick sounds of our bodies colliding and the deep bangs of the bed frame slamming against the wall filled the room.

"Xander . . ." A broken sob cracked out of my throat.

"Say it." He slammed into me mercilessly again and paused. "Tell me what you want."

"Fuck me," I managed to piece together through a string of unintelligible moans and sobs. "*Please.*"

Slamming into me, he delivered what I'd begged for.

Eliciting moan after moan. Pushing me closer. His thumb finally pressed on my clit and his savage strokes became so insurmountably pleasurable nothing could abate what was coming.

Complete oblivion.

My ankles mere inches from my head, he pushed even deeper, rolling his hips, and hitting the spot that lit up every neuron in my body. The pleasure began to push through the haze, my nails dug into his back.

My vision became starry, distant specks of light in a dark expanse. Then, like crashing back to reality suddenly, it became blinding.

The flash. The electric heat. The mind-altering high.

Every feeling burst at once as he slammed into me without any regard to the filthy symphony of screams. Sheer euphoria overcame my senses, my body quaked with an orgasm. The magnitude of which I'd never experienced before. Seconds later, my vision cleared and the aftershocks rolled through me.

I could barely register what was happening, my body trembled trying to make sense of the rush it had just experienced.

He leaned in close, still buried inside me.

"That's one." His rough whisper scraped against my ear. He slowly moved my legs off his shoulders and pulled out of me. "Turn around."

Heat moved down my spine.

I turned and got on all fours. My unsteady muscles struggled to balance on the mattress. I could barely catch my uneven breath as his hands took a firm grip of my hips.

Xander positioned himself behind me. "You okay, Poppy?"

Goose bumps swept across every inch of my skin. All I could muster was a faint nod.

His hand ran up my back and took a fistful of hair. With a hard push he was completely inside me again. After the first orgasm, I was so wet our thighs were covered in my arousal.

"Fuck," he cursed under his breath.

His other hand ran down my back and began to massage my breast, before giving my nipple a hard pinch.

I panted a broken cry for more.

"*My* Poppy. On her hands and knees. Taking every inch of me so fucking well."

He yanked my hair harder with each thrust. Pain splintered along my scalp in concert with a carnal gratification. Just like last time, it wasn't long until his rough hands became the keys to my release.

"Yes . . . God . . ." I cried out, tears forming in the corners of my eyes. "Harder."

He grunted; his fingers moved from my hair to lace lightly against the column of my neck. His thumb gently grazed back and forth against my skin.

"Is this too much?"

There wasn't a thing about him that I feared, and *God* did it feel good to relinquish control to a man who knew how to use it.

"No." I needed to feel it. Controlled and completely free at the same time. "More."

I barely heard his chuckle over the renewed roar in my ears.

"That's my girl." His velvet tone betrayed the ferocity of his strokes. All the tension found its release in each savage thrust.

Pushing my head into the pillow, Xander *fucked* me.

Hard and deep.

Like my body was his to tease. His to play with. His to shatter and put back together.

He hit the spot inside that made my toes curl and my muscles jump.

"That's it, Poppy, come for me." Pleasure strangled his voice; his hand kneaded my hip in a viselike grip.

The bed rattled against the wall. The next orgasm crested with waves of chills and broken moans. The pleasure exploded along the base of my spine and completely unraveled. Tears and saliva soaked the pillow.

Moments later, Xander let out a deep guttural groan and jerked forward. The first peek of vulnerability from him since before the party.

After a few moments of stillness, Xander laid a few gentle kisses along my spine then slowly pulled out. His cum dripping out of me was surprisingly the most erotically gratifying thing I never thought I'd enjoy. The idea of it sent a delicious chill up my spine.

He rolled over and pulled me into his arms. I rested on my side; our legs intertwined.

Sex with Xander broke something deep inside me that I never wanted fixed. I didn't care how I looked, how I sounded, or what the consequences were.

All I cared about was the serene calm that floated over me. One I had never been able to pin down for very long.

Sweaty. Exhausted. Looking like I'd just been properly fucked. I felt amazing.

"You're beautiful," he whispered softly, tucking some errant strands of hair behind my ear.

His words settled in my heart even though I knew better than to let them. But I didn't care. I basked in it. We didn't talk about what this was. Xander was known to not have long-term girlfriends and I'd just finally found my own freedom. Maybe this was something we both could use. If we split amicably later, I'd deal with whatever that felt like then.

The voice in my head that told me not to trust how I felt was completely silent.

For now, for once, I wasn't worried.

"Good thing we have the entire floor." I yawned and nuzzled my head into the crook of his neck. "We were a little loud."

Xander ran his fingers up and down my spine slowly. A deep, joyful, chuckle reverberated through his chest.

"They'll probably think we're on our honeymoon," he teased quietly. I glanced up at him, partially delirious, and found myself lost in his hypnotic smile. "We *were* instructed to sell it."

Chapter 27

XANDER

In comparison to Penelope, every illicit substance I'd misused in the past had the addictiveness of a breath mint.

I found myself falling asleep only to wake up, needing her. Another kiss, another taste, another moan slipping out from between her impossibly soft lips.

The reaction proved I was right; that crossing the line with her was probably a bad idea. After the time we spent together on this trip, I saw parts of her I'd never known. I was hooked.

With a soft moan, she turned in bed. Her inky black hair fanned across the white pillows. I looped an arm around her waist and pulled her back to me. An arched smile ran up her mouth.

"We've made a proper mess, haven't we?" She pulled her arm out from under the sheets and turned the ring along her finger.

No anxious pitch. No jumbled words rushing out of her mouth. She was at ease.

"I like Messy Poppy," I whispered in her ear. "She's a lot of fun."

She hummed softy in agreement before she sat up. The blanket fell off her shoulders and she pulled it around her. "Maybe you have it right."

I sat up and pulled her into my lap, she shifted to straddle me.

"What do I have right?" I asked as I leaned in and dropped a few tentative kisses along her collarbone, lining them up her neck to that spot that made her lose it last night.

Her body jerked forward when I got to it.

"Your standard operating procedure for relationships." She ran a hand through my hair. "You're stuck with me for a year. May as well have a bit of fun."

"You look like Poppy . . ." I teased, moving my hand up her side until I got to the curve of her breast. I ran my thumb over her nipple a few times. "But you don't sound like her."

She muffled a moan with her light and airy laugh. My other hand gripped her hip, encouraging it to grind against me.

"Is that alright? Some fun inside of our arrangement?" she questioned softly. Her fingernails gently scratched down my scalp, sending shivers down my spine. My cock twitched.

"Nothing serious," she added quickly, like she was trying to assure me it wouldn't happen. "Have some fun this year. No harm done, right?"

No harm done. It was the whole reason I kept relationships short and surface level.

Despite what I was sure would be a fucking brutal comedown from this high, maybe the risk was worth it. If she didn't want this after the year, I'd figure out how to manage.

I didn't want to jostle this careful balance we found with what I really wanted: to hold on to her and never let go.

She wanted something less intense, so I'd give it to her.

Besides, it wasn't like avoiding my feelings for her was working.

"Whatever you want." I flipped her onto her back.

"You're sure? I know this may be redundant since Xander Sutton doesn't typically want to be serious anyway." She pushed her fingers through my hair. "But I don't know what I want yet. And it seems a shame to stop doing all of *that*."

She smiled at me impishly.

"That's fine, Poppy." I pressed a kiss against her lips. Penelope wanted all of it—companionship, passion, the complete chaos that only love could summon—and even though she'd made it so incredibly clear she hadn't seen that with me, maybe the crash after this wouldn't be so bad. "We'll do whatever you want. If you want more, less, or anything in between, all you have to do is ask."

Maybe, hope fluttered stupidly in my chest, there wouldn't be a crash.

"I want to stay in bed," she said.

I glanced back at the clock. We had to go if we wanted to make it before high tide.

"That's too bad." I began to pull away. She whimpered and looped her legs around my torso, encouraging me back down to her. I groaned. "We have to get dressed. I have a surprise for you."

She sighed with a fleeting disappointment. Her brows lifted. "A surprise?"

She unhooked her legs, and I got out of bed.

* * *

PENELOPE DIDN'T ASK many questions when we got on the boat. She spent the hour-long ride laid out on the sun deck with no cover-up this time.

"If you're trying to impress me with a private island," Penelope said, taking my hand as we reached the island and I helped her onto the dock, "you'll have to try harder."

Surrounded by the turquoise embrace of the South China Sea, the small private island just east of Singapore had a house and was in the middle of relatively calm waters.

Perfect for someone to learn to surf.

I ran both hands along her waist and leaned in to whisper in her ear. "You know I like a challenge."

"So, is that where we're going?" She eased back into me and looked ahead to the little bungalow.

Tucked between the lush foliage, the thatched roof whispered in harmony with the ocean breeze. There was a plunge pool, a teak patio that wrapped around the entire structure, and all we'd need for a night on the island.

"No." I grasped her chin lightly and turned her head to the beach. There were a couple of boards and surf gear waiting for us. "That's what we're doing."

This island was the first thing I thought of when I saw that list.

Well, maybe not the *first* thing.

I made the call to a private concierge service while Penelope was asleep last night to arrange it all. We'd stay here for a night before heading back to Singapore late in the day tomorrow. We'd enjoy one last night there, maybe a final stop at the night markets. Then, we'd fly back to Manhattan.

"I don't think so." Penelope continued walking down the dock but once we hit the sand, she made her way to the house.

"Poppy." I took her hand and pulled her into me. "It's on the list."

I wanted her to know that everything on that list, both sides, was safe with me. She could trust me with her desires, fantasies, anything.

"Why not do something else on the list?" She threw her arms around me, pressing her barely clad body against mine. With a purposeful roll of her hips, I began rethinking surfing.

My mind wondered where she'd locked up this version of herself. A surge of blistering possessiveness rushed through me at the idea that she was like this with anyone else.

"I plan to." I leaned down and grazed my teeth against her neck. "Later."

I took her hand and led her toward the beach, but her heels stayed dug into the sand.

"I'll fall off that thing."

"And I'll catch you." I pulled gently again and this time she followed.

"Or I'll fall in the water."

"Or that," I chuckled. "If you're not having fun after twenty minutes, we'll go inside, and I will make it up to you."

Her defiant scowl cracked. "Deal."

"Great." I playfully smacked that perfect round ass. "Come on, Poppy, time to get wet."

Penelope picked up the basics of surfing quickly. After many attempts to stand on the board, it clicked, and Penelope was surfing.

Well, sort of. Penelope successfully stood on the board and mostly bodyboarded, but she did it.

Most importantly, she had fun and I got to float along the water and watch the brightness fill her eyes. The same brightness I saw at the night markets and the botanical gardens.

An hour later, Penelope and I walked up the shore and stuck the boards deep into the sand.

"Technically, that was surfing." She beamed as we walked up the beach. The teak steps that led up the patio to the bungalow creaked as we walked up them and she stopped and turned to me. "Thank you."

"I didn't do anything," I told her. I held her hips. She was a step above me, so we stood eye to eye.

"You did." She looked down and took a few steps back. I followed. "That list . . ."

"Yeah?" I backed her against the wooden post on the side of the steps.

"I wrote it"—she faltered—"parts of it—because they were things . . . sometimes I have trouble asking for what I want."

"You can ask me for anything."

The air between us shifted from breezy to heavy.

"Thank you for encouraging me to do this." She nodded, looking down again, turning her engagement ring a few times next to the wedding band.

The sunset sparkled off the diamond, throwing facets of light all over her.

I didn't say anything, rather I pulled her in for a kiss. With a quiet gasp, Penelope's tense frame immediately relaxed and she gave in, opening her mouth and deepening the kiss.

Her fingers ran through my hair, yanking to keep me close.

I leisurely tugged one of the strings that held her bikini top around her neck. "Where are we going, Poppy?"

The top came loose and with a final pluck to the flimsy strings that tied around her back, it fell to the ground.

"Inside," she answered without hesitation.

She drew me in to another heated kiss backing herself into the bungalow, pulling me in with her. I hooked a finger under the string-tied waistband of her bikini bottoms and they slipped right off.

Stopping in front of the bed, I took a second to admire her. The remnants of the sunny day melted across the horizon, casting a warm glow through the window and over the luscious curve of her breasts. Her peaked nipples begged to be touched, licked, sucked.

I didn't believe in a God, but fuck, if divinity existed it was in front of me.

Completely naked, lying down in the bed, with her arousal glistening between her thighs.

I leaned over her, an arm bracketed on either side of her body. "Tied up or blindfolded?"

The heat concentrated into a heavy, pleading sigh that filled the silence. My heart beat in a slow cadence with the pulse nearly bursting through my groin waiting for her answer.

Indecision flickered to life in her eyes, quickly turning into something else. "Both."

My lips crashed back onto hers with a tortured groan at the knowledge that she was her true nature for me. She pushed her boundaries. She let me in and, fuck, it was the hottest thing I'd ever experienced.

With a newfound impatience, I pulled myself off of her, took off my swim trunks, and walked over to grab the extra neckties I threw in my bag *just in case*.

"If it's too much, tell me to stop," I whispered to her as I took the first tie and blindfolded her with it.

She nodded, so I took the second tie and slowly circled it around both wrists before tying it to the rails on the headboard.

I dropped my mouth to the nape of her neck and dragged my teeth along it.

"Xander." Her wrists pushed against the tie while her hips rolled against me.

I chuckled lightly. "I'm going to map every inch of your skin with my mouth. You're going to have to be patient."

Her stomach dipped and bowed as I kissed my way to the slickness between her thighs. After months of telling myself I didn't feel what I did—that I didn't want what I knew I needed—I had to remind myself to take my time.

Spreading her legs apart, I heard her wrist knock against the headboard again. With a voracious grunt, I took her aroused clit into my mouth and sucked on it lightly at first.

"Oh," she mewed softly with a sharp inhale.

I'd imagined a million different scenarios where I had her in my arms, in my bed, writhing on my cock. But *this*?

Fuck.

I had to fight the overwhelming urge to bury myself in her. My thumb replaced my mouth on her clit and I spread her thighs further apart and fucking devoured her.

An impolite shriek ripped out of her. A string of delirious pants and moans began to spill out from between her lips.

I sank a finger into her. She was so wet I glided right in and another followed seconds later.

"Darling," she pleaded. It came out breathy with her back bowing up from the mattress.

The antagonistic nickname turned into something else now that she cried it out when she needed me. I moved with intention, slowly so she could feel every single inch.

"That's it, Poppy." Her pussy clenched around my fingers while she dripped down them. I pushed even more until I was knuckle-deep. "Come for me."

I hooked my fingers and moved faster, stroking the spot I knew intimately.

Her shrieks and moans became more frantic. Her walls tightened against my fingers as I teased and licked her clit with my tongue and finally her muscles went taut.

A full body shudder rolled down her as she began to come down from it.

My cock throbbed, ached, fucking nearly split watching her orgasm. But I needed to be deep inside of her before I let go.

I reached up and started to untie her wrists from the headboard. "Turn around."

Chapter 28

PENELOPE

There was a sensory overload that came with being unable to see or touch him while he could do just about anything he wanted to me.

My heart roared as it began to come down from the haze. I could feel his finger glide along my wrist. Seconds later the tie that affixed them to the headboard loosened.

Over the last two days, I was experiencing a new, overwhelming sensation every few hours with him. I'd had orgasms before, on my own, but never like these. The ones that made my vision blur, that felt like every drop of blood was set ablaze as it rushed through my body.

"Turn around." His gravelly tone, set between heavy breaths, settled low in my stomach.

The mattress dipped as he began to move, putting his hands on my hips to help me turn. The blindfold stayed tightly wrapped around my head as my trembling muscles worked to steady me. I turned around, his hands kneaded my hips.

I never gave much thought when I added those two items to the list. All I knew was that when I used my vibrator at home, that was the scenario I imagined. The idea of being completely under the control of a partner during sex was wildly arousing, but something I kept to myself.

It wasn't as though I had a partner who knew what to do with that power, until now.

"You have no idea how good you look, Poppy," he said slowly. His hand spread along the small of my back while the other gripped my hip.

I couldn't see him, but my imagination conjured up just how filthy the scene was, making it almost more erotic than if I'd witnessed it with my eyes. Tied to the bed, blindfolded and completely at his mercy. The only other souls for miles were the birds that were most certainly startled away from the sheer volume of the sounds we were making.

"Tied up, coming on my mouth." His hand moved up my back, he slowly teased my entrance. Shivers erupted all over my body.

"Xander," I gasped as he slowly entered me, teasing for a few moments, allowing me to feel every inch of his cock stretching me as he went in.

Then, with another heavy breath, he pushed all the way in. A needy whimper escaped my lips.

"Fuck." He released a loud, tortured groan.

Taking only a few seconds before he was fully unleashed, I felt every inch pushing, stroking, taking me apart. Second by second. Inch by inch.

Another orgasm began to swell deep in my core.

He was relentless. The heat began to coil and twist at the base of my spine. His hand roved up my stomach and caressed my breast, before giving my nipple a hard pinch.

I screamed but at the same time waves of electric pleasure crashed over every muscle fiber. It became muffled as I drowned in the overwhelming pleasure.

He continued fucking me through my orgasm and with a deep, low groan his body tightened and he succumbed to his own.

He stilled and after a few moments, the blindfold loosened and the saturated sunset flooded into my vision.

I collapsed onto the bed.

"You did amazing, Poppy." He held me close and kissed my head.

His praise felt like basking in the sun. I never thought I'd do something like that, but God, did that feel good.

* * *

THE NEXT MORNING, a series of vibrations across the nightstand woke me. I shifted and turned in bed. Xander's arm fell from around my waist to my lap as I sat up.

> **Olivia:** Before you go back to Manhattan, maybe you and Bella can talk.

> **Olivia:** She doesn't talk to me much, but even I can tell she misses you.

> **Olivia:** Don't hate me for suggesting it.

I read them, pushing the hair from my eyes as the morning breeze swept through the room. The white linen canopy around the bed billowed, filling and deflating as the air passed through it.

With a sleepy groan, I looked down at Xander and the emerald peeked out from his slowly opening eyelids. He let out a long yawn.

Xander was a dichotomy between mesmerizing and menacing, kind and sinister. It was enthralling to see up close.

The charisma that could disarm a madman one moment. Then, he was the man who stripped away every single layer of propriety with a ruthless determination.

And in the morning, he was as innocuous and lovable as a golden retriever.

"What's wrong, Poppy?" He sat and dropped a kiss on my shoulder.

"I think I need to go see my half siblings." I leaned my head into his chest. He shifted slightly and put his arm around me.

"Arabella and Silas?"

I nodded.

He didn't know much about my family, by design. But it was time I told him more, especially since I told him I wanted to preserve the peace and that would likely mean relying on his legendary good nature when inevitably Silas acted out.

"And I need to tell you something." I sat up and straddled him on the bed. "You asked me about the merger and Maddox months ago when all of this happened."

His grip tightened on my hips. Maddox always seemed to elicit that response in him. An uneasy tension, which was precisely why I wanted to address it.

"When the news of the merger and our arranged marriage came around, I was in London with Sloan. Maddox came to see me and at first, we sort of accepted it. We figured it was time to start acting the part."

"You can skip the details." His warning felt razor-sharp. My heart fluttered at the jealousy.

"It's nothing like that," I assured him. I hadn't been with Maddox since London and even then, sex with him felt like a chore. "I just want you to know that the reason I try to keep things with Maddox amicable is that he's sort of stuck in the same situation I am. I don't think he realizes it but his family sees him as a pawn as well and, I dunno, I feel bad that he's collateral damage. That's all."

The idea that Xander might be carrying around the suspicion hurt, and I didn't want him to. Wherever this went, I didn't want him believing that there was something left between Maddox and me.

"It was never Maddox," I added. The whole point in bringing up this story was to give Xander an idea of all the reasons I walked away that night at the masquerade. For him to at least understand that if it were simpler, if there had been less going on that cluttered every available neuron, I wouldn't have. "He just . . . seemed like the most reasonable option for a long time."

"And now?" He tucked my hair behind my ear.

"That day in my foyer when I—how did you put it?—blindsided you with a proposal," I teased and he chuckled. "It was the first time I *really* considered another way, and now the path of least resistance doesn't seem fair."

And I couldn't go back to being the people-pleasing Penelope.

"But, I don't want to fight," I added. I wanted this to be behind me. "Maybe if I talk to Silas, once and for all, I can make some peace. Move on."

"I'll come with you."

"No." I leaned forward and brushed a kiss against his lips. "I have to do this myself."

Chapter 29

PENELOPE

The next day, I arrived at Arabella's home in one of the poshest subdivisions in Singapore. She and her husband, James, lived a few houses down from Silas. The expansive lawn was punctuated with elaborate gardens and rare flowers that filled each breeze with a warm floral scent.

Even though my brain told me to be aware, I was overcome with nostalgia for the atmosphere I didn't know I missed.

After three hard knocks, the staff let me into Arabella's house. Straight through the hallway and into the salon where Olivia said Arabella had tea every afternoon.

"What are you doing here?" Arabella placed the cup on the table and stood. "Olivia said she was coming to apologize." Her eyes moved slowly down my body, assessing me.

"May I come in?" I shuffled my weight between my legs beneath the archway at the end of the hall.

She crossed her arms. "Why?"

I took a step forward into the room. Then a few more until I was on the opposite side of her coffee table. "Bella, you're my baby sister. I wanted to see you."

Her shoulders dropped with a heavy sigh and eye roll. "Well, here I am; you see me."

I took a seat on the tufted tuxedo couch across from her. "I'm sorry I haven't visited."

"Me, too," she whispered to herself and a silence blanketed us.

"The house is lovely." I looked around and tried to figure out how exactly to have this conversation. I missed her. I missed home. But she was a different person. I was sure she had her own life, and I simply wanted to be a part of it again. "You always had a talent for design."

Arabella smiled briefly and looked around the room. Her sterner expression softened, maybe in pity, either way the anger felt less pronounced.

"I missed you," she admitted quietly. "You've been gone a long time."

"I didn't stay away because I didn't want to see you," I rushed to say before reminding myself not to dump every thought I'd had over the past few years on her at once. "Being here hurt. It stung," I explained. But then, I'd spent a day with Olivia and went to the gardens with Xander. It felt nice. "But I realize now how much I've missed it, too. How much I've missed you."

It wasn't home but nowhere was home. This was close, though.

"I'm sorry for snapping at you," Arabella added after another extended pause. "At the party. You were being civil, and I was being rude."

"It's alright."

"I do understand . . ." she offered. Her eyes flickered around the room again, like she was trying to find the words. "You had opportunities and I sort of . . ." She twisted her fingers. "Well, I never really had anything but this."

"Bella . . ." My heart sank hearing it. She was perfect. She'd gotten everything she'd wanted. Right?

"I understand why you left, that's all," she explained. "I sort of resented you for it, but if I was smart enough to have a career, I think . . ." She took a deep breath and ran her hands over her skirt. "Well, it makes sense. It would've been silly to waste all your talent."

I wanted to fill the air with all the ways I wanted us to get back on some solid footing. Make up for years of being strangers to each other. It would take time. But finally, it didn't seem impossible. That was too much for one day. Too much for a single visit. This was the long game.

Another silence fell in the room. A little less awkward this time, more of a comfortable one, with Arabella and me deep in thought.

"It was rather badass that you missed grandfather's funeral." She smiled as she picked up her tea again. "Father spun himself into a tizzy."

My grandfather was a cruel man and the only nice thing my father ever did for me was keep me away from him. And after the divorce, my grandfather took his anger out on Eleanor. In turn, Eleanor took it out on me. And then I ran away from it.

In an attempt to break the cycle, I might have inadvertently allowed it to continue by leaving Arabella behind. I was always jealous that she was loved, but I hadn't been here for years and all that venom had to go somewhere. She was *different*, that much was certain.

"Grandfather dying while yelling at a member of his staff seems fitting, doesn't it?" I mused.

"The demons finally dragged that man back to hell." Arabella giggled lightly and raised her teacup. "Hear! Hear!"

And with that, the tension was gone. Even though there were decades of unresolved conflicts. Resentment and abandonment to discuss. In that moment, we were sisters again. The ones who ran through our childhood home, making a mess, and trying our best to clean it up before Eleanor punished me for it.

"I know I missed a lot." I sighed. "I thought maybe I could explain it away. Chinese filial piety seemed to have skipped me."

Going to the States and pushing my marriage back sealed it in everyone's mind that I was the problem even though I spent my entire life up to that point trying to constantly find solutions.

"Either way," I went on, "I'm happy to finally see you now."

She didn't smile but a hopeful glint in her eye made me feel better. The anxiety wore down.

"At least you avoided the Chen-arranged marriage," Arabella murmured, pulling her sleeve down a little further, odd choice in clothing for a muggy Singapore late-summer day. Although, the air-conditioning was blaring.

"What did you mean?" The change in Arabella's demeanor made me curious again. She was always happy in her marriage or so I thought. It was convenient for the family, but she was happy about it. Right? "When you said that my *choices* would affect the family?"

She had to mean the wedding and the merger, but I didn't think things were that dire.

She rolled her eyes. "Everyone used to go on about how smart you were."

"Bella," I pleaded.

Her hands curled around a glass of tea. "I don't know specifics, but finances are strained. Have been for a while."

"Are you alright?" I asked. Arabella received her inheritance and married well, I assumed she'd be fine as long as the money wasn't wasted.

The parallels between Arabella and my mother were striking. In choosing to stay in New York for work, I might have lost relationships, but I kept my autonomy.

"Yes, but I think you were Silas's golden ticket."

I was afraid of that. It meant Silas would probably try to salvage things. Before she could say anything else the sound of people walking echoed in the hallway.

"Arabella." A loud warning gritted across the room to my sister.

We looked over to see Silas and James walking in. Silas's trademark scowl juxtaposed brilliantly with the relaxed T-shirt and joggers. Arabella straightened in her seat. "James and I just returned from a round of golf. We were planning to get lunch. Why don't you join us?"

"Alright," Arabella agreed, sounding resigned. Her eyes glanced past me with a warm smile. "It was nice to see you, Penelope."

"Bella . . ." Worry and a steely protectiveness overcame my senses. But I wasn't here for years and James was her husband. It made sense she'd go but it just felt *off.*

Arabella disappeared down the hallway; I took a few steps to follow after her when Silas's voice stopped me.

"Finally taking an interest in the family?" he baited when Arabella was well out of earshot. I could hear her front door open and close.

I was hoping to leave on decent terms with both, maybe the chance at reconciliation with Arabella if I visited more.

I turned to see Silas run his thumb over his knuckles slowly. He took a seat.

"I didn't come here to fight," I stated diplomatically.

"No," he mocked with a sarcastic coo. "Just to pry about the company. I heard that bit you asked Arabella."

"Well, someone should keep an eye on it," I ventured. It sounded like he was floundering a bit. How very on-brand for Silas. "I can only assume you're not doing a very good job, *little* brother."

Technically we were only three months apart since my father never stopped his affair with Eleanor for something silly, like his marriage.

"You did surprise me, you know." He skated past my insult. "People-pleasing Penny was defiant. I didn't expect you to marry some random American. I was only trying to expedite the merger. I assumed you'd marry Maddox in the desperate hope to finally have a family."

A cruel mocking frosted his words. It hurt because it was true.

"What do you want, Silas?" I asked, exasperated. We could go back and forth with insults all day, and all I wanted to do now was go back to Xander. To not let Silas steal the happiness I felt when talking to Arabella.

"End this farce of a marriage and honor your real commitments. Come home. Beg for the Xus' forgiveness—they'll accept, you know how they live and breathe to have a grandchild with both Eastern and Western titles."

I scoffed. "Even if I were to agree, which is ridiculous, you realize Maddox may feel differently now?"

He leaned forward with a menacing smile. "Maddox will do anything his parents tell him. Why do you think he was ever interested in *you*?"

I flinched. I knew I was a pawn, but it didn't hurt any less to hear it.

"For good measure," Silas added, "I will help you arrive at the right conclusion."

"If you were half as smart as you think you are, you'd find a way to move forward with the merger without me," I retorted patronizingly. "And I'm not afraid of you."

The Xus weren't the only other option for a merger, right? This felt cruel. There had to be another reason Silas needed this with Xu Enterprises.

"Maybe you should be," he advised calmly. "I don't think you know your husband as well as you think you do. But I've been watching closely ever since the engagement with Maddox was announced, as an insurance policy of sorts."

I didn't know what he was talking about, but a chill ran through my veins.

"You have no idea what you're doing," I warned.

I hated that Silas knew me so well. That he knew the best way to bring me to my knees was to make me responsible for everyone else's well-being.

"I think I do, Penny."

The nickname scraped against my heart for the last time. The one he created. Because he liked to say that like a penny, I was essentially worthless. I got to have that little gem all throughout childhood. He was always a little jealous to be untitled amongst the higher echelons of society he liked to pretend he fit with.

"A piece of advice, Silas." I turned to leave. "If you're going to take aim at us, don't miss, because we won't."

My entire body trembled as I got into the car that was waiting to take me back to the hotel.

I couldn't make sense of every emotion that swirled in my head. The chance at that reconciliation with Arabella, with Singapore, felt further than ever. And now, I'd dragged everyone I knew in Manhattan into it.

And while my mind was a mess with worry and self-imposed guilt because I was the one whose decisions started all of this—some clarity did ring through.

The circumstances had changed again but this time I didn't allow that bitter chill to bleed over everything here—Arabella, Olivia, Singapore. This time, my mind didn't need to run to a safe place where it tricked me into pinning that feeling on the place, and that was oddly freeing.

Chapter 30

XANDER

I should have gone with her.

Penelope got back to our suite in Singapore sort of dazed. She sat quietly for a few minutes before she told me everything.

"I'm sorry." She turned the stemless wineglass in her hand before placing it down on the table in front of us. Wrapped in a plush robe, her hair still wet, she leaned her head onto my shoulder and looked out at the city skyline. "I don't know what he knows, but he was smug."

On the balcony of our suite, we watched the late-summer sunset as it painted the sky. It was our last night here and I had planned to take her out, but she came back so stressed I figured she might prefer to unwind privately. So, we ordered room service.

"You have nothing to be sorry about," I insisted.

After she told me what happened, I suggested she take a bath to relax, and I resisted the urge to join her, knowing that was probably the last thing she needed. After that, we settled out on the balcony.

"I thought about calling Sloan," she admitted, sitting back up and turning to me. The horizon blazed with tangerine and coral hues, casting a golden glow along the curve of her cheek. "But outside of some ambiguous threat against us, I didn't have details. He's probably bluffing."

Us. That had to be the first time she referred to everyone who cared for her in Manhattan as *us.*

My heart leapt.

"Probably best not to call Sloan," I teased softly. "Why release the Kraken if you don't have to?"

For the first time since she got back, her sadness snapped open with a deep and joyful laugh. A long one. Her body shook, and she leaned into me.

My entire world stopped when she did that.

When she laughed.

It reminded me of that night in her kitchen after the Hightower party. When a loud, unfettered laugh burst out of Penelope. It bounced around her sparsely decorated kitchen and resonated in my mind at all hours. The memory played back like a movie.

Leaning against Penelope's kitchen counter, I had just finished telling her the story of how Sloan set me on fire, literally. On fire. To this day she claimed it was an accident.

"That did not happen." Penelope leaned forward in her seat, resting her elbows on the countertop as a few final giggles made their way out of her.

"Sloan claims it was an accident." I chuckled.

"Sloan Amari is many things. Accidental pyromaniac was not one I was expecting."

"Allegedly accidental."

She giggled again. My heart surged at the sound of it.

Penelope's laughter quieted and she took another large sip of whiskey. She was drinking faster than I'd ever seen her before. When I stopped her at the entrance of the party, Penelope looked like she was thinking a thousand things a second. Instead of going inside to the event, I suggested a drink. She pointed out that it was New Year's Eve and every bar in town was probably overflowing. So we ended up at her place.

"Jeez, slow down." I moved the empty glass a few inches further from her on the counter. "Something wrong?"

"Family thing," she said with a deep sigh, her shoulder slumped, and the strap of her yellow gown slipped down it. "What's that Tolstoy quote? All happy families are similar, but unhappy ones are unique."

Her face was a little rosy and her temperament a little less than buttoned-up. She was relaxed, vulnerable even.

"Yeah, something like that." I reached out and slipped the strap back up her shoulder.

Our eyes caught for a moment before she looked back at her drink.

"From what Sloan's told me, it sounds like you had wonderful parents."

I did. They were there for everything. Every practice. Every game. Every achievement, even the ones Marcus and I didn't think were worth celebrating. They celebrated them.

I nodded.

"What do you do when your family may not be worth having?" She reached down the counter, grabbed her glass, and finished the last bit.

"Make a new one."

She turned to me; a melancholy smile tugged at her cheek. The delicate lines along the column of her throat shifted with a hard swallow.

With a deep breath, she sat up and refilled her glass and mine even though I hadn't finished my first drink yet.

"What about you?" she asked, shaking her head slightly. "What has you upset?"

"Nothing," I assured her.

I saw Reina earlier that night. The only woman I've ever loved . . . thought I loved. The ghost of our relationship haunted me for years. And while seeing her tonight wasn't fun, for the first time, I felt nothing for Reina.

The loud burst of laughter that popped out of Penelope earlier was helping me realize why.

I stared, unable to look away. "Nothing important, anyway."

Penelope's head nuzzling into my neck pulled me from the memory of that night.

"I thought she might be able to help. You know Sloan, Miss Fix-it," she said after a long pause.

Penelope yawned and began to quietly explain her plans for the upcoming week, like saying her day-to-day schedule helped calm her down.

She drifted to sleep on my shoulder and the reality of Silas's threat settled in.

Concern lodged firmly in my chest. For years, Sloan and Tristan sort of acted like a cleanup crew for me when I spun out. There was plenty to see if someone could dig it up. And if they could find all of my sordid past, they could find CeCe's past, which was just as colorful. Or, maybe, figure out how it was that we were so effective at hiding our scandals: the close proximity to the American political dynasty that was the Alders family.

Or Silas could find nothing, since Sloan and Tristan were meticulous when they cleaned things up, and maybe this was nothing. Either way, we were leaving Singapore a lot more tangled than we arrived.

* * *

PENELOPE

THE NEXT MORNING, after a week in Singapore, we boarded the jet to return to Manhattan.

I stopped on the last few steps up while boarding and turned to take a last look at Singapore. I hadn't really decided when I'd be back. Now that I'd met all the terms for my inheritance, all I needed to do was run out the clock and deal with whatever hell Silas had in store.

In a little less than a year, I'd have everything I wanted when I started this. Problem solved. Yet, anxiety scratched at my heart.

Before we left the hotel, I called Arabella. She assured me she was fine. The call was short, but it was nice to hear her confirm it.

"Are you okay?" Xander pressed a kiss on my head when I stopped.

I nodded and continued my way into the jet. He'd been absolutely wonderful since I got back from seeing Arabella yesterday.

But something was weighing on him. His eyes flickered occasionally, adrift in thought.

Once we were settled on the plane and it completed its ascent, the flight attendant made her way to us. "Can I get you anything, Mrs. Sutton?"

He was still looking down at his phone, awaiting something, but a smile curved across Xander's mouth.

I turned my ring around my finger.

"No, thank you," I told her.

She politely excused herself to the galley and shut the door behind her, leaving us to our seclusion.

"Are you alright?" I watched as his eyes moved around the phone he was staring at.

"Herrera." Xander looked up, running a hand through his hair. "I want to get the deal with him and Dawn Capital done before anything . . ."

"Before Silas uses whatever he knows." Guilt constricted my chest. "I'm sorry."

He took my hand and stroked the back with his thumb. "Look, there are things about the past—"

"You don't have to tell me," I interrupted, gently stroking his knee.

"I know," he whispered, leaning forward and tucking a strand of hair behind my ear. "I want to."

Chapter 31

XANDER

I didn't talk about the time that directly followed my parents' death because I was pretty ashamed of how I handled it. While Marcus was the adult and took care of all the arrangements, I lost control. And every time I did that, someone had to clean up my mess.

Namely Sloan. Sometimes Tristan.

"It's not one thing, it's a million," I confessed. "After my parents died, I sort of spun out. Drinking, partying, drugs. All of it. Mostly cleaned up thanks to Sloan and Tristan, but there's a lot of fodder if someone went looking."

"*If* Silas finds anything," Penelope encouraged, "nobody would fault you."

"I don't care if it gets out," I blurted. The first place my mind went to when Penelope told me that Silas leveled some ambiguous threat was the press, because that would be the easiest target. "I just want you to know about it."

The second thing that popped into my head was the look on Selena's face whenever something unsavory got printed about Henry. It happened less now, but I could tell it hurt her—because it was a lot easier to take a hit than watch someone you loved do so. Not that I thought Penelope felt for me even a quarter of what Selena felt for Henry, but at least she wasn't caught off guard.

Penelope nodded, squeezing my hand.

"It was only ever *bad* twice," I assured her. "Once when they died and once after Reina and I—"

I stopped, realizing where I was going. Reina was a relic of the past and the last person I wanted to talk about with Penelope.

"Reina and you . . ." An encouraging smile and gentle squeeze on my knee.

"Yeah. After we broke up, Sloan suggested a trip, we went to Istanbul," I explained, trying to gauge how Penelope felt as we moved into much more serious territory than we ever had. "After that, it was like a dam burst. Every memory I'd managed to keep from following me became this unstoppable highlight reel. I just needed a break. For a second. I was a mess that week and Sloan and Tristan had to pick up the pieces. I drank, took drugs, ended up in the hospital because I was pretty out of it."

Penelope's eyebrows rose.

"I was fine, after that. A while after. I started trying to handle things better."

I didn't venture near things that got me that close to the edge again. Like relationships. I kept them brief and surface level so I couldn't possibly hurt like that again. And I held on tight to the people I had, the ones I knew I wouldn't lose. I didn't let them go.

"During those times," I added, looking down at the floor, "I felt like I was drowning and no matter how hard I tried, I couldn't come up for air."

Everything that hid in the corners of my mind came to life all at once that night. Sounds of metal screeching. The sound of blood-curdling screams. Reina walking away. Feeling like I was completely alone, even though I wasn't. Every single terrible thought I'd ever had surrounded me with no escape.

That breakup felt like a marker in time.

After that, my life went on, but a part felt frozen. The part that closed itself to entertaining any bond that might break. That was, until Penelope.

"Hey." Penelope lifted my chin. "I'm glad you're alright, now."

I smoothed a hand down her back. "Listen, about Reina."

"You're allowed to have had a past and have been in love." An upward inflection at the end of her sentence almost made it sound like a question, but she moved past it quickly. "I don't know if you recall, but I was engaged for a time."

I smiled at her attempt at levity.

"I can't go back to that place, and I won't," I assured her. I swallowed against a tightness in my throat. Stability looked different for everyone. For me, it was having everyone I needed to keep me steady. My family. Home.

The fear of being that hurt, completely untethered, it kept me close to home. Close to my family. The people that were around for good, that I wouldn't lose. That kept my world on its axis.

"But fair warning, I'm a little broken."

"No," she gently disagreed. She looked at me impishly, shaking her head. She leaned in and rested it against my shoulder. "Just a bit bent."

Chapter 32

PENELOPE

Aspiring to touch the heavens, Xander's penthouse was perched on the top four floors of the Manhattan Tower. The crown jewel of Billionaires' Row, the tower overlooked Central Park on its north face and lower Manhattan from the south. His penthouse unfolded between 360-degree views of the city, the floor-to-ceiling windows in every room dissolving the boundary between the clean, sleek interior and the kaleidoscope of Manhattan outside. It would've been a little unsettling if I didn't know they were all one-way views.

I turned the shower faucet off, and the waterfall nozzle dripped to a stop. The warm steam enveloped the Makrana marble bathroom.

We arrived back in Manhattan a couple days ago after our week in Singapore. Since summer was winding down, we came straight into the city. And all my things arrived earlier in the morning, so I spent my Saturday helping the staff find a place for the many boxes that littered the well-organized home.

It was a fairly peaceful morning. That was, until a courier arrived with another folder of documents. I suspected it would have come from my family, but I wasn't expecting a court summons.

I tore through the documents. The summons was from the State

Department—calling my work visa into question—filling my head with a thousand different concerns on how or why this was happening.

So I decided to retreat to the tranquil allure of the guest bathroom's steam shower to relax. I wrapped a towel around my torso and stepped in front of the vanity. I took a smaller towel and patted my hair dry as I looked out the large windows.

"Poppy?" Xander's voice echoed through the halls.

My bones jumped at that shot through the quiet space.

"I'm in here," I squeaked, suddenly feeling incredibly awkward even though the man had seen me bare naked in a variety of different positions over the last week.

I'd spent the last couple nights in Xander's bed, but I figured I should probably pick a guest room to stay in for the near term. I was enjoying the freedom of the arrangement; it was the thrill of exploring parts of myself I kept hidden with the safety I felt with Xander. But we hadn't talked living arrangements and, since I had time today and an excessive amount of anxiety from the summons, I figured I could channel that into organizing.

"What are you doing in here?" Xander walked in and looked over the boxes neatly stacked against the wall. He looked around the room until his eyes fell to the opened summons on the chaise at the foot of the bed.

Before I had a chance to answer, he picked it up and his eyes ran over the words.

"What's this?" He turned it to the back and read the rest.

"A summons." I explained it was one of the reasons I'd started unpacking and making myself busy that morning. "Apparently, my work visa is suddenly being called into question."

Xander ran a hand down the slope of his jaw as he read through the papers. Including having the Chen family lawyer evict me from the house in Manhattan. This would be the second thing to happen that felt *targeted*. "And without that as your reason to live in the States, this is forcing you to go to the State Department and clear it up or provide another."

"I'm guessing Silas is attempting to call the marriage into question. Legally," I explained, feeling my words sort of smash together as they rushed out of my mouth.

"Don't worry." Xander's seriousness melted off him, leaving behind a playful arch to his lips. "I'll take care of it."

"Oh." My shoulders relaxed. It was sweet, but I could take care of it myself. I didn't need him to fix it. I felt a little more comfortable with taking on potentially inflammatory tasks with my family every day; it was a little empowering. "No need, I already called the State Department and let Tristan know, see if he can't expedite something. I may need to go to the courthouse, but hopefully it will be settled soon."

Xander nodded again.

"So, what are you doing in here?" he repeated, putting the summons back down on the chaise at the foot of the bed. Then, slowly, his eyes moved up my body.

I became very aware that I was still in my towel.

"Getting dressed." I held the towel tight against my chest.

"Yeah, I can see that," he noted casually, looking over a few of the open boxes. He'd left earlier in the morning to go to the Augustus to meet his brother and Henry. "I mean what are you doing in *here*?"

"You never actually told me which guest room to take, so I simply chose the first one I saw," I explained.

"You have a room," he reminded me softly; his attention went to the box on my bed. "The one you've been sleeping and screaming in for the last few days."

My cheeks heated.

"Well, I thought maybe you'd want some space," I reasoned.

"Do *you* want space?" he asked simply, still not looking up at me, spending more time examining the box. Now all the blood had rushed to my face.

He was looking at the box labeled *Nightstand*.

"That's . . ." I began, but sputtered out.

I swallowed hard, a little mortified, when he pulled out my hot-pink vibrator. The only thing that was ever successful at consistently getting me off. With the notable exception of my new husband.

He paused and turned it in his hand.

"Still haven't answered my question." A smirk tugged at the slope of his jaw. His eyes shot up to me, pinning me in a heavy stare. "Do you want space?"

A familiar electricity sparked between us. He had that look in his eye. The one that always preceded an orgasm.

"Well . . ." I rolled my teeth over my lip. It was the start of a carnal game and, God, I was enjoying the play. The embarrassment melted away as quickly as it came, because with Xander, I wasn't afraid to ask for what I wanted. "Maybe I do."

He prowled slowly over to me; I backed up until the bathroom doorframe stopped me. His tone adopted that flirtatious hitch.

"Is that so?" He pushed me gently against the doorframe that led into the still steamy bathroom. Cool drops of water fell off my hair and skimmed along my skin.

My blood heated with expectation, knowing all that came next.

I swallowed against a dry throat. "Maybe."

He chuckled lightly and leaned his head against mine. My legs nearly buckled under the weight of his gaze.

"Shower, bed, window," he whispered. "Where are we going, Poppy?"

My stomach flipped. Moisture began to gather between my thighs.

"Why don't you . . ." The steam that was so soothing just a few minutes ago felt suffocating now. I rested my hand on his chest. "Why don't you pick?"

"That's not what I asked." His tone took on the teasing volley. He clicked the button, and the familiar buzz filled the room. "What do you think about when you use this?"

Moving the towel aside, he pressed the vibrator right at the bottom of my navel.

The controlled tremors ricocheted down my legs and through my core. My hips bucked.

"Who do you think about?" He continued his line of questioning with a possessive undercurrent.

Goose bumps pebbled all along my skin.

"Lower," I whispered.

"You need to start answering my questions, Poppy," he groaned against my ear, moving the vibrator to just above my clit, teasing me. "Who do you think about?"

I swallowed hard. Nothing lit a controlled burn in my body quite like when Xander asked how I wanted to be taken. To make me say the words. To demand what I wanted. But he wasn't the only one who could play. "Theo James."

It was the first name I could think of, and I wasn't going to give him the satisfaction of knowing he'd often been the man I imagined.

A look he tried to hide behind a lazy, self-assured smirk didn't fool me this time.

"Oh yeah?" he taunted and pressed me harder against the doorframe, clicking the button again; the smooth silicone vibrated faster. "Anyone else?"

I gasped and rolled my hips against it. The rough pulses sent ripples through my lower half. "No . . ."

"You sure?" Envy sparked and chipped at the emerald in his eyes.

He began to rock it back and forth along my clit, teasing me by pushing it lower only to pull it back.

My hands curled around his shirt; I pulled him closer. "Xander . . ."

He rocked it faster, giving me the brief flashes of ecstasy when he'd allow it to rub against me and fill me only to take it away seconds later.

"Are you sure, Poppy? You're not thinking of anyone else?" He pushed the vibrator inside of me. I was so wet it slid in with ease. He held it steady with his fingers while his thumb pressed slow circles on my clit. "Because either you're really fucking wet for a man that isn't here. Or you're lying."

His thumb stroked me more firmly. My head tipped back against the solid doorframe. I was close.

My nails dug into his back. The heat concentrated in my core, ready to burst at any second. My breath shallowed, my vision began to blur.

Then, it stopped. The room came back into perfect view.

Paradise stolen with one click.

My hand grabbed his wrist and held it like a vise as he pulled away.

"If you don't play along," he teased, "nobody wins."

I whimpered and tugged on his shirt. "Don't stop."

"Do you know what I get if I win?" He clicked it back on and ran it over my clit.

I nearly screamed.

"Xander," I begged in a broken sob.

"I get to fuck every one of those lies right out of you." His teeth dragged along my neck. "Now, where are we going, Poppy?"

"Shower."

Before I knew it, my towel was discarded on the floor along with his clothes and the warm water was pouring over me. Xander's muscular chest pressed against my back and his erection was hard against my skin.

"Do you want to come?" he said between light kisses on the nape of my neck. He massaged my breast with one hand—passing a taut nipple between his fingers—while the other turned the vibrator carelessly in his hand.

"Yes," I grated out, leaning my head back against his shoulder.

His hand smoothed down my stomach and his fingers stopped just above my clit. A jittery fog filled my mind as the steam filled the shower.

"Should I use this?" He passed the vibrator between his fingers while the other hand teased my entrance. "Or do you want my cock?"

The water gently lapping down my body, mixed with the static building in my core, made me impatient. I was so aroused I felt slickness between my thighs despite the water falling over me.

I wanted all of it, to be completely overwhelmed. "Both."

He maneuvered me away from the waterfall faucet and bent me over, my arms braced against the cool marble ledge on the built-in bench.

"Did you ever wonder." He pushed into me slowly. Bubbles of pleasure popped along my spine as he moved, inch by inch. "About how I'd feel fucking you when you used this?"

Yes. Too many times.

"Xander." The pleasure climbed along every nerve ending.

Tempting. Teasing. Pushing me closer.

Holding the vibrator lightly against my clit with one hand, he thrust into me slow at first. The familiar anticipation climbed higher. The buzz echoed in the steam. Electric waves moved down my legs; they began to wobble.

"Or maybe. How it would feel when I took you to the edge and stopped." He clicked it off.

"Xander!" I cried out. Feeling like all the air in my lungs was pulled out of me, I bucked back, begging for friction when he refused to move.

"Poppy . . ." he drawled.

"*Please*." My heart felt like it might stop with all the ways he stole my release. At that point, I'd beg to get any of it back.

But he gave it all. A click paired with a hard thrust and all that restraint seemed to dissipate into the steam. He pushed into me rough and quick, diving deeper.

The water trickling to the floor. The indecent echo of our bodies slamming together. The wicked buzz from the vibrator. All crashed together with the impossibly pleasurable sensation at the base of my spine.

It burst in concert with a string of moans and broken sobs. The climax crashing so hard over me that nothing else registered.

It wasn't until moments later after a harsh grunt that Xander's movements slowed. I blinked again, and as though I was moving frame by frame, the sound of the water shutting off came next. Then a towel wrapped around my body and his arms holding it and me close.

"I thought unpacking would be boring," I murmured, my heavy eyes closing. I leaned back into him, feeling the rise and fall of his chest.

He smiled against my neck. "While we're on the subject, your things are in the wrong room."

I could barely think let alone understand what he was saying. "Hmmm?"

"I'm not coming over here if I want to make you scream in the middle of the night," he told me. "I'll have your things moved to our room."

"Oh." My heart fluttered. I guess he didn't need space. "Okay."

He lifted his hand and passed the vibrator between his fingers again. "And bring this with you."

Chapter 33

PENELOPE

A week of getting settled in my new home—for the year—Xander suggested we go to the club after our weekly Sunday brunch. I think he caught on that I was feeling a little restless, the issue of my visa was still pending and even though it had only been a little less than two weeks since getting back from Singapore, I felt like maybe I'd left too soon.

"Poppy." Xander's voice pulled me from my thoughts.

I hadn't been back to the pottery studio in a while and I was having a project delivered there that I wanted to start on, but I wasn't expecting Xander would join. He wasn't particularly artistically inclined.

"The studios are down the north wing." I pointed to the elevators as we walked by them. We just missed the corridor to the studios and kept walking toward the galleries.

"I know." His smile taunted me as we continued down the hallway.

When the summer wound down and every high-society family returned from Newport, Nantucket, or the Hamptons, the Augustus Club in Manhattan began to effervesce with a renewed vitality.

I preferred it in the summer and usually spent my time there when Sloan and her friends went to the Hamptons, but as autumn began its slow conquest over the city, I was happy to see it coming. I missed the fizz of the busy club.

"There's a private collection being shown this weekend." I read the placard on the door aloud to Xander.

The Augustus had a well-appointed arts center. There were studios and galleries as well as open workspaces.

"Yeah, I know." Xander led me around the corner to the back entrance of the exhibit hall. "They haven't opened it to members yet."

"Oh." I cocked my head. "Then, why are we here?"

Xander didn't say anything, he only smiled and lifted some of the clear plastic sheeting that covered the double doorway.

We took a few steps into the exhibit space. Most of the paintings were still in their protective carriers, but even with the covers on many of them I could recognize the works a mile away.

My eyes swept over the deep reds, the mustard yellow, the colors that saturated art of that era. "This is Norman Rockwell's collection," I sputtered.

My heart thumped erratically. It was on the list.

Xander ran his arm around my waist. "The museum is under renovation, which means no visitors for the rest of the year."

"So, you brought the museum here?"

He shrugged. "It was the least ambiguous goal on that list."

The line I'd written on my list was "Norman Rockwell Museum." He had no idea which of his paintings I wanted to see or why.

My eyes homed in on the only painting that was fully uncovered, hanging on the wall. My mouth fell open.

"I told them to put that one up first." His voice played softly over the excited hum that filled my ears.

I turned my ring along my finger. It was probably one of Rockwell's most famous pieces: *Freedom from Want*. An idyllic family rendered in oil paint, sitting around a Thanksgiving table, right before the feast.

I tried to buy the piece; it was on auction once. Without my inheritance, even with my salary from the firm, I couldn't afford it. The final bid went over fifty million dollars, so this piece, the one that was stuck in my heart, was impossible to see unless someone enchanted the private collector and persuaded them to allow the Augustus to show it.

"How did you manage to find the collector?" I whispered.

"I can be convincing. And the Sotheby's art dealer was willing to bend the rules when I bought out her gallery," he said quietly as his hand rested on the small of my back. "She gave me the name of the private collector."

"And you used the legendary Xander Sutton charm to convince them to show it?" I surmised.

"Yeah," he answered curtly. "And it did not work. He refused to allow one of his pieces to be shown here."

I looked up at him speculatively.

"He wasn't open to lending it, but he was open to something else and the new owner is a lot more considerate," he explained.

The realization wrapped around me slowly. My heart stopped before it picked up like a roaring engine.

"You bought it?" I managed to choke out before looking back at the piece that I was sure I'd never be able to see with my own eyes. A quiet tremble ran through my muscles. I looked back up at him. "You own this?"

"No." He shook his head. "You do."

He nodded in the direction of the small golden plaque beneath the painting.

The light reflected off it and I read the inscriptions. "*On loan.*" Just below it was my name. "*Penelope Chen-Astor-Sutton's private collection.*"

The only thing on the list was that I wanted to visit the museum. I hadn't mentioned this painting. Or every feeling that was tied to it.

Every sentiment clogged my throat. He considered me and what I wanted. A simple courtesy but one I was never granted before. Xander took time to consider the things I said and the things I didn't say. He spent enough time thinking about it that he was able to figure out this one piece without ever being told. With a deep breath I managed to choke out, "How did you know?"

"I didn't. I was just thinking about that night you were drunkenly musing about Tolstoy's family dysfunction." He pressed a kiss on my head. A circuit clicked in my mind—that night in my kitchen. He carried that tiny scrap of information with him and turned it over in his head enough times to know it was *this* painting. "I thought maybe this one was your favorite. Was I right?" he whispered, his thumb running slow circles in the same spot on my back.

I nodded and, even though he didn't ask, I told him. I wanted him to know. "I spent the summers in Singapore and my mother went to the farm—the one where she lives now, outside of Glasgow. I always imagined in some alternate universe if I was in a *real family*, on that little farm . . ." Emotion welled at the base of my throat. "One that didn't . . ."

Tears stung the corners of my eyes.

It was all too much. The lengths he must have gone through parsing details from that night to come to the correct conclusion, finding the collector, buying it for me. All so that I could have this one painting that made me feel so many things all at once.

"They aren't the only family you have." His hand moved soothingly up and down my back.

I nodded. I understood what he meant, that I had a life here, too.

But I missed Singapore.

Maybe I should have stayed longer.

Maybe I shouldn't have left. I hated questioning myself, not trusting what I felt. That feeling of rejection I always felt when I went home was still there, but so easily smothered by the joy in Olivia's laugh. Or the occasional biting remark Arabella would let slip.

Xander's eyes flickered along my face, his jaw became tight.

"Why don't we visit again soon?" he offered, knowing it was what I was thinking about.

I nodded.

I'd texted Arabella and Olivia. A couple short calls. Restarting a relationship that was on hold for years took work and was made even harder by distance.

A visit sounded wonderful even though we'd just been there. But it felt like adhering a Band-Aid to a gaping wound.

He didn't say anything else. His eyes wavered around the other pieces and then back to the one in front of us.

"They look happy." I sighed, taking it in even though I had every detail of it committed to memory.

I remembered seeing it as a girl and wondering what it must have been like to be one of them. All seated around a table where everyone wanted you there. I always found myself picturing this when I pictured my future. A silly perfected version of happiness.

"It was the forties." Xander's voice lifted with a playful lightness, like it was a reflex to not let anyone around be anything other than content. "A lot of American housewives were on drugs."

I shook with a reluctant laugh at the dark humor. I tried to contain my smile, but it refused to cooperate. "Are you ever serious?"

"Yeah, I am." His hand continued to slowly stroke my back, voice dropping to a whisper. "When it comes to you."

I was trying not to let my head interfere with something that felt so good. Giving in to the attraction with Xander allowed me to finally indulge in passion and all the things I'd ignored for so long. For now, I didn't want to question it, I wanted to float along and enjoy it.

"Thank you for this," I murmured softly, unable to sort through everything I was feeling. I looked down.

Seemingly understanding without a word, he held my chin with his thumb and forefinger, lifting it so I could see the mischievous glint through the mossy green. "Nothing on that list is safe."

I smiled and basked in the warmth of his touch and the reprieve he'd granted me by not pushing the subject of us.

The reality began to dawn on me. I knew what this relationship was supposed to be; exactly what I'd asked for: a year to get what I needed so I could figure out what I wanted.

Except now maybe, what I wanted was a few things.

Chapter 34

XANDER

Senator Fitzgerald Alders wasn't exactly a friend, but I'd met him so many times that we were friendly. And he was an effective tool in getting the Senate inquiry opened on the Hightowers.

"I had my secretary take care of everything so it shouldn't be a problem now," Fitzgerald said, looking over the visa documents in question. "Sorry you had to deal with this, but the concern came from high up."

"From?" I asked as Penelope and I got up from our seats at the end of his desk.

"You know I can't tell you that." Fitzgerald handed the papers back to Penelope.

The Alders family was the epitome of honesty—at least publicly. High society nicknamed them "the quiet Kennedys"—in that none of their dirty laundry ever made it out of the house.

"We're terribly sorry for the mess," Penelope apologized, putting the documents away.

"Really, it's no trouble." He got up from behind his desk and motioned to the door. "But if you'd like to return the favor, convince my cousin to run."

Penelope looked between us speculatively.

"Sorry." I slapped a hand on his shoulder. "Work would be a lot less interesting without Tristan."

"I had to try." Fitzgerald chuckled and looked to Penelope.

"And congratulations, Fitz," Penelope added just as she turned to the door, looking over her shoulder. "I saw your stellar cross-examination of the Hightower executives. Terrible for the firm but you certainly looked presidential."

Fitzgerald shot a quick questioning look to me, but the classic politician smile came back in a flash. Good thing, because my mind kept replaying her calling him *Fitz*.

We said our goodbyes and turned to walk down the hallway. "I didn't know you were so *close* to the senator," I said. Why were they on a nickname basis?

"Maya's close to the whole family and I've helped her with a few things that were Alders adjacent over the years," she noted offhandedly as we stopped at the elevators. "I went to the Newport house. It's lovely."

I pressed the down button. "You stayed with them?"

She sighed, sounding almost bored. "Last summer."

"Last summer?" I repeated. That was when she was apparently too busy to come to the Hamptons with us.

"You sound surprised. Rohan is close to them, too," Penelope added as she typed something on her phone.

Rohan and his little sister, Maya, *were* close to the Alders family. And all of what she was saying made perfect sense. I knew the envy was misplaced. It was stupid to be jealous. And yet . . .

"Is that why you and Tristan are close?" I spat. "Maya?"

"I'd hardly say we're close. But Tristan is kind and dependable. A good friend to have." She rolled her eyes and kept texting.

I ignored the fact that she was right, and I owed a lot to Tristan for his unwavering loyalty.

"You just described a golden retriever," I scoffed.

I was not this guy. I didn't get possessive and territorial. But she stirred something primal in me, a need to keep her all to myself.

"Did I?" She lifted a brow. A knowing smile curved along her cheek. She knew she was driving me crazy.

"You're not jealous of the good senator, are you?" she teased. She clicked the side of her phone and tucked it in her purse.

"Of course not," I grumbled. "There's nothing to be jealous of."

"I don't know about that." She reached for my tie and neatly fastened the knot. The gentle pressure sent a ripple through my body. The elevator rang and jostled to a stop. "He is rather handsome, isn't he?"

A spark lit in her eyes.

I grabbed her hand right as the elevator opened. If she wanted to play a game, we could play.

My eyes darted around the hallway, and I saw an open office. Without any explanation, I pulled her into it. Sex in a public place was on the list.

"I'm sure the campaign strategist won't mind," I told her, locking the door behind us. The dark office looked like it hadn't been used in months. Maps and rolled-up posters were littered in the corners and hanging on the walls.

"Xander." Penelope's eyes went wide in warning. But the look in them revealed she wanted to spar.

I loosened my tie. "Don't act innocent when you started this."

She pressed her lips together, but the corners of her mouth tipped up. "I guess you're right. But you have to admit the Alders men are quite polished."

A few streams of light peeked through the closed blinds, casting shadows along her cheek.

"Poppy . . ." I warned, and gripping her hips I pushed her gently until she stepped up against the desk.

She smoothed her palms over my lapels, looking up at me innocently. "Some women find that attractive."

My hands moved under her skirt; I ran a finger along the satin that spanned the curve of her hips. They slowly rolled against me.

I leaned in and whispered along her neck. "Poppy."

My thumb grazed along her clit and her breath hitched.

That was all it took to feel my pants become impossibly tight, my cock pushing against my zipper.

Fuck, the things this woman did to me. It was a look. A bated breath. A shaky sigh and I was done for.

"I never said that I—" She sputtered, the pleasure cracking fissures in her words. Her eyes closed, her teeth running over her bottom lip as her hands braced on my shoulders. "I never said I was one of those women."

My thumb pressed harder against her clit. Each swipe a little firmer, her fists pulled against my jacket.

"Then, why are you instigating?"

A few soft whimpers began to blend together when I refused to give her a second of reprieve.

"I . . ."

She leaned forward so her groin ground against the base of my hand, her lips pressed against my shoulder, muting her moans. I pushed the panties aside and I sank a finger into her.

"Is it because you want a reaction?" I goaded her on. Tiny sparks popped all along my muscles, she felt so fucking good. I fought the strong urge to sink myself into her, my cock beating in cadence with my heart's drumbeat.

"Or a reminder . . ." I gritted out. Her pussy clamped around my finger, tight and wet, and I pushed another finger in, using the base of my hand to rub her clit. "Of who does this to you?"

Rocking back and forth, quickening the tempo, her skin sheened with a thin layer of sweat.

"Xander . . ." she moaned softly.

I moved harder and faster, twisting and curling my fingers until her walls tightened and rippled around them.

She shook as the orgasm crashed over her, letting out a muffled shriek into my shoulder.

I kept moving until the jerks and tiny tremors subsided, her body leaned further into mine, fucked limp by my fingers.

"Sit on the desk," I whispered impatiently, needing to bury myself inside of her. "And spread your legs."

"No." Her heavy-lidded eyes looked up to mine as she slowly pulled away.

They didn't leave mine for a second, stuck in a heated stare as she pulled my hand out of her. I watched as she took it, opened her mouth, and sucked my drenched fingers clean.

Fuck.

"On the desk," I grated out more forcefully this time.

She shook her head again, running her tongue along the pads of my fingers as she released them. The defiance in her eyes burrowed down to the base of my hips.

Fuck.

"No." Her calm tone warred with uneven breaths and flushed skin as her agile fingers made quick work of my belt.

"Poppy." The strength in my warning crumbled with a deep shudder.

"Careful with that tone, *darling*," she whispered softly in my ear while she got my rigid cock out of my pants and stroked it slowly. "Remember who you're talking to."

She sank down to her knees.

Electricity shot up my spine at the fucking sight of her. There was nothing hotter than when Penelope initiated. When she made it known that she wanted something.

I grasped her chin and tilted her head up to me. "I'm talking to *my wife*."

She licked her lips and instead of a sultry retort, she slid my cock slowly into her mouth, her eyes never leaving mine.

Chills ran down my body. My fingers tangled into her hair.

"That's it, Poppy." I let out a long, pleasure-filled sigh.

Encouraging her to go deeper, she eagerly complied. Stacking her hands on each other as she bobbed and occasionally choked trying to get my shaft entirely inside of her.

The pressure at the base of my spine grew more impatient as she pumped, sucked, and grazed her teeth along my length.

"You look good like that," I groaned, trying to hold on even a little longer; the tableau of her was too gratifying to lose just yet.

She was mine. In Singapore. In Manhattan. In a government building, coming on my hand, then sucking on my cock.

All *mine*.

And I couldn't let her go.

She hummed, sending unruly vibrations along my shaft. My fist closed in her hair.

Fuck. I was close.

"Poppy," I warned. It only spurred her on. She moved faster and deeper until I couldn't hold out any longer.

Every synapse erupted with pleasure and following a guttural grunt, I released in her mouth. A mix of sweltering heat and satisfying chills moved through me. She continued to bob up and down, slowing just as my vision started to clear.

Her hair was a mess around my hand. She looked up and the column of her throat shifted as she swallowed. Only then did she smile as she released me.

The world went from moving in slow motion back to reality.

She stood up and I caught my breath. Realizing exactly where we were, we quickly got ourselves together.

"This little hiccup was rather fun." She tightened my tie. She smiled, doing a final check then reached for the door. "If this is the best Silas can do, then I'm not worried. We can wait him out the year."

In that moment, I found another way to ease her mind. I opened my mouth to tell Penelope about my plans for SunCorp—we had an advantage we could levy against Silas. But then closed it. My plans had always been risky, but if SunCorp fell through, all of this would be for nothing. And while I trusted Penelope implicitly, she was a lawyer—and a lawyer who had once represented Dawn Capital, and still worked for the same firm that represented Hightower. Getting her involved at this stage would be irresponsible. I needed to get the remaining pieces lined up, and once I was sure the deal was solid, I'd tell her everything.

I would need to meet with Herrera again and nudge him along. In that moment, I remembered something else. Something Penelope might love. Something to show her just how serious I could be when it came to her when saying it felt impossible. That if it was a matter of waiting for her to feel the way I did, I'd wait as long as she needed—anything to not lose her.

"Come with me to Jalisco next week."

"Jalisco?" She opened the door and took a look down the hall.

We walked out back into the hallway casually, like we hadn't just had sex in a government building. I put an arm around her waist. "I'm closing a deal with Herrera, and I need to get it done as soon as possible."

She took my hand. "Alright."

I'd tell her once it was all sealed and done. Right now, everything felt so fragile. It felt like a dream and I would do anything not to wake up.

Chapter 35

PENELOPE

Xander's penthouse had three balconies that you could walk out onto.

The one off Xander's bedroom was the only one I hadn't seen, usually because I tried not to get too wrapped up in him in the morning since that tended to mean I'd run late for work. This morning it meant that we missed Sunday brunch at Sloan's.

After I got dressed, I found myself there. Large glass panes extended up as protection to anyone out there on a windy day, but unlike the other balconies, at the edges they seemed to taper inward. The additional glass was tinted soft green.

The cool wind whipped by, and my attention was drawn to a few planters along the wall. The largest terracotta one in the center was filled with poppies.

My heart skipped a beat.

My poppies.

I stared at them for a moment before running my fingers over a few petals, needing to feel them to prove to myself they were actually there.

Poppy.

A swirl of emotion began to swell in my chest, sending a delightful tremor through my body.

I faintly heard the sound of the glass door opening and closing.

"You usually disappear by now." Xander walked past me, handing me a mug on his way to the glass parapet.

I smiled, the flutter in my chest became a whirlwind.

"Are these mine?" The poppies were in a same planter, with an identical one next to it, also thriving. "I gave them to Maya."

He turned, glanced at the plant, then looked back out onto the city. "Yeah. I said caretaker, not undertaker."

"Don't be dramatic." I ran my fingers around the satin petals.

"I saw them in her office," he explained. "She forgot to water them and thought coffee might help."

I grimaced. "Oh. Well, thank you for caring for them in my stead. I promise I won't kill them."

"You say that like you're under the illusion that I'm giving them back," he scoffed lightheartedly.

I couldn't explain the feeling. The best comparison was it felt like I'd been wearing a corset for years and it finally loosened. Maybe it was the brisk air or maybe I was hallucinating at such a high altitude, but I was practically giddy looking at them.

Like finding something I'd lost, only to realize how much I missed it.

"Why didn't you tell me you had them?" I asked. The wind whistled by me, and I opened my mouth to ask again, but stopped as I turned and saw the look on his face become more somber.

Whatever crossed his mind in that moment swept the excitement away in the wind.

"You'd try to take them back," he pointed out casually, walking back to the door even though he'd just come out here.

"Well, they *are* mine."

"No, now they're mine." He shook his head and he closed the space between us. He took my chin in his hand and gently pressed a kiss against my lips. "And I don't want to let my poppies go."

His eyes bored into mine, a kaleidoscope of sincerity and maybe the slightest hint of fear keeping him from saying exactly what he meant.

My heart skittered because when he looked at me like that, it made me believe that his carefully guarded heart was mine.

A rush of emotion, akin to what I felt looking at that painting, crashed over me. A blissful anxiety mixed with excitement—this wasn't me figuring out what I wanted anymore. It wasn't simply the two of us enjoying our sexual chemistry.

It was more.

It was so much more.

"Don't make plans for later. We're going to be *busy*," he whispered.

A shiver rolled up my spine. "I'm going to the Augustus with the girls. They'll be here soon."

He groaned and pressed another short kiss on my lips before going inside.

With everything going so well, a part of me was waiting for the reality to set in. For Silas to make good on his threat, because I was sure what he'd done so far wasn't it. Or for something to yank away the cloud I felt like I was floating on.

My gaze lingered on the poppies, feeling both heavy and weightless at the same time.

* * *

FOR A MAN with an infallible memory, Xander had a surprising number of framed photographs and they adorned almost every wall of his home. All along clean lines with very simple, symmetrical framing.

"It was my choose-your-player party." CeCe's voice pulled me from my thoughts as I looked at one of the many pictures.

The four of us girls—Selena, Sloan, CeCe, and I—were meeting here and going to the Augustus Club together. Selena was warming up to the idea of spending some time there and Xander suggested she come along to the arts section. It was nice since Sloan—at any moment she and I were alone—was practically bursting with glee and withheld questions about the state of my relationship. She knew Xander and me well enough to pick up that we'd moved past acting the part.

She was respecting our privacy, and it was clearly difficult for her to hide her excitement as Xander and I found our footing. Which was beginning to feel strong and permanent.

"Hmmm?" I looked over at CeCe and Sloan as they walked over. I found myself stopping at different photographs every day, some of them had an obvious backstory. Others made me curious.

"We all went as different *Mortal Combat* characters. I was Kitana. Sloan was Mileena," CeCe explained.

I looked over the photograph again. The five of them, Sloan, Tristan, CeCe, Xander, and Rohan in one picture. Each a different *Mortal Combat* character.

"Are those real swords?" I asked, noticing Sloan's costume came with two long daggers that were swordlike, with ornate handles.

"Japanese steel," Sloan confirmed with a wide smile.

My eyes widened. I looked at CeCe for confirmation and she nodded as though validating something mundane.

"Marcus took them from her within five minutes of getting there. Concern for fratricide," CeCe added.

"I wasn't going to hurt anyone," Sloan assured offhandedly.

I laughed and looked at her. "Was it that bad between you and Henry?"

"Things weren't great." She shrugged. The last few years, from what I'd witnessed, their relationship was on the mend. Lately, it was hard to tell there was ever any animosity between the siblings. "The choose-your-player party was a few months after the official succession plans for Amari Global were announced. I wasn't handling it well."

"Yikes," I said to myself.

"Family drama is evergreen if you let it be." Her eyes scanned over the next picture, the one of her, Xander, Henry, and Marcus. All at her law-school graduation. It was the focal point on the wall; it caught your eye immediately when walking in. "The constant barrage of shots at each other wasn't sustainable. It was either give peace a real chance—be around each other and make amends—or live with a grudge forever. Peace is nice."

That sentiment settled in my chest.

I'd found peace here. But it was at the expense of my relationship with Arabella. Visiting Singapore again, after years, stirred up everything I'd missed. Liv, Bella, and a home I ignored because I was trying to protect myself from how I felt there.

"Is that why you considered staying in London?" I asked. After our assignment in London, Sloan entertained an offer to stay there despite Manhattan being her home.

She shrugged. "It was always the easy option to remove myself from it. But Henry is here and if I wanted to fix things, I needed to be *here*. He was trying, so I had to try, too."

A dull ache sharpened: Sloan was right.

The sound of Selena's telltale heels entering the entryway pulled us from the conversation.

"Sorry, I'm late. Blame Henry," she called.

CeCe laughed and turned to walk back to the entryway. Sloan and I followed a few steps behind.

The heavy truth of what I wanted had been weighing on me more since returning from Singapore. I glanced around at all the photographs on the walls. "Why all the pictures?"

Sloan's smile was gloomy. "I think he likes to have the good memories handy."

Chapter 36

XANDER

The crisp morning breeze rustled through the pages of a rolled-up newspaper Sloan was carrying under her arm, with a cannister of oats held between her hands. The autumn leaves sprayed the park in reds and oranges. She approached the bench we always sat at in Central Park.

"You know, for a man who loves a game, you sure can suck the fun out of a hostile takeover," she grumbled lightly, taking a seat next to me.

I chuckled.

My new counsel—at a different firm—sent a formal offer for a complete buyout of Hightower Energy. Thanks to Sloan, I knew it was only a matter of days before the board would vote Victor out and so I figured I'd settle this easily. An inflated offer was sent to the board yesterday before the opening bell on the New York Stock Exchange. They gladly accepted it knowing the stock would plummet, thinking they got a deal.

They did. But I wasn't concerned. It would skyrocket once I secured Herrera. And now I had the shiny object to lure him in with.

"Cleaner is better. Fewer waves," I attested.

She handed me the cannister and let out a long sigh. "And, in case you're wondering, I figured it out."

Feeding the ducks in Central Park was a tradition we had for years.

"What are you talking about?" I asked.

"The endgame." Sloan put the newspaper aside. I held the cannister open and she took a scoop of oats out.

"What do you mean?" I asked again, except the sudden elevation in my heart rate and the turn my stomach just took meant I already knew what she meant.

I wasn't even sure why it made me so anxious. I'd always planned to tell her.

She raised a brow; concern battled with her will to push. Instead of saying anything, she stood and walked to the water's edge, spreading the oats evenly over the surface for the ducks. Like she was waiting me out.

Tradition aside, the ducks were when Sloan and I talked. Actually talked. After years of me falling into bad habits when I couldn't handle the changes in my life. Losing my parents. Losing Reina. Spinning out in all manner of unhealthy ways—drinking, drugs, all of it.

This random activity became mandatory and every week we made time to make sure everything was okay. And if it wasn't, we fixed it.

"Xan, look." Sloan's face went rigid when she turned back to me and took her seat again. "I didn't press about this earlier because it felt great to take those horrible people down. But SunCorp will make extended-life batteries. And I'm going to venture a guess here. Chen Tech might be able to use it?"

"Xu Enterprises, too," I added, feeling anxiety push air out of my lungs. "But yeah, I want to have a say in the same industry Chen Tech and Xu Enterprises operate in."

"Why?" Sloan wondered glancing up in thought. "How could you know Silas would try something?"

"I didn't," I admitted. "But they both used familial obligation as a means of control over Penelope. So I wanted a means of control over them. If she was being forced into something and needed an out, now we have a way to set terms." Silently, I acknowledged the other reason. This gave me a way to sort of hold on to her. Nobody would be able to pull her back to Singapore, unless she wanted to go. And that was the root of my anxiety.

Sloan's smile stretched across her face. Her brows lifted; her chest filled with air. The fact that I'd asked her to skirt professional ethics didn't even register on her face because I was sure she was wrapped up in what I'd just confirmed for her. The thing that was going to come bursting out of her mouth any second.

"You love Pen!" she exclaimed in hushed glee.

Obviously. So incredibly obvious that it scared the living shit out of me every day, knowing that she might still go. I tried to show her all the ways we could be happy, together, here. I tried to tell her—without the terrifying act of actually telling her—how much I cared for her by showing her that all I wanted was to make her happy. To be the one she could be completely herself with.

"Sloan." I pleaded for her to not overreact to the news.

I'd been in enough relationships when I didn't feel *that* feeling to know when I did. That connection, the magnetic draw to someone else you just couldn't fight. I felt it for Penelope that night in her kitchen and the next morning with the poppies.

Sloan smacked a hand over her mouth. Stood up. She took a few steps to the water's edge, turned to the ducks and lifted her hand off her mouth momentarily. "He loves Pen."

"You know I hate it when you talk to the ducks like I'm not here."

"I knew it." She whipped around, pointing at me, looking a little maniacal. She turned her head to the ducks. "I knew it."

I couldn't help but smile.

A fourteen-year-old Sloan bull-rushed into my life and became my sister. My confidante. My best friend. I knew why I couldn't leave Manhattan when Reina asked and so did Reina. The Amaris were my family as much as Marcus was and, after everything, I refused to ever lose my family again. They all held me together and without them, I wasn't sure I wouldn't fall apart. And that's what made telling Penelope feel impossible. I wanted to hold on to her, *here*.

"When are you going to tell her?"

I could tell her about our new position of power, but it wasn't sealed yet. She didn't ever need to know the lengths we went through to get it. That didn't matter now. It was done. "Tell her what?"

Sloan's mouth hung open and she smacked my shoulder with the back of her hand.

"Jesus, Sloan." A crack splintered down my arm and I rolled it back. "Not the ring hand; we've talked about this."

"Xan." She crossed her arms. "When are you telling her you did something absolutely batshit because you *love her*?"

"I feel like corporate espionage isn't really Penelope's love language."

Everything felt so perfect. I was terrified to let anything change.

Once it was done, giving her this information—leverage over Silas—meant she had all she needed to go.

She probably would.

And I wasn't ready to face that yet.

"What if she doesn't . . ." I murmured.

What if everything, all of this, dropped me back to exactly where I started. Her choosing to leave and me left with nothing but all the pain.

"It's not so scary," Sloan ventured quietly. "A leap of faith."

"Said the woman who took five years to admit she had feelings for my brother," I mumbled.

Another smack against my shoulder warned me to be serious. "I mean it, Xan. When you find the right person, everything that felt impossible just isn't anymore. Tell her."

"I will," I said, so unsure I knew Sloan could hear it in my voice. "Stop worrying. I'm happy."

She shook her head. "'Happy' and 'not sad' are two different things. Chase happy, Xan."

Chapter 37

XANDER

The next week, when we arrived in Jalisco for the weekend, Penelope was content with working on one of the massive sunporches of the Spanish Revival–style compound that sat in the middle of nearly one hundred acres of agave fields in Jalisco.

She planned to do some work there while I went to talk details with Alejandro about the sale.

I put a hand up along my brow, squinting in the bright sun even though I was wearing sunglasses. Instead of talking in Alejandro's office, he preferred to walk the fields.

"CEO of Hightower Energy," Alejandro mused as I followed him down one of the perfectly lined rows of agave.

"You can't rename it, sorry," I joked.

He chuckled. "All of this to secure my portfolio?"

Past the neatly manicured desert-style garden and pool were rows and rows of agave plants. Alejandro was a man of many interests, one of them being distilling. His first venture had been turning his family's small batch distillery into one of the largest tequila producers in the world. This was what had made his family wealthy, giving him the money to finance his other visions. Next, he decided to use some of that land for massive wind farms that were capable of providing energy for nearly a quarter of the country's requirements.

"You happen to have a good hand," I told him. "Why not play it?"

"Seems a little too good, doesn't it?" he asked speculatively.

"Or serendipitous?" I offered. "Turn the largest energy producer and carbon emitter—a global nuisance—into a completely clean energy company."

He sighed and knelt down next to one of the plants. "I never cared for the distillery. It was my father's. He made me promise not to let it out of the family's hands. The fields, the lands, all of it."

"The distillery and all of the other ventures owned by your family will stay that way," I reminded him. "I'm only interested in your developments in clean energy."

He ran his hand down his jaw. "But why me?"

Alejandro knew his technology would change the world. But he was also skeptical. He knew how precious the tech he had was and wanted to make sure he didn't lose control over it.

"You need capital to make your tech scalable. We want to fund it and we want you to run the project. It's that simple." I raked a hand through my hair. "You'll head Hightower and do everything you've been doing at a much larger scale."

SunCorp, Herrera's clean energy venture, was small, so he was right in being suspicious: he'd go from running a small but mighty energy company to literally being the most powerful man in that sector.

He nodded in the direction of the distilleries. "We both know I wouldn't have brought you all the way here if I wasn't seriously considering it, but I'm curious why you came all the way here just to settle my concerns."

"Because this is just as important to me as it is to you," I assured him. "You have all the leverage here. You can refuse at any time."

But he wouldn't. No matter how noble, every leader of a company was persuaded by power. It was simply a matter of how much. And this deal gave him all that he could ever ask for.

Only a fool would say no.

Chapter 38

XANDER

A few hours after a polite dinner with Alejandro and his daughter, Penelope and I walked to the back of the property.

"Did you bring me out here for a tryst?" Penelope followed me outside. The warm air swept past as we turned off the corridor toward an off-road side-by-side waiting for us. "Because I was planning to work."

"It's a surprise."

Penelope opened the door skeptically and took her seat and buckled herself in. "Is this even safe?"

"Most fun things aren't," I told her. The engine roared when I turned the key.

When he was in the Hamptons, Alejandro mentioned that he would stargaze at the edge of the southern agave fields as a kid and on clear nights, the onyx black of night was blinding with starlight.

He was right. As we pulled away from the compound, after the dust the tires kicked up was well behind us, the deep orange sunset gave way to a diamond-studded twilight.

"First breaking and entering and now abduction?" She gave me a cheeky grin.

We passed the neat rows of agave and neared the end of the property, rolling up and down small, dusty hills on our way.

"Only you look at something fun and turn it into a federal crime."

"I'm a dual citizen of Singapore and the UK, residing in the US, whom you've abducted in Mexico," she teased. Her hair whipped in all directions as we finally came upon our destination. "It would be an international crime."

I chuckled.

The long stretch of mostly level ground began to fill with soaring hills. I stopped right where the valley tapered away and the mountainous terrain began.

I checked my watch. It was still a little early.

"Stargazing?" Her neck was craned back, staring at the sky. It was late enough into the evening that it was dark, but not dark enough yet.

"Your list can be very ambiguous." I got out and rounded the vehicle, then helped her out of her side.

"Stargazing is not on it," she reminded me.

The valley was punctuated with soaring rocky peaks on either side.

"The Astra meteor shower happens every year around this time." I pulled the blanket out of the back, laid it down, and Penelope took a seat. She leaned back on the palms of her hands and watched the sky.

"Shooting stars," she deduced slowly.

That was on her list.

I nodded. "We should be able to see it here."

Herrera wanted to meet in New York, but when I realized I could use the trip to knock something off that list, I took it. I might have been the one to insist we visit so I could get Penelope in a part of the world where she would be able to view the Astra meteor shower perfectly.

"What's all this for?" She opened the basket and pulled a few things out of it. Some glasses and a bottle of what I thought was a cocktail.

"I had to be here, and it happened to be on your list."

It was mostly true. She wanted to see shooting stars and I couldn't bring those to Manhattan, so I brought her to them.

"Thank you, Xander."

I shrugged. "What are first husbands for?"

She smiled. Her attention went back to the sky, the darkness enveloped everything, making each meteor striking as it passed.

"Why shooting stars?" I asked.

"It's childish, but wishes," she admitted softly. She took a sip from the drink in the glass, not taking her eyes off the horizon. "Well, just the one wish really."

I looked at her expectantly, hoping she'd tell me.

She looked down at the drink. She turned it in her hand. "I wanted to go home."

The words curled around my chest, pushing all the air from it.

It was something I recognized in Singapore and chose to ignore. She wanted to be there so badly she'd conformed to everything she thought she had to be in order to find a place. It was her home no matter what she'd found in London or Manhattan.

"But I didn't know where that was," she added, putting the drink down. "I always assumed once I saw one, I'd have it figured out."

"Have you?" I asked, knowing how much my entire world was tied up in the answer I knew, but I prayed I didn't hear. That she'd figured out what she wanted and it was an ocean away.

Her lips parted for a second before closing. She turned back to the sky. "Radiant, aren't they?"

"Yeah." I watched her as she watched the sky. The starlight swept over the delicate curve of her cheek. "Radiant."

I wanted to press her on it. But at the same time I wasn't sure I wanted the confirmation that she wanted the one thing I couldn't give her, a life away from home. My home. The one that kept me together all these years.

The deal was all but done. I could tell her everything now: how I planned to put Herrera in charge of Hightower Energy, how it would provide her with leverage and power. The kind that made any future available to her because she wouldn't need to fear Silas's retribution. And once this year was up, there was nothing left to keep her here.

I opened my mouth, but no words came out.

My chest tightened, reminding me of the last time I was in this position.

Losing Reina hurt, a wound that didn't heal for years—losing Penelope would be insurmountable. The fear, icy and piercing, became all I could feel. It told me to hold on tighter. Or at the very least, not to let go.

Not yet. Not when everything *could* work out. Because there were moments, ones that were becoming more frequent, when I'd hold her and everything felt too deep and serious for either of us to ever walk away.

She swayed a bit. "You know how to get back, right?"

Her voice, running up a few octaves playfully, pulled me from the constriction along my ribs.

"God, I hope so." I tried to shake off what I was feeling. "Because you certainly can't drive us back."

She laughed. *That* laugh. A real one. The one that was loud and a little boisterous. Impolite. Each heavenly disharmonic note echoed along the fractures in my heart.

Chapter 39

PENELOPE

CeCe was easily one of the nicest people I'd ever met in my life. A couple days after returning from Jalisco, she and I took seats next to each other at the pottery wheels in front of floor-to-ceiling windows that offered a view of the West Side.

CeCe sat in front of a messy slab of clay as she attempted to throw a new piece. I took one that I'd already thrown, and the clay had dried. Today, I planned to put some details on it.

"Thank you for inviting me along again." CeCe sat up straight on the bench and focused keenly on her work. The mound of clay was slightly higher and turned a bit more like a bowl.

Ever since getting back from Singapore, I'd been coming to the Augustus Club more often to work on a project. I usually came alone, but after inviting the girls a few weeks ago, I realized how much I'd probably missed out on not inviting them sooner.

"Thank you for coming." I pressed the pedal of my pottery wheel tentatively. The light streaming in from the windows we sat in front of cast a shadow that moved slowly with the turning wheel. "It's been nice to have company."

I worked on more details, taking a looped texture tool and making a few delicate lines.

Since Sloan was busy with wedding details and Selena and Henry were in LA visiting her mother, CeCe and I came here together.

We began our work. She told me about helping plan the Central Park Conservancy Gala next week, one we'd all attend.

"I heard about the painting," CeCe said over the subtle hum of the pottery wheel a few minutes later.

My heart skipped. I stopped my work to glance up at her, but she remained focused, pushing her thumbs into the center of the clay to begin shaping it.

She'd probably heard from Sloan, since I had it hung in my office after the weeklong showing ended, and Sloan smiled with so much withheld excitement that she looked exactly like her mother did on the patio that day that flipped our entire world upside down.

"Yes, it was sweet." I could feel my entire face heat up.

The whole lot of them—the girls: Sloan, Selena, and CeCe—all took their turns to quietly nudge the subject since we were back from Singapore. Sloan, who acted like the mother of a teenage daughter desperately trying to be "the cool mom," was terrible at pretending she didn't have a vested interest. She was my first friend here and things working out with Xander meant she'd be my sister.

Guilt twinged my heart for a moment.

Whether the guilt was misplaced or not, it didn't matter. I had a sister. And I missed her. Ignored her for years in deference to being here.

"It's nice. To see him like this," CeCe stated as her hands worked their way up the short bowl, pulling the clay with them. Bringing the edges higher. "It's been a while."

Another twinge.

I let the pottery wheel stop and decided to work on details that didn't require my full attention now that I was distracted. "A while?"

"Well, yeah." CeCe's cheeks lifted up in a wide smile as she pulled the bowl into standing higher; it was the first time she'd been able to make something that tall and stable since coming here with me. She watched it carefully, so focused it seemed she didn't realize where this conversation was going. "Romantically, anyway, he hasn't been like this since—"

She stopped herself and her hand slipped. The side of her bowl flopped onto itself.

"Reina?" I finished for her. She didn't say anything, she didn't look up, so I went on. "What happened between them?"

I had to know. Xander didn't talk about her, obviously that would be a little weird.

It wasn't jealousy, or I told myself it wasn't. But it was wanting to know *why* something bad happened. Like knowing the cause might placate the fear that it would happen to you.

To rationalize that you'd never be in that situation.

"They were young." CeCe shrugged; her eyes scattered all over the pottery wheel. She blew a few puffs of air upward to the strands of her blond bangs that fell in her face, since her hands were still covered in clay. "Who stays with the person they met in college anyway?"

I meant what I said to him in Singapore. I wanted to explore this thing we had between us, but I wasn't sure where it would go. At the time, I wasn't sure where I *wanted* it to go.

But now I was.

Ever since that day with the painting, it felt like everything was telling me that this wasn't just real, but it was also . . .

It felt like it was meant to be.

But the intrusive part of my mind reminded me that while I hadn't known this deep and all-consuming feeling before, Xander might have. And I just needed to know why it hadn't worked then.

"Is that all? Or is it a secret?" I mumbled to myself, a little resentful that I didn't know him as well as all the others even though he'd never once tried to keep something from me.

He told me about Reina, not what broke them up, but I didn't ask either.

"It's not." CeCe stopped her wheel and turned to me. "We just . . . I dunno. The rule is if it isn't your story, you don't tell it."

I knew what she meant, like Xander's vague mention of something that happened to CeCe in Paris. When CeCe was ready to share whatever happened there with me, she would.

The whole group had a way of looking out for each other. Sometimes keeping secrets between them only for the sake of the person they were meant to safeguard. In this case I suspected it was my husband's heart that required protection.

"Reina's a journalist," CeCe explained. "She got a job to be an international correspondent for a little while. A little while turned into the foreseeable future."

I nodded. "So, she left."

"Yeah."

"And Xander stayed."

Because why would he leave? He had such deep roots here. Who could possibly compete with the gaggle of best friends, the deeply loving—albeit meddling—family.

"Yeah," CeCe repeated.

"And he sort of—" I stopped myself.

Xander told me what happened after. Falling apart around a broken heart, something he seemingly protected himself from over the time I'd known him. Until now . . .

"But that's the past," CeCe added brightly.

She looked back at her haphazardly fixed bowl, smiled, and slowly used the peel to pull it off the base and I did the same.

"And if there's one thing I know"—she went on as we both

stood and walked to the sinks to wash our hands—"it's that the past is best when it's left there."

She dried her hands and offered me the towel.

"Trust me," she added, and adjusted her headband to let down her golden hair. "It was a long time ago. A lot has changed."

A lot *had* changed. Between the painting, all the items he tried to check off my list, the way he showed me a side of himself he hid from others. It all told me that this was real.

I nodded, feeling a heaviness fill my lungs despite the bright realization.

It should have made me float on air, but instead I focused on Reina. The striking similarity between the situations was impossible to ignore, as much as I wished I could.

We made our way to the end of the studio when she stopped and looked down at a large tarp covering a project with my name written on it.

"What's this one?" CeCe asked.

"Oh nothing." It was something I'd been working on since my things were delivered from the Hamptons. I wasn't sure why I was working on it, but I couldn't help myself. "Long story."

In the last few weeks, I'd become very comfortable asking for what I wanted, thanks to Xander. I'd realized that I wanted two things. I suspected they might be in direct conflict, but now I knew what they were.

And the dread of having to face that made me wish I never knew.

Chapter 40

PENELOPE

By the time I arrived at the Central Park Conservancy Gala, it was in full swing. I walked through the towering gables, each adorned with twinkling lights, and made my way to the main ballroom overlooking the pond.

The park surrounding the Loeb Boathouse was lit with string lights hung along the wooden beams inside and along branches in trees surrounding the pond outside.

The crisp fall air wisped around the bursting autumnal oranges and reds that checkered the trees.

I was a bit late and told Xander I'd meet him here since I got caught up with some work at the firm, but when I did arrive, I saw Sloan standing beside Marcus and her brother and Selena. The four stood there, a few steps off from the entrance, silently watching. Although the appropriate word was probably *staring*.

"Who is that?" I asked Sloan, her vision fixated on the woman in the poorly fitted black dress.

Across the room, in a corner on her own, she tucked her light brown hair behind her ear. Her eyes wide and body tense, she shifted her weight between her feet, the fabric of her dress bunched and rippled awkwardly.

I couldn't help but feel a little bad for whoever she was.

"Is she back?" Sloan murmured, lost in thought, and I knew she didn't hear me. She glanced around the room, no doubt looking for CeCe for any additional information.

My first thought was that the mystery woman was a patron of the conservancy. When I watched as her eyes stopped on Xander I had a feeling about who she was. Then, when I saw genuine surprise sweep along his face when he saw her, I knew.

It was Reina. The ghost of Xander's past, here, in the present.

The question I found myself needing answered was right in front of me.

"Oh," Sloan stammered as she looked at me then to Marcus and Henry, who both gave her the same unsure look. "She's . . ."

"Xander's ex," Marcus cut in plainly. I looked at Marcus but from my periphery I could see the two walking toward each other. "From a very long time ago."

I nodded and I couldn't stop my attention from moving back to them.

"I'm sure whatever she has to say won't take long. Come on, let's get him," Sloan decided; the high-society coating melted off her. I didn't know who she was trying to protect: me or Xander, probably both, but she looked ready for battle.

"No." I took a gentle hold of her wrist. I tried to smile through the deep ache in my chest. "There's no harm in talking. We're all civilized adults in polite society."

"It's nothing," Sloan assured me, but the confidence in her tone didn't hide the uneasiness that painted her face. "It was forever ago."

"Exactly," I agreed. "An ex is hardly a reason to make a scene."

With that, the four took my hint and made themselves scarce. I tried not to watch as the two made conversation. I hated how quickly the sight pulled me from the high I was riding in anticipation of seeing him.

"I got a strange call one New Year's morning a couple years ago, asking how to care for a houseplant in dire straits." Madison's voice broke my stare. I looked away from Xander and Reina to a comforting smile from Madison. "It didn't click until much later. But I always thought it was her."

A sharp pain wedged itself between my ribs.

"They have history, that's all," I insisted. "It's nothing."

"Oh, I know." Madison's voice picked up into a cheerful pitch. She gently swirled her glass, the wine made graceful laps around the crystal goblet. "I've heard his nickname for you."

"Pardon?"

"Poppy." She smiled demurely. "Those poppies are from you, aren't they?"

"Yes," I answered. My brow wrinkled together.

"The greenhouse was an engineering feat. He had it built for the flowers."

"Greenhouse?"

"That balcony, it functions as a high-altitude greenhouse. Withstands hurricane-force winds. It's new," Madison explained. "That's why I was there a couple times last spring. I know the society gossips said we were still dating, but he needed some help with getting engineers and filling out the space with other plants. I had a few suggestions for him."

The realization blossomed slowly like a flower in the springtime sun.

"You'd think those poppies sprouted diamonds the way he worried about them," Madison added.

"His mother loved to garden," I muttered blankly, feeling every knotted muscle in my body relax.

"Did she?" Madison shrugged, her tone even, almost bored. "He never really talked about her with me."

"I suppose I should let them finish their conversation," I said, despite wanting nothing more than to pull him away from this party.

"Interrupt or don't. It doesn't matter. He's charming for everyone," she pointed out as she began to walk away. "But from what I can tell, he's completely serious for only one person."

"Madison," I called quickly. She stopped and turned back to me. "Thank you."

For a time, I wondered how it was that none of his exes harbored any animosity toward him. It felt unnatural. But the more I got to know and understand him, it was obvious.

Xander never did anything that might make him lose someone. So even relatively meaningless relationships were treated with care because when you were scared to lose people, you didn't discard them—his charm was a survival tactic.

"Don't mention it, Mrs. Sutton." She gave me a knowing smile, and floated along the party, mingling with her guests.

His exes had all come and gone with civility because they were something of placeholders in his life. It was easy to remain friendly when nobody's heart was broken. Relationships without true depth meant you couldn't possibly drown.

But I wasn't a placeholder.

A rush of warmth seeped through me because, in that moment, the truth that I was too nervous to let myself believe was right there in front of me.

I was the person he was holding a place for.

Chapter 41

XANDER

T alking to Reina felt like a lesson.

Or the universe's way of shoving me in the right direction.

She was still the kind, free-spirited woman I'd known years ago. Seeing her again confirmed what I felt that night I ended up spending with Penelope. And it almost felt like fate she was here, pushing me to tell Penelope what I'd known for months, filling me with a hope that it would end differently than it had with Reina. Penelope was conflicted between Manhattan and Singapore, but if she felt even a fraction of what I did, she'd stay. We'd figure something out.

Reina explained how she ended up at this party. She was one of the volunteers asked to come and mingle since she'd be talking to donors. "Well, I'll think twice before I volunteer for the next Amherst Media Initiative," she joked, though her eyes held a hint of concern.

Our relationship was a lesson I needed to learn. One that I was learning sort of late, but better late than never. There were people who came into your life to leave it and that was fine because they were never meant to stay. Reina was never meant to stay.

"You don't have to do that," I assured her. I didn't love the idea of Penelope having to run into her, but seeing her occasionally at an event, or not, didn't really matter to me. "Manhattan is a big island and there are plenty of parties to go around."

"Yeah, well." She shifted her feet. "It's never really been my scene."

Outside of the major difference that broke us up, seeing Reina, here in this setting, gave me a clarity about her that got foggy over the years. We were similar when we met but my life had changed drastically since we first got together—back when I was twenty-three.

We grew in opposite directions, to a point where she felt unrecognizable now. I'd spent so long focused on holding on to her, or the idea of her, I never stopped to see that there was nothing left to even hold on to. Based on the look on her face, she felt the same.

I shrugged. "I don't mind it. I sort of enjoy the parties."

From the corner of my eye, I caught a glimpse of Penelope.

The yellow silk sparkled in the night. A thin collar held the delicate fabric around her neck and the rest flowed down along her chest, leaving her back bare.

I knew I was staring and that it was probably incredibly rude, but I couldn't make myself care. Talking to Reina felt like talking to anyone else, while being anywhere near Penelope felt like being pulled closer and closer to the sun.

My chest warmed when Penelope's eyes finally met mine.

"It was nice to see you," I said to Reina, unable to look away from Penelope.

I could faintly hear her say something, but it was completely drowned out by my own heartbeat. My legs moved to Penelope without instruction and, before I knew it, I was beside her. Exactly where I belonged.

Her teeth ran over her lower lip. She turned her ring around her finger.

Her ring.

My heart dipped. It was hers.

I loved watching her turn it when she was thinking, or nervous. I loved seeing it sparkle on her finger when it caught the light. I loved knowing that where she was, a piece of me was with her.

"Poppy," I said slowly, drawing closer.

A smile tempted the corners of her mouth. "Is the theme of this party The Night of Girlfriends Past?"

"Poppy . . ." I teased. "You're not jealous are you?"

She shook her head. "Of course not."

She had no reason to be. Whether it was in the glaringly bright lights of Manhattan or under a blanket of stars in the desert, she was all I could see.

"Good." I ran my hands over her hips and pulled her close.

My fingers dragged leisurely down her spine, stopping at the hem along the small of her back.

"Xander." She ran her fingers through my hair. "Why do you have my poppies?"

I was wondering if she'd bring them up again. I wasn't hiding them but at the same time I was advertising that I desperately held on to the tiny pieces of her I was allowed to have.

"A piece of you was better than nothing," I confessed.

But now a piece wasn't enough. I wanted all of her because she already had all of me.

Her breath caught and her hands slid down to rest on my chest. "And that night, the masquerade. You were going to tell me something."

"It doesn't matter."

"Why?" she pressed gently, quietly.

"It's not true anymore," I whispered against her lips before laying a light kiss on them. I pulled back so I could look into her eyes. "I was going to tell you that I didn't want you to leave because I wasn't ready to let you go."

At the time, the only thing I knew was that I didn't want to lose her.

"That's changed?" Her throat bobbed with a hard swallow. She looked at the floor.

"Yeah." I leaned my head against hers, catching her eyes again. Despite the tremble that ran through my muscles, I was never surer about what I needed to tell her. A truth I'd known for a while. One I wasn't going to trip or stumble over. When I said it, I needed her to hear the resolute clarity because there wasn't a single doubt in my mind. "Now I don't want you to go because I'm madly in love with you."

I pulled back and cradled her face in my hands.

This feeling. One that was fused to my bones and every part of my being. This was love. Real love. The type you couldn't let yourself lose, the type you hung on to—desperately if you had to—because nothing could compare to this feeling.

And nothing could heal losing it.

"I'm thankful I can't forget things because every smile, every laugh, every time you call me *darling*, they play in my head, filling the time before I see you again. It could be a day or twenty minutes but, fuck, Poppy, it's too long."

My voice trembled with emotion. My thumbs stroked away the stray tears that streaked down her cheek as a quiet tremor moved through her.

I kissed her once, unable to resist.

"Every piece of my heart belongs to you."

It might have been riddled with cracks and haphazardly stitched back together. But it was hers.

"Xander, darling." Her voice quivered with a shaky breath. "I love you, too."

A feeling I couldn't figure out washed over me. It was like coming up for air and finally being able to breathe, filling me with a hope that I'd avoided for years. One that told me I wasn't going to lose her.

Forgetting that we were in the middle of a society event, I pulled her into a kiss.

With a soft moan, she deepened it; her hands slid up my chest and laced around the back of my neck.

"Poppy . . ." I whispered into the tangled mess of our heavy breaths.

I could feel her body brace as another sob attempted to break through when I pulled away. "Take me home."

Chapter 42

PENELOPE

Xander's touch was velvet as we entered the penthouse. Unlike most nights where things escalated quickly, he was patient on the ride back home.

Gentle strokes along my back, feathered kisses down my neck. The air between us stretched impossibly thin, but he kept an unhurried pace.

Making no detours as we entered the house, I took his hand and began leading him to our bedroom. He stopped me in the grand foyer. Looming behind me, he ran his hand down my hips, splaying along my stomach.

"Darling." My nipples hardened against the silk. I let my head lean back onto his shoulder. "You can rip this one."

"Maybe another night," he whispered along the curve of my neck as the short zipper slowly traveled down around my hips. "I'm in no rush."

The metallic zip spread heat along its path. His palms burned as they slipped beneath the fabric and let it fall down my body.

His words from the party played in my head.

Hearing that he loved me didn't feel like a surprise. It felt like the slow culmination of a long, drawn-out path that was equal parts beautiful and terrifying. All leading to something entirely new.

It felt like dawn.

Something we'd both known was coming, but now was so bright we couldn't possibly hide from it. And we didn't want to. Not when basking in it felt so good.

He lined kisses down my back, until he was on his knees at the base of my spine. He looked up at me with a devious grin as he helped me out of my heels. "Where are we going, Poppy?"

His words throbbed in my ears.

I wanted him, impatiently. But I also wanted to relish the feeling, the one I'd been searching for only to find it directly in front of me.

"Take me to bed," I murmured.

I didn't want to think of anything other than how good it all felt. How perfect we were together and ignore the hard truths that lay before us.

With a slow groan he stood and captured my lips. After a few extended pecks, he deepened the kiss languidly. Sliding his tongue leisurely against mine. I savored the taste of him. The way every single touch was heavy, but I'd never felt lighter. Every anxiety washed away with each fused breath.

He began to maneuver us to the bedroom, careful not to pull away from the deep, aching kiss.

He watched patiently, the moonlight streaming over his sharp features, when we made it to our room, and I began removing his clothes.

Another kiss brought us to the bed, and we became tangled in each other. Our hearts beat in tempo together. Slow hands grew firmer with intensity as I straddled him.

I sank onto him, gradually. Taking him inch by inch. My hitched pants laced around his groans until he was completely buried inside me. I let a suspended beat pass between us before my hips gave him a pleasing swivel.

His muscles grew taut, straining against the overwhelming pleasure but he didn't take control.

"Poppy . . ." His heavy-lidded eyes finally closed, and his head pushed back against the mattress.

Now was usually when he'd flip me over. Instead, his fingers grooved into my hips, not pushing or pulling, patiently waiting for my next move. His neck drew tight lines along the column of his throat.

Emotion strangled my voice as I began to rock against him faster, my heart pounding in my ears.

"Darling . . ." My nails carved into his chest, the tempo finally reaching a fever pitch.

He pushed himself up just as the orgasm began to crest. I rode him faster. Sweat misted my skin, fog blurred my vision, and the pressure pushed past its restraints. His arms wrapped tight around me, holding me when all of it broke over us and we climaxed together.

My head leaned against his as the aftershocks rolled through.

He pulled me into a long, adoring kiss; his lips painted the beautifully imperfect version of a fairy tale I'd longed for.

"The poppies . . ." I whispered, refusing to move even an inch away. I didn't know why I said it, but they kept appearing in my mind. He'd held on to them all this time.

"They're mine." His satin tone brushed against my cheek. He ran a thumb along my collar. "I'm never letting them go."

I smiled. I couldn't think of a better caretaker.

* * *

THE NEXT MORNING, I woke to a rustling that echoed through the halls.

Xander had a staff, but they weren't around-the-clock. I could hear a bit of shuffling, a short thud, and then silence again. Probably one of the few staff members that took care of tasks at odd hours.

I glanced over to Xander, sound asleep, and carefully stepped out of bed. His shirt from the night before was in the doorway, so I quietly slipped it on and made my way downstairs to the large brown box awaiting me in the living room.

Sitting in the middle of the open-concept main floor, the large brown box stuck out. I knelt down in front of it, my heart racing, and slowly pulled the tape back.

The delivery was from the Augustus.

My piece was finished. I pulled the sides of the box away, careful with each fastener. Once the box was removed, the entire piece sat completely covered in bubble wrapping.

"Poppy?" Xander walked out to the living area with a yawn, his eyes squinting as he adjusted to all the light streaming in.

He sat down next to me on the floor.

"Sorry I woke you."

"Don't be. I don't like sleeping without you, anyway." He leaned in and kissed me. I then turned back to my task, unwrapping it slowly. "What is that?"

"It took some convincing to allow a jeweler to use the club facilities," I explained as I got up on my knees and began to carefully remove the protective wrapping around it. "And then of course, I wasn't allowed to actually help. Given the danger around melted metal . . ."

I looked back at him and realized I wasn't making a lot of sense, but I had his complete attention as if I were.

"I took the globe, the one I broke. I took the pieces and had them mended." I pulled back the last protective covering.

The globe was its same painted ceramic. Navy blue oceans and amber-colored continents. Silver lines that designated different latitudes. The only, extremely noticeable, difference was the large golden seams that covered the cracks.

"I was thinking about what you said that day, when I broke

it," I told him, running my finger down one of the golden seams. "Maybe things are meant to be broken, so we learn how to fix them."

That day was the first time I started feeling comfortable enough to let out some of the pressure that built in my head. He was the first and only person I felt that way around.

He didn't care if I broke something, as long as I was alright. It was simple, but to me it was foreign.

"It's called kintsugi," I went on, turning the globe to see all the places the gold snaked around it. "The Japanese art of repairing broken pottery with gold or silver. The idea is that the cracks shouldn't be hidden; they should be celebrated. They're a part of its history and make it more beautiful."

I turned to him.

His countenance was a canvas of emotion. His mouth hung slightly open. Beneath the easygoing mask, an ocean of feelings threatened to breach his well-leveed composure.

"Poppy," he whispered. His throat bobbed with a hard swallow.

I moved to sit in his lap and his arms tightened around me.

"There isn't anything broken that can't be fixed," I told him. A simple fact I learned that day.

"I love you," he said gently, but definitively, like a promise. I hummed softly in overwhelming happiness. I heard those words last night at the party, while we made love and after, and I'd never get tired of hearing it. "And I love this."

"You don't have a list, so I had to improvise."

"I don't need a list." He kissed along the back of my neck. "I have everything I *need* right here."

Chapter 43

PENELOPE

I felt like I was floating on air.

I found myself staring at my ring. Daydreaming about seeing my husband, ignoring all the inconvenient truths I didn't want to think about. The ones that became so loud over the last few days, I knew we had to have the conversation sooner rather than later.

The conversation that figured out where we'd be past the terms of this marriage.

A loud knock on my office door jarred me from my thoughts.

"Sorry to interrupt." Maya's unsteady voice came through from beyond the closed door. Each thump became more forceful and frantic. "But this is important."

"Come in." I shuffled a bit in my seat.

Maya opened the door, her eyes bewildered. Her hair was askew as if she'd been raking her hands through it while running around the halls.

"What's going on?" I rose, hearing a commotion in the hallway.

"Sloan is being questioned by agents from the Federal Trade Commission. They're escorting her to their offices."

A feeling of vertigo kept me stationary for an extended pause with a sudden blaring ring in my ears. Everything felt jumbled, moving in slow motion.

Then the sound of Maya's voice shot everything back to full speed. She tapped her foot with an expectant expression. "Let's go," I finally answered.

My mind kicked into autopilot, and I rounded my desk to join Maya. Just as I left my office, three agents accompanied Sloan down the hallway. We followed a few steps behind them.

Every partner, associate, secretary . . . everyone was watching.

Working at a large law firm in corporate law meant that this type of questioning wasn't too far-fetched. But the spectacle was new. Something was going on.

As she walked, Sloan turned her head to look over her shoulder at Maya. "Get Declan. Tell him to meet us at the federal offices."

Declan Parsons—Maya's boss—was a senior partner in litigation, but made a name for himself as one of the best defense attorneys in the country.

Maya nodded and scurried quickly to the bull pen to get her things and fetch Declan.

"Sloan," I called after her, keeping in pace. My mind flipped to all the next steps. "Don't worry and don't say anything until Declan gets there."

"It's a voluntary questioning. I'm not being charged with anything and if I can help these fine people . . ." She turned to smile politely at the two federal agents. "I'm happy to help. Once my counsel arrives."

"We appreciate that, ma'am," one of the agents, a burly man with sandy hair and his arms neatly folded on each other, answered.

"May I see your credentials?" I asked sternly to the two agents—a man and woman, both with stony facades, who clearly had no idea who they'd been tangling with. Nobody was above the law, but if someone were, it was a member of the Amari family.

The agents looked at each other and held out their badges for my inspection.

"I already asked, Pen. I'm complying with an inquiry received by the Federal Trade Commission." Her voice remained calm, stoic. It was the tone Sloan put on when she was nervous. The outer exterior of confidence, a tranquil surface, with a storm beneath.

I knew better than to ask any more questions to Sloan about what was going on with the two federal agents a couple of feet away. I handed back the badges and smiled politely.

"We'll get this sorted," I assured her.

"Of course," Sloan agreed. She craned her neck to look out the window and down to street level. I followed her gaze and noticed press lining the entrance. Her shoulders dropped and a sigh was barely audible over the sounds of the office picking back up. "Great. Press."

My eyes shot up to the two agents. "That is wildly inappropriate."

"The FTC has no interest in a scandal." The other agent with pin-straight brown hair responded. "We would never alert the media."

"Then how do you suppose they knew that Sloan Amari would be questioned today?" I crossed my arms.

Silas.

Nausea rolled through me.

Sloan was silent as she got into the elevator.

I caught the next elevator down to the lobby to see a swarm of reporters waiting to meet her there.

"Shit," I cursed to myself, and walked out beside Maya to an array of flashes aimed at Sloan.

Summoning all of her mother's stoicism, Sloan was stone-faced. She turned and said a few things to Declan, who nodded and motioned for Maya to follow him.

Before I could say anything, all three were in the black SUV and on their way.

I walked back into my office in a blurred state of shock.

I took a seat at my desk and pulled out my phone to let Xander know what had just happened when my phone lit up with a call.

My heart sank.

It was Silas.

"What did you do?" I answered without waiting for whatever he wanted to say.

"Misery loves company."

"What did you do?" My voice hardened to steel.

"Nothing, Penny," he stated calmly. "I simply called in suspicious behavior. Whatever the FTC makes of it is none of my business."

"What are you—"

"I told you I was keeping a close eye, and I couldn't help but wonder. What could a billionaire leading a venture capital firm want with someone like you?" He noted grimly, "We needed to bribe the Xus with your titles, yet here he is wanting seemingly nothing. Doesn't that strike you as odd?"

I knew I was nothing more than a bargaining chip for a lot of people who sought to control me, but even so, it hurt to hear it.

"Whatever you're getting at, just spit it out." The shakiness began to bleed into my voice.

"Did your husband know the merger would fall apart? I'm guessing he did," Silas went on, taunting.

My stomach turned.

I remembered the drive to the Hamptons after I slipped on his mother's ring. He knew about the merger and I told him about Xu Enterprises, not thinking it was all that important at the time—I was reeling from everything else.

"It wasn't a secret," I reasoned.

It also wasn't front-page news, the pessimistic part of my mind reminded me. Someone had to go looking for that information.

"But it was fortuitous," he pointed out. "Being married to you meant he'd know when the merger might fall through, so he can strike at just the right time."

"He wouldn't do that," I snapped.

"He already did, with Hightower Energy. Why do you think your friend is being questioned as we speak?" A long pause came from the end of the phone. "Dawn Capital just acquired it."

I was speechless as I put it all together.

I had no idea about Dawn Capital's current dealing because after the wedding, Dawn Capital retained other counsel due to our conflict of interest—or I thought that was the reason they left the firm. But if Xander was planning to take over Hightower Energy, then it would have raised red flags since our firm also represented the Hightowers. Switching counsel would avoid scrutiny.

When I didn't answer Silas went on. "Isn't that convenient, they struck at the perfect moment, too. A takeover just days before the board voted down Victor Hightower. With the perfect company all lined up to take over—SunCorp."

My mind put together the strings of information it knew. Hightower was implicated in many crimes, all of which were well outlined in the whistleblower's documents.

The ones Senator Alders took to the Senate oversight committee.

The ones Sloan, as the Hightower account's counsel—had access to.

"That doesn't mean anything," I insisted.

Even if what he was implying—that Sloan aided in bringing down Hightower Energy—were all true, it didn't mean it had anything to do with Chen Tech. Either way, I couldn't believe Xander set any of this in motion to take something from me or my family.

"Your husband now has control over a global energy company and SunCorp—who owns the technology that every tech-related manufacturing company will need," he stated. "He is waiting out the demise of Chen Tech. And that has *nothing* to do with you?"

My mind reeled.

"You are his pawn," Silas continued. "At least Maddox was clear with his intentions. Did you ever stop and think that maybe your family may know best?"

"I know what's best for me," I retorted on such a shaky breath it almost came out a sob. The revelations began to make me question my intuition, every single choice I'd made. Again.

He chuckled humorlessly. "Clearly."

"What do you want, Silas?" I tried to regain some composure. He called for a reason and it had to be more than gloating.

"A compromise. The Xus are the only company that will merge with Chen Tech given its financial constraints."

"Whose fault is that?" I hadn't driven the company into the ground; he had.

"Fine, I admit it. I'm not the best leader, but misery loves company," he repeated. "So, I am going to come at this from another angle. You can still save your family's company. Or you can watch it fall down. I wonder how Arabella will feel being collateral damage because you couldn't do the one thing she did without argument."

Every single person affected by this spun past my vision. Once again, I'd be blamed for doing something that was only meant to give myself a chance at happiness. And now, I couldn't trust my own intuition. And maybe I couldn't trust Xander either.

I had to speak to him before I let this consume me.

"Silas," I warned.

"The choice is yours. You can finally be worthy of this family. Or you can turn your back on it and let your friends in Manhattan deal with me slowly releasing all the fun tidbits I've collected over the years. Today was just a tiny little sample." He laughed without humor. "Now that Xander has what he needs from you, let's see how long it takes for you to lose that family, too."

The call ended and I sat there in a state of disbelief.

Chapter 44

XANDER

Amari Heiress Questioned by Federal Agents

I swiped away the headline. The press got a shot of Sloan getting into the SUV with the federal agents that went to question her.

I was in a meeting with Tristan when he got the call, so he and I went to Sloan's place and waited for her there. Given he was the one who facilitated sending the files to Fitzgerald's Senate office, he was well aware of what was going on. Not so much the motive behind it, but he knew what we'd been planning.

He wasn't really fazed by any of it. Tristan was used to being the go-between. He kept himself out of the family dynasty by providing political capital from time to time—like with Fitzgerald and the Hightower hearings—and that meant the Alders family usually owed him a few favors. Favors that he loyally gave to us when we needed them.

"Fitz talked to Liana Blackwell." Tristan walked down the hall to the kitchen after making a call to his cousin. "Head of the FTC. He was her staunch supporter during her Senate confirmation."

I was waiting in the kitchen, checking my phone to see if Penelope called me back. She hadn't yet, but it was late afternoon. Maybe she was still working or caught up with any fallout at the office.

A sense of dread wrapped around my chest. I knew I'd have to tell Penelope about this now. Before, I could rationalize that it gave her plausible deniability to not know, but now she'd have questions and I wasn't going to lie to her. I'd tell her all of it, it *was* a little batshit, but it was meant to help her. And it felt like now she'd stay regardless of pressure from Silas or not.

"And?" I clicked the side of my phone.

"Sloan is being asked to make a statement about her work with the Hightowers. The FTC is following up on a tip about potential insider trading."

"Which is ridiculous because no trades between myself, my family, or anyone were made with the Hightowers altogether." Sloan's voice filled the room. We looked over our shoulders and she walked in, her hair in a bun and a scowl on her face. She turned toward the living room and sat down on the couch. She motioned for us to follow.

"And that's easy to corroborate," Tristan added, conciliatory. "Don't worry."

"So, why bring you in?" I questioned.

Nobody in our circle was even invested in Hightower, that was easy to prove.

Insider trading. Very illegal. We hadn't done that, we just happened to know when the Hightowers went down because we happened to be the ones who brought them down.

Sloan laughed a little deliriously. "Because it *does* look suspicious when pointed to directly. My client's entire company tanks and then my close friends swoop in. I'm not concerned, obviously people know we're close, so the implication is something I assumed we'd deal with. That's why there is nothing to find. I'm just surprised anyone was paying *that* close attention."

"Right, they'd need a lot of evidence to prove that's related," Tristan added.

"And they have none." Sloan perked up, she tucked her legs beneath her. "Based on their questions they're building a larger case against the Hightowers."

"There's nothing to prove you broke—" Before I could say "attorney-client privilege," which was exactly what Sloan broke in handing over those documents to Fitz, she interrupted.

"It's complete speculation. All of which, I vehemently deny," Sloan challenged.

"And the firm?"

Sloan laughed. "They know that I am fully cooperating with the FTC's questions. It is hardly the first time a big law firm has had questions from the feds. We're not exactly working for the weak and downtrodden. The feds keep going after me, I'll counter with a malicious prosecution suit. Bury them in work they can't afford, looking for evidence that doesn't exist."

Tristan took a deep breath and sat down on the chair across from Sloan. "Any idea who called in the tip?"

"You think it was Penelope's brother?" Sloan speculated. "He has an axe to grind, right?"

I shrugged. The news was public so technically it could have been anyone. But there was no proof to substantiate it and whoever it was had to be paying extremely close attention. It made sense it might be Silas.

"Go home, tell Pen," Sloan instructed when I stayed silent. "Everything. I trust her."

I nodded. "You're okay?"

"I'm fine. Tristan and I can figure this out. I'm sure Henry and Marcus are going to come barreling in here soon even though I told them everything is fine."

"Given that those files, the ones that ended up in Fitz's chief of staff's hands *mysteriously*," Tristan added, since nobody was going to say the quiet truth out loud, "are part of the reason Fitz is the frontrunner for the next election cycle, I'd say that you've banked a lot of favors with Fitz and my grandfather."

I turned and made my way to the door, checking my phone but no calls or texts from Penelope.

When I got home, I couldn't find her around the house, the kitchen, any of the bedrooms. I called her again, but no answer.

Panic started to bleed into my veins until I walked back into our bedroom one last time and looked out to the balcony.

Next to the poppies, her back against the glass wall, was Penelope.

I walked outside into the chilly autumn air.

She looked up at me; her eyes were puffy and a little swollen.

My heart dropped.

"We need to talk," she told me quietly.

Chapter 45

PENELOPE

The frustrating thing about being an adult with a fully formed frontal cortex and critical-thinking skills was that while anger felt *so* cathartic in the moment, once logic set in, it was fleeting.

All you were left with were simple truths.

I knew whatever the explanation was, it wouldn't be nearly as tumultuous as I'd created in my head hours ago. It would be nuanced, and I'd be upset. But I also knew Xander and unless I was truly blind—which after thinking this over for hours, I knew I wasn't—there was probably a decent explanation.

One I needed to hear.

"We need to talk." I looked up at him momentarily then stared blankly at the horizon.

After sitting in a state of numbness for about an hour in my office, I knew I couldn't possibly get any work done. I came here, and every muscle felt sore. I tried to lie down, but I saw my poppies and just sat there. I figured he'd find me once he returned.

Xander sat down beside me; he tried to take my hand but I pulled it away.

"Silas called. It was him who called in the tip," I told him. "Is Sloan alright?"

Whatever the explanation was, Sloan was surely in on it. That knowledge actually helped, after the initial shock wore off, and I could think—that fact helped steady me. There was a reasonable explanation. There had to be.

"Yeah," Xander said quietly. Looking at me instead of the early autumnal sunset, the one I refused to pull my eyes from. "She'll be fine."

After spending hours wondering how I'd have this conversation, I knew where I wanted to start. "Why did you agree to this marriage?"

The first thing I needed was to understand what he was thinking that day, out on the terrace when *he* told the lie. The one that launched this entire thing.

"What?" He turned to me; his brow furrowed.

I faced him and tried to keep that steely feeling, but it swept away the second I finally met his gaze. My detached facade crumbled immediately. Because I loved him and no matter how logical whatever argument he gave me was—he'd lied and it hurt.

"Why," I repeated, my voice dipped before I immediately pulled it back together. "You told Beatrice we were engaged. You went along with it when I gave you an out. Why?"

His brows rose, forming lines along his forehead, surprised. As if it were obvious. He turned his entire body so that he was facing me. "Poppy, I spent seven months trying and failing to figure out how I was going to grin and bear it while you got married. In that moment, I saw a way to hold on to you a little longer." His voice shook before he said the rest. "I took it."

"It had nothing to do with the Chen-Xu merger?" I asked, knowing what Silas said was not the explanation. But I needed to hear him say it. "Or wounding companies enough to take it over. Like you did Hightower?"

Hurt flickered in his eyes, but he answered with resolute clarity. "No."

"You didn't know Chen Tech was in a precarious financial situation?"

"No, but after we were in Singapore it was a safe assumption."

"So, you expect me to believe that it's purely coincidence? That you now happen to have control over the technology that both Chen Tech and Xu Enterprises would need after their merger?"

"Well . . ." He rubbed the back of his neck, looking down at his lap.

"Now is not the time to omit something," I warned. "Start from the beginning."

"Originally, Sloan and I wanted to take down the Hightowers because their automotive tech division made the automatic braking systems that failed and killed hundreds over the course of a decade. My parents were two of them. The company covered it up."

I wanted to stop him because suddenly this felt like it went a lot deeper than I thought, but he kept going and I let him.

"When you told me your family or Maddox's was going to use whatever influence they had to get you back in line, I took what I knew about Xu Enterprises and changed the plan. I asked Sloan to make sure the Hightowers went down, quickly and publicly, so I could buy them out. I used the open CEO seat as incentive for Herrera to sell majority stake in SunCorp to Dawn Capital."

"So, now you control both," I surmised.

He nodded. "Herrera is tiny. Put him at the helm of Hightower, it has global reach. Nobody would be able to compete. Xu Enterprises still needs things like extended battery life for their devices. The kind Herrera already developed. Maddox would need to play nice to continue."

"You took down Hightower to install your preferred leader, with the technology you'd need to have some power in the exact market Maddox and Silas were participating in." I strung it all together. "Do I have that right?"

"Yes."

"So instead of Maddox and Silas having power over me . . ." I demanded, hurt wedging itself between my ribs. "You do?"

"No," he faltered, taking my hands and this time I didn't pull them back. I believed him, but I needed the rest. I needed his motive. "Look. I never planned to use the power. I just wanted it available." He squeezed my hand a little tighter. "I know you act in the best interests of the people around you, and sometimes you feel trapped by your familial duties. I wanted to make a way out. If you ever needed it. If either your family or his had something that made you feel like you had to do what they asked, then having power over their future meant you could dictate terms."

The scattered colors of the now setting sun dispersed along his irises as they became glassy. My mouth hung open.

"I wasn't ever going to use it against your family if you didn't need it," he asserted quietly. He looked down at my ring. "This was also a great business deal. The world would have a clean energy company replace Hightower—one of the world's worst carbon emitters. Win-win. You have to believe that I would never use that power unless you wanted me to."

Emotion welled in my chest. Hurt from the lie. Love from the motive of it all. Pain knowing this conversation wasn't close to finished.

"Xander . . ." For some reason I wasn't surprised. The scheme was crazy, but the sentiment, from Xander, was almost predictable. "I believe you."

That was what he did, he held on to the people he didn't want to lose. His heart was in the right place. But that didn't mean it was right.

"But you can't do that," I whispered, pulling my hands from his. Swallowing a lump in my throat, one that threatened to push tears from the corners of my eyes. "You can't hold on that tight or you put me in the same position I've been in my entire life. Where someone else is attempting to pull the strings—no matter how well-meaning. I've already lived that life."

"It was never my intention," he pleaded, leaning his head against mine.

He pulled me to him like he needed physical assurance I was there. Putting both hands on my waist he gently eased me into his lap. I went willingly because it was so tempting to just let this be it.

"You made me question myself," I admitted with a bob in my throat. That's probably what hurt the most: that just as I was finally trusting myself, this flipped it all on its head for a few hours and it felt like being in a tailspin. "Question you."

"I never meant for any of this to cause you any sort of pain," he whispered into my ear. "I'm sorry."

The initial razor-sharp pain of the lie had dulled because like all things with Xander it was rooted in good intent. It was out of love or fear. I wasn't sure which. But it was meant to protect me.

Which only made the next part harder.

"I know." I swallowed a shaky breath. I turned a bit in his lap and ran my fingers through his hair, wanting nothing more than to feel him hold me. A shuddered breath rippled out of him. "You cannot *ever* lie to me again."

"I swear to you I won't." He took my hand and kissed it gently.

I nodded.

I believed that, too.

His arms wrapped around my waist and he held me close. I shifted and leaned my head against his chest. A deep, cutting betrayal would have made the next steps easier. But Xander would never hurt me, that much was clear. I had to forgive the lie of omission, which would take time, but that didn't change the fact that I loved him.

We sat like that, entwined in each other silently for a few minutes before I finally summoned the courage to have the conversation we'd postponed but Silas's interference brought to the forefront. We couldn't keep ignoring it, no matter how tempting it was to float along as we were. The ache moved through my muscles.

I pulled away and shifted to face him. "I need to go to Singapore to settle this."

"We'll leave tomorrow," he said quickly. "I know all of this was a . . . lot." He rubbed the back of his neck. "But it's a means to the same end. You can use SunCorp's new position as leverage with Silas or—"

"I need to do this," I interrupted. I needed to do this for myself. I trusted myself, finally. And this lie might have shaken it, but I needed to follow this through. "And you need to stay here." His body tensed. The arm he had around my waist tightened like he was physically trying not to let me go. "I know you're sorry and I *do* forgive you."

I asked for the truth, and he gave it to me.

I asked for assurance it would never happen again, and he gave it to me.

I *could* have used all of it—the secret and the omission—to be angry and hold on to some hostility. I could let it break us if I wanted to.

But my instincts told me not to, and I had to trust them.

The fact was that despite the lingering ache, I understood. I'd never forgive his keeping secrets again, but I had a confidence he never would.

Because he wouldn't risk losing me.

And that, right there, was the conversation that might *actually* break us.

"I need you to stay here because I need you to think on our future."

"Poppy—"

"Just listen," I begged quietly.

He nodded.

"I'm not sure how long it'll be, but I think I want to stay in Singapore." I looked down, unable to look him in his eyes, knowing how much it would hurt him to hear this. "And then from there, who knows. I haven't had my chance at adventures and I'd like to have a few."

My first ever decision for myself was moving to New York instead of home to Singapore and that decision was riddled with guilt over the years. I didn't want to live like that anymore. I finally had the strength to be loud and ask for what I wanted.

Thanks, in large part, to him.

And I wasn't going to keep second-guessing it. I was going to make my decision based on what I wanted, not what scared me. He had to do the same.

"Okay." He pulled me onto him so I was straddling his legs, making it impossible to look anywhere but into his eyes. "We'll move to Singapore."

I could hear it in the rapid cadence of his words—the fear. He was making a split-second decision, weighing the outcomes quickly in order to keep moving forward. To keep playing. But not playing to win, simply playing to *not lose*.

To not lose me. It felt knee-jerk, born of fear, and I couldn't let him make this decision that way.

"It's not that simple," I asserted, trying not to feel the pain that was so palpable radiating off of him. Heartbreak and fear. "We can spend this year, the marriage contract, wherever. You don't have to come. You don't have to pick up your life. Asking you to leave home is an enormous task. I know that."

"*You* are my home." His tone became more agitated. Anxious.

"It's more than that, Xander." My heart twisted. He had to be ready for it, on his own. No gaggle of friends to unquestioningly protect his heart for him. "You have to fully understand what you're giving up, because I can't be those things. I can't make Singapore Manhattan. I'm one person. I can't be every single friend you love and you're leaving behind. Putting all your happiness on me is too much pressure."

I spent too long taking responsibility for other people's well-being; it was exhausting.

With the sun now fully set, twilight enveloped us.

"I don't expect you to be anything other than who you are," he insisted, his voice cracking.

The anguish in his voice tore at my heart. All I wanted was to give in, kiss away the pain, and make us both feel better. I held his face in my hands and leaned in to kiss him. His arms wrapped around my waist, keeping me firmly planted there. As I pulled away, he captured my lips again desperately.

My hands spanned across his chest and I pulled away.

"You have to think about this and *really* give it thought. Because I need to know that you're doing this because you love me. Not because you're afraid of losing me. I deserve the first one, not the second."

It had to be love that steered this decision, not fear. The exact emotion I could see so clearly in his eyes.

"Okay." His throat shifted with a hard swallow. "You go. I'll stay here."

"For now," I added, hoping his love for me was greater than anything else. It felt that way, but no matter how much it hurt, I needed him to be sure. "Once everything is settled we can figure things out."

His arms pulled me in, holding me close. I let him, laying my head along the crook of his neck. He didn't say anything, rather held me like that for a while before it became too chilly to be outside.

We quietly went to bed knowing that the next few weeks would be more painful than tonight was.

Chapter 46

XANDER

The familiar feeling of Penelope's short, perfectly rounded nails running along my scalp sent tiny sparks down my neck, pulling me awake the next morning. My heart skipped. A smile formed on my face.

Then, everything we talked about the night before flooded me.

"Poppy." My eyes blinked open and I sat up quickly.

"I'm sorry I didn't wake you earlier," she whispered, sitting on the side of the bed. I glanced at the clock on the wall; it was just before nine. "I know you didn't sleep much last night."

The curtains were still drawn but the light peered in along the sides. She had to have been up early. We must have slept in shifts because she'd fallen asleep in my arms and I watched her for hours. I was unable to keep the anxiety of everything to come from blaring in my mind, keeping me awake. I must have fallen asleep right before dawn.

"Wait," I pleaded, still groggy. I ran my hand down the side of my face and started getting out of bed when she stopped me by laying her hands on either shoulder.

The strength in her resolve wavered for a second.

"We talked about this last night," she reminded me. "I'm heading out. I talked to the firm. I'm working remotely the next few weeks while things get sorted."

Last night, after we came inside, we lay in bed and we talked a little more. Not about us, but about the path moving forward. What she planned to do; she needed to talk to Arabella. Then Silas and Maddox. While the idea of her and her ex drove me a little insane, I trusted Penelope with everything. My heart, my future, all of it.

Her assistant booked a flight for this morning, but she refused to take the jet because it was impractical for just her. She wanted to handle the Silas situation as soon as possible and finally put it behind her. So she could move forward.

She must have packed quietly while I was sleeping. At least I didn't have to watch it happen.

"I wanted to say goodbye," she admitted softly. My chest constricted, pushing the air from my lungs. "For now," she added quickly.

Her eyes drifted to my nightstand, mine followed. My heart dropped into my stomach when I saw the familiar black velvet box.

"Penelope." Panic bled into my voice. The knee-jerk reaction to hold on tighter when I felt her slipping away. We weren't ending it.

"I'm wearing my wedding ring and I am still very much *your wife*," she assured me, not that it helped. Her thumbs gently swiped back and forth along my jaw, keeping my eyes locked on hers. "I never actually tried to take off the ring after that first week in the Hamptons. This morning was the first time I tried. You were right, it slipped off when I stopped clawing at it." A tiny smile moved up her lips. "I just want you to know that if that box doesn't come with you when you come visit in a week, I understand. Moving forward, this arrangement can look however you'd like it to."

I opened my mouth to tell her all the things I wanted to: I didn't need to think about it, that she was my everything.

But Penelope needed to know that if she asked, I'd let her go. And I had to learn to stop holding on too tight.

"Okay," I whispered, feeling completely powerless.

"Remember what you promised me." She leaned in and brushed her lips against mine. "I deserve a man that's by my side out of love, not fear."

I nodded.

She wasn't just asking for what she wanted, she was demanding it. And even though it was killing me, I was so fucking proud of her.

"I'm going to spend the week at Olivia's, figure this out with Arabella. But I'll call you when I land."

She stood and I fought every urge to get up and stop her. Beg her, plead with her to stay. Instead, I tried to deal with everything I was feeling. The sheer unstoppable pain of watching while the person I loved more than anything walked out hit me all at once.

The anxiety, the fear, all of it.

*　*　*

I SAT AT my kitchen island, staring at the ring, going over everything Penelope said on loop.

I need to know that you're doing this because you love me. Not because you're afraid of losing me.

She was right—a lot of my actions were born from fear.

It wasn't just not telling her about Hightower. I was so terrified that I'd get used to her and I'd be devastated if she were gone, that I told myself it was better to never know how good it would feel to be with her. Then, when we first crossed the line in Singapore, I could have told her I wanted so much more, but I didn't. I took whatever she was willing to give out of fear she would pull away if I asked for more.

It wasn't fair to me either.

The sound of footsteps pulled me from my thoughts.

"Pen called me," Sloan explained into the silence without being asked. She took a seat next to me. "Told me she's going to Singapore and wanted to give you some time to figure some things out, so I thought I'd check in."

"Are *you* okay?" I asked, remembering everything else that happened yesterday. Besides, it wouldn't be long before we talked about what happened with Penelope. There was still the matter of what Silas kicked up. "With everything that happened?"

"Liana Blackwell, on behalf of the FTC, is thankful for my cooperation even though I provided no additional insight and Senator Alders corroborated my story that his Senate office received a private couriered—anonymous—packet of documents. It's not unheard of that an employee might be fearful of retribution from a giant like Hightower," she explained.

"And the firm?"

"I told them the truth. I was questioned; I complied. Nothing further. It's over now. Thanks to Fitzgerald, it's going to stay over."

"I'm sorry I put you in that position," I mumbled.

"Don't be," Sloan countered sternly, almost threateningly. The only time Sloan was truly upset with me was when I *didn't* ask for help. "It may be murky ethics, but I have the moral high ground, the Amari last name, and powerful friends. I always knew I'd be just fine."

Sloan loved to say that laws were only ethical to the people they served, and she worked for a lot of morally bankrupt people. Ethics was in the eye of the beholder. With crimes ranging from tax evasion to criminal negligence resulting in the deaths of hundreds over the last decade—nobody was mourning the Hightowers.

"My morally gray best friend," I said with a chuckle, the first splinter of laughter since Penelope left.

"Everyone needs one." She grinned proudly. "And what about Pen? She's all set to deal with Silas?"

"Yeah." I didn't know what Penelope planned to do with the information I'd given her, but she wanted to talk to Arabella first.

After a few minutes of silence, I began to tell Sloan what Penelope and I had talked about, mostly to hear it out loud instead of in my head over and over. A little because I knew Sloan would be trusted counsel.

She sat quietly and did not interrupt even once as I went through it all.

"Are you okay?" she asked minutes after I finished, and she took it all in.

No. I felt like I was coming apart at the seams. But I was managing at least. Trying to do what Penelope asked.

"I'm holding on too tight," I admitted.

"Unfortunately, that seems to be an Amari-Sutton quirk. The trauma bonds that bind," she said quietly, like it was to herself. The four of us did it—got overly involved—because we wanted to keep things from coming undone. It was hard to see when it felt so reflexive. "We all sort of have a blind spot to it."

"I love her. Of course I'd be scared to lose her." I stared at the ring; it sparkled in the morning light.

"Imagine being Pen. Maddox only wanted to be with her because he was scared that his parents wouldn't give him the power he wanted."

My eyes snapped up to Sloan. My molars ground together for a moment. Maddox and I were *nothing* alike. "I love her."

Maddox never did. Not like I do.

"I know," Sloan defended gently, putting a stabilizing hand on my shoulder. "But now, to be faced with a man who might be making a knee-jerk decision because he's scared of something else—as valid as the fear of losing her is, Xan—if it were me, I might wonder what happens when you're not scared anymore. Will you still want to be in Singapore? Will you still want all the things you say you want now?"

I huffed, frustrated. She was right. "So, what do I do?"

I was trying to give Penelope what she wanted. But how did I know I wasn't scared to lose her more than anything else? Because right now I was fucking terrified.

With a few extended beats of silence, I looked at Sloan, who pursed her lips in thought.

"Well, how do you face a fear?" Sloan asked but didn't wait for me to answer. "Head-on, right? Scared of flying, travel around the world. Scared of water, jump into the deep end."

My brows rose. "Remind me to tell Marcus that *he* should be the one to teach my nieces and nephews to swim."

"Humor to avoid a difficult conversation. Classic Xan." She rolled her shoulders back, showing uncharacteristic patience. "Look around. You're living your fear. She's gone. She may not ever come back. She could live there, you'd be here, she meets someo—"

Pain sliced through my chest.

"Sloan!" I snapped, closing my eyes as if that might help my mind to not picture all of that. What the hell was her point in reminding me of the fact that Penelope was gone?

"My point is, you're dealing with it." She gave me a reassuring squeeze on my shoulder. "Much better than you have in the past. I've seen you fall apart, Xan."

"I know." I looked down at the countertop. I knew how much she'd done to keep me together over the years.

Sloan yanked my chin to look at her. "And here you are. In one piece, putting one foot in front of the other. Proof that if your worst fear comes to fruition, you'll be okay."

"Yeah . . ."

"If all of that did happen. If you two end it. And one day she came back and asked you to put yourself through it again. Would you?"

Months ago, I was terrified at the thought of losing her because I knew that pain would be unbearable—sitting here without her proved it was—so I held on tighter to avoid that hurt. But feeling it now made me even more sure that I'd deal with it a thousand more times if it meant making her happy. "Yes."

"Why?" she asked quickly.

"Because I love her." I answered just as fast, realizing exactly where this questioning was supposed to lead me. I dropped my head with a short, exhausted chuckle. "So much more than I'm afraid to lose her."

A bright smile swept across her face. "I'm proud of you."

I was a little proud of myself, too.

A surge of emotion welled in the back of my throat. God, I wanted to see Penelope. Hold her. Tell her that nothing could compete with how much I loved her. Not fear, not hurt, not the comfort of home. Nothing.

"And if it helps"—Sloan pushed her shoulder against mine, pulling my mom's ring out of my hands to examine it—"I think this ring is proof that when you love people, you never really lose them. It'll work out, don't worry."

"Yeah?" I cleared my throat. "How can you be so sure?"

"Well, I think what happened that day when Penelope put this on was divine intervention." Sloan handed the ring back to me. "Lily must have known it was Pen."

I choked out a laugh. There wasn't a person in the world who was less religious than Sloan. But she summoned spirituality when trying to drive home a point.

"That or you did." I blinked away mistiness in my eyes.

I often found myself going over that day in Penelope's foyer, the one where we got engaged, accidently. It didn't add up.

Sloan never let anyone handle my mom's ring. My mom and Sloan were close, and Sloan treasured anything that once belonged to her, but Sloan refused to wear her ring. She never gave a reason other than that it "didn't feel right." Ever since Marcus proposed and that ring was moved from the safety of the Sutton vault a couple of times, you would think Sloan was coordinating the movement of a diamond collection, not a singular ring.

It was four modest carats compared to Sloan's engagement ring, but didn't go anywhere without an armed guard. Yet Sloan had Penelope pick it up. Then she had me go get Penelope because she and Marcus were running late.

"Why did you have Penelope pick it up?" I asked, tucking the ring back in the box.

A slow smile, one that she tried her best to stop, arched up her mouth. She looked down at the countertop. "In my defense, I thought it might spark a conversation, not a wedding."

A laugh made its way out of my chest followed by a sharp ache. The reality that my best friend wasn't going to be twenty minutes away was settling in; a growing pain I'd avoided for years. I was doing the one thing I never thought I could: I was leaving home, the only place that felt permanent. Safe.

But safety at the expense of my own happiness wasn't what it seemed. It was cowardice, and for Penelope I wanted to be brave.

Sloan stood from the seat and walked out of the kitchen. A minute later she walked back in with a large frame in her hands.

"Until we can have a new one with all of us. Pen and Selena included." Sloan sat back down and stared wistfully at the picture. The four of us at her law school graduation. "Wherever you two land, take this with you. Here, Singapore, wherever."

Saying the thing she was feeling—a necessary melancholy—without saying it, I took Sloan's sentiment for what it was.

Things were changing in a very real way now, something she

tried to get me to talk about months ago, but I did what I always did and maneuvered past it. It took years for Sloan and me to resolve the fact that we were each other's emotional crutches. Too scared to venture into a relationship for our own reasons, we hid and pretended we had everything we needed.

Falling for Marcus helped her see she didn't need her crutch anymore.

And, finally, I wasn't scared to go without mine.

I ran an arm around her shoulders and gave them a squeeze. "I'm going to miss you barging into things that don't concern you."

"You shouldn't." Sloan's voice faltered. She looked down, running her hand over her cheek, but looking back up at me with glassy eyes. Her pride wouldn't let her cry, but I knew she was about to. With a deep, shuddered breath, she went on, "I'm not going to stop doing that."

I smiled. "One foot in front of the other?"

She nodded. "Don't forget that."

How could I? It was the message written on the back of my copy. A reminder that no matter what happened, life went on.

One foot in front of the other.

"Don't become the crazy Central Park duck lady when I'm gone."

Chapter 47

PENELOPE

I never experienced autumn or winter in Singapore growing up since I spent the school year with my mother in London. Singapore in the autumn was cooler and less hazy than the summer, although it rained nearly every day.

"I can't believe this is my first time seeing your business venture." I curled my legs underneath me on the sofa as Olivia handed me a glass of wine, then one to Arabella who sat next to me.

When I arrived last night, still not having decided which home in the tower Xander purchased that I wanted, I stayed with Olivia. She was excited when I called to tell her I'd be in town for a few weeks. She was even more excited that Arabella, who'd become something of a recluse by Olivia's definition, was willing to come and spend time with us as well.

Based on what she told me when I got here, Arabella hardly ever went out these days.

"Well, I had to keep myself busy." She took a seat next to me on the couch, opposite the balcony. The doors were open, allowing the warm evening breeze to drift through the enormous penthouse.

"This makes me feel incredibly unproductive as—"

"An incredibly successful lawyer?" She rolled her eyes. "Well, look where that got you. A handsome billionaire who loves you."

Olivia's smile dropped when she noticed Arabella's uncomfortable shifting.

"Not that work is the only place to gain fulfillment," Olivia quickly corrected.

"Of course not," I added.

"No, it's nice," Arabella insisted quietly, looking up at the two of us with a wobbly smile. "Having a purpose outside of love and marriage. I'm happy for you."

"Well, you know love and marriage isn't exactly the order it went." I turned the glass in my hand.

I told them the truth about my marriage with Xander, primarily because I needed to get Arabella's blessing to give Silas an ultimatum. If Silas didn't take my offer, it would affect Chen Tech and Arabella's personal wealth. She was married into the Lau family, which would offer some financial protection. But I couldn't make her collateral damage—I had to know she'd be okay on her own.

"Either way, it seems like he's been rather perfect," Arabella said with a warm, sympathetic smile. She looked perfect herself. Her hair was neatly arranged behind a headband. Her makeup was flawlessly applied. She was wearing a conservative long-sleeved, high-collared dress even in the warmth. "The arrangement worked for you."

There was an almost longing pitch in her voice.

Of all the people in my family, the one person I knew would understand why I did what I did with Xander was Olivia. But with Arabella, I didn't know what to expect. She'd been so happy to take on the role ascribed to her that a part of me always assumed she judged me. That she thought I was selfish or stupid to choose myself rather than a seemingly perfect man in the perfect family.

But when I explained all of it, she seemed happy for me. She listened intently when I told her about my life before it flipped upside down a few months ago. She seemed almost yearning for something similar.

"It worked for now." I sighed. "He's at home, figuring things out. Home has always been one place for him."

"If he's a smart man, he'll chase you around the world if he has to," Olivia pointed out.

I smiled.

I knew Xander would do that—chase me around the world. It was the crux of the issue. He wanted to do whatever *I* wanted; he needed to do whatever would make him happy, not simply placate his fear. Even if it meant he would hurt awhile first.

"Yes, well." I took a deep breath, blinking away the mistiness in my eyes every time I thought about Xander, missing him so viscerally it ached in my bones. "First things first, Silas."

I didn't want Arabella to end up like my mother, solely dependent on others. Watching Chen Tech fall down would be cathartic, but I couldn't do that to Arabella—not without at least discussing it with her first. I wanted her to have her own nest egg. And hopefully the plan went off without a hitch and she'd be fine, but if not, I would be here to help her find her own independence.

"I'm sorry about all he's done. I didn't know he was holding your mother's financial well-being over your head like that, Pen, truly," Arabella added.

Over the last couple of years, Silas had become increasingly volatile and controlling. Olivia considered herself lucky to have been an outsider like me; it saved her from having to deal with him. And Arabella attested to it.

"I never let you in, it's not your fault," I told her.

"Still." She looked down at her lap, twisting her fingers. "Telephones work both ways and I sort of fell into myself the last few years."

"Fell in?" I looked at Olivia, who looked just as bewildered as me.

"Mother is convinced it's just a bout of melancholy," she admitted, looking up at us for a second before her gaze fell to the floor. "All my accomplishments were wrapped up in who I married and turns out I don't really have any of my own. I sort of resented you because you had a real life."

She still looked down, but I could see her eyes becoming glassy.

I was always a bit resentful with how much love she was showered with, bitterly reminding myself that she was the daughter they wanted.

I told myself that she was fine.

Except she wasn't. Up close, I could see all the pain etched behind the illusion.

The guilt welled in my chest. "Arabella, I should have been here . . ."

"Back to the topic at hand." She looked up, sounding more assured. "Let Chen Tech fall if it has to, if he won't agree to your terms. Don't back down in some attempt to protect me. It's my own stupid fault for not achieving anything on my own."

"You're not stupid," I told her firmly.

"I am. They all made me think I was special, and I believed it. They told me I was the good one. My reward was a proper marriage and . . ." She swallowed hard again but this time the tears streamed down her cheeks without regard to her perfectly made face. "I was an idiot, and I took my anger and resentment out on you. Ignoring you and telling myself it was your fault for leaving, not my own for having nothing for myself."

"Hey. It's alright. I should have been here." I wrapped my arms around her and let her release a quiet sob into my shoulder. "I won't do it again. I promise."

She took a deep breath and ran her index finger below her lower eyelid, attempting to clean up the tiniest bit of smeared mascara. "Do what?"

"Let you feel like you're on your own, because you're not."

She smiled.

The lesson that I'd learned with Xander echoed in my mind.

"Nothing is so broken it can't be fixed." I smoothed my thumbs over the last stray tears along her cheeks. "I promise."

Chapter 48

PENELOPE

I met Silas at his house instead of his office the next day.

We walked through the marble-tiled floor to the back of the house where Silas was waiting for me in the solarium that sat nestled between towering vines crawling up the windows and lush flowers on every side.

His forehead wrinkled when I was led in. "Made a decision, have we?"

"I am sick of feeling like I've done something to deserve not having a place here," I admitted, taking a seat across from him on a tightly woven white wicker chair.

"So, you've finally decided to earn it?"

The implication set my jaw on edge. What had he ever done to be treated like a member of this family? Absolutely nothing, yet I was the target of everyone's criticism. Every decision I made was wrong.

"No, Silas." I sat down, forcing my shoulders back down, I reminded myself not to waste any more emotion here. "But I'm not here to fight."

I went over each option with Arabella, point by point. I knew what we wanted and how we'd get it. And I quietly thought to myself about how Xander's interference made the perfect way out.

"I'm giving you an option. Because you're right. I won't let the company fail," I admitted. "So, your options are to leave me alone. Leave Arabella alone and never interfere in our lives again. In turn, I will save the merger for you."

His brows shot up.

More than anything, I wanted to protect Arabella's future. Like my mother, her well-being was out of her hands and I never wanted her to feel financially trapped.

"Finally taking your place with the Xus, are you?" he questioned almost mockingly.

"Let me handle the details. All you need to do is agree." I slapped the file in front of him and he leaned in with an unsurprising excitement. He reviewed the new merger agreements, picking up a pen with some enthusiasm. Every single term was the same except for one. Instead of leaving the issue of eventual leadership open, it was written clearly in black and white. "Maddox will be the leader of the newly merged company."

Silas dropped his pen and tenuous smile.

That was the only way I was going to get Maddox on board. He could lead that branch of his family's company. It was a step down from what he truly wanted—leading the family company as a whole, but it was something that would entice him. An opportunity to stay close enough to that leadership spot that I was sure he'd find a way into it eventually.

I just needed him to agree as well.

"And option two?"

I sighed. "Let Chen Tech fail. If you continue to harass me or my friends, you can see what happens when you play outside your skill level. And probably go bankrupt in the process."

"So, your fix is to either have your family company led by someone else or let it fail?"

"Eventual leadership was always going to be up to the board.

Did you really think you'd have a chance given all you've done to Chen Tech so far?" I argued politely. I wanted to let go of all the painful feelings of resentment, not let them bleed into this conversation. I wanted to be free of it. "We both know Maddox would have done the decision-making given your . . . inaptitude for it."

The wicker seat cracked as Silas leaned into it. He crossed his arms and thought about it for a few extended seconds. "I'll need to have someone review—"

I stood up. "You have until the end of the day."

His head bobbed back like he wasn't expecting my response or firm line on the offer. "And Maddox. Xu Enterprises. They're already on board with this?"

"Leave that to me, little brother." A patronizing tone snuck in when I hadn't meant it to. I turned to leave but stopped for a moment. "And for the record, this is the last mess I am ever going to be tangled in. So much as breathe my name again, and I promise you, Silas, you will regret it."

I didn't stop to gauge his reaction.

I didn't care.

* * *

A CAFÉ ALONG the water in the Marina Bay district was where I asked Maddox to meet me. Sitting here filled me with what felt like a warm hug from the inside. The familiar sound of water slapping against the docks, sending a salty mist along the railings a few feet away made my mind run wild with all the days I could spend here.

My lips turned up in a slight smile under the warmth of the early afternoon sun. I felt like I was home.

"Does your husband know you're having lunch with me?" Maddox's voice yanked me right out of that fuzzy nostalgic feeling.

I shook my head clear for a second, but the excitement at the final step before I was free of all of the obligation ran through my muscles in an impatient buzz.

"If there is one thing my husband knows," I said, looking down at my coffee, seeing my wedding band along my finger. I smiled bittersweetly, I missed him. "It is that I love him completely. And he trusts me, completely."

I called him this morning just to double-check that my plan was okay with him and SunCorp, because I did plan to use that leverage he'd so painstakingly retrieved for me.

"Alright." He shuffled a bit in his chair, looked down at the menu, then crossed his arms. "What is this about?"

"I have a proposal for you."

"No." The answer shot out of his mouth on the heels of my words.

I looked at him, confused, but he refused to look at me.

"See." He squinted as he looked out onto the water, sunlight making the gentle waves sparkle like sheets of diamonds along the surface. "It's rather inconvenient when someone just shoots down your proposal."

"Maddox," I pleaded with an exasperated sigh. "I am not sorry for choosing my own happiness, but I am sorry for how all of this shook out. And how it affected your future."

I was.

I hated that choosing my happiness came with collateral damage, but I wasn't apologizing for it anymore.

The corners of his mouth relaxed to the point where he was almost not scowling. "Alright, then, get on with it."

"Continue the merg—"

"No," he answered just as fast. This time he turned his head to glance at me then rolled his eyes and released a heavy breath. "Be sensible, why would I continue the merger now? The only appeal was one to my parents. Now that it's not an option, why sign on to a failing company? We'll wait and simply acquire it when it's circling the drain."

I nodded and pulled out the folder with the specifics detailing release and production timelines for SunCorp's solar cell–powered extended-life batteries. The tiny ones that would fit into his gaming systems.

"What is this?" He turned completely so that his entire body was facing me and not the shoreline. He paged through the proposal.

"If you continue with the merger. With all the previous terms— our marriage excluded, obviously—you'll head the newly merged company *and* get priority when these hit the market in a few months."

He could order them all for the foreseeable future. Put out the line of new gaming systems at any scale he wanted and have no competition for years while others attempted to catch up. If he wanted an argument to bolster his claim to run the whole company one day, this would be it.

"And if I refuse," he pondered slowly, deeply entrenched in the offer.

He wasn't going to refuse.

"Well, SunCorp is owned—at least the capital behind it is—by someone I happen to love dearly. And he will do just about anything for me," I explained. "Like make sure you're the absolute last in line for this. Maybe put your competitors ahead of you. Play favorites. He does love a game."

Maddox looked up slowly from the papers, confusion grooved deep between his brows. "Was your deranged husband going to blackmail me?"

The side of my mouth couldn't help but curl upward.

All the anger and hurt from that night felt like a distant memory even though it was only a few nights ago. Proof that I was right to trust my intuition and not fly off the handle like I initially wanted to. Xander would never do anything to hurt me and it would have been ridiculous to react any more than I had in that moment.

Balanced. Trusting in myself to hear and believe the truth.

"Only if I asked him to."

His stony exterior, looking like he might yell at me at any moment, broke with a surprised boom of a laugh. "Who are you?"

"Same person, different priorities," I answered simply.

A few chuckles rolled through him and then he stopped, realized I was serious, and his upper lip curled. "Well . . . it's off-putting."

"Noted," I said sarcastically. I leaned against the wicker back, content. "Now, do we have a deal?"

"Fine." Maddox pushed his chair back and began to get up. "I'll call Silas."

He took his copies and quickly left with a polite wave. If I ever wanted assurance I was never more than a means to an end for him—that was it. Not that I cared. I was just happy to finally have some peace.

Leaving the café, I decided to walk back to Olivia's—which after walking a mile in 80 percent humidity—I realized was a terrible idea.

Just as refreshing cool air from the air-conditioning in Olivia's building whipped around me while I passed though the automatic glass doors, a text from Xander came through:

Xander: Formal request to add an item to the list:

Dinner on the roof of the Marina Sands

Saturday night

He'd given us space this week. He called only when I asked him to, texted good morning and good night and a daily "I love you."

Other than that, he was doing what I asked. Figuring it all out and proving that he could plan his life around *our* needs, not his fears.

Maybe we'd finish this year and then date like a normal couple.

Maybe we'd just pick up where we left off.

I hoped he loved me enough to accept free fall without fear. Love in all its chaos and uncertainty. I was strong enough to handle whatever came out of this.

But, God, I wanted him to be the happily-ever-after I was so sure he was.

Me: Request formally accepted

Chapter 49

XANDER

I got Penelope's text this morning and texted Sloan to get a few plans in motion since I was busy packing for at least a few months.

Just as I finished getting a final bag packed—because I planned to go there for as long as she wanted to be there—I heard a couple of voices bounce off the walls in the grand foyer.

I walked out of the bedroom and toward them.

I'd planned to meet Penelope in Singapore this week and she'd seemed lighter in the short conversations we'd had. I was giving her time and space not just to prove that I could but also to remind myself that I loved her way too fucking much to ever let her feel like I was trying to control any part of her life. It was never my intention but that was what I got stuck on all week.

"You can't hold on that tight or you put me in the same position I've been in my entire life."

No matter how well-intentioned, I could never make her feel that way again.

And if there was ever a day she needed me to let her go, I would. I prayed there wouldn't be. That I'd always be able to make her happy, but at the end of the day all that mattered was that she was happy.

Because that was love, and true love was fearless.

"See, he is planning something," Marcus told Henry and pointed to the bags as they walked in. They looked up at me as I came down the central staircase. "You okay?"

I nodded. "Yeah."

I *was* doing okay. Not great. But okay.

Over the last week, everyone found a reason to check on me. For the first time in a long time, I didn't feel any shame in it. No bombardment of memories that made me feel guilty for needing them. It was what family did and what we'd continue to do.

I tried to get my mind off of things with poker, occasionally. I even tried that pottery wheel Penelope used at the club that we'd planned to do together before all of this. I was really bad at it.

We stood there for a beat when I got down the stairs and to them in the foyer. I waited to hear whatever explanation they had to "drop by" today.

This was Henry and Marcus's third visit.

The first one was hours after Sloan. The second was an insistence on boxing at the club, which made no sense to me because I didn't find any joy in beating the shit out of a friend like they seemed to.

"Are you going to ask?" Henry wondered to Marcus as they both wandered around the foyer.

"It was your question," Marcus quipped back.

"It was only my question because you won't shut up about it," Henry defended.

They had a tendency of doing that—carrying on a full conversation between themselves while in another one.

"I hate to interrupt the gossip." I pinched the bridge of my nose. "But what do you want to know?"

"You're going to go to her, right?" Henry asked bluntly. "*Move* to Singapore, grand gesture, you know—happily ever after."

An annoying side effect of Marcus and Henry being close for so long was that now I had *two* overprotective big brothers.

"You two are getting a little overly involved," I stated wryly. "It reeks of Sloan."

"Us? Overly involved?" Henry glided past the comparison and looked at Marcus. "Hey, Marcus," he said with faux curiosity. "How did that invitation for the alumni gala a couple years ago end up on your desk?"

I saw where Henry was going with this. It was me.

Two years ago, Sloan was the host of our alma mater's annual alumni gala. All the invitations were sent out with Sloan's name and signature, including Marcus's, which went to Sutton Industries. He'd been gone for two years by that point, and he needed to come home, so I made sure it didn't go to the Manhattan office, rather the London one. Where I was sure he would see it. If he thought Sloan was the one who sent it, I had a feeling he'd come back for the event. Sloan missed him and it was obvious how much it hurt her that he was gone. I figured seeing her again might finally be the kick my brother needed to pursue her.

And I was right.

He came home and months later he and Sloan finally got together. And the rest was history.

"I don't know, Henry." Marcus played along, wrinkling his nose. "Who convinced Selena to try out the arts facilities at the Augustus to help her feel more comfortable there?"

That was me, too.

"Point taken," I conceded.

Born out of a fear of losing someone, I tried to play in the background to push things in the right direction. To keep us together.

"And, yeah, I'm going to Singapore," I answered.

I didn't need to fix things, make them perfect so that everything would go as planned. I couldn't control what happened to us. But, as long as I had Penelope with me, none of that held the same power it used to.

Henry slapped a supportive hand on my shoulder with a reassuring squeeze. "Look at that, all grown-up."

This last week proved that I could go through the ringer and make it through unscathed. Relatively unscathed. I would always be a little scared to lose the people I loved; it was natural, but not so much so that the fear drove my decisions or my actions.

"Oh yeah? Like when Henry Amari went from walking red flag to lovesick puppy?" I retorted back.

"I won't miss the snark," Henry countered flatly. "And yes, exactly like that. You know when Selena was thinking about moving back to LA, I had my assistant start getting the process ready for me to head Amari Global from there."

It was Henry's way of saying that the stability that all of our collective meddling made was an illusion and we had to plan our lives for change.

"What?" Marcus asked, face scrunched looking at Henry. Clearly offended. "You didn't tell me that."

"Oh, I'm sorry, should I have told you I was considering it?" Henry crossed his arms and cocked his head. "When you were a virtual ghost for two years?"

I smiled at their bickering, and a little ache moved through my chest wondering if or when I'd be back here with enough frequency to catch it again.

Growing pains.

Marcus's serious facade cracked with a chuckle.

He looked at me, ignoring Henry.

"Mom and Dad lived in France for years before coming back here," Marcus reminded me.

"And they were happy," I added. My parents, after college, moved to France for my mom to study literature. My dad worked and they only came back to the States when he decided on medical school. They were never the "play it safe" types.

They had a love that was fearless.

And, finally, so did I.

I smiled, realizing why Henry and Marcus stopped by today. To be sounding boards, reassurance that everything would be okay. Tell me all the ways that this was the right move.

"They'd be proud of you," Marcus said with a deep inhale. He glanced around the open foyer at all the many photographs that filled the walls.

I let a silent moment pass.

"If I'm there for the long haul, or somewhere . . . you're going to visit, right?" I asked, not expecting the dip in my voice.

The one that made Henry's high-society stoicism falter.

"Obviously," Henry barked out, then mumbled something about me being an idiot for even asking under his breath.

"It's cute that you think Sloan would give us a choice," Marcus deadpanned.

I laughed.

Not because it was funny, Marcus was never really all that funny, but because he was different. A good different. The less-serious version of himself I hadn't seen in years; a version I chalked up to Sloan's influence.

Everything had changed.

We'd all moved on, forward.

And nothing about that scared me.

Chapter 50

PENELOPE

That Saturday, I looked at my hand as I entered the elevator at the lobby of the Marina Sands hotel. It looked different without the engagement ring next to the wedding band. Lonely.

The last couple of days with Olivia and Arabella were stressful, but that time did also help me solidify that I wanted to stay. For a while at least. Maybe one day in a few months or a few years, I would be ready to leave. But not just yet.

I spent the entire time getting ready and going to the Marina Sands in a state of anxious excitement. I adjusted my dress again, the canary yellow silk with an elaborately beaded collar fell perfectly against my skin. And because I knew it would drive him a little crazy, it was completely backless.

I went over all the iterations tonight could be. Maybe he wanted to start over together, without the pressure of marriage. It would be prudent and sensible. I wasn't rushing toward a happily-ever-after. I wanted happy.

And while I still didn't know *where* happy was, I knew *who* it was.

The loud ding from the elevator as it completed its journey pushed me out of my head and into the present.

A warm, humid breeze filled the elevator as the doors opened to the rooftop. The expansive outdoor bar was empty, but the space was punctuated with high-tops and nothing else. Not a soul around.

My eyes stopped when they found him, standing in front of the door that led into the rooftop restaurant. His alluring smile pulled me forward.

My next few steps felt like I was walking on mud. They were unsteady and hurried until I was in front of him.

"Hi, Poppy." He smiled, so devilishly handsome I had to resist the urge to pull him in and kiss him right there.

I ran my hands down the dress. "Hello, darling."

"You look . . ." His voice lowered, the heat of his stare warmed every inch of my skin.

"You've given it thought?" I couldn't help myself. We could have sat for a nice dinner or at least entered the room, but I couldn't wait.

"You were right." He reached out and ran a few fingers through my hair. A delightful burst of sparks ran down the back of my ear and along my neck. "I was scared and my initial reaction was knee-jerk to hold on to you. But I spent the week realizing I did need some time."

My heart wobbled in my chest, nervous for what came next, but his gentle fingers ran along my skin reassuringly.

"Not because I need more than a second to know you're the one. My one. I realized something. Every person that came into my life and every single one that left it was a lesson. I thought it was that I had to hold on tight or I'd lose the person I loved. But it was actually a lesson in resilience. All so when this moment came, I wouldn't mess it up."

Every butterfly in my stomach took flight. I felt weightless.

"What if in six months, it's not Singapore anymore?" I blurted, anxiety pushing the words out of my mouth, second-guessing— old habits died hard.

"Here or Manhattan or Tokyo or Bali or wherever the hell you want to go. Take me with you, or have adventures on your own and then come back to me." His hands slid along my hips and pulled me close. "And not because I'm afraid to lose you—because I *want* to be with you, however you'll have me. My heart is yours. Whether it is perfectly intact or riddled with cracks. So do your worst. Break whatever you want. I'm not scared; I can take it." He leaned his head against mine. "I dare you."

My throat clogged with emotion. The tears pushed against the backs of my eyes, but with a deep inhale I kept most at bay.

"This isn't a game," I quipped, trying and failing to lift the heavy weight and get a handle on all the tears that streaked through my makeup.

"No, it's not, because I've already won," he whispered. His thumb pushed away a few of the stray tears.

The words throbbed in my ears. A quiet sob racked my bones. "You're sure?"

His hand moved over my cheek and my head tilted back. Time stilled, the vast expanse filled with the meaning of all of it. A new life for both of us. He slowly pressed his lips over mine and pulled me into a soft kiss.

Like the one after the conservancy gala: lazy and slow. A gentle passage to what we'd become so familiar with. It had only been a week, yet I missed the taste of him. Rich and sensuous. Sweet and strong.

I missed it all. The warmth of his breath mingled in mine. His velvet touch when his deep longing revealed itself. With a soft moan, I deepened the kiss and pulled him closer. The desire finding new urgency as the world faded away and all I could feel, hear, breathe, was him.

A slow groan rumbled up his chest. His hands splayed over my bare back, finding the hem of the dress, and his fingers traced up and down it.

Teasing.

"You cannot rip this before dinner," I whispered as he pulled away slowly.

"I won't." He laid a final peck on my lips. He pushed away a few final tears with his thumbs. "Not before dinner, anyway."

He didn't move. We stayed in that suspended moment. The soft breeze, the traffic below, and the faint sounds of the ocean began to reemerge.

"Shouldn't we go in?" I whispered.

He cocked his head to the side and the corner of his mouth tipped up.

"In a second." He looked up in thought or like he was listening for something. I tried to listen more carefully; I could hear faint hushed whispers and a few chairs moving.

"Xander . . ."

"I realized something else. When you took off the ring." His hands moved down my body to clasp mine. He slowly knelt down as he pulled a familiar box from his pocket. "I never *actually* proposed."

My heart tumbled. A tremble moved through my entire body as I realized what he was doing. "Xander . . ."

"Not that I don't love what happened at your house that day, but we need a proposal story for the spreadsheet." He knocked three times on the doors. "A real one."

Before I could say anything, the doors opened to a long table. Seated around it was everyone. Our entire group of friends: our family. An encouraging look from Sloan and CeCe. A quiet chuckle from Tristan. A rare smile from Rohan. Everyone was there: Henry, Selena, Marcus, Jackson; Olivia and Arabella, too.

Every word got tangled in my chest. "How did they? When . . ."

The tears pushed through and streaked down my face.

"They're a little louder and less easy to control. Definitely wouldn't sit still for a painting." He glanced over to them then looked back to me. "Our version of a Norman Rockwell."

The trembles gave way to a quiet sob.

"Lots of things are going to change, but them? We're stuck with them because when you love people, you can't *really* lose them."

I hiccupped a laugh. "Good."

"And you're stuck with me. All I want is to spend the rest of my life without a plan, figuring it out as we go." He began opening the ring box. My ring sat inside, waiting for me. "Penelope Kath—"

"Yes." I pushed my shaking hand a millimeter closer to the ring.

His head dropped with a corresponding laugh that was short and shaky. A moment later, he lifted it again. "You have to let me ask you at least *once*, Poppy."

I nodded.

"Penelope Katherine Chen-Astor, will you marry me?"

"Yes."

In a flash my ring was back on my finger and he stood, wrapping me in his arms and pulling me back into another kiss. The sound of claps and cheers went from loud to muffled. Another kiss that I could melt into. In the arms of the man that flipped every notion I had about myself on its head and changed my entire world in the process.

We pulled away; the sounds of the room began to slowly bleed back into my senses.

"You forgot Sutton," I playfully corrected him.

The serenity I always found in his eyes was accompanied by something else. I could see an entire life for us in them. "Penelope Katherine Chen-Astor-Sutton."

I yanked on his lapels to bring his lips to mine. "Much better."

Chapter 51

XANDER

Once everyone left to head back to Manhattan, Penelope and I spent some time getting settled into our lives in Singapore.

Since I was a founder at Dawn Capital, working from Singapore was a pretty easy sell. Especially since the people I had to convince didn't need any convincing. CeCe had arranged for all the things I needed for work to get shipped before she even left for the proposal. And the partners at Penelope's firm were already preparing for her to be remote from Singapore, regardless.

After a few weeks, everything was settled in Singapore with Chen Tech and our new penthouse, so we flew to Manhattan to spend Christmas with Sloan and everyone there. I think Penelope was a little nervous to deviate from that tradition even though I told her Christmas in Singapore sounded just as good.

Either way, after a raucous Christmas at my childhood home in the suburbs outside of Philadelphia, we flew to Scotland while the few necessities we wanted moved to Singapore were flown over and organized in our new home.

"Now, once the shares transfer this summer, these highlighted accounts will have a small portion that's been liquidated. That's your way to keep up with expenses." Penelope sat patiently next to her mom at the sturdy wooden kitchen table, weathered and worn from years of use. "The rest of the shares are in your name and will be managed by Dawn Capital. Anything you need, you can draw from your liquid assets in your bank accounts."

I turned the mug in my hand and leaned against the stone archway that opened up to the kitchen.

An hour north of Glasgow, Victoria Astor lived quietly among sprawling hills in an old stone manor that the Astor family owned for generations. She had a small staff because it was becoming abundantly clear to me that she had no idea how to run her own life, let alone an entire estate. It seemed like she enjoyed the life but not anything that came along with managing it.

"Can't you do this for me, dearest?" her mother complained, running her fingers through her auburn hair as Penelope gently tried to get her to sign the paperwork. "You know I abhor these types of things."

Victoria was used to Penelope taking care of everything. Now that Penelope had arranged for her mom to have a manager to keep an eye on her investments, Victoria could finally take some responsibility on her own. Knowing her mother, Penelope set some checks in the process so Victoria couldn't do anything outlandish with her wealth since the shares in Astor Media were worth around two-hundred million pounds.

"I know, Mother, but you have to get used to doing some of it on your own," Penelope cooed softly, introducing Victoria to a life where her daughter wasn't the one who had to do everything for her. One where Penelope was able to free herself from some of that responsibility. "I've hired an executor for the estate. They'll take care of most things. Any questions can go to them, and if you're nervous you can always ask me."

"Or me," I interjected as I peeled myself off the wall and took a seat next to Penelope. "I'll take care of anything you need."

It wasn't just an offer because I happened to be a banker and running the capital firm she'd store the investments in, but I was tired of having to see Penelope be the one run ragged doing everything.

A smile stretched across Victoria's face. "Well, alright, then."

The pen scrawled across the last line that Penelope flagged for her mom to sign.

It was a little unsettling, seeing how much Penelope had been responsible for. She was her mom's personal secretary from the day she could read.

Penelope leaned her head on my shoulder for a fleeting moment, before popping back up and stacking the papers neatly together. "I'll send these off first thing tomorrow."

She stood up and walked out of the kitchen, leaving me and Victoria alone at the table.

"My Penelope seems different." Victoria turned her head, watching Penelope leave the room to put the papers in a folder. "Happy."

"If ever she's not"—I looked her in the eye—"I'll fix it. I'll take care of her; you don't have to worry."

She smiled proudly. She took the book at the end of the table and opened it to a bookmarked page and began reading. "I never worry. Nobody *needs* to take care of my Penelope."

No, but someone *should.*

And from here on out, it was me. I was going to do everything in my power to pull things off that never-ending list in her head.

I didn't say anything. I only nodded.

A few quiet minutes later, Penelope returned to the table, but Victoria's attention was squarely in a book by that point.

With an almost silent sigh she sat down at the table.

"Are you okay?" I asked.

With another deep breath she nodded and leaned into me. "Why do I feel like I just ran a marathon?"

"You work too hard, dearest," Victoria said offhandedly, her attention still in the book.

Ignoring the urge to point out that maybe she was the reason Penelope always seemed to run at 150 percent, I kissed Penelope on her head.

"You'll have some time to relax soon," I whispered.

She sat up, an excited twinkle in her eye. "A surprise?"

"Something like that."

* * *

PENELOPE

WHEN WE LANDED in the Faroe Islands the day after I took care of all of my mother's financial paperwork, I had a feeling about what he was up to.

Now, walking into the cabin that was a remote home with multiple one-way glass domes, I was sure of it.

The aurora. The last item on the list.

Xander led me inside. The glass dome at the end of the room granted us an uninterrupted panoramic view of the Arctic wilderness that lay beyond. Spread as far as the eye could see, it was a pristine portrait of crisp white beneath the muted glow of the twilight sky.

"How long until we can see them?" I asked, taking the coffee from the attendant that greeted us when we got off the all-terrain truck.

He chuckled. "How'd you know?"

"Remote islands in the north Atlantic during the winter. Far off from light pollution." I flicked a glance over my shoulder as he helped me out of my parka. "You're really not that clever."

He chuckled again.

"We should be able to see them in half an hour." He handed the coats off to the other attendants as they made their final touches and put away our luggage.

Inside the cabin, the large domes were the focal points, but the ambient light cast a soft, golden hue across the room. The warmth of the wooden furnishings juxtaposed the frozen canvas just beyond the glass.

"How will we pass the time?" I sat on one of the plush blankets.

The blankets and fur adorned the comfortable seating area, inviting us to sink into their embrace.

Xander took a glance over his shoulder, offering a quick thank-you to the staff as they left the cabin. He took a seat beside me and whispered, "I can think of a few things."

His breath just barely grazed along my shoulder; an eruption of goose bumps pebbled along my skin.

"But I want to give you something first." He reached behind the couch and pulled something from the bag he'd deposited there.

I leaned forward and put the coffee on the beveled wood table ahead of us.

He handed me a stack of papers.

A realization pushed forward as I glanced over the blank cover page. The date on our divorce papers was approaching in a few months and it was something I'd completely forgotten about. My heart rate picked up.

"I had Sloan send these." Xander's hand gripped my thigh gently, as if reading my thoughts. "And all we need to do to nullify them is sign on the flagged lines."

I paged through the same papers I signed months ago. Seeing

the addendum Sloan and Maya had added. One to nullify the divorce clause and keep us married—for good.

"You think of everything, don't you?" I whispered.

A tremor moved along my body. His arm moved from my thigh to my shoulders, and he shifted to allow me to lean into him.

All the competing interests, the compromises, all of it was silent. Xander gave me the one thing nobody else ever had.

Peace.

And he kept giving it to me. A mind clear from clutter. Anyplace he could pull an item from it, he would.

"I didn't want you to have to worry about this later," he answered.

I signed my set and Xander signed his. Before I could neatly stack the papers and tuck them away, he took them and leaned back to return them to his bag.

"I love you," I told him, leaning back into him.

"I love you, too." He pressed a kiss against my head, pulled a blanket up around us, and turned his attention up at the night sky. The darkness had fully blanketed it by that point.

Every star was visible, an array of diamonds along a silky onyx horizon. It wasn't long before the first flashes of the aurora came into view.

The occasional silhouettes of distant mountains were only visible in fleeting moments between the dancing greens and yellows.

"Nothing on that list is safe," he whispered in her ear.

"You've just crossed off the final item, darling."

"Don't worry. I'll think of some more."

Chapter 52

PENELOPE

A couple of months after returning from our trips to the States, Scotland, and Denmark, we'd settled into a new routine in Singapore. Xander took absolutely no time to make friends. We'd joined a social club here and it wasn't long before he knew more people in Singapore than I did.

It was a relief. He might not have liked change, but Xander was more adaptable than he gave himself credit for.

His easy grace with strangers abated the occasional guilt when I recollected how happy we all were over the winter holidays.

"You still don't like raspberries?" I questioned. I watched from my seat at our intimate two-person table as Arabella's face fell when the tiny chocolate tarte she ordered was placed in front of her.

Weekly lunches with Arabella helped remind me of everything I had here. The part of my heart that felt cracked healed as my sister and I found our footing again.

"No, I like them, but why would you put fruit in a dessert?" Her upper lip curled a bit as she took the back of her spoon and pushed the raspberry compote off the top, careful not to disturb the mousse. "It ruins the fruit, and it ruins the dessert."

"Then why order it?" I took a spoonful of ice cream that I ordered for that exact reason.

"Habit. It's sophisticated." She shrugged, looking at my dessert wistfully. I pushed it to the center of the table, and she sank a spoon into it. "James was always a little judgmental when I ordered something that wasn't dainty."

"Speaking of James . . ." I said quietly. After we returned from the holidays away, I began to see a clearer picture of Arabella's relationship with James.

Things like finding out that he was controlling and often discouraged her independence, making her feel isolated and like she was unworthy of pursuing ventures that might make her feel fulfilled outside of homemaking.

"I'm going ahead with it." Arabella nodded, stirring her spoon around the tea. "The divorce."

I tried not to interject my own bias. I tried to help her make the decision she wanted. But even so, I felt like I could cry with relief. "I'm proud of you."

Her cheeks lifted.

There were a couple of our weekly lunches that bled into dinner when Arabella would weigh her options over hours of conversation. She begged me to not speak a word to anyone. She'd told me that she wasn't in physical danger, but I had trouble feeling like she was safe when they were in the same house.

"This calls for champagne." I politely motioned to our waiter.

A loud, nasaled laugh squeaked out of my sister. The same one from when we were girls. "It's a little early for that, besides, that's not all."

I still ordered the champagne. I was at least celebrating. "It's not?"

She shook her head. "I was chatting with your friend CeCe while she was here back in November. She worked at *Vogue* and planned a lot of events there."

I nodded. Before CeCe abruptly left *Vogue* she did quite a bit in terms of getting the right people at the right parties for them.

"And then after I decided to go ahead with the divorce, I started thinking about what I wanted." Arabella looked down at her lap, twisting the napkin. "And you inspired me to take a chance."

My heart squeezed a bit. The knowledge that this relationship could have been one we had for years stung, but it was quickly washed away by the hopeful smile on Arabella's face.

"Did I?"

She nodded. "It turns out that *Vogue* has an opening in their event management team. I've planned a million parties."

"Arabella . . ." The pieces slowly fell into place.

"I've never left home for anything past vacations. And I was always so jealous of that life you had. Glittering and glamorous in Manhattan." She chewed on her lower lip.

My mouth hung open just slightly.

"Are you . . ." An almost delirious fog began to clear. "Moving?"

"I know you planned to stay in Singapore awhile . . ." She straightened in her seat. "And I know you stayed here for me."

"Not just you." I reached across the table for her free hand. She was a part of it. Of course, she was. In the last four months, we'd done more to repair our relationship than we had in years. I was happy we stayed. "For me, too."

"Really? Because I've never really been on my own. I could use a big sister's advice from time to time." She smiled nervously. "Maybe we can test that good nature your husband has, and you can go back with me? I'm sure Liv would understand and visit."

"Xander will probably be open to the idea," I assured her. My entire chest lightened at the prospect of going back, before the reality of what else that meant settled in. "And James?"

Divorces, especially international ones, took time.

"I'll have the lawyers serve him the papers once I'm in Manhattan." An inflection curved the last few words upward.

As both a lawyer and product of an international divorce, I was well aware of just how hard that would be. "That's going to be messy."

"You have no idea," she mumbled quietly to herself. A silent moment passed, and she looked at me with conviction. "I can't stay."

"Well, this time, I'll be with you every step of the way."

I'd have to settle another move with the firm. But they were amenable to a remote setup before, and I had a feeling once Sloan found out I planned to move back, she'd move heaven and earth with the rest of the partners to make sure it happened.

Chapter 53

XANDER

Sloan and Marcus's wedding celebrations took place over the first week of June. Just in time for the start of summer.

After five days of celebrations—a *mehndi*, a *sangeet*, a *Vidhi*, and a few dinners sprinkled in between—that stretched from the Hamptons to the Amari country house, back to Manhattan, Sloan was exhausted.

She'd fallen asleep twice while getting ready for the final ceremony this morning: the wedding.

My phone buzzed inside my tux's jacket pocket, but I ignored it as I opened the door to Sloan's dressing room.

"You're supposed to be sitting." I walked in to see Sloan pacing back and forth.

"I can't sit still. I'm excited." The scent of jasmine and sandalwood wafted past her as she walked. "I'm getting married, Xan."

"I know." I chuckled. A few more buzzes in my pocket in rapid succession reminded me that she needed to take a breather. "You're supposed to be sitting."

Marcus, who was normally a little extra cautious when it came to Sloan's safety, was a menace. He and Henry both were. I got calls or texts every hour or so when the happy couple wasn't in the same room together asking how she was, if she'd eaten, if she was tired.

"Pregnant women run marathons," Sloan pointed out.

I rolled my eyes at the comparison. Sloan once signed up for a 5K. It ended with her vomit on my shoes and sitting on a curb a quarter of the way through, eating doughnuts.

"You threw up in the first half of the Alumni 5K." I pointed to the tufted chaise. "What's your point?"

"I'm just saying," she groaned. I helped her onto the chaise, careful with the ornate *lehenga* skirt so the hand-stitched gems didn't catch on the fabric. "You don't need to treat me like I'm made of glass."

Sloan was pregnant.

It was very early on. When we landed in Manhattan a week ago, before all the festivities began, they told me, Henry, Selena, and Penelope.

"I know you're fine." I pulled the ottoman to the side of the chaise and sat on it. "But to appease your crazy soon-to-be husband, just relax for five minutes and I'll tell him you were napping this whole time."

"Thanks, Xan." She closed her eyes. "Oh, by the way—"

"I said relax," I repeated, exasperated.

"I can't do that." She gestured directionless with her hands; eyes still closed. "Have you talked to Pen yet?"

I ran a hand down my face. At least she was sitting. "About?"

"Oh, you haven't." She opened one eye, smiled smugly, and closed it.

We didn't really keep important secrets, so I knew this had to be silly or a surprise. "Does it have anything to do with what you and Penelope have been giggling about without me?"

Sloan, Selena, and Penelope kept sneaking off and talking amongst themselves. I didn't know what they were planning but I hated being left out of it. More than that, I wasn't prepared for how much it bothered me when Penelope had secrets, even silly ones, with anyone else.

"Jealous, Xan? Don't worry, she still likes you."

"She loves me," I corrected. "And you're deflecting. What's going on?"

"Ask your wife," she insisted.

"No, I'm asking you." I gave her a hard stare, but she didn't break.

Instead, she crossed her arms defiantly.

"Would you mind getting me a little snack? The baby is hungry." She said it with a haughty look, knowing it would work.

"Does that work on Marcus?"

"Every time." She grinned. "If you don't want to get something to eat for your *niece*, I can always ask Uncle Henry . . ."

She grinned even wider when I stood up.

"This conversation isn't over."

"Okay but have it with your wife." She shooed me out of the room.

"And *jalebi* please!" she shouted as the door closed behind me.

* * *

PERCHED BETWEEN THE soaring tower that was Rockefeller Center, historic St. Patrick's Cathedral, and a number of Manhattan landmarks, the lofted rooftop venue Sloan had chosen for the reception was picturesque.

High-top tables lined a sparkling reflective pool and fountain. Grass spread alongside a granite path with small plants and greenery punctuating the outdoor oasis. The views from all angles were of the stunning city on all sides.

My eyes found Penelope in a second, leaning her arms against the decorated balcony, she looked out at the city. The warm summer night's breeze swept along her deep green *lehenga*.

"There you are." I bracketed my hands against the balcony on either side of her.

After the two ceremonies, and cocktail hour, the reception was in full swing. As predicted, Sloan and Marcus were nowhere to be found and I wasn't about to go looking.

"Beautiful, isn't it?"

It was. The rooftop garden was lush and perfectly manicured, if it weren't for the soaring buildings that stretched up in all directions, you'd forget you were in Manhattan. It was a reprieve from the reception inside.

"You know we should probably plan ours." I wrapped my arms around her bare waist.

There was a serene calm being out here, not just because the entire building and the surrounding ones were closed and emptied to ensure privacy, but being back in this city was always wonderful.

"Our what?" She leaned back but turned her head to me.

"Wedding."

It was almost a year since the one we had on the beach in the Hamptons.

"We had our wedding, darling." A wistful look swept across her face. She took a deep, contented sigh. "I don't want another story."

I didn't either. Our wedding was a lie that ended up becoming the truth. But Arabella and Olivia missed it. Her mom did, too. I didn't want her to look back on that day with any regrets.

"Not a new story." I pressed a kiss against her hair. "A rewrite. I think a few characters were missing."

She laughed, shook her head, and turned in my arms. "Olivia and Bella will be around for the next chapters. But that day . . . it's perfect."

"You're sure?"

She nodded and looked down at her ring. "Besides, you're never getting this ring off my finger again."

"Trust me, Poppy." My thumbs stroked circles on her hips. "It's not what I like taking off of you."

She ran her teeth over her bottom lip, and I started thinking of all the rooms we could sneak off to for a little while.

"I know that look." Penelope's voice dropped to a warning. "The Mishra design team hand-stitched every single gem on this dress. You cannot rip it."

"I'll be gentle." I brushed a kiss against her lips. She eased slightly, leaning forward into me.

"Only with the dress," she negotiated.

"Deal." I leaned in. "If you tell me what you, Sloan, and Selena have been giggling about the last week."

Not knowing something about her bothered me more than I liked to admit.

She straightened, pressing her lips together, but the corners of her mouth tipped up.

"Seriously, what is going on?" I wrapped my arms around her waist tightly.

"I'm sorry, darling, I was trying to make sure I had all my *ducks* in a row before I asked you something." She grinned.

"And that something is?"

"Well . . . we were talking about Sloan's Park Avenue town house." She casually threw her arms over my shoulders. The moonlight glinted through her eyes. "Since she moved out two years ago it's been empty, and Arabella would love it. Lots of shopping and fun close by for her to make friends."

"Penelope . . ." My pulse ticked up.

"With her divorce, she wants a new start. And she's chosen Manhattan for it." Penelope ran her teeth over her lip again, this time she looked a little nervous. "What would you say to another city?"

My heart leapt. I was happy anywhere she was, but I would be the first to admit I missed it here.

"It's a good thing we didn't pack up the whole penthouse," I teased.

"I warned you. And you said it yourself: I have no plan."

I smiled. "Nope. Just a spreadsheet and an engagement ring."

"So, then . . ." She shifted her weight between her legs. "Is that okay? Moving back?"

"I'll follow you to every corner of the world. You know that."

"Then, ask me the question." Her arms slid down my shoulders, resting on my chest. A hopeful timbre squeaked through.

"Which question?"

She scrunched her nose and yanked on my lapels. "You know the one."

I chuckled. "Where are we going, Poppy?"

She looked up at me with a grin that still filled my entire chest with warmth; excitement sparkled in her eyes. She gazed out at the Manhattan skyline, blanketed in darkness but lit up in all its glory, muted only by her blinding light. "Home."

Epilogue

PENELOPE

One Year Later

Anchored along rolling hills by sweeping stone walls, the Amari Castle in the French mountains looked like it was plucked from a fairy tale. Ivy vines, lush and green, climbed up the exterior, while the soaring ceiling and archways stood in grandeur inside.

I walked briskly through a long corridor, glancing out the large windows along the way. Outside, just in front of the acres of vineyard vines, the ceremony was being arranged. The elaborate altar sat prominently in front of carefully arranged rows of seating.

I continued on, knowing the groom was nervous. And it was rather adorable.

"Is she okay?" Henry turned immediately at the creaky wooden door to the room in the castle that the wedding coordinator designated as the groom's holding area.

Sloan, Xander, Marcus, and I all congregated in the room while we waited for the ceremony to begin. The other three played with baby Meera rather than helping the groom remain calm and I felt a little bad for Henry.

"She's perfectly well," I answered.

Henry seemed nervous but not about getting married. More so about how Selena was doing.

"Yeah?" He remained tense, but the lines along his forehead disappeared.

I nodded and Xander crossed the room to me, closing the door as I stepped further inside.

"Feeling any better?" Xander asked me. His voice—deep and strong when it was serious—always sent a delightful shudder down my spine.

He ran his hand along my belly. Now well into my second trimester, the telltale curve at just the right spot along my dress gave me away. That or the fact that Xander's hand was permanently affixed to my stomach whenever he was within arm's reach.

"Yes, I just needed some fresh air," I excused loudly for everyone to hear because the entire family began to get just as overly protective when they heard that we were expecting. "And a walk. It's a lovely day."

A warm summer wedding along the slopes of the Vosges Mountains was both picturesque and a great place to settle some of the lingering nausea.

"Henry, if Selena didn't run away when Mom encouraged her to start on the Amari heir at any time," Sloan said from her seat beside her husband on the chaise along the wall. She looked down at her daughter, Meera, fussing quietly in a bassinet. "She's not running away now."

Marcus chuckled. The two were completely and utterly enamored with their three-month-old, rightfully so, it was almost impossible to get a straight conversation out of either.

"And over the mountains would be the hardest way to do it," Marcus added, picking up a temperamental Meera, who immediately calmed in her father's arms. He rocked her gently. "If she really wanted to run away, she'd have done it at the prewedding events in Paris last week."

Henry's unsure look went back to me, apparently the only member of the family who was here to make him feel better.

"Selena is practically giddy," I assured him, walking over to the bar cart and handing him the glass he hadn't touched. Selena was a vision in her lace wedding dress, not a single concern on her face, only a quiet excitement that was so apparent it filled the bridal ready room. "She and Isabelle are giggling over something about the throne room."

He smiled with obvious relief. "Thank you for checking on her." I nodded.

"Are you sure you're feeling okay?" Xander asked again, concern running deep in his mossy green eyes.

We found out I was pregnant in Morocco. I'd always wanted to go and so we spent a couple of months there working and living without much plan at all. About halfway through the stay, I was racked with terrible nausea and fatigue.

I was a couple of months pregnant.

"I'm sure, darling," I reassured him, reaching my hand into the inside pocket of his tux where I knew he probably put those ginger candies that settled my stomach. I smiled when I was right and pulled one out. "The mountain air does wonders."

Once we knew I was pregnant, we decided to head home to tell everyone and prepare the penthouse. Arabella was over the moon when we told her. At the time, I wanted to nest a bit, perched high above Manhattan in our home. One we'd fill with a family. My heart skipped at just the thought of it.

"We can stay a while longer after the wedding. Maybe go to the Riviera," Xander suggested gently, knowing I was probably feeling a bit restless. He was right. "A few weeks on a beach in Nice, a little time in Monte Carlo."

"I do love a poker table," I whispered on his lips, throwing my arms over his shoulders.

A sly smirk inched up his mouth. "Me, too."

Meera's cheerful giggle pulled our attention, and I glanced over to the large grandfather clock in the corner.

"We should probably get to our seats." Sloan stood, running her hands down her dress.

"Come on, give her here." I walked over to the bassinet and gestured to Marcus to hand my niece over. He reluctantly did so when he checked the time. The ceremony would be starting soon.

Meera squirmed a bit with a couple of angry squeaks when she was parted from her father, but she settled just as quickly. Of all the adults that vied for Meera's preference, she was often content in my arms.

"You and Uncle Henry can compete all you'd like," I teased Xander as Sloan and I made our way out. "I'm her favorite."

Extended Epilogue

XANDER

Five Years Later

I partied more than my fair share in life.

Ibiza, Amsterdam, Berlin.

Nothing was more exhausting than my kid's birthday. And this was just the small one we had with family before the actual party in a week.

"Daddy." Lily pulled on my pant leg, looking up at me with her bright green eyes. The carefully placed ribbons in her hair were lopsided in the sea of onyx after hours of playing with her cousins. "Is it time yet?"

Toys and games were scattered all along our living area. Sloan, Marcus, Henry, Selena, and Penelope were chatting while the kids played.

"We may want to spin the globe before this little one falls back asleep," Penelope said softly, rocking our son, Luca Sutton, in her arms. It was his birthday but since Luca was too young to spin the globe, his big sister, Lily, kindly offered.

And reminded me every few minutes that she was going to do it for him.

"Sure, why don't you go get your cousins," I told Lily gently and she was off in a sugar-fueled flash.

When Lily was one, we helped her spin it and that decided where we'd go next. Now it was a little tradition for our little family. One that everyone else was happy to come along on.

Seconds later tiny giggles could be heard getting louder as their feet stampeded in a quake down the hallway.

Meera Sutton—the oldest—darted around a corner first, followed by Lily right on her heels. The tornado of dark black hair and ribbons was chased by Maxwell, Meera's little brother and the twins—Esme and Aisha Amari—who held each other's hands as they haphazardly ran behind them.

They all darted right to the globe sitting in the corner. Once there, they waited for us.

"Okay, my love." Penelope bent down to Lily, giving her a kiss on the head. We gathered behind the kids. "Spin it for your baby brother."

Lily nodded, spun it, and landed in the ocean. She did that for another few spins before a brief negotiation with Meera ended with both of them pointing to somewhere in Brazil.

The two smiled, looked at us like tiny versions of Sloan and Penelope side by side, having accomplished the task.

"Okay." Henry knelt down to scoop up his little girls, one in each arm. They squealed with laughter. "Rio?"

"Sounds wonderful." Penelope leaned into me. Luca fussed and cried a second before drifting off to sleep in Penelope's arms. Both Lily and Luca looked like Penelope with the notable exception of their eyes. Those they got from me.

Lily sped off toward the kitchen and, before I could turn to go get her, she was back.

"Daddy." Lily chaotically held a cupcake in her hand. "You didn't eat your cupcake."

The lopsided cupcake with more sprinkles than it could handle and frosting everywhere looked like something she made especially for me.

I smiled, expecting it to taste like an entire bucket of icing. I took a bite and stopped when what felt like gravel moved between my teeth.

"Lily?" I began, not opening my mouth again, looking around for a napkin.

"I made it." She beamed, her smile stretching all the way across her cheeks.

"Lily, he loves it," Sloan cooed loudly from a few feet away, a manufactured smile painted along her face. "Don't you, Xan?"

Lily looked at me expectantly, her eyes filled with pride.

"I do. I love it." I kissed Lily on the forehead and forced down whatever the fuck that was. "You made this?"

She nodded her head with so much excitement she looked like she could burst. "We used the stuff from the garden."

Dirt. I was eating dirt.

Luca had a June birthday. The official start to summer. And with his first birthday and Lily looking exactly like her mother but acting exactly like me, we'd had our hands full.

I forgot this was usually when we kicked off the annual prank wars.

I shot an unamused look to Sloan. Meera caught Lily's attention and they ran off. The rest of the kids taking that as their cue to chase.

"What?" Sloan moved out of the way as the kids raced past her. "It's summer. And that one was your wife's idea."

Over the last couple of years, Selena, Sloan, and Penelope created an alliance. And I hated to admit it, but they were hard to beat.

Especially because Marcus and Henry were my teammates and generally deadweight.

I stood, choking down the rest of what was in my mouth. Penelope laughed quietly, walking over to the corner of the room and laying Luca in the portable crib we kept there.

"You picked the wrong side, again." I shook my head, downing a glass of water that sat on a console table. Following behind her, I wrapped my arms around her waist.

"I'm not worried." She leaned back into me and turned her head to give me a baiting smile. "Penelope Sutton does not lose."

I chuckled, basking in the warmth of her smile, glancing around at my life as it was now.

My house was a mess. My family was chaos. My world was unpredictable.

It was perfect. A kind of perfect I never imagined I'd have.

I laid a kiss on her shoulder. "Game on, Poppy."

Playlist

Single Soon – Selena Gomez
Something Blue – VOILA
Happy Face – Jagwar Twin
Numb Little Bug – Em Beihold
Magic in the Hamptons – Social House, Lil Yachty
Good for You – Selena Gomez, A$AP Rocky
Paradise – Coldplay
Girls Just Want to Have Fun – Cyndi Lauper
Dangerous Hands – Austin Giorgio
Fix You – Coldplay
Me And My Broken Heart – Rixton
A Sky Full of Stars – Coldplay
Willow – Taylor Swift
Stargazing – Myles Smith
All of the Girls You Loved Before (Taylor's Version) – Taylor Swift
Death of a Bachelor – Panic! At the Disco

Acknowledgments

To the readers: Thank you for reading and supporting my work. Your reviews, messages, and emails have meant more to me than you will ever know. I save them all and love every single one.

To my husband: You are the man that fictional men strive to be. In you, I found a partner and the truest love there is. One who stalwartly follows while I chase a dream and pushes me forward when I'm too scared to do it for myself.

To my family: There's no way you're reading this because, as discussed, you aren't reading this book. (But thank you for buying it.)

To Dimpy, Lenny, Kerri, Angella, Levina, and (my co-Queen) Jen: Our friendships have withstood time, distance, and all of life's changing seasons. The characters in this series are connected though a strong found family—thank you for being mine.

To Britt: Your care with these stories have made them what they are today. Thank you.

To Salima: You've been here from the start. Thank you for supporting me in my journey no matter how far away you may be.

To Shaye and Lindsay: A lot has changed since we met, right before I released *The Spare,* and I cannot imagine doing all of this without you two. I'm grateful to call you ardent supporters, trusted advisors, and, most importantly, friends.

To Kimberly: Thank you for believing in me and my work. Your care and unending support mean the world to me.

ABOUT THE AUTHOR

AVA RANI is a contemporary romance writer who writes stories with equal parts spice and swoon. Expect big cities, diverse backgrounds, strong female leads, and plot twists.

She fell in love with reading and writing again after a decade of working in another field. In a burst of creative energy, she wrote this series.

When she's not writing, she loves to travel (fifty-three countries so far), perfect her pecan pie recipe, and introduce her toddler to every ice cream flavor imaginable (for purely academic reasons, of course).

Delve into the interconnected world of the Biotech Billionaires series, filled with hot CEOs, glitzy penthouse parties, rich family alliances and betrayals!

THE SPARE

The Spare is the first book in a series of interconnected standalones in the Biotech Billionaires universe.

Gossip Girl meets *Succession* in this steamy romance about a tenacious Indian-American heiress who's ready to prove she can lead her family's business, and her best friend's brother, a CEO hiding a secret that might be worth billions.

THE HEIR

The second book in the Biotech Billionaires series, a sparkling romance about a newly minted CEO and the "billionaire babysitter" hired to rehab his playboy image—but falling in love could be the worst scandal of all.

THE CHARMER

When a charming billionaire and a reclusive lawyer tie the knot to outsmart an inheritance scheme, sparks fly and unexpected love blossoms in this sizzling romance.